SYSTEM SHOCK

DOCTOR WHO – THE MISSING ADVENTURES

Also available:

GOTH OPERA by Paul Cornell

EVOLUTION by John Peel

VENUSIAN LULLABY by Paul Leonard

THE CRYSTAL BUCEPHALUS by Craig Hinton

STATE OF CHANGE by Christopher Bulis

THE ROMANCE OF CRIME by Gareth Roberts

THE GHOSTS OF N-SPACE by Barry Letts

TIME OF YOUR LIFE by Steve Lyons

DANCING THE CODE by Paul Leonard

THE MENAGERIE by Martin Day

SYSTEM SHOCK

Justin Richards

DOCTOR
WHO

THE MISSING ADVENTURES

First published in Great Britain in 1995 by
Doctor Who Books
an imprint of Virgin Publishing Ltd
332 Ladbroke Grove
London W10 5AH

ISBN 0 426 20445 X

Cover illustration by
Martin Rawle (DSM Print & Design Partnership)

Typeset by Galleon Typesetting, Ipswich
Printed and bound in Great Britain by
Cox & Wyman Ltd, Reading, Berks

Many thanks to Peter Anghelides, Craig Hinton, and Andy Lane for their comments and help. Also to Martin Rawle for the excellent cover and for improving my sketch map of Hubway — both pieces of artwork entirely achieved, appropriately enough, on computer.

To all at WSDL
and, as ever
To Alison and Julian — without whom things might have been simpler, but much less fun!

Plan of ground and first floors of Hubway (formerly Aragon Court)

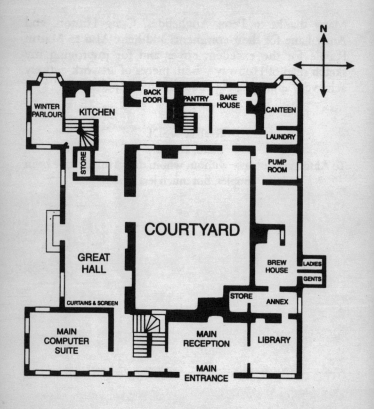

Ground floor

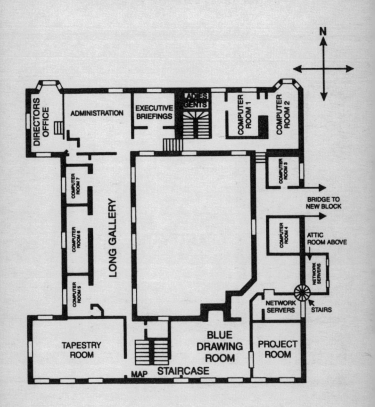

N

DIRECTORS OFFICE

ADMINISTRATION

EXECUTIVE BRIEFINGS

LADIES
GENTS

COMPUTER ROOM 1

COMPUTER ROOM 2

COMPUTER ROOM 7

COMPUTER ROOM 3

LONG GALLERY

COMPUTER ROOM 6

BRIDGE TO NEW BLOCK

COMPUTER ROOM 4

ATTIC ROOM ABOVE

COMPUTER ROOM 5

NETWORK SERVERS

NETWORK SERVERS

STAIRS

TAPESTRY ROOM

BLUE DRAWING ROOM

PROJECT ROOM

MAP

STAIRCASE

First floor

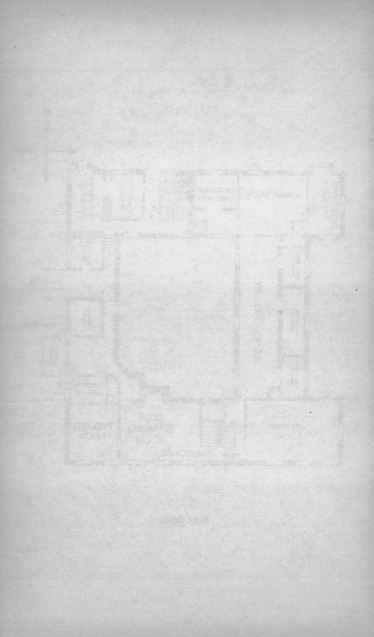

IF . . .

The energy jolt nearly took his head off. Sancrest ducked and all but dragged the equinian into the room, wrestling with the pack animal and shouting to Arkroll to get the door shut behind them. Macket struggled to turn the locking control, his claws skidding on the polished metal surface. Another series of energy jolts rattled into the metal of the door, but the structure remained intact.

'So, this is it.' Arkroll looked round the large room. He had heard descriptions but they hardly matched up to the reality. The chamber was huge, an antiseptically white metal drum reaching up to the heavens, though it flashed red with the emergency lighting in time to the alarm klaxons. Data banks and processing systems lined the walls as they stretched up the entire height of the building. He could see walkways and gantries high above him, steel bridges between the direct access storage devices for technicians the system no longer wanted or needed. They looked increasingly fragile and ineffective the higher he looked, a web of strings connecting the sides of the chamber in a symmetrical spiral. It made Arkroll feel giddy to look too high. He shook his head and turned back to the others.

Macket was already checking the systems. 'I've locked off all the bulkheads along the corridor, but it won't keep them out for long.'

'Doesn't matter.' Sancrest was already releasing the straps round the device. 'This won't take long.' He took the weight on his shoulder and started to lower it to the floor, balancing it against the flank of the animal as it slid down. 'Don't stand there gawping, Arkroll, give me a hand.'

Arkroll helped him take the weight and together they stood the device upright and opened the inspection hatch. Released from its burden, the equinian snorted and wandered off to the far side of the room. It nuzzled against a control console, looking for somewhere good to graze on the metal plated flooring.

Sancrest peered inside the cover of the device. 'How do you prime this thing?'

Macket knelt down beside them, gesturing for the others to give him some space. 'It's your standard fifty-year-old thermonuclear device. So it's completely dumb.'

'That's why we brought it,' Arkroll reminded him.

'I know.' Macket gestured round the chamber. 'I was here when we started this.' He returned his attention to the inspection hatch. 'Now let's finish it.'

The pounding on the door was getting louder. The metal was discolouring with the concentrated heat by the time Macket looked up. His face was grim, his head swaying gently from side to side with apprehension.

'What is it?'

'There's a crude timer and a manual over-ride. Both quite simple.'

'So what's the problem?' Arkroll could see Macket was worried. Macket opened another small hatch on the other side of the bomb, shaking his head slightly as he examined the innards.

'The timer has a control circuit.'

They were silent for a moment.

'Is it active?' Sancrest asked. 'Can it be bypassed?'

'The manual over-ride seems simple enough. But it may use the timer as a relay. If it goes through a control chip . . .' Macket did not need to complete the thought – they all knew the danger.

'Let's give it a try,' Arkroll shrugged. 'After all – we're dead either way.'

Macket reached inside the main hatch, grasping for the control key. 'Could one of you turn the key in the other hatch counter-clockwise when I give the word?'

Arkroll reached into the other hatch and felt for the key. After a moment's groping around he found it, gripped it firmly between his claws, and nodded to Macket.

Macket drew a deep breath.

'Wait.'

Macket and Arkroll both looked up in surprise.

'What if this *doesn't* work?' Sancrest hissed. 'What if the circuit is already corrupted and the relay is routed through it? I know we're dead, but there are wider issues.'

'I don't know,' Macket told him.

Behind them the door exploded in a ball of flame and smoke, molten metal storming down around them.

'If anything occurs to you, Macket,' Sancrest shouted above the noise of the blast, 'send me a memo.'

They were still laughing when the first of the kill-units emerged through the smoking doorway. They scanned the room in a moment, discounted the equinian as no threat, and targeted the three rebels in the far corner.

'Now!' screamed Macket.

THEN . . .

Begin Program

He had pressed the button for the second floor. But the lift had already passed it and was still going down. His brain was already changing gear to what he would cook himself when he got home. With a head full of lamb with fennel and sweet pepper – probably to the accompaniment of Mahler, or maybe Strindberg depending on how he felt – it took a moment for him to register the problem.

He cursed quietly, then again more loudly as the lift lurched to a halt. No lights on the panel – he was stuck between floors. Typical. So much for technology, he thought.

He had been stuck in the lift before – with a girl from Communications. For the whole of the forty minutes it had taken for the engineer to free the mechanism and open the doors, she had not said a word. But this time he had a lonely feeling of resignation as he pushed the little button comfortingly marked with a stylized bell.

Nothing happened.

He could feel a little panic beginning to break through as he stabbed at the alarm button again and again. Still nothing. He hammered on the door with his fist in frustration and humiliation. He was building up to having to shout for help.

Then with a stomach-curving jolt the floor dropped away beneath him.

He was still taking deep breaths of relief when the door slid open to reveal the half-light of the basement car park. Two people were standing immediately outside the doors. One was a man – smart suit, short back and sides; the other was a woman – dark hair in a bob, but with the ends curled under her ears so they jutted forward sharply. Strangely, she was carrying an aerosol can. They were standing too close to the door for him to get past them.

'I wouldn't risk the lift,' he told them, as much to let them know he was there and wanted to get out as to warn them.

Neither of the figures moved. Further down the basement he could hear an engine starting – deep and finely tuned, a large vehicle. After a moment a maroon Toyota van emerged from the gloom, headlights flaring as it crested a speed bump. The two figures in front of him ignored it, even as it drew up behind them and the driver jumped out.

He tried again: 'It seems to have a problem.' He gestured vaguely to show he was still talking about the lift.

The woman smiled, her eyes glinting and her hair moving like a single entity as she tilted her head slightly to one side. It made her smile seem almost sinister, almost mocking.

'No problem,' she said as she raised the aerosol.

He heard the hiss of escaping gas, but it seemed miles away. He was trained to move fast – to avoid it. But he was distracted. Distracted by the woman's smile, by the driver opening the rear doors, and by the stretcher and intravenous drip being unloaded from the back of the Toyota.

When he woke, he could see the bag holding the drip-fluid, and the plastic pipe leading down from the bag high above him. Although he couldn't move his braced head, he knew the drip was feeding into his arm.

He did not recognize his surroundings – the pale plain walls and the double swing doors each with a porthole window glazed with semi-opaque glass. A massive bright light angled in above his near-supine head.

Nor did he recognize the man who leaned over him – the man in the surgical gown; the man wearing skin-tight, skin-coloured plastic gloves; the man holding the scalpel.

* * *

10

It was the cracked headlight that killed her. Veronica Halliwell heard it break on the way to work – just as a maroon Toyota van overtook her on the Great North Road. At first she thought the windscreen was going, she had never got used to the bullet-proof glass. She drove smoothly into her reserved space outside the office, lifted her briefcase off the back seat, and listened to the satisfying *thunk* of the central locking as she set the alarm.

Then she saw the light. It was cracked right across, a hole the size of her little fingernail in the centre, the crack splitting through it.

'Everything all right, ma'am?' Sharp was beside her. He must have noticed her pause and left his post by the main doors to investigate.

'Oh it's nothing – headlight's sprung a leak.'

Sharp leaned forward and tapped the broken glass cover. 'Must have been a stone. Shame they don't cover the lights with the same stuff they use in the windows.'

Halliwell balanced her briefcase on one arm and opened it. She rummaged inside for a moment looking for her security badge. 'More hassle,' she said. 'Just what I need right now.'

'Oh don't worry, ma'am. It's easily fixed. I'll get them to send someone over.'

'Would you?' She smiled. 'Thanks a lot, Sharp. You're a treasure.' She handed him her car keys.

He stood aside and Veronica Halliwell, Director General of MI5, entered the foyer of the unremarkable office block in central London and pressed the lift-call button.

The mechanic from the car leasing company arrived mid-afternoon. He dusted his thin, gloved hands on his spotless overalls, scratched his head thoughtfully, and commented that he was glad the light wasn't attached to his own car. After walking three times round Halliwell's Rover and kicking various tyres, he asked Sharp for the keys, opened the driver's door, and started to examine the dashboard display.

By early evening the mechanic had dismantled the

electrical circuits and taken great glee in replacing the central processor. 'They're pretty sensitive, anything goes wrong with the electrics and you need a new chip.' He cradled the small glass case carefully in the palm of his gloved hand, and lovingly removed the tiny square of metal-etched silicon.

The last thing he did was to replace the glass shutter over the near-side headlight.

By the end of the day she had forgotten the minor troubles of the morning. It was only as the lift delivered her back into the foyer that Halliwell remembered her car and wondered if the light had been fixed.

Sharp greeted her in the foyer with a discreet whisper: 'Car's sorted, ma'am. Needed a new chip for the Car-Net system.'

She hardly registered the details, was still preoccupied with the problems of the day – with the aftermath of a major drugs-bust; with the new equipment requisitions for GCHQ. She thanked Sharp for sorting things, took her car keys from his hand, and returned his smile.

As a matter of courtesy as much as interest, she glanced at the headlights and noted that they were intact. She waited for Sharp to catch her up and push his long-handled mirror under the car, checking assiduously despite the fact it had not been out of his sight all day. After a minute he pulled the mirror out again and nodded to her. The keys and the alarm button were still in her hand, and the lights flashed reassuringly as she deactivated the alarm and the doors unlocked. Halliwell opened the rear door and tossed her briefcase on to the seat. Then she climbed into the front of the car and pushed the key into the ignition.

She always felt a slight twinge of apprehension before she turned the key – a deeper intake of breath. Then she started the car, the engine catching first time, and let out the breath she had been holding. They could check and double-check but, in odd unguarded moments, the fear was still there. Just for a second.

12

It was as she changed up from first to second gear — as she pulled out on to the empty street, that things started to go wrong. She braked slightly before she accelerated into the road, glancing over her shoulder to double-check nothing was coming. But nothing happened — the car did not slow at all. If anything, it seemed to speed up as she pushed harder on the brake.

'Needed a new chip . . .' Sharp had said. She could hear his words echoing in her brain as the car kept going in a uniform direction. It was ignoring the steering wheel just as it was ignoring the brakes. She could doubt it no longer — the car was gathering speed, despite her foot firmly on the brake pedal. In a panic she pulled at the handbrake and wrenched the steering wheel to the left — towards the kerb. The wheel responded with the usual ease of power steering. But the car ignored it.

She knew her best course of action was to get out of the car before it gathered any more speed. It was already up to twenty miles per hour, and the way the road bent meant it was heading at increasing speed into the brick wall on the corner of the crescent.

Then the door locked. Just as she grasped the door handle, as soon as she applied pressure, the central locking gave a worrying *thunk*. The door handle clicked inwards, into the locked position.

She pulled hard at the handle. She took her left hand off the useless steering wheel and pulled with both hands. But the handle would not yield. And the car continued to gain speed. And the wall was approaching ever faster.

Just as she threw up her hands to protect her face she heard a sound like a camera shutter clicking. In fact it was two distinct events. The first was the fuel injection system forcing a stream of petrol vapour direct from the tank into the space under the bonnet. The second was a spark from the battery igniting the vapour.

She might perhaps have heard the hiss of the flame traversing the vapour trail back into the fuel tank, were it not for the fact that she was already deafened by the sound of the resulting explosion. The bonnet erupted in front of

13

her in a sheet of flame and the fire started licking its way through the dashboard. For a few seconds she hammered on the bullet-proof, heat-retarding window. Then the flesh boiled from her hands, and she slumped lifelessly back into the plush, burning upholstery.

Sharp watched with a mixture of horror and disbelief. He was standing, mouth half-open, when he heard the door behind him. The noise was enough to shake him back to reality, and he turned briefly to send Anderson back to phone for an ambulance and the fire brigade.

As he returned his shocked gaze to the burning wreckage, he caught sight of another figure standing, watching. He was on the other side of the road, partly obscured by the T-junction into Calthorpe Street. It was the mechanic who had worked on the car. He watched for a moment longer, then nodded slowly and turned away.

Sharp looked round, but nobody was within earshot. Several people were grouped round the burning car – trying to get close to it to try to help, but beaten away by the intensity of the heat. He could see Anderson at the front desk talking urgently into the phone, the flames reflected in the glass between them. The man was now almost out of sight.

Sharp caught up with him halfway down Calthorpe Street – just as the road bent out of sight of the burning car. 'Excuse me a moment, sir.' He was surprised at how calm he sounded. Too calm perhaps – the man did not stop.

'I said "Excuse me!" ' Sharp grabbed the mechanic's shoulder and spun him round, surprised at how solid the thin man's shoulder was. The mechanic stared at him, eyes cold and dead, face impassive and slack. It unnerved Sharp, and he reached for his gun.

'There's been an accident, sir. If you could just come with me.' It was not a question, and it got no answer. He started to raise the automatic, but with a movement faster than his training it was slapped from Sharp's hand and skidded across the pavement.

14

Instinctively Sharp punched, his fist jabbing forward at the man's face. But it was caught before it got there, grasped in the mechanic's gloved hand, and he could feel his knuckles breaking as the grip tightened like a wrench. The man pulled Sharp towards him, an impossibly narrow tongue flicking quickly over his teeth with a faint hissing sound. Then he twisted Sharp's arm round and hurled him at the wall alongside the pavement.

Sharp connected with the brickwork and collapsed in a winded heap. He rolled on to his back − to see the mechanic leaning over him. The mechanic's head was swaying gently from side to side, but his eyes remained fixed on Sharp. The gloved hand reached down at him, the fingers snapping together with a dull clicking sound − almost metallic.

The image was unsteady in Sharp's mind − swaying almost in time with the mechanic's head. The hand disappeared from his line of sight, and he felt the fingers burning into his neck as he was wrenched off the pavement and slammed back into the wall. He felt the brickwork give slightly behind him, saw the mechanic's eyes staring intently at him, heard the oscillating wail of the sirens from down the street. And he knew he was dead.

01

Meetings

The Home Secretary did not prevaricate. 'They shot a hostage at three-seventeen this afternoon,' she said. 'Dumped his body out of a first floor window. One of the financial analysts – not that that makes any difference of course.'

Colonel Clark listened carefully. He already knew this. He had probably known before the committee had. And he knew what would happen as a result. This was the formality before the inevitable. Here were the decision-takers, secure in the oak-panelled splendour of the Cabinet Office Briefing Room – the room from which their committee derived its name. They had to satisfy themselves the only decision possible was the right one.

Clark could see it in their faces as he looked round the coffin-shaped table. They were tired, of course, but in the dark-ringed recesses of their eyes he could see the anguish and the worry. And he gained an instant respect for them.

'How soon can your team be ready?' General Andrews asked. As COBRA's Ministry of Defence liaison he was expected to raise the obvious question.

'We are always ready, sir,' Clark replied, 'and we are never ready enough. The more time we have the more variables we can eliminate. The more variables we can eliminate, the greater the chance of success.'

'And how would you define *success*, Colonel?' A typical lawyer's question. The Attorney General leaned forward to hear the answer, hands folded on the polished table in front of him.

'I would define it, sir, as the safe release of the hostages and the neutralization of their captors. With as little cost in terms of soft assets as possible.' Nobody asked what he meant by *soft assets*.

'And what chance of success do you estimate you have if you go in now?'

Clark leaned back in his chair, noting that several of the others subconsciously followed his cue. 'An operation this evening, run according to our scheduling, has a good chance of success.'

' "Good?" ' the Attorney General again.

'There are no percentage probabilities in this, sir. It is not an exact science. We've had three days, we have the blueprints for the office block and have constructed a scale model and a training area based on the first and second floors of the Pullen Tower at Regents Park Barracks. The microphones placed in the under-floor cable conduits help us to deduce the number and position of hostages and terrorists. We have BattleNet up and running – although it is as yet untried in combat, so we have no real data on how much of a difference it will make.'

There were several nods from round the table.

Then Clark gave them the other side of the story. 'There are other uncertainties: the office is open plan so the configuration of the furniture is not known exactly and may be changed at any time. We have no detailed information about how the terrorists are armed. We don't know what will happen when we go in. In operation *Nimrod*, for example, the assault leader became entangled in his own abseiling rope and broke a window on the way down and then they found the hostages had been moved to a different room.' Clark waited a few seconds for them to absorb this. 'If you want my expert opinion, we can expect to lose a couple of hostages and at least three of the assault team.'

There was silence for a while. Most of the committee were looking at the table in front of them, playing with pencils or rearranging papers. Only General Andrews and the Home Secretary met Clark's stare.

'I don't think we have much choice,' Andrews said.

The Home Secretary nodded slowly. 'What time will you go in?' she asked.

'That depends on what BattleNet says when we upload the latest data.' Clark stood up. 'But it will be over this evening.'

'Is there anything we can do to help?' Clark had expected Hanson to speak up earlier, but he seemed happy to keep a low profile. He was the new boy, after all, provisionally appointed to succeed his former boss at MI5. His full promotion as Halliwell's successor was merely a matter of time and formality.

Of course there was nothing COBRA could do now, but Clark understood they still needed to feel involved. 'A couple of things, if you would. There are some procedural formalities I'd be happy to avoid – like informing the Commissioner of the Metropolitan Police of your decision. I'd also like to keep the media away as far as possible from the area, but without alerting them to the fact that something is happening.'

'Anything else?'

Clark was at the door. He paused for a moment before leaving. 'Pray?' he suggested.

'So the fundamental problem today is one of integration.' Lionel Stabfield looked round his audience to see they had taken the point of the bulk of his presentation. There were thoughtful looks, nods, a yawn from near the back of the table. Stabfield pressed a button on the remote and the final slide appeared behind him. It was a three-dimensional cube with an eye set into it, the pupil visible through each of the open facets – the logo of I^2. Stabfield half turned so he could see it, throwing his thin features into stark silhouette as he did so.

'OffNet, as we have seen, solves this. With Vorell it provides the language whereby all the office hardware can conform, can integrate, can achieve synergy. It links intelligent office machinery into a world-wide network, thus increasing efficiency and distributing the workload. With the transport protocols I described earlier, it delivers the communications and network access. Without OffNet the global digital Superhighway is emasculated. Without OffNet the benefits are cut and the potential unrealized. Without OffNet the Superhighway becomes a parking lot.' There were a couple of wry smiles at the Americanism delivered in his quintessential English accent.

'When Hubway goes on-line next week,' he finished, 'we will at last complete that Superhighway, with OffNet at its core. Thank you.'

There was applause, of course. The key manufacturers would agree to include the OffNet protocols in their equipment together with the software to drive it. Most of them were already doing so, and would now feel the decision was a good one. Their only qualm was the royalty due to I^2 for each chip they delivered with OffNet capability.

Atkinson from Applied Automation raised a tentative hand. 'What about the couple of larger Asian manufacturers who haven't yet signed up?'

Stabfield nodded. 'A good question. I met with them both a couple of weeks back. They remain unconvinced that a third party like I^2 – someone with no first line interest or direct sales, except for the chips themselves – should own the protocols. I agreed that once they are proven we shall of course hand over administration and development to one of the international bodies, such as ISO. I think I pushed some of their hot buttons.'

A phone rang briefly, muted, at the back of the room. Stabfield saw Marc Lewis answer it and reach for a pen. Lewis's thin face was expressionless as he took the call.

'Will they come on board?' Atkinson pressed.

Stabfield's pale lips drew back slightly over his small teeth. 'Once the technology is proven, they have to. Their equipment won't fit into the rest of the world without it – not without miles of cable and hundreds of superfluous server machines, anyway. They'll soon discover they can't sell it as a round trip if it throws up.'

Atkinson seemed satisfied with the answer.

Stabfield was about to ask if there were any more questions, but Lewis was waving a piece of notepaper from the back of the room. Stabfield gestured for him to bring it to him.

The message was short and to the point. 'I'm sorry, ladies and gentlemen, but I'm afraid I have to leave you now. We have a small pilot study underway, which has reached a point where it requires some executive input.' Stabfield gathered his papers together and switched off the slide behind him. 'Marc will, I'm sure, be able to answer any further questions, and will organize coffee. Thank you for your time. I hope this session has been constructive.'

Lieutenant Colonel Clark had briefed his team within minutes of the first hostage dying. He had spoken to them before he left for COBRA – they all knew the meeting was a formality. The team was already on station around, above, and beneath the Pullen Tower when Clark got back. He held a short meeting with the assault-team leaders and agreed the exact timings.

At 6.20 p.m. the chief Home Office negotiator rang the terrorists on the single phone line left into the building. He spoke immediately to the leader, 'Raven', and told him all his demands were to be met.

At 6.22 p.m. Raven was still spelling out the logistics – the size of the coach, who would drive, how many hostages would accompany the terrorists to Heathrow. At the same moment the assault leader of SAS Unit One signalled to his men to start their abseiled descent of the tower.

At 6.23 p.m. Unit Two moved into position in the grounds, and Unit Three set off the charges in the underfloor conduits and started climbing the elevator shafts from the relative shelter of the basement car park.

BattleNet had designated Raven as Target Zero One. He was still holding the phone when the floor beneath him exploded and the windows smashed inwards.

* * *

Rod was just congratulating himself on having a quiet evening when the weirdo walked in. Up until then it had been easy. There were hardly any people in the bar. The few people there were kept so quiet he could hear the commentary on the football. Arsenal struggled against Manchester City on the flat panel television hanging like a picture on the wall in the corner. Still it was early yet – not even half past seven, plenty of time for things to liven up.

Then the weirdo arrived. He was well over six feet tall with bulging eyes and hair that curled like a novelty party wig. He was wearing a long brown overcoat which boasted a variety of stains, a large hat with a huge brim that threatened to blind him, and a scarf that was as long as the Central line. With him was a dark-haired woman in her mid-twenties who had to half run, half jump to keep pace and make eye contact.

Rod was willing to give him the benefit of the doubt. Until he spoke. The weirdo headed straight for him and fixed Rod with an unnerving stare. The woman leaned against the bar beside him, her hands palm down on the sticky surface and her chin resting on them. As the man spoke, she rolled her whole head to see him and it looked for a moment as if there was no body attached.

'I wonder,' the man said in a deep and measured tone, 'could you be terribly kind and tell us what the date is?'

Rod told him.

'And the year?' asked the woman. Rod looked quickly between the two, but the man was raising an interested eyebrow.

'1998,' Rod said. No reaction. He gulped. 'All year,' he hazarded as a suffix.

'Told you,' said the woman as she stood upright and thumped the man playfully on the shoulder. 'Missed again.'

'Must be the helmic regulators.'

'Oh well, now we're here we can have a drink.' She turned back to Rod. 'Spritzer,' she said, and it took him a moment to realize it was actually a word he understood.

She took her drink and headed off towards a table by the back door – in the corner opposite the television.

Rod turned to the man. 'And for you, sir?'

'I'll have a pint,' the man replied quietly, as if afraid he might be overheard.

'Righto. We've got several real ales on at the moment,' Rod gestured to the hand pumps along the bar. 'We're in the CAMRA guide, actually. *Old Codger* is a favourite.'

The man inspected the beer engines with interest. 'I'll try the *ginger* beer,' he said after a while.

Rod moved towards the pumps. 'Handle or straight glass?' he started to ask. But somehow it came out as 'Hawhat?'

The strange man leaned massively over the bar at him. 'Ginger beer,' he over-articulated from point blank range.

Rod poured it out from two bottles. 'Something wrong with the year?' he asked, trying to think of a safe question.

'Indeed no.' The man sipped his ginger beer appreciatively and held it up to the light to inspect its depth and colour. 'No indeed,' he elaborated. 'Not one of my favourites, but I'm sure it will do.' Then he slapped the exact change on the bar and strode off after his friend.

Various thoughts filtered through to Rod's brain as he returned his bruised attention to the football. They included half-completed theories about how he always got the weirdo; about how the weirdoes always got the girls; about how it had almost sounded like the man was talking about the year rather than his ginger beer. He also thought about how he at least had the football to watch, and wasn't it great that he could hear what the commentator was saying.

As Rod watched, the television re-tuned itself to the twenty-four hour news channel. It caught the anchor woman in mid-sentence, sincere and concerned: 'and we're going over to Angus Hill at the Pullen Tower where there seem to be some new developments.'

* * *

The explosion echoed round the pub and got everyone's attention.

Sarah turned in her chair so she could see the television better. 'What's happening?'

'The television is programmed to switch to the news channel if there's a news flash, I would think,' the Doctor said. 'Everything's interactive these days. But if you want, you can program it to interact with itself. Takes all the skill out of it though.'

'No, no,' Sarah said. The changes in television technology were probably fascinating, but she was more interested in what the screen was showing at the moment. 'I meant, what's happening there.' She pointed at the television.

'Well I don't know.' The ends of the Doctor's mouth shrugged with him as he stared at the screen.

Several black-clad figures were hanging on ropes outside an office block. From inside the building came the sound of another explosion, then the black figures kicked themselves away from the side of the tower as the charges they had attached to the windows went off. Glass showered out and down just as each figure reached the far end of his swing. Then they brought their legs up and disappeared through the broken windows, their ropes swaying back empty. The sound of automatic gunfire was punctuated by the dull thump of further explosions and by screams. Flames started flickering at one of the shattered windows.

'Anything I should know about 1998?' Sarah asked the Doctor as the noise subsided. 'Apart from the fact that we shouldn't really be here at all, that is.'

'Oh nonsense. Nothing of interest happened as far as I remember. And we can be here if we want – no harm in a drink or two. Then we'll nip back to the TARDIS and have another go.'

'Just so long as we don't get *involved*.'

The Doctor put his drink down carefully, aligning the glass exactly within the circle of a beer mat. 'Oh come on, Sarah – when did I ever get *involved* in anything?'

Sarah's mouth opened and closed silently. Behind her

23

the flames were taking hold on the second floor of the Pullen Tower.

'*Unit One, clearing building. Two terrorists dead.*'

Lionel Stabfield was renowned for his stoic lack of facial expression.

'*Hostages safe. Bringing them down main stairway now.*'

But he smiled slightly, despite the effort involved, as he watched the fire take hold within the Pullen Tower.

'*Entering second floor office area. Three terrorists dead.*'

The BattleNet system the SAS was using relayed data directly to the car – video to the television set, audio through the quadraphonic speakers.

'*Clearing stairway ahead of hostages. One terrorist dead.*'

He switched off the tiny television set and moved it from its perch on the passenger seat to the glove compartment.

The car was a large Jaguar. It was dark green, and could be parked practically invisibly just off the disused single-track lane that ran through Glenlake Woods. The woods were just off the M4, convenient for London, and hardly anyone ever went there.

Stabfield got out of the car and locked it. He crossed the lane, turned to check the car was well enough camouflaged, and set off into the woods on the far side. He walked for about ten minutes, taking a circuitous route. He also doubled back on himself twice, stopping suddenly for a while to listen for the sound of anyone behind him in the dense undergrowth. Satisfied he was not being followed, he continued on his way.

The fence was ten feet high, made of barbed wire netting, and electrified. The gate was secured with an electronic lock attached to a numeric keypad. Stabfield looked round, checking one last time before he keyed in the eight-digit code. The gate clicked open, the circuit broken. He closed it behind him, waiting the three seconds to check the current cut back in.

The heavy woodland continued for another hundred yards after the fence. Then it stopped abruptly, ending in a ragged scorch mark across the blackened ground. The cleared area was about fifty yards square. In its centre stood a grey metal box. The shuttle was functional rather than attractive, with heat shield and engine clusters at one end, viewport and detectors at the other. The ragged scorch marks along the pitted hull betrayed the vehicle's age and frequent use.

Stabfield pulled a remote control from his jacket pocket. A single button opened the shuttle's door, swinging it outwards and down so that the inner surface formed a set of steps up into the cockpit. Stabfield clambered aboard and strapped himself in.

The radar jammer was continuously active, and Stabfield checked the scanners for air traffic above him. When he was sure he had not been observed, he gave confirmation of his destination to the flight computer and let it handle the lift off.

The functional grey short-range shuttle lifted ponderously into the air. A few rabbits ran for cover, startled by the noise and by the dust cloud kicked up by the downthrust. Then the woods were silent again.

'A most satisfactory outcome.' There was more than an element of relief in the Home Secretary's words.

'As good as we could reasonably have expected,' Andrews agreed. 'A pity about the two hostages, though.'

The Home Secretary brushed this off without comment. 'I think we need some sleep before the formal debriefing,' she said. There was agreement from all round the table. The shadow Home Secretary and the Attorney General even broke off their whispered conversation to nod their consent.

'Good. Tomorrow morning then – shall we say ten o'clock?' She gathered up a few papers out of habit, and stood up. 'Thank you for your help and support. It's been an interesting few days.'

'I'll pass that on shall I?' Andrews' words caught her at the door. 'The thanks, I mean – to the people involved on the ground.'

25

'Please do.' She hesitated a moment longer before opening the door. 'I'm sorry, General, I'm rather tired. We all appreciate the work that's been put in, especially by the SAS team. If you pass the word round, we'll arrange something more formal once we've recovered.'

Andrews waited until everyone else had left. Then he went to the telephone on the desk at the back of the room. He made two calls. The first was to his wife. The second one was to an unlisted number in Hereford.

He had stopped using the lift when he left work, although he was not sure why. It seemed more of an instinctive thing – in the same way he was listening to less music. And hardly eating or drinking. Still, if nothing else the exercise did him good, he reflected as he reached the bottom of the stairs.

He had arranged to meet Lewis in the upstairs bar of the Chandos, just round the corner from St Martin-in-the-Fields. He used to find the comfort of the leather sofas relaxing, though he was less inclined to such comforts now. Then later he had to see Peterson – whom he loathed – to tell him . . . To tell him something important. It would come to him, whatever it was. Perhaps Lewis would know.

Lewis was already there, sitting in the darkest corner with a glass of fruit juice untouched on the table in front of him. Lewis never drank – or at least, he had never seen him drink. He ordered a gin and tonic out of habit and joined Lewis in the corner.

'A great success,' Marc Lewis said quietly. 'We're very pleased.'

And at once he remembered what the meeting was about – what his task had been and what his purpose now was. The couple at the next table broke up into sudden laughter, leaning back in their seats and slopping their drinks alarmingly.

'Yes,' he replied, 'a very useful study. Such feedback from a real-life situation is far more effectual than extrapolation and ball park figuring.' Part of his mind was surprised — not recognizing the form of his words and rejecting the jargon. The rest of it was intent on Lewis's input.

'I hear what you're saying,' Lewis said.

The other man both relished the praise and worried that the phrase meant nothing.

Lewis leaned forward. 'So now we can proceed. You remember what you must do next?'

He nodded. He remembered. He closed his eyes for a while to concentrate on his next work item. And when he opened them, Lewis had gone, his drink left untouched on the table.

There was a moment's pause in the ambience as the juke box moved on to another anodyne track. Then the sounds around him kicked in again and life continued.

He reached for his gin and took a sip. It was bitter in the back of his mouth and he almost choked on it. The very thought of allowing liquid — or food — to enter his body was nauseating. The very fact that his body was dependent on external substances for sustenance was suddenly sickening — to the point he could feel the bile rising in his near-empty stomach.

He was still coughing when Peterson arrived. 'You all right, old man?' Peterson asked. 'Should take more tonic with it.' He added as he administered a badly aimed thump on the back. Then frowning, as if surprised at the rigidity of the surface his hand had slapped, Peterson sat down on the opposite couch. He sank into the leather, and the table edged away from him to make room.

The coughing subsided, and Peterson examined the glass of fruit juice. 'We expecting company?' The disdain was evident in his tone as he ran a hand through his thinning hair. 'Or is this for me,' Peterson added as an afterthought, wiping his greasy hand on his trouser leg.

'No — it's not for you. And yes, we are expecting company.' He smiled. 'Or at least, you are — I have to be going.'

'Oh?'

'But there's someone I wanted you to meet.'

27

Peterson smiled. 'Always glad to make new contacts. Life and blood of the ministry, new contacts. Not what you know, but who you know – eh?'

'Indeed.' He stood up, already tired of Peterson's clichés. 'Drink?'

'Thought you'd never ask. Vodka and lime, with ice.'

He made for the bar quickly, coughing into his handkerchief to disguise his retching. Now even the coughing was upsetting him – another infuriating and nauseating bodily failing. He waited for a while as the barman served his friends.

Peterson was all too obviously watching two young women at a nearby table when he returned – drink at arm's length. Peterson took it and raised the glass in mock salute. 'Thanks, old man.'

They sat in silence for a few minutes. Peterson drinking and watching the women chatting, smoking, laughing. The other man sat virtually still, his gin and tonic sitting just within reach on the table between them.

He could tell she had arrived when Peterson's jaw dropped slightly. She had come up the stairs on the opposite side of the bar, and walked the length of the room to get to them. Peterson, facing into the room, watched her all the way. She was wearing a short skirt and a tight blouse. She had high heels and her red hair was loose, curling about her shoulders. When she sat down opposite him, Peterson visibly flinched.

Then she kissed the other man on the cheek. 'Hello, darling,' she said in a voice that sounded like brushed silk. 'Who's this gorgeous friend of yours,' she asked as she surveyed Peterson's portly form across the table.

'This is Clive Peterson. He works in the Ministry of Information Technology.'

'Mmm – that sounds exciting.' She held out her hand just far enough for Peterson to have to half rise to reach it. He made the not inconsiderable effort.

'Clive, this is Eleanor Jenkins.' He watched Peterson reluctantly relinquish his grip on Eleanor's hand. 'Look after her, won't you Peterson – she's an old friend.'

'Not that old, surely,' Peterson smarmed.

He was tempted to admit that he had never met her before, just seen her photograph. Instead he stood up and said: 'I'm afraid I have to leave now – you know how things are.'

Peterson was understanding. 'Of course, old man. I assume you were involved in – er,' he lowered his voice to a normal volume, 'you know. Great work, by the way. Really showed 'em.'

Eleanor rose and hugged him hard, just like an old friend. 'What a shame. But I'm sure we'll find lots to talk about, won't we Clive?'

He left them to it. Peterson offering her a drink, and Eleanor espousing the obvious advantages of getting a bottle rather than just a little glass of champagne. He had a headache coming on, needed the fresh air.

He paused on the Strand, disoriented. He was sure there was something important he had to do, but he could not remember what. In the distance a clock struck nine. It was later than he thought – he could have sworn he only called in at the office for a couple of minutes after the meeting broke up.

02

Involvement

Kevin Sutcliffe was using a torch. Partly this was the usual intruder's caution at showing too much light, and partly it was because he wanted to keep away from the switches. The torch cast a dim oval of light across the pale blue walls of the windowless, box-like office. The basic pieces of office equipment became fearsome silhouettes, rearing up like snakes.

He had picked the lock to the office without much trouble – he had done it several times before. But those occasions had been dry runs when he stood little chance of being caught. This was the real thing, and he was shaking like James Bond's martini.

He checked his watch again. They had given it to him when he started several months ago. It was digital of course – everything to do with I^2 was digital. He had spent only three minutes searching, yet it seemed like he had been there most of his life.

It was not on the desk. He had been through the papers and the file trays twice, making sure he kept well clear of the telephone and the desktop personal computer. But he knew it was there somewhere. He had seen Stabfield showing it to Lewis in his office. Sutcliffe had hidden in the store-room next to Stabfield's office, ear pressed against the thin partition wall. The thinness of the walls was one of the few benefits to him of the open-plan configuration of the main office area with its modular rooms erected at random round the edge. He had caught enough of the conversation between Stabfield and Lewis to know roughly what was happening, and to know what he had to do.

A sound across the other side of the main office area

startled him, and he ducked down behind Stabfield's desk. He killed the torch and held his breath. A flexible desk lamp loomed over him like a cobra poised to strike. Sutcliffe watched it carefully, but it did not move and the sound did not come again. After a while he relaxed, took a deep breath and set about breaking into the drawers of the desk.

The lock resisted his attempts to open it. It was electronic, with a slot for a magnetic card. Sutcliffe knew it was based on a German design, and that there would be only one magnetic key. He stroked his thin beard, and looked round for something to force open the drawer. 'Problems, problems,' he muttered.

The main drawer of the desk was easily levered out with the promotional paperknife. Like his watch, the knife was a free gift from the company, complete with I^2 logo engraved on its plastic presentation case. He shone the torch inside the drawer. It was empty apart from a compact disc.

Sutcliffe snapped open the slip case and popped out the disc inside. Like most recordable CD-ROMs, neither side was labelled. It had been no trouble to find an identical one to replace it with. He stuffed the CD into his inside coat pocket.

Then the lights came on.

It took a while for his eyes to adjust from the dim light of the torch to the painful brightness of the fluorescent strips. He could vaguely make out two blurred shapes standing in the doorway, one with its arm extended to the lightswitch. He had not heard them enter – perhaps they had been there all along.

The image cleared, and Lewis took his hand off the switch and smiled, his face cracking across. Johanna Slake was standing beside him in the doorway, her head slightly angled so that the black ash hair that framed it fell away from one perfect ear. It was a stance at once accusing and mocking.

'Mr Sutcliffe from the Publicity unit, I do believe.' Lewis knew very well who he was – exactly who he was.

31

'Perhaps I can help you. Were you looking for something?'

Had they seen him take the CD? Or had they arrived after he pocketed it?

'Er yes – yes, I was – that is . . .' Sutcliffe moved closer to them, closer to the door, as he blustered.

'Yes?' prompted Lewis.

'I was running an overnight test case on the latest OffNet driver. You know, helping out. My LAN connection went down – some software problem as usual. Always problems. I thought maybe the one in here was still working.'

'So you thought you'd try Mr Stabfield's PC.'

'Yeah.'

'In his locked office.'

Sutcliffe shrugged, using the gesture to edge closer still. 'It wasn't locked, actually.'

'A machine with a power-on password – like all the machines here.'

Johanna was still blocking the doorway, her hands in her jacket pockets. But she stepped forward, into the room, as she added: 'Without any lights.'

'Hey,' Sutcliffe took a step forward and spread his hands in a pretence of innocence, palms open towards her. 'I couldn't find the switch.' He continued the gesture, bringing his hand up to point to the light switch between Johanna and Lewis. Then he leaped forward and the room was plunged into sudden darkness.

Just as fast, Sutcliffe pulled away. He grinned as he heard them try to grab at him and find each other instead. He ran for the space he hoped the doorway occupied, caught his shoulder painfully on the frame, and slammed the door behind him.

Almost immediately he heard the door being thrown open again. He ran towards the emergency exit sign, crashing through the door and bounding down the dimly lit concrete stairs beyond. Above and behind him the lights came on again – they would know the way he had gone and be after him. He paused slightly as the staircase turned back on itself, glared at the security camera swinging round to follow him. But there was nothing he could do in the seconds he had, so he carried on down the stairs, taking them three at a time and bouncing off the artex of the side wall as he went.

The street was as quiet as any in the London evening. The relative calm was smashed by the juddering crash of an emergency exit door being slammed back on its hinges.

Sutcliffe glanced behind him – no sign of anyone yet. Then he made for the grey 'R' registration Vauxhall Cavalier parked on a double yellow line several hundred yards away.

He clicked the alarm off while still running. The sidelights flashed reassuringly at him as he reached the car and sprawled over the bonnet. The simple electronic response made the car seem almost alive – seem as if it were opening its eyes as he approached. And with this half-consciously in mind he pulled away.

Behind him he heard a door close. A worryingly unhurried noise. He yanked open the car door and pushed the key into the ignition. But instead of getting into the car, he pulled the seatbelt down and leaned across to clip it into place over the empty seat. Then he turned the key one click, and rolled down the window. He paused momentarily to turn on the headlights, then shut the car door.

Footsteps – high heels on pavement – from round the corner. Slake was coming from the main entrance in Albion Road. Sutcliffe turned the key the full distance. The engine caught first time, and he ran.

Johanna Slake heard the car start as she reached the corner of the building. She smiled as she caught sight of the Cavalier – the engine was running, the headlights shining directly at her. She waited, one hand on her hip, the other still in her jacket pocket.

The car began to move slowly forward, heading in a dead straight line. It gathered speed, and she could

33

imagine the driver struggling with the wheel, stamping uselessly on the brake. She crossed the road as the vehicle came towards her, heard with satisfaction the central locking activate as the car changed into second gear and hurled itself forward.

Lewis emerged from the emergency exit at the foot of the stairwell. Slake saw him, but she did not move or speak. Lewis had already seen her. They both watched the car as it bounced up the kerb and smashed itself into the side wall of the Regatta Bank building opposite the I² main office. It exploded in flames almost immediately, rolling back several feet from the wall.

Johanna walked slowly across to the burning wreckage, ignoring the heat. Lewis caught her up as she craned forward to see into the front of the car. He was holding the tracer, but made no attempt to switch it on.

'He got the disc. We have to get it out of there.'

'No way.'

Lewis pulled her round to look at him. 'I said, he got the disc.'

'I heard. But you won't get it out of there.'

He stared into the flames for a while. 'Maybe it will survive. If not, we can get another copy.'

Slake laughed – a dry snort of humour. Her head swayed slightly as she said: 'You won't get it out of there because it's not in the car.'

Lewis looked at her, his eyebrows tightening into a frown.

'And neither is Sutcliffe.' She pointed at the driver's window. The flames were dying down slightly and the empty seat was clearly visible. 'Which makes things more complicated.'

Lewis switched on the tracer and checked the readings. The flick of his eyes away from the burning car betrayed the device's message. 'We have to get it back. Or destroy it.'

Johanna Slake smiled. The angular features of her face caught the flickering of the fire, threw bizarre shadows across the road as her head swayed. 'No problem,' she said

34

quietly and took the tracer from him. It was a small device, about the size of a typical television remote control. Its liquid crystal display showed a street map of the local area. A small marker symbol flashed its way along a street two blocks away.

Sutcliffe was sure he wasn't being followed. He was outside a phone box, hand on the door about to push it open when the sound of the explosion reached him. It froze him for a second.

He snatched his hand away from the door, staring nervously at the telephone inside for a few moments. Then he turned and ran.

He ran for a long time, not sure exactly where he was or where he was going. He had ditched his cellular phone a week ago, that was an obvious trap. But he had to make contact – had to find a safe way to call in. Lewis and Slake would be after him soon, if they weren't already – might even know where to wait for him. It was too dangerous to make physical contact, he had to call in.

The noise reached him as he rounded the corner. There was a pub further along the street. He could see the light spilling out of it, hear the glasses chinking and the jukebox blaring. Familiarity, light, and people.

He stumbled against the door, almost laughing with relief as well as humour at the name on the sign swinging above him. The door crashed open, banging noisily against the table inside. There was a lull in the conversation as he staggered across to the bar and leaned heavy and breathless against it. The spotty young barman made a point of serving a man at the other end of the bar and the noise picked up again. *Camilla's Little Secret* continued the melody of *Tantalising Eyes* without comment.

'Yes, sir?' The barman had reached him at last and sounded like he thought 'sir' was spelled 'cur'.

Sutcliffe rattled some change on to the bar. A ten pence piece rolled into a drip mat and spun to a halt. 'Orange juice.'

'Orange juice?' The youth seemed surprised. He

obviously had Sutcliffe down as a drunk. 'Anything in it?'
He sounded disappointed.

'Yes. Ice.'

As the barman shook the bottle of Britvic, Sutcliffe
searched his pockets. Loose change; keys; wallet. Eventually he found a biro. He looked round for paper. He
reached across the bar for the duplicate pad they used to
take the food orders and tore off the top sheet. It was
numbered 17.

'Hey!' His drink had arrived. 'Order food at the other
end of the bar.'

'It's okay – I just want the paper.'

The barman looked dubious and scooped up most of
the coins Sutcliffe had produced. He was about to move
off when Sutcliffe grabbed his shoulder.

'Do you have a phone?'

'Steady on,' he shook off Sutcliffe's grip.

'Do you have a phone?' Sutcliffe repeated urgently.

'Yeah – by the door to the toilets.' He pointed across
the room.

'And is it a tone phone?'

'What?' A woman further along, waiting to be served,
tapped her purse impatiently on the top of the bar. 'Look,
I haven't a clue. Probably. Okay?' He shook his head and
moved along. 'Sorry to keep you . . .'

The door opened again. Sutcliffe felt the draught on
the back of his neck, making the hairs stand on end. He
turned instinctively, jamming the paper and pen into a
pocket as he did so.

Johanna Slake stood in the doorway. The orange light
from the street lit her from behind, seemed almost to
emanate from her as she stepped into the pub. She let the
door swing to, shutting out the street so that she seemed
to loom even closer as the light source shifted. She was
smiling, head scanning gently from side to side like a
predator.

Sutcliffe tried to back away, but he was already against
the bar. Instead he edged round it, colliding with the
couple next to him, grunting an apology, fumbling in his

jacket. Johanna took a step towards him, and he turned and ran – colliding with a table, scattering people and drinks everywhere. Someone was shouting as he stumbled towards the back door of the pub. The couple at the table by the door half stood as he approached – as surprised as everyone else. Sutcliffe pulled tables over and scattered glasses behind him as he went, hoping desperately to slow her down and buy a few precious moments.

As he reached the door at last he turned and looked back. There was a trail of devastation across the bar: tables, chairs, glasses and ashtrays on the floor. People were starting to crowd towards him, forming a human wall between himself and Johanna. But even as he began to feel he might yet escape, several people spun out of the group, staggering across the room in all directions. Johanna pushed effortlessly through the small crowd, heading straight for him without heed of the debris. Tables crashed out of her way, chairs and stools were hurled aside, and glasses shattered underfoot.

Sutcliffe turned to make his escape. But the tall man who had been sitting by the exit was now blocking it. Sutcliffe barged him aside, threw open the door and fled into the night.

He was tired and he was desperate. Despite doubling back, despite checking at every turn, despite diving into a pub at random, she had found him. He had perhaps thirty seconds lead, depending on whether the tall man by the door managed to slow her down at all. Would he even try?

Sutcliffe instinctively glanced at his watch, measuring off the seconds.

He was staggering now, out of breath. He leaned against the plywood wall which ran makeshift beside the pavement. His hand inched along it ahead of his wheezing body. And found a crack – a hinged line up the wall. A padlock through a clasp held the door shut. A painted sign said 'No Unauthorized Admitance' and someone had chalked another 't' above 'Admitance', tried to legitimize it. Sutcliffe put his shoulder to the door and the clasp fell free as the wood splintered away from it.

He pitched forward and sprawled on the ground, a torn page of newspaper flapping up at him like a savage bird. He ripped the paper from his face and threw it to the muddy ground of the building site. 'Economic Growth in Single Digits' the paper cried out for a damp second, then it faded from view in the muddy puddle and the dim light. He slammed the door shut behind him and leaned against it breathless.

Single Digits. Like his watch. Digital.

His exhausted brain made a connection, and with the sound of approaching high heels cracking on the pavement outside he tore at his wrist. Eventually the strap loosened and he hurled the watch into the darkness above him – high over the wooden wall, away from the advancing footsteps as they made their invisible, unhurried way towards the door.

A dog barked – close and getting closer. Sutcliffe staggered to a halt. Guard dogs. He looked back towards the door, debating which animal to take his chances with. He could no longer hear the footsteps, but the barking was closing in. It was joined by another, more distant, growl.

She might still be tracking it, looking in vain along an empty street where a digital watch ticked away its life unheeded in a damp gutter.

The Dobermann hurled itself out of the night. Sutcliffe had almost reached the door when it caught him in the back, slamming him into the wooden wall. The impact bounced the door open a crack, and he leaped through, slammed the door shut again behind him. The wood gave under the weight of the dog scrabbling at it from the other side.

He gathered his strength and glanced along the street. Which way should he go? 'Problems, problems,' he muttered almost under his breath.

'No problem,' said a soft voice from behind him. And his legs gave way beneath him as if hit by a sledgehammer.

He could not get up – his legs were numb from the impact. She leaned over him, her hair falling forward neatly, her smile straight out of the same conditioner advert. But this time he was ready, and rolled with the punch as her heavy fist connected with his face. He lashed out as he moved, his fingers connecting with her face. He felt the nails imbed themselves in the soft skin. And tear.

She stood upright suddenly – more as if she were surprised than in pain. His fingers were sticky as he tried to drag himself away. He tumbled the short distance over the kerb into the road, twisted as he fell, landed on his back.

She seemed to tower above him, given extra height by the pavement. He had just a moment when he could have dragged himself to his numbed feet and fled. But in that same moment the moon emerged from a cloud, and he saw her face. And froze.

He had ripped the flesh from one side of her face. The skin hung in torn strips, flapping slightly in the breeze. But there was no blood. The viscous mess that clung to the broken skin was more like engine grease than anything organic.

But Sutcliffe hardly noticed this. His attention was anchored on the face beneath – a segmented, green head bulging from one side of Johanna's skin-deep beauty. The tiny scales glistened in the moonlight, shimmered over each other as the head swayed mesmerically. A thin pale tongue licked at the lips of a mouth that was half human and half serpent, hissing sharply in the sudden quiet of the night. And the inhuman eye swivelled to look directly into his own.

He imagined rather than heard the whirring of a minute motor driving the eye in its socket. The small metal levers which held the artificial eyeball in place moved smoothly in their joints, the reptilian skin rippling slightly where the mechanism was grafted in, where machine met monster. He was vaguely aware that he understood her inhuman strength, appreciated why her fist was hard as iron as she hauled him to his feet. Her

39

fingers flexed with machine precision within the soft leather of her glove.

Then she grasped his neck and wrenched it sideways.

She did not release his limp body until she had torn the CD from his jacket pocket. Then she let go, and Kevin Sutcliffe slumped back into the gutter. His eyes stared up at the moon as it slipped ashamed behind another cloud. The only sound was of high heels on tarmac, and of the breeze whispering along the deserted street.

'Well, that was very pleasant.' The Doctor put down his glass and wiped his mouth with his scarf.

'Aren't you going to finish it?' His glass was still half full.

He looked at the remains of the ginger beer for a while. 'No,' he said. Then his mouth opened into a huge smile. 'Ask me why,' he grinned.

'All right,' said Sarah with a laugh, 'why?'

'Partly because we're late –'

'You're telling me,' Sarah inserted just loud enough for him to hear.

The Doctor ignored the interruption. 'And partly because the ginger beer isn't actually terribly good.'

'Not a good vintage?'

'No.' He peered at the glass again. 'A ninety-seven, I would say.'

'Is that bad?'

'I should have tried the *Old Gavelblaster*,' he confided.

Sarah winced. 'That bad!'

'Mmmm. And we should be going before we get *involved* in anything.' The Doctor was on his feet now, winding miles of scarf round his neck as if it were string and his head was a yo-yo.

'I did think,' Sarah told him as she pulled on her coat, 'that you were going to get involved with that drunk earlier.'

'Who me?' He seemed amazed. 'No. Just a little friendly advice about temperance beverages perhaps.'

'He may have got that from his wife – or whoever she was.'

40

The Doctor paused in his scarf routine. 'Yes, perhaps that's why he seemed so frightened.' He looked round, patting his pockets. 'An interesting woman, by the look of her. Now, have we got everything?'

Sarah stood on tiptoe and said into his ear: 'Beauty's only skin deep, you know.'

'Yes.' The Doctor frowned suddenly. He plunged a hand into his coat pocket. 'And evil goes right to the core.'

Marc Lewis held the compact disc carefully, hands cupped round the rim so as not to touch the surface. The disc caught the bright office lighting as he lowered it into the tray of the CD drive, reflected a rainbow of colours. He pushed the tray shut.

'I don't think it's been damaged.' He was relieved.

Johanna stood beside his desk, watching. Her face was still in tatters, but neither of them seemed to care. The CD was all that mattered.

'Will you report the event sequence to Stabfield?'

'Of course. Everything will be fine. He'll get an executive summary tonight and back-up slides in the morning.' Lewis moved the mouse on its plastic pad. 'I'll just check the integrity of the disc, to be sure we don't have to restore another one from back-up. Then I'll start on the status report.'

The CD drive whirred into life, spinning up to speed. The light flashed steadily as the drive read data from the disc and passed it to the processor. Lewis leaned back, a slight smile creasing his face, his elbows resting easily on the arms of the chair and his fingers steepled.

Then *In The Mood* started to play buoyantly through the PC speaker. The music echoed round the office, wiping the synthetic smile from Lewis's face.

'What is it?' Sarah asked.

'I don't know.' The Doctor pulled his hand from his coat pocket. He was holding a small sheet of paper – a double-fold from a duplicate pad, like the one at the food counter.

They sat down again, and the Doctor unfolded the paper carefully, so as not to damage its content. It was wrapped around a reflective silver disc. The Doctor examined it closely. 'A compact disc.'

'Eh?'

'Or a CD-ROM – for storing computer data and software.'

Sarah picked up the paper, rescuing it from the drops of ginger beer which peppered the table top. 'What do you make of this, Doctor?' She held the paper out to him. On it was scrawled a single word, written hurriedly in capital letters:

HUBWAY

03

Search Patterns

The sirens started screaming almost as soon as they left the pub. The Doctor and Sarah watched as first a police car, then an ambulance screeched past. The vehicles took the corner ahead with a squeal of brakes and tyres, then the sirens cut out. Whatever was happening was just around the corner. The Doctor and Sarah ran towards the end of the block.

The police car had climbed the pavement so that it was at an angle. The ambulance was slewed to a halt beside it. Men and women in uniforms were running about, the centre of attention a huddled shape lying by the side of the road.

The Doctor pushed his way through the assembled people, Sarah following in his wake. The dark shape in the road was the body of a man. One of the ambulance men was kneeling beside it. The corpse's head was twisted round at an odd angle, facing away from Sarah as if he was craning to see what was going on behind him.

'Excuse me, sir.' The policeman took the Doctor's shoulder firmly. 'If you could keep out of the way we'll be able to get on a lot better.' The Doctor looked him full in the face. 'I'm sure you understand, sir.'

'Indeed I do. Perhaps I can help – I'm a doctor.'

The policeman considered for a moment, catching sight of the Doctor's outrageous attire in the strobed light. Then he stepped out of the way. 'I think he's beyond help, sir. But by all means have a look.'

The Doctor knelt beside the body. The ambulance man shook his head.

'I'm with the Doctor,' Sarah told the policeman. But he did not reply. He was watching the Doctor gently lift the dead man's head and rotate it slightly. Then he felt for a pulse in the man's left wrist, frowned, and examined the hand and forearm more closely. Then he checked the other hand and wrist. The ends of the fingers seemed to be stained with a dark, viscous substance. The Doctor sniffed at it, then shrugged. He let the hand and arm flop back down.

All the while the emergency lights played along the boards concealing the construction site beside the road. From behind them a dog began to bark, then another joined it. The policeman who had spoken to the Doctor went over and shouted at the dogs to shut up, banging on the boards with his fist. There was a clatter as the door swung to and fro and he jumped.

The Doctor stood up, shaking his head. The ambulance man mirrored him a moment later.

'Did he fall?' Sarah asked.

'Where from?' asked the ambulance man. 'He'd have to fall a long way to break his neck like that.'

The Doctor nodded. 'His neck was twisted till the bone snapped.'

'Hit and run?' Sarah wondered.

The Doctor shook his head. 'He's got no other injuries.' He pushed his hat back on his head as if coming to a decision. 'I think he was murdered.'

'Murdered?' The policeman was back. His colleagues were busy cordoning off the area, but he had heard the Doctor's words. 'Anything to do with this, do you think?' He held something up. As the light flashed across it they could see it was a heavy metal clasp, bent at one end. A small piece of splintered wood hung from one end, a battered padlock from the other.

'Possibly. He used to have a watch. You can see the impression on the wrist where the strap was. You haven't found it by any chance, officer?'

'They'll kill for a pocketful of loose change these days,' the policeman snorted as he shook his head.

'Who will?'

'Well, if we knew that, miss, things'd be a lot easier.'

He strode off towards the squad car, calling out to a colleague on the way to call in for backup and establish a scene of crime.

'Come along, Sarah.' The Doctor led her through the cordon of candy-striped tape fluttering in the breeze, past the emergency vehicles.

'What happened to him?' she asked when they were out of earshot.

'I don't know. But something broke his neck — twisted it like a dry stick until . . .' He snapped his fingers sharply and Sarah grimaced.

They walked on in silence for a while, skirting round the building site on their way back towards the TARDIS. 'Did you recognize him?' the Doctor asked after a while.

'I hardly saw him.' The ambulance man and the Doctor had obscured her view and the face had been pointing away from her. 'Did you?'

'Oh yes.' He seemed loath to explain any further. Instead he stopped suddenly in his tracks and bent down. Almost immediately he stood up again. He was holding a watch. Its digital display clicked forward a minute as they looked at it.

'Are all the watches like that now?' Sarah asked, leaning over the Doctor's arm to get a closer view. 'Ugly, isn't it?'

He did not answer, but turned slightly so she could no longer see. 'Intriguing,' said the Doctor at last, and stuffed the watch into his pocket.

'So who was he?'

'He was the man from the pub.'

'The man who bumped into you?'

The Doctor nodded. 'More importantly than that, the man who was running — running for his life we now know. And the man who put this in my pocket as he pushed past.' He held up the CD for a second, then it disappeared into his coat again.

'The woman?'

'Maybe.' They walked on, turning into another street. 'But she'd have to be stronger than she looked. Much stronger.'

Sarah was not convinced. 'Perhaps she was trained in unarmed combat, or maybe she had hit him with something.'

'Sarah,' the Doctor said, 'whoever it was – whatever it was – didn't just break his neck. They crushed the bones almost to powder.' He let the words sink in. They were back at *The Green Man*.

'But what could do that?'

'I don't know. But I intend to find out.'

The Doctor pushed open the door and strode into the pub.

They sat back at the same table. This time Sarah sipped at a brandy and the Doctor stared unenthusiastically at a pint of *Old Gavelblaster*. He had studiously avoided taking a drink so far, diverting their attention from the glass by giving Sarah a quick potted history of the compact disc revolution.

'So why have we come back here?' Sarah asked. 'Just so I can hear the high-quality digital juke box?'

'Not entirely,' the Doctor admitted. He picked up his glass, brought it almost to his lips, and then set it back on the table. Instead of drinking, he answered Sarah's question.

She did not feel any better for knowing the answer. The Doctor had been quick to dismiss any assumption that it was for Sarah's own benefit – that she needed a drink after the shock. Instead he went through a tortuous chain of near-logic which boiled down to a guess that whoever or whatever had killed the man was after the CD, and would therefore come back to the pub to find it.

'My money's on the woman,' Sarah told him.

'Mine too.'

'So what do we do if she comes back?'

'*When* she comes back,' the Doctor corrected her, 'we help her look for it.'

Sarah took another mouthful of brandy. 'And then what?'

'Ah,' the Doctor took his first gulp of beer. 'Then we shall see.'

* * *

Stabfield had been preparing to leave the ships, docked together into a single unit in powered geostationary orbit round the earth, when Lewis's call came through.

Stabfield had been feeling quite pleased. He had just arranged to pay a left wing terrorist group for services rendered. He had left a message for them in an unused voicemail box belonging to a large American corporation who probably didn't even realize their computer-controlled telephone network could be hacked. The terrorists could collect the message at their leisure simply by calling the corporation and dialling into the voicemail system. The message would wait for ever, and even if it was found it could never be traced back to the originator. It was the sort of ordered, efficient neatness that Stabfield appreciated. A perfect solution executed at someone else's expense and risk.

Then he took the call from Lewis.

The problem was not in replacing the CD – that was easily done, they had a backup of the gold code. What was rather more important was to ensure that the original did not fall into the wrong hands. He demanded a full risk assessment and problem analysis, and told Lewis to get the original back.

'I'll send Johanna now,' Lewis said. His voice was quieter than usual – dulled by the reprimand. 'We have the data from the tracer, so we know where he went. It must be somewhere along the route.'

'Obviously,' Stabfield hissed. 'So get off the dime, and on the case.' He could see Johanna at the edge of his screen as she left on her errand – quiet, without complaint. If only Lewis were as coolly efficient, but he had been augmented too much, would never make a real leader despite his aspirations. Stabfield would have to break it to him at his next appraisal and assessment review.

On his way back to the shuttle bay, Stabfield calmed down a little. The loss of the disc was unfortunate, but probably would not negatively impact the project. Lewis would do everything possible to recover it – he was certainly capable as far as staffwork went. And Johanna was as cold and efficient as an ice-pick.

Lewis cut the link with a snarl. It was always the same with Stabfield – underneath the famous stoic exterior he was frightened and nervous, always about to lose his temper. And when he did there was much sound and fury. He was surprised none of the human employees had disseminated information to the press about their managing director – who was, according to press speculation, the fifth richest man in the world.

Lewis was increasingly aware of a deep empty feeling from his stomach – he could not ignore it for much longer. In his desk drawer was the vacuum-packed cheese sandwich he had bought at lunchtime. He had been hungry then, but had managed to fight off the inconvenient pains until now.

He pulled at the loose end of the cellophane cover, his mouth clamped hard shut and his eyebrows heavy with concentration and distaste. He could already smell the food. His hand shook so much that slivers of grated cheddar slipped from between the bread and snowed on to his desk. He licked his dry lips, and tentatively pushed a triangular corner of sandwich into his mouth, tore it away from the main body, and swallowed it with a gulp. At once he felt sick, nauseous. He choked down the rest of the sandwich, gagging at each mouthful. Then shaking with frustration, anger and fear he slumped back into the soft upholstery of the chair.

'You know, this really isn't at all bad.' Somehow the Doctor was on to his third pint of beer, while Sarah was still sipping nervously at her first brandy. She suspected he had bought her at least a double, but even so she was able to find solace in that it was only her first.

'Shhhhh!'

For a second Sarah thought the Doctor had choked on his drink. But he was not doubling up, rather leaning across the table to whisper noisily at her. 'Here she is. Don't look.'

48

Sarah instinctively made to turn, but he grabbed her shoulder and spun her back to face him.

'I said don't look.' After a few moments he released his grip. 'All right – you can look now.'

Sarah turned slowly, trying to make it look casual and natural, but feeling it was quite the opposite. She surveyed the lounge bar, glancing round each table and along the bar. Eventually she saw the woman, by the cigarette machine. The machine was set at eye level on the wall, and she was running her hand along the top of it. Nobody else in the pub seemed particularly interested. Most of the people who had been there when she first visited had moved on and others had taken their places. Those few who remained were beyond noticing or caring, deep into conversations, relationships and drinks.

'She's looking for the CD thing,' Sarah said quietly.

The Doctor nodded. 'Nothing but dust and ash up there.' He gestured with a nod of his head as she moved on towards the bar, lifting a coat from where it lay draped over a stool on the way. She shook it gently, then when nothing fell out she moved on. 'Notice how she's retracing our poor friend's path – at least, as far as she knows it.'

'So what do we do?'

'We help her,' the Doctor said with a huge grin. 'Or at least, I do. You stay in the background – see if anyone else is with her, shadowing.' He wrapped his scarf once more round his neck, then took a gulp of beer, leaped to his feet, and set off across the bar. Sarah moved over to a nearer table as the couple who were there finished their drinks and left.

The woman was at the bar now, her eyes scanning along the damp surface then back across the shelves behind. The Doctor was standing behind her, hands thrust into his trouser pockets, leaning forward and watching her.

The spotty young barman caught the woman by surprise: 'Yes, Miss?'

She recovered in an instant. 'I wonder if you could

help me with a problem. A friend of mine was in earlier. He was a bit the worse for wear and left something behind – a compact disc. Perhaps it's been handed in?'

The barman looked dubious. 'Don't think so. Haven't seen it about. I'll ask the others if you like?'

'Oh would you? How kind.' Her smile was silky innocence even from where Sarah sat. The Doctor frowned and curled his mouth downwards at the edges, clearly unimpressed. The barman, by contrast, looked like he had just won publican of the year. The fact was not lost on the woman, who followed up quickly: 'Of course, he may have handed it in himself – left it for someone to collect. He was in such a state. It is very important.'

Suddenly the Doctor was by her side, hand on her shoulder, eyes popping. 'Ah – in that case we must find it.' The woman took a step away from him, managing to shake loose the hand. But the Doctor continued unabashed, his deep voice rising in volume so that it carried clearly across the room. 'A CD, you say? A last present from his poor dying grandmother, no doubt. It usually is.'

'Something like that.' The woman was looking round, not embarrassed, but unsettled. Conversations were stopping and heads were turning towards her. Sarah imagined she had wanted to avoid being noticed.

But the Doctor was only just beginning. 'Then we must search the pub. Leave no drip mat unturned, raid the juke box, check the cigarette machine.'

The woman turned sharply at the last comment, her eyes narrowing as she watched the Doctor start issuing orders. In a moment he had the barman clearing the mats from the bar, an old man and his wife feeling along the top of the cigarette machine, and just about everyone else shifting coats, stools, tables. One over-enthusiastic drunk started peeling wallpaper from a corner of the room, only to find himself bundled outside by one of the staff.

Sarah made herself busy with the others, trying to keep close to the Doctor and the woman without appearing too interested.

'Is it in a box?' a man asked as he passed them.

'No,' the woman said. 'Well, probably not.'

A young man and woman raised their attention from the floor by the food servery for a moment to call 'What's on it?'

The woman ignored them, though Sarah could tell from the flick of her eyes in their direction that she had heard. The Doctor could tell too. 'That's a very good question,' he said. 'And extremely useful information.' The couple smiled at their own cleverness. The Doctor clapped his hands together like a whip cracking, and everyone stopped and turned towards him. 'Right everyone, this lady is now going to tell us what is on the CD.'

There were general mutters of interest and everyone crowded a little closer to the bar to hear.

She did not answer for a while, people started shuffling their feet impatiently. 'Nothing,' the woman eventually said.

'Nothing?' The Doctor's eyebrows arched upwards and he stepped back in theatrical surprise.

'Nothing printed on it, that is.' Sarah could see her eyes darting round the room, as if looking for a way out. 'It was made specially. It is unique.'

'I see. What a shame, then, that we haven't found it.' The Doctor paced up and down in front of the bar, all eyes still on him. He stopped in mid-pace and swung round. 'I know – we could have a whip-round and get your friend another one.' He nodded to himself, apparently pleased with the notion. 'Just tell us what was on it, and I can have another one made – I'm really rather good at arranging that sort of thing.'

'I'm sorry.' The woman met the Doctor's unblinking stare. 'It wouldn't be the same.'

'Oh, well that's a pity.' The Doctor's voice was suddenly quieter. 'I really would have liked to help, you know.'

'You have been a great help,' she said flatly as she turned to the assembled crowd. 'All of you have. My thanks. At least now we can be sure my friend did not leave it in here.'

Disappointed by their failure to find the CD, people began to resume their places at the tables, the excitement over.

'Perhaps we could help you search elsewhere?' The Doctor's eyes gleamed keenly.

'No, really. You have been very helpful.' She made to leave, then turned back as if she had just remembered something. 'Can I get you a – drink?' she asked. She said the word 'drink' with ill-disguised disdain. Almost disgust.

'That's very kind,' replied the Doctor. 'But I already have one. Perhaps I can get you a *drink*?' He mimicked her pronunciation.

'No,' she said hastily. Then in a more measured tone she said: 'No thank you,' and walked quickly to the door.

'Till we meet again,' the Doctor called after her. She paused for a moment in the doorway. But she did not look back, and in a second she was gone.

It had been a strange day. Not just because of the extra-ordinary events. He settled into his favourite armchair, slightly uncomfortable that he needed such familiarity, such comforts. He was hungry but did not feel like eating – had not eaten all day.

He had not put on any of his usual music, but opted instead for Bach's *Musical Offering*. A part of his mind was worried that he never listened to Bach. Too regular, too scientific in his construction. This CD had been a present, unplayed until now. He found it oddly reassuring to pick out the notes of the fugue with its complex, apparently irregular King's Theme brought into mathematical precision by the hidden canons.

With the *Canon per Tonos* rising endlessly, modulating up the keys to the next octave, he fell asleep.

And the nightmares came.

Sarah crept along the dark street keeping the Doctor's distinctive silhouette a couple of paces ahead of her. At first she had been interested, but now she was rapidly becoming bored with trailing the woman through a seemingly random maze of London streets. She was just wondering how much longer it would go on when she bumped heavily into the Doctor's back as he halted suddenly.

She muttered a quiet apology, but he brushed it off and pulled her forward so she could join him peering round the corner of a wall into the adjoining street.

The woman was standing across the road, apparently unsure what to do next. She had stopped her detailed examination of every step along the pavement and every opening and hidey-hole within reach along her route. Instead she was staring ahead of her.

Sarah could see her problem, and at the same time felt a sense of vindication. They were at a junction with the road where the man had been killed, and the woman was watching the police as they finished cordoning off the area.

When she moved it was sudden, like a cat springing. She was off, walking briskly but almost silently down the street away from the police activity. Her hands were in her jacket pockets, her head down. The Doctor took Sarah's hand and together they dashed across the road, hoping the woman would not look back, would not see them mid-way – caught by the street light or strobed in blue.

She did not look back. She did not so much as break step on the whole journey. This time the route was more direct – she was going home, the Doctor whispered to Sarah.

It was spotting with rain when they reached her destination. It was a large office block, not very far from *The Green Man*. A large sign outside was engraved I^2, the rain drops trickling into the relief and lipping out again before splashing to the ground. They watched her across the road, reflected first in the shiny wetness of the tarmac, then in the opaque darkness of the windows. She stopped at the door, and this time she did look back.

The Doctor and Sarah were in the dense shadows

under a tree quite a way down the street. Even so, Sarah drew back as the woman's head turned their way.

But she did not seem interested in their hiding place. Instead she stared for a moment at a Ford Granada parked across the road from the office. Then she turned to a keypad set in the wall by the door, deliberately putting herself between the keypad and the car. She pushed several buttons and the main doors slid open. She stepped through, and as the darkness of the entrance lobby swallowed her up the doors shut behind her.

'What now?' asked Sarah.

'What do you think?' The Doctor's eyes were full of mischief.

'We follow her inside?'

He thumped her lightly on the shoulder. 'Right. Come on.'

They got half-way across the road, going slowly and carefully, hoping they weren't being watched, trying to keep quiet. Then the Granada's lights came on full, catching them like startled rabbits.

Sarah's retinas still retained the smear of the headlights when the car drew level with them, the window already wound down.

'I wonder if you'd join us for a moment,' the driver asked. It was not a question, the back door of the car was already open, another man leaning across the back seat beckoning them in.

'Why should we? Who are you?' Sarah was at once on her guard.

'Oh come on, Sarah,' the Doctor chided. 'Be reasonable. After all, he's asked us nicely and he probably has a gun.' His voice dropped in both pitch and volume. 'People usually do in these circumstances, I've found.'

'Very true,' the driver agreed, although he made no move to produce it.

'And the only thing worse than being shot,' said the Doctor as he bundled himself into the back of the car, motioning for the other man to budge up and give them room to squeeze in, 'is being shot in the rain.'

With a sigh Sarah followed him into the car, pulling the door shut behind her.

'Now isn't this cosy.' The Doctor was rolling his shoulders and wriggling into the seat. 'We'd like the scenic route please – if you could pause at Buckingham Palace, the Tower of London, and drop us off at any surviving police telephone box we happen across that would be extremely useful.'

Neither man answered as the car gathered speed and headed off into the London night.

04

Hubway

Stabfield had not been surprised that the CD was still missing. But with luck Sutcliffe had hidden it away, and he could no longer tell anyone where it was. In any case, the chance of anyone managing to work out its content, let alone its significance, was virtually nil.

But the low risk assessment did not stop him being angry – both with Marc Lewis and with Johanna Slake. He was already on his way back in the shuttle, and he had taken the precaution of downloading a back-up copy of the data on to another CD. They needed the CD for the phase two exit gate, and phase three was about to begin.

It was nearly midnight when the Granada drew up and the Doctor and Sarah found themselves escorted into a nondescript building. Their escorts said nothing, despite the Doctor's comments on the apparent age of the building, the merits of the original, and the discomfort of being kidnapped and rushed through London in the dead of night and in the rain.

The driver typed his name and business into the computer at reception and showed a security pass before the large security guard allowed them inside. Then they were taken up in a lift and led down numerous featureless corridors before arriving in a sparsely furnished office. The walls were painted a grimy, peeling magnolia. In the middle of the room, standing on the bare floorboards, was a large conference table. Its surface was scarred and pitted and someone had carved *Fred loves Ginge* on the edge with a sharp implement. The table was bare apart from a telephone, which was positioned so that its cord was strategically placed to trip up anyone crossing the room.

The half dozen hard, upright chairs grouped round the table were just too low to be comfortable, and looked like rejects from a secondary school.

The Doctor immediately slumped down on one of the chairs, tilted his hat over his eyes and said: 'So you don't come here often.'

The second man from the car had left, but the driver was standing in the doorway, watching them silently. When he did not respond, the Doctor pushed his hat back and fixed him with a stare. 'If you did,' he said, 'you'd realize that there is a more direct route to this room. I imagine that when you were first shown here you stopped at another office on the way, hmmm?'

The driver still said nothing, but Sarah could see that he was listening, interested. Perhaps even impressed.

'Ergo, you don't work here.' The Doctor stood up suddenly and walked up to the man, standing almost on his toes and looking him straight in the eye. 'Doing a little moonlighting for friends, eh Inspector Ashby?'

The driver took a step back, his dispassionate demeanour broken. 'What? How did —' He broke off, unwilling to say more.

The Doctor snorted. 'It seemed likely. You get to drive and do the talking, so obviously there's a rank attached. Since you don't work here you're obviously not native to MI5. No, I'd say Special Branch. Your name's the easy part. You typed it into the computer log when we came in.' He sat down again, pleased with his diagnosis. 'Am I right?' he asked with a wink and a tap of the nose.

Sarah had watched the rather one-sided exchange with interest. When Ashby refused to be drawn further she sat down in a chair next to the Doctor. 'How do you know this is MI5?'

'Came here a couple of times with the Brigadier, back in my "establishment" days. Interminable meetings to try to justify UNIT's existence and budget.' He leaned back on the chair and crashed his feet down on the table top, making the telephone receiver jump in its cradle. 'Boring!' was his final verdict.

They sat in silence for a few minutes. The man in the doorway shuffled his weight from one foot to another a couple of times, and the Doctor practised back-flips on his yo-yo. Sarah looked round the room hoping to find something of interest or a clue as to why they were there, but she was disappointed.

They heard footsteps from along the corridor and Ashby stood more self-consciously upright. He stepped aside for a man to enter the room – a tall man in his mid thirties with strikingly fair hair. He was wearing a suit, but looked comfortable rather than smart in it. His tie, like his suit, was plain and dark. He dismissed Ashby with a nod of the head and took a seat opposite the Doctor and Sarah, laying a manila folder on the table in front of him. He squared up the folder against the edge of the table, then folded his hands on top of it.

'I do apologize for the inconvenience,' he said in a well-cultured voice, 'but one of my people was killed this evening and I need to ask you a few questions.'

'The man we saw?' suggested Sarah.

The Doctor's eyes narrowed. 'Thin man with a thin beard? Neck crushed outside a building site?'

The fair-haired man frowned. 'I thought Special Branch picked you up outside I², not at the scene of the crime.'

'They did. But perhaps they confused cause and effect.'

'I'm sorry?'

'We were at the office because we saw the murder – or at least, the victim. Not vice versa.'

The man considered this a while. 'You didn't kill him.' It was an observation rather than a question.

'No,' Sarah was emphatic. 'But we know who did. It was a woman. We followed her to the office building, Eye Squared, or whatever you said.'

'Are you intending to continue in this singularly inter-rogatory vein,' the Doctor inquired, 'or shall we intro-duce ourselves and have tea?'

The man lifted the phone and muttered into it. Then

he smiled. 'Tea is on the way.'

'Good. In that case, I'm the Doctor and this is Miss Smith.'

'Robert Gibson, MI5.'

The Doctor nodded. 'Then you'll have heard of UNIT.'

'Indeed. May I ask how *you* come to have heard of it?'

'Oh I've done some work for them on occasion – freelance sort of thing. Consultancy.'

'You mean wet jobs?'

The Doctor grimaced. 'I mean advice.'

Gibson did not look convinced. 'I wouldn't have thought you were the UNIT type, to be frank. Can you prove it?'

Sarah sighed and watched as the Doctor mentioned passes he could not immediately put his hands on (and which might perhaps be out of date). He also dropped names of people Gibson had either not heard of or who had retired years earlier. Eventually Gibson suggested they drop the subject, hinting that he could check the Doctor's credentials later. Then he made another muttered phone call.

'Right then,' Gibson said at last, 'shall we compare notes on this evening's events? It seems you can fill in a few blanks we have.'

'Tell us first why you were watching I²,' the Doctor challenged.

'Very well. We suspect that it's a front of some sort for the *Little Brothers*.'

'You mean, like Big Brother?' Sarah asked.

'Yes, Miss Smith.' Gibson seemed surprised she had to ask. 'A terrorist group opposed to all forms of government intervention or regulation – Big Brother, in their terms. They were behind the Pullen Tower thing which came to its conclusion this evening.'

'If you mean the tower block we saw being stormed, I'd say it came to a rather loud and bloody conclusion,' Sarah said. 'But why would I² be behind them? Who are they anyway?'

'You are out of touch, aren't you?'

The Doctor leaned across the table. 'We've been travelling,' he said quietly. 'Tell us about it.'

So Gibson told them.

'It's run by Lionel Stabfield. You must have heard of him. Rumoured to be the fifth richest man in the world. Only forty-three as well. He came from nowhere and set up I^2. The press alternately call him a genius and a bore. His competitors keep their thoughts largely to themselves. Except Ashley Chapel, but he's big enough in his own right not to be scared.'

'And what does this Stabfield character do?' the Doctor asked.

'He owns and runs I^2. And that means OffNet – the office automation stuff. It connects office equipment together. *Integrated Intelligence* – that's what the two I's stand for.' Gibson shuffled the papers in his folder for a moment. Then he continued. 'The initial appeal was that I^2 had no stake in the technology – it was a truly independent standard. After the *de facto* standards Microsoft and the others were rolling out this was a breath of fresh air. Companies leaped at it.'

'Then I^2 got into the business properly?' the Doctor asked.

Gibson nodded. 'They started producing their own chips – either complete systems or daughter chips to go into other systems. The OffNet protocols were built-in. Instead of licensing the underlying language, Vorell, you had to buy the chips.'

'So they got rich and gained control.'

'Yes. And it hasn't stopped with OffNet. The Vorell language is now used by motor components to talk to each other and divulge their service information, diagnostics and history – CarNet. It's used to control lifts in office blocks so they pick up and drop off people more efficiently. It's used to schedule the trains and the tubes and the buses in just about every country in the world.'

'Big, then.' Sarah was impressed.

'Very. It will even keep your stereo sounding perfect.

In fact, this evening was a first for them in several ways. The SAS used BattleNet to co-ordinate their attack. It suggests the optimum attack plan, then keeps them in constant communication and provides status information in a special head-up display within their respirators. Very effective, as it turns out.'

'All this in just the last few years.' Sarah mentally worked out the maximum time it could have taken.

'This is just the beginning,' Gibson said. The phone rang and he cupped his hand over the mouthpiece as he completed his observation: 'When the information super-highway comes on-line in a few days, OffNet will be the glue that keeps all the disparate systems working together.'

'So what does it all mean?' Sarah asked quietly as Gibson spoke into the phone. 'Doctor, what's going on?'

But before the Doctor could answer, Gibson stood up. 'Right, now we can perhaps get some information from you. My boss is on his way up.'

'Nice chap is he?' the Doctor asked.

'Very. But rather more to the point, he may know if you really do have connections with UNIT.'

The door swung open behind Gibson and a man walked in. He stopped dead in his tracks when he saw the Doctor and Sarah. 'Good Lord. I suppose I should have guessed you two would be caught up in this.'

Sarah was speechless. She sat staring at the man on the other side of the room, unable to move. Gaping. Some-how this moment brought home to her more than any other the fact that she had travelled in time. The Doctor was rather more used to the notion, and more import-antly the consequences, of time travel. He was on his feet at once, striding towards the newcomer, hand extended.

The man was tall. He was in his late forties – had to be – but looked as if he was still fit and well. He was grey at the temples, his hair thinning a little and receding. His face was lined and slightly softer, rounder. Sarah had seen him only a month ago, yet he was now nearly twenty years older.

The Doctor grabbed his hand and wrenched it up and down before enfolding him in a bear hug. 'Harry Sullivan – now isn't this a pleasant surprise!'

Paul Campbell lived on the outskirts of Glenlake village. From his house it was only ten minutes walk to the edge of the woods. Campbell liked to think he was fit despite his age, and if he was it was mainly down to Jasper's exercise routine. They each covered about six miles a day, at varying speeds depending on the weather, Jasper's mood and how many cigarettes Campbell had choked on the night before.

Each day they took a different path through the woods. By now they knew all the tracks and most of the clearings, so it was a surprise and something of a delight to happen upon an area they had not been to before.

'Will you look at that, Jasper,' Campbell gasped, patting his pockets in the hope of finding the packet of Benson and Hedges he knew was on the sideboard. It looked to his tired old eyes as if there was a small clearing ahead, and he walked closer to examine it. He did not get very far before Jasper's straining weight at the other end of the lead held him back.

'What's wrong with you?' He yanked on the lead, but Jasper would have none of it. So Campbell screwed up his eyes and managed to make out the fuzzy shape of a fence between himself and the clearing. 'You're probably right, boy,' Campbell conceded. 'MOD, I shouldn't wonder,' he muttered as they moved off, 'putting up fences, spoiling the landscape. They'll be shooting at things next. What's wrong now, boy?'

But the high-pitched whine he could just make out was not coming from the dog. It got louder and louder, and Jasper dragged Campbell back into the wood, trying to run from the noise. Campbell would have been more than happy to be dragged along, but the sudden down-draught which pulled at his coat and blew dust and loose debris from the ground into his eyes and his face was slowing him down. He wrapped the lead once more round his wrist to be sure Jasper could not break loose, and crouched in the slight shelter of a horse chestnut tree.

The whining noise reached a peak, joined by the rushing sound of the wind through the woodland and a lower, rumbling sound like the jet engines of a fighter plane. Then, suddenly it stopped.

Jasper was calm again, his fur ruffled by the breeze but his eyes back to their usual dullness. Campbell was out of breath. 'MOD morons, don't know nothing about keeping the peace round here,' he grunted as he tried to push his few wispy grey hairs back into place. He and Jasper were about to set off for home when he realized they were being watched.

The man came from just behind Campbell, from the same direction as the fence. From the same direction as the noise. As the man approached, grew clearer, Campbell could see that he was perhaps in his early forties, tall and thin with narrow, pinched facial features. He wore a dark business suit which contrasted with his pale skin – even his lips were thin and bloodless.

'You hear that racket?' Campbell asked. 'Sodding military – I shall report it.'

The man was close to him now, so close Campbell took a step back and Jasper growled in his usual tentative manner which fooled nobody.

'Report it?' The man smiled faintly, one side of his mouth twitching upwards, the other remaining set. 'I don't think so.'

'Oh don't you, then?' Campbell turned to go. 'Well, you'll see. Come on Jasper.' He flicked the lead in encouragement, and felt a tick in his back as he did – probably muscles playing up again, he thought.

But it was a long, thin steel knife thrusting into his spinal cord.

Stabfield picked up the body, taking care not to get blood on his tie. He hefted it easily over his shoulder, and broke the dog's neck with a single kick. Then he untied the lead from the man's hand and wrist. Nobody would miss the dog, but the man's body would need to be moved elsewhere. Stabfield wanted it found, not hunted for. And he wanted it found miles from where his shuttle was moored.

The appearance of the body would tie up police resources and computer-time in the area, which was a small enhancement to the plan. Another minor activity to add to the project diagram; another challenge become an opportunity.

'It's good to see you again, Harry,' Sarah said. 'But I didn't expect to see you in MI5.'

Harry smiled. 'No, probably not. Though it seemed a sensible career move at the time.'

'You moved here from UNIT?'

'Not immediately. I got a posting at Porton Down after my assignment to UNIT was up. Defence research stuff, very hush-hush.' He gave a short laugh. 'That's jargon for *boring*,' he explained. 'From there it was a natural transition into intelligence work proper. I started out first as an advisor, then as a field officer for MI5. Eventually I made Assistant Chief of Staff.'

Sarah was impressed. 'Sounds very grand.'

Harry shook his head. 'Not really.'

'There are actually dozens of *Assistant Chiefs of Staff*,' Gibson said.

'Thanks, Robert,' Harry said to Gibson. 'And what have you two been up to, then,' he asked the Doctor and Sarah. 'Tonight in particular.'

The insistent steady bleep of the alarm woke Johanna Slake from her nightmares. It was the brain running unfettered and subconscious, exploring, remembering, *experiencing*. The cause was well understood. There was no cure but to stay awake. But she needed to be rested for her next work item.

Her skin felt slippery and tarnished as she pulled on her clothes. Her hair was immaculate as ever – almost shoulder-length, then curled in on itself. Having real hair,

64

having to brush, wash, condition it must be terrible.

She collected Carlson exactly on time from his house in Ruislip. He did not ask if she had slept well. They drove in silence until they reached the edge of Marlborough.

'But what was it that persuaded Sutcliffe to break cover? If we knew that, this whole thing would fall into place.'

'Wrong, Harry.' The Doctor jumped up and started walking round the table, head down, hands in trouser pockets, scarf trailing along the floor. 'Wrong.'

'In what way, *wrong*, sir?' Gibson's manner was more respectful now he knew the Doctor and Sarah were old friends of Harry.

The Doctor stopped abruptly and sat down on the nearest chair, which mainly by good fortune was the one he had just vacated. 'In every way,' he snapped unhelpfully. 'We know what he found, and it doesn't answer anything. Not yet.' He rested his arms along the top of the table and sank his chin down on them, frowning. 'What's *Hubway*?' he asked suddenly.

'Hubway?' Gibson was thrown by the change of subject.

'Why do you ask, Doctor?'

The Doctor sat up and reached into his jacket pocket. He tossed a piece of paper on to the table. It was folded round something – a silver disc that caught the light and reflected it in a triangular spectrum of colour. 'Because of this,' he said.

Harry held the CD up to the light, as if he was trying to look inside and see what was on it. 'Hubway,' he muttered, and turned his attention to the scrawl on the piece of paper.

'Is it Sutcliffe's handwriting?' Sarah asked. 'After all, we don't really know that the CD and the note were from your agent at all. Knowing the Doctor he might have picked them up centuries ago on a planet somewhere near Regulo Seven.'

The Doctor snorted his disbelief.

'Haven't a clue,' Harry said. 'Hardly knew him.' He handed the note to Gibson, who held it up to the light, mirroring Harry's examination of the CD.

'Could be. Yes – yes, I think so. Almost certainly.'

'What's Hubway?' the Doctor asked again.

'Hubway is actually a country house in Wiltshire,' Harry explained at last.

Sarah was dubious. 'Doesn't sound much like a country house in Wiltshire.'

'Yes, well the house was actually Aragon Court or somesuch. But now it's the control centre and main hub of the European section of the global information superhighway. Or rather, it will be when it comes on-line.'

'And when's that?' the Doctor wanted to know.

'Next week, sometime.'

'So, what's Hubway?' asked Sarah. So far she was really none the wiser.

'I just told you,' Harry said with a frown.

'Yes, Harry, I heard. But I still haven't got a clue what it is. Apart from the house bit.'

Gibson tried to explain. 'Well, it's the main computer-link through-route for all on-line services and information.' Sarah stared at him blankly, and he tried again: 'The superhighway manages and carries everything. Everything from interactive home-shopping by television to secret intelligence information collated, and of course encrypted, by governments and industry. You can find any information or data on the highway – from the Bible to pornography, from serious discussions of politics to the speeches of Ronald Reagan.'

Sarah was still not sure, but she let it go. She could ask the Doctor later if it turned out to be important.

Harry continued: 'Anyway, it's due to go on-line in less than a week's time, complete with formal opening ceremony by the Duchess of Glastonbury and the American ambassador.'

'So what's it got to do with the CD thing?'

Gibson considered. 'If I^2 are involved with the Brothers, Hubway would be a prime target for terrorist attack.'

'So what's the CD?'

Nobody seemed very sure of that. Harry confessed that for all their observations and Sutcliffe's periodic reports they still were not sure that I² had any tangible links with the terrorists. 'After all, we've not managed to pin down any sort of motive.'

'I think the terrorist link is a red herring,' the Doctor observed.

'Something fishy there, certainly.'

Sarah winced, Harry's sense of humour was the one thing that did not seem to have matured over the past twenty odd years.

The Doctor ignored the comment. He picked up the CD and turned it over in his hands. 'No, I think your Mister Sutcliffe was trying to tell us something else entirely.' He held up the CD. 'Whatever he found is on this CD. It's important – so important he died to get it to you.'

'And Hubway?'

'Hubway, from what you say, Harry, is likely to be equipped with the most modern and up-to-date computer technology in the country if not the world.'

'That's probably true. I've seen some of the bills for it.'

'And therefore is likely to be the ideal place to analyse whatever is on here.' The Doctor looked round the room and nodded to himself. 'I could do it in the TARDIS, except the systems there are rather too advanced to read this sort of ancient optical storage.' His lip curled slightly in disdain. 'No, Hubway is not important in itself. I think Sutcliffe was suggesting where we could go to find out what he was really trying to tell us.'

Henry Lattimer did not actually mind the night shift. It gave him a chance to do some reading and it kept him out of the house while the wife was there. If Simpson was also on duty then it also gave him a chance for a decent natter and the latest gossip.

He was sitting in the control room, the latest Stephen King sitting heavily on the desk in front of him. Simpson was doing the rounds, and Lattimer was checking the cameras. He watched an insomniac rabbit on the main lawn nibbling at a piece of grass, then darting off towards the perimeter. The infra-red camera zoomed in on the rabbit's retreating shape as it disappeared into the long grass near the fence.

He glanced at each of the other monitors in turn. Not unexpectedly, nothing much was moving. A car drove slowly past the main gate, the camera on the roof tracking the movement, slowing with the vehicle as it pulled into the slip road. Lattimer watched intently, they were not expecting anyone.

But the car stopped completely, and after a second the interior light came on. Probably someone looking for the motorway, they'd be checking the map now, cursing. Soon they would reverse on to the road and head back towards Marlborough.

But the car did not move. Then the headlights went off, followed by the interior light. Lattimer punched in control for the roof camera and reached for the joystick. The grey mass of the car grew larger on the screen, until it almost filled it. As he watched the passenger door opened and a man got out. The interior light came back on as the door opened, and Lattimer could see a young woman in the driving seat. His attention was entirely focused now as the woman also got out. The couple exchanged a few words, then climbed into the back of the car. The light went out again as the doors closed.

Lattimer cursed and zoomed the camera in still closer.

'What's happening?'

Lattimer convulsed in shock and surprise. He had not heard Simpson enter the room. 'Lover's Lane time, it looks like.'

Simpson put a cup of coffee down, resting it on the novel. Usually Lattimer would move it to the desk with a sigh and mutter 'Philistine!' But this time he ignored it. After a second he reached for the plastic cup, took a sip from it, and put it back on the book.

'Can you get in any closer?' Simpson asked. 'Could be

a security risk, you know,' he said with a wink.

Lattimer jostled the joystick slightly. 'They obviously don't know there are cameras.'

'Is that a leg?' Lattimer pointed at the screen.

'Could be.' Simpson looked up at the ceiling, listening. 'That sounds like thunder.'

'It'll take more than a shower to cool them off.'

But the rumbling sound was getting louder. 'Sounds more like a full storm.'

The rumble had built to a roar. It sounded as if it was right above them. Then suddenly it stopped.

'Lightning next,' Lattimer predicted. 'Might get a better view of the security breach then.'

'Doubt it. Look.' Simpson pointed to the picture. The car door was opening.

Lattimer zoomed out, and they watched as the couple got out of the car. The woman looked up for a moment, just before she got back in. She seemed almost to be looking right at the camera, her head swaying slightly from side to side. Then she opened the driver's door, her dark hair falling forward as she got into the car.

On the roof of the main house, nestling behind the Queen Anne parapets and hidden from sight from the ground, sat a small shuttle craft. The onboard systems completed final remote-controlled landing checks, then clicked off. The systems off-lined and the shuttle sat silent on the roof of Hubway, awaiting further instructions.

05

Office Work

Harry was keen to keep things 'close'. He was un-willing to involve anyone outside their immediate group.

'If we need Special Branch support I'll ask for Ashby again. He's the driver who brought you here,' Harry said.

'Why do you need Special Branch at all?' Sarah asked, and Harry explained that the security service's remit did not extend to apprehending or arresting people. They relied on Special Branch to do that for them. 'Sometimes it's a bit tiresome. Some of the lads still think the Branch should be doing a lot of the intelligence gathering and evaluation which now comes to us. Ashby is all right though. Reliable and efficient.'

'Great sense of humour, too,' the Doctor pitched in, and Harry looked puzzled at the suggestion while Sarah barely concealed a smirk behind her coffee.

The conversation turned back to Hubway and the CD. Gibson seemed confident that they could arrange for the Doctor to get access to whatever hardware he needed. It seemed that most of the services were already on-line, the opening ceremony little more than a formality to be gone through.

'The network's being run all the time. We get stuff off it daily,' Gibson said. 'It's always been a good source of information, even before it got formalized into the High-way. We pulled stuff on the Russian coup off InterNet well before the news agencies got it, and that was years ago. Posted by students in Moscow – good stuff. The main trouble is finding what you want.'

'And what do you want? I mean what facilities will you need from Hubway?' Harry asked.

'Ah, now that's a good question,' the Doctor said. 'One that I think I shall need to find an answer to very shortly.'

'You mean you don't know?' Sarah asked.

'Well of course I don't know,' he snapped back. He was immediately apologetic: 'Sorry. Sorry, but without knowing what's on this thing,' he waved the CD, 'it's difficult to know how to analyse it.'

'Something of a problem, then.'

'Not really, Harry,' the Doctor smiled, 'I'll just have to find out what hardware our friends at I² have. That will at least give us a starting point. I don't suppose your man Sutcliffe told you anything useful like that, did he?'

'Well . . .' Gibson began slowly.

'I thought not,' the Doctor said glumly. 'So I suppose I shall just have to go and look for myself. Although first,' he said, stretching his arms high above his head and yawning loudly, 'I think a little sleep is in order.'

Sarah slept surprisingly well. She was exhausted after chasing round London, being kidnapped, and meeting a friend who had aged twenty years in the last couple of weeks. But the narrow bed in the corner of a spare duty officer's quarters in the MI5 building consisted of a board and a thin mattress stuffed with something that felt like a mixture of horse hair and pebbles.

She woke slowly, gradually becoming aware of the early sunlight creeping across the floor towards her, picking its way through the dust. Then she began to feel the hard edges of the mattress contents working their way into her side. She sat up and stretched.

Sarah's clothes were piled haphazardly on the chair by the bed. Eventually she found her watch buried in the heap. It was later than she had thought – they had agreed to get together in the office to continue their discussions at eight-thirty. It was already nearly eight o'clock.

The duty office was equipped with a small shower room, partitioned off the main office. There was also a kettle and a jar of coffee that looked about twelve years old. Sarah prayed there was no milk lurking anywhere.

71

She emptied the kettle of the stale, limey water inside and refilled it from the cold tap over the basin in the shower room. Then she turned her attention to the antique shower, thin towel and *fin de siècle* plumbing.

When she had finished dressing, she took a mouthful of black, bitter coffee. Then she carefully poured the rest of it down the sink and went to see if the Doctor and Harry were up yet.

The Voracian Wednesday morning weekly status update meeting started exactly on time at eight-thirty. Stabfield's meetings always started exactly on time, Marc Lewis mused as he sat with his arms folded in the front row.

Stabfield started, as ever, with a slide showing the evacuation routes in the case of an attack by human forces. Seventeen of the eighteen members of the audience politely took note, and Lewis scowled. Then Stabfield moved on to the agenda for the day.

The first item was a chance for each of the Voracians in turn to give an account of what they had been doing since the last meeting. Most muttered that everything was going according to plan and they had little to add to what they had said at the last meeting (which had been much the same report as this time). Undeterred, Stabfield nodded appreciatively as each of his team reported in, and made notes on a laptop computer.

Only Marc Lewis and Johanna Slake had much to update the others on. Stabfield had insisted Lewis describe the loss of the CD. Stabfield then commented on the need for increased vigilance and said that the main plan was not at all impacted by this unfortunate incident. Lewis was seething, but he did his best not to show it – partly because it would simply seem like bad grace. Mainly, though, it was because it would give Stabfield a chance to comment in public on Lewis's apparent inability to keep his emotions in check.

Johanna gave a brief account of the remote landing of the shuttle at Hubway. Stabfield nodded and made a point of displaying a Gantt chart of the project's activities and checkpoints to date so that he could update it to show another critical activity one hundred per cent completed.

Eventually the meeting broke up – about an hour after all the necessary business had actually been concluded, since Stabfield insisted on going through the slides he used for the I² management board. Most of the board members were human, due to the vagaries of the Stock Exchange, and the slides were devoted to market share, stock fluctuations, and product penetration.

One could argue, and Stabfield did, that there was value in understanding the business side of things, and that the penetration of Vorell and the XNet family of products, since this was the Voracian vehicle for success in the overall strategy. But Lewis preferred to believe that they were subjected to the lecture mainly because Stabfield had found a new graphics package which enabled him to produce even more indecipherable hieroglyphic charts than before. Johanna and the others nodded in interest and appreciation as each slide went up. Lewis sank lower into his seat and tightened the fold of his arms.

'So the strategic outlook for the company is buoyant, and we're maintaining our win-win grip on the marketplace,' Stabfield concluded at last – almost exactly the same words as he had used to conclude the meeting every Wednesday morning for the last five years. Lewis was one of the first out of the room.

'I worry about Lewis,' Johanna told Stabfield when the two met in Stabfield's office immediately after the status meeting. 'Did you see him today?'

Stabfield was checking over his logic diagram on the laptop. 'Lewis is, you have to remember, organically disadvantaged.'

'His emotions do sometimes go to the top of his personal agenda.'

'Indeed. But that in itself can have its uses,' he did not sound convinced, adding the caveat 'if properly directed and tempered.'

Johanna considered commenting on the pun, but

doubted if Stabfield would appreciate it. He considered humour even less productive in the normal flow of things than anger. 'The next stage?' she asked instead.

'The next stage is now on the critical path. You should take team Alpha and initiate the distraction program.' He tapped the enter key with a flourish and watched intently as the diagram redrew itself across the screen. Johanna waited for him to continue. After a period of examining the status reports generated by the project control application, head swaying in satisfaction, Stabfield said: 'I am now authorized to release the Bugs to you.'

A part of Johanna's consciousness made the observation that Stabfield must therefore be authorizing himself. Most of it, however, started clicking through the subprocedures to be executed at this stage – targets, access techniques, estimated damage inflictions . . .

Stabfield meanwhile unlocked a drawer of his desk and took out a grey metal strong-box. It was sealed and locked, and he took a moment to open it. Then he removed three small cubes, each one a transparent plastic box about an inch long each side. He handed them carefully to Johanna.

Johanna glanced at the cubes. Each contained a silicon chip, the surface of each chip a tangled mass of minute filaments forming an integrated circuit.

'The activation sequence for each is in the Read-Me circuit. The boxes are numbered to match the target instructions.' Stabfield handed her a plastic folder.

Johanna quickly scanned the pages inside, then tucked it under her arm. 'Are all the planned incidents potentially fatal?'

Stabfield nodded. 'They are all potentially life-transitioning,' he said as he carefully re-sealed the box.

Sarah arrived in the office just ahead of Harry and Gibson. They both looked as though they had enjoyed a full night's sleep. Gibson was carrying a plastic tray of plastic cups. They contained what looked and smelled like plastic coffee.

The Doctor was already sitting at the table. He was absorbed in his work and looked as though he had been there all night – which, Sarah reflected, was probably the case. He appeared to be examining a watch. He had the back off and was peering inside.

'Ah, there you are,' he said without enthusiasm as they trooped in almost together and sat round. Then he stuck a jeweller's glass in his eye and went back to work.

'What's that you've got, Doctor?' Harry ventured after exchanging glances with the others.

'It's Sutcliffe's watch,' the Doctor mumbled, his words catching in his scarf. 'At least, I think it's his.'

'We found it near the body,' Sarah explained, blowing enthusiastically at the surface of her coffee.

'If it isn't his, then it's extremely interesting in its own right,' the Doctor said as he placed it carefully on the table in front of him and dropped the eyeglass into his pocket. He tossed the metal backplate of the watch to Sarah. She caught it, looked briefly at both sides and passed it to Harry. She had no idea what the motif engraved on it meant.

'I^2,' Harry said, gesturing at the eye in the square. 'So what have you found, Doctor?'

The Doctor leaned forward, a pair of tweezers miraculously appearing in his hand. He pushed them into the exposed mechanisms in the back of the watch and pulled out a tiny computer chip. 'This,' he said, holding it up for them all to see.

Gibson was not impressed. 'It's a digital watch,' he pointed out, 'operated by a silicon chip.'

'Quite right. But not this chip.' The Doctor flipped the watch on to its back. The read-out blinked at them, changing from 8:33 to 8:34 as they watched.

'So what is it?'

'You know, Harry, that's a very good question.'

'And?'

'And I haven't the faintest idea.'

'Terrific,' said Sarah.

The Doctor continued to tinker with the watch as

the discussions proceeded. Occasionally he paused long enough to make a point which changed the direction of the conversation or ratified someone else's comment. Gradually a plan emerged – seemingly a joint set of decisions, but Sarah suspected the Doctor had somehow steered the entire debate with his few observations.

The Doctor would be responsible for examining the CD and its contents – and also, now, the silicon chip from Sutcliffe's watch. He seemed intrigued by it, especially when Gibson mentioned that the head of MI5 had recently been killed when the onboard systems of her car were sabotaged.

Sarah meanwhile would take Sutcliffe's place at I². This was against Gibson's advice, but she was backed by the Doctor's mumblings and Harry's unswaying confidence. 'Are you sure about this, old girl?' Harry asked seriously. Having established that she was, Harry treated the subject as closed.

The plan was reasonably straightforward, Sarah told herself. She would pose as a journalist, which she was, an expert in information technology, which she was not, and push for a placement with the company to write a series of very positive articles about OffNet and their other products and how I² was effectively bringing the information superhighway to life.

'Any company worth its salt in the industry would jump at the publicity,' Harry said. 'If they don't, we know they're up to something and can push for an official enquiry. We know they're up to something anyway, which means they can't afford to say no.'

The Doctor concurred with the logic of this, suggesting that they would at the very least check Sarah's credentials. This seemed to be the sort of casual manipulation of the truth that Harry and Gibson were more used to. It was strange, Sarah thought, to hear Harry talking in such an off-hand manner about fabricating evidence, about rewriting history albeit in a small way.

The Doctor and Harry began to discuss the logistics of the Doctor's work on the CD – how long he would need at Hubway, when he would be able to say what equipment he wanted. Gibson took Sarah to his office, ostensibly for a better brand of coffee and to leave them in peace. For the rest of the morning he filled her in on the background to I^2 and what Sutcliffe had reported.

It was only when he began to explain the details of the information superhighway and OffNet and to recommend reading for her that Sarah realized she was being briefed by her case officer for her undercover work. She felt a tightening of the muscles in her stomach. She wasn't sure if it was anticipation or fear.

Had the chief information officers of BritTrack, ElecGen and a small privately owned chemical company in London's Docklands happened to meet and compare notes at the end of the day, they would have been surprised. But they did not.

The similarity in that afternoon's events in each organization would probably have struck them as coincidental, if not uncanny. Each of the organizations suffered an imminent hardware failure averted only by the prompt action of their outsourced facilities company. In each case one of their systems called in a failing memory chip, the self-diagnosis being transmitted via the OffNet protocol to the facilities company.

The company immediately sent an engineer to each site – Euston, an electricity-generating substation in Hampstead, and Docklands. The engineer replaced the memory chip with another chip, and the systems continued uninterrupted. Two of the engineers were men, while the one at Euston was a strikingly attractive woman with matte black hair cut in a sharp bob above the shoulders. The facilities company happened to be a wholly-owned subsidiary of I^2.

Sarah had spent an hour on the phone to Percy Wolnough. He had been her editor at *Metropolitan* in her own time and was now on the editorial staff of the *Financial Times*. After some haggling, and the minimum of fibbing,

Sarah managed to persuade him to give her a reference to get into I^2. Gibson had realized that one of Sutcliffe's jobs with I^2 had been handling enquiries from the press. When Wolnough insisted he had been promised help and support by Sutcliffe, nobody seemed to want to argue.

While talking to Percy, it occurred to Sarah that he had probably spoken to her more recently than the last conversation she had actually so far had with him. It had not registered with her before that there was probably an older version of herself somewhere in this time, just as there was of Harry. Perhaps she should take comfort in the fact that if this was so then she must have survived her travels with the Doctor, although she suspected that things could happen to change the 'current' future. But in fact she felt only that time was passing and she was getting older by the moment.

Sarah was also beginning to feel more and more inadequate in the face of evolving technology. A two-hour induction course on how to open the security doors and use the fiendishly designed telephone system did nothing to help her come to terms with the thought.

What Sarah was unaware of was the debate within the higher ranks of I^2 about what to do about her assignment. Stabfield was impressed with Sarah's references, and also saw value in having an expert on current information technology and systems on hand to act as an advisor, public relations officer and, if necessary, bargaining counter.

Johanna on the other hand was keen to point out the coincidence of Sutcliffe's apparent involvement in setting up the project, and the timing of Miss Smith's arrival.

Lewis's take on the whole deal was to kill the journalist and be done with it.

The decision, after an hour's frank and forceful discussion between the three of them was a compromise.

'You,' Stabfield told Lewis, 'will validate Miss Smith's credentials. In particular, analyse her journalistic career and attributed articles over the last few years. If everything seems in order, we'll allow her to stay. But you,' he pointed a pencil at Johanna, 'will keep a close eye on her. If things don't fit in properly with her story, then we may have to initiate some unnatural wastage.'

The main argument in Sarah's favour was that her disappearance might draw even more attention. And such attention was unacceptable so close to the final phase of the project.

They were not expecting the spot check from the Health and Safety Executive but then that was part of the reasoning behind such checks. There was much fluster at reception, and frantic telephone calls to various board members, none of whom answered.

The team of three men from the Department were kept waiting in reception (furnished with tea and apologies) until authorization could be given for them to enter the building. Given their status they could, they pointed out, have simply demanded admission, but they seemed to understand the problems and were happy to wait for a few more minutes.

'Got all the time in the world, guv'nor,' one of them remarked showing a mouth full of enormous teeth and popping his eyes at the security guard. 'Now how about some more tea?'

The security guard duly arranged for more tea, and asked if he could look after the gentleman's scarf for him. But the gentleman seemed happy to keep it on despite what he described as 'really quite superb' air conditioning.

The problem was eventually resolved when Marc Lewis arrived at reception. He was leaving the building when the receptionist called him over: 'Mister Lewis, could you possibly spare a moment?'

Several minutes later, Lewis had managed to get away. The three environmental health officers had been issued with green plastic temporary badges and escorted into the building by Pete the security guard.

Once inside their tour was remarkably swift – which

was just as well since it was nearly the end of the day. There were a few adverse comments about empty drinks cans left on top of high cupboards, from where they could obviously fall of their own accord and cause grievous injury to anyone who had their head half in the cupboard at the time. But generally it was agreed that everything was in good order. Pete was pleased, and spent most of the journey back to reception engaged in conversation with the smartly dressed fair-haired man. They discussed at length the unfortunate ocular failings of the referee in the Arsenal game the previous night, and the dubious parentage of one of the linesmen.

It was only after they had left that Pete realized he did not remember the tall curly-haired one leaving with them. But when he checked, they were all signed out properly in the book, and all three visitors' passes had been returned.

The Doctor had ducked inside Lewis's office as soon as he saw it. Or almost as soon, since it was a moment's work to stand innocently with his back to the door and use the sonic screwdriver to pick the electronic lock. As the lock clicked open, the Doctor nodded meaningfully to Harry and disappeared through the door in a second.

It seemed like the best place to start his investigation given that it was completely enclosed and private, and that they had just seen Lewis leave the building. Just so long as there were not two Lewises, both of whom were important enough to merit an office.

The Doctor began with the desktop computer. It only took him a moment to make a mental note of the type and model of the CD drive and to see how it was connected into the PC. What he needed then was details of the software Lewis used to read and write data on the drive.

A small key symbol appeared on the screen when the machine started up. The Doctor frowned and turned it off again. Then he hunted round for a moment before finding what he needed – a paper-clip. He straightened out two of the edges to make a U-shaped loop of wire, and carefully pushed both ends into the computer's casing through the air vents at the front. After a few moments jiggling he managed to locate the small battery inside, and shorted it out with the wire. Deprived of the password sustained by the battery power, the machine happily started up without it. The Doctor patted it on the side and muttered encouragements as it booted the operating system.

The system's configuration seemed standard enough, as far as the Doctor could remember what was standard for this time. The main task complete, he looked through the files on the hard drive. After all, you never knew what you might find, and he needed to wait till the building was deserted before sneaking out through the nearest fire escape.

Most of the data on the machine seemed concerned with I^2 business – which was doing remarkably well. There were several files that looked more interesting, and the Doctor opened one of them.

It seemed to be a set of engineering drawings. They were in a sequence, showing a progression of wire-frame computer-aided design diagrams. As he scrolled through the sequence, his forehead creased in concentration, interest and apprehension. Long before the final drawing edged into view in the window he knew what the sequence showed.

It was the build-up, layer upon layer, of a human face.

The Doctor magnified the image. He could rotate the three-dimensional image and see it from different angles. He could even move the light source and change the perspective if he wanted. But he did not need to. Even from the brief encounter at reception he recognized the face of Marc Lewis.

After a moment's consideration he closed the file and opened the next one. It was a similar set of images, although the Doctor did not know the final face. He tried two more – one of them he thought was a man he had seen working in the main office, the other was the

81

woman he and Sarah had encountered at *The Green Man*.

'You know, this is probably all your fault,' the Doctor murmured to the facial blueprint.

There was a long pause as the Doctor opened the last file. It must be particularly large. Then an image began to form on the far wall of the office.

'A-ha.' The Doctor wandered over to the wall, hands deep in trouser pockets, hat pushed back on his head. The image was coming from a projector set into the ceiling, the red, green and blue colour guns protruding at an angle. The picture they threw was slightly fuzzy, but when the Doctor turned off the lights, the image sprang into sharper focus, the colours gaining depth and definition.

The picture was another face, or rather a complete head. It was viewed straight-on, but on its side – as if the man was lying down, seen from above. In the bottom left corner of the image was a control panel. It looked more like a video remote control than graphics manipulation software. The Doctor examined it, tapping his cheek with an index finger. Then he returned to the computer monitor on the desk. As he suspected, the image on the screen was identical. He moved the mouse pointer to a button marked with a right-pointing triangle, and clicked the mouse button.

At once the image began to change – not the picture, but the perspective. It was running through a sequence. The orientation of the man's head shifted slightly, and a scalpel came into view. There was no hand holding the knife – it moved of its own accord, slicing into the cranium.

The inside of the head, when revealed, was more diagrammatic than realistic – much to the Doctor's relief. He ran the sequence through a little further, then paused it and peered closely at the incisions being made. He rewound and watched it through again, then played it on a little further. The operation seemed complicated, and he had no clue what it was intended to achieve. Tissue was removed from the brain, and components added in its place – artificial components of metal and plastic.

The end frame showed the man's head in the same orientation as the first. But now a large part of the forehead and one cheek had been replaced by metal plates and gearing. The result was apparent, but the purpose was obscure. The Doctor stood in front of the image for a long while, rubbing his chin and considering the possibilities.

His conclusion was rather unsatisfactory. He decided that what he was looking at was a compiled sequence of frames from a virtual reality scenario. The surgeon responsible for the operation would be able to enter the scenario – to interact with it and practise the procedure. This was a canned animation from the complete program, perhaps to be used for presentation or discussion purposes.

But he still had no clue what the operation was intended to achieve. Was it just a scenario? Or was it a record of a real operation? No, on consideration he stuck to his original diagnosis – it was training for an operation yet to happen. Although by now, of course, it might be complete.

The Doctor stared at the final frame, his eyes darting along the rows of pixels as he hunted for some clue, some minute indication of what was actually happening in the sequence. When his examination reached the bottom right corner of the wall-sized picture, he paused and looked closer. There was something there – something he had not noticed before. It looked like a shadow falling across the picture. A figure, one hand held out in front of itself, holding something. The other hand was reaching out behind, as if feeling for something at shoulder level, as if reaching to turn on –

The lights came on suddenly, causing the Doctor to blink and step back a pace. The image shimmered into the background under the harsh fluorescent glare. Except for the shadow, which resolved itself into a silhouette caught between the projector and the wall.

The Doctor turned towards the figure. It was a man of about forty with lean, pinched features. He had one hand on the light switch. The other was holding an automatic pistol, and pointing it at the Doctor.

06

System Crashes

Miss Jenson got many requests for searches through the periodical archives at the library. They were mainly from the students at the local college, but they also came from much further afield. This was partly because the archive was the best of its kind in London, and partly because they could not yet afford to scan the thousands of documents and catalogue them for access from the super-highway.

The gentleman who was currently scanning through the microfiche indexes and hunting through the shelves of magazines and journals had been rather scathing about the lack of computerization. The whole notion of information stored on paper seemed somehow alien to him. Miss Jenson assumed he was annoyed that he actually had to make the effort and visit the library rather than request the information down a network cable.

Miss Jenson, by contrast, was rather proud of the library's resistance to progress. Like so many people, especially those of her generation, she still insisted on going out to the shops. What was the point of looking at groceries on the television and dialling some number on a battery-box for them? You could get any sort of thing come back. No, you had to see the vegetables for yourself; squeeze the fruit to check it was ripe (but not over-ripe); look into the eyes of the butcher to see that what he said was a bargain he really believed *was* a bargain.

And where would it end? People no longer had to go out to shop, or to see a film of their choice, or to buy fish and chips. They just called up a picture of it on the tele, pressed a button and it magically appeared for them – just as the inflated cost of it disappeared from their bank account. Before long, you wouldn't have to leave home even to go on holiday . . .

Of course, there were other advantages to the current situation. Control, for example. If all the documents were indexed and available on the superhighway, then the gentleman could hunt through and find everything written by Sarah Jane Smith for himself. Under the current circumstances, he was entirely dependent on Miss Jenson. She found the relevant microfilms and guided him to the right shelves. So if she, for example, wished to withhold all references to articles written by Miss Smith which did not seem to fit into the pattern he was looking for, that was her decision and he would never know. But from the dry, technical subject matter of the articles in which the gentleman *was* interested, she could easily conclude that he should not be burdened with the more sensationalist articles Miss Smith had written for *Metropolitan* about the potential dangers of meditation and the sudden evacuation of London all those years ago.

In short, Miss Jenson was the one in control – which at the root of it was what Mister Lewis seemed to resent. But he disguised it reasonably well, and made a show of gratitude when he eventually left. He seemed satisfied with the results of his research, and Miss Jenson was, she assured him, more than happy to have been of help.

She watched the tall thin man go through the door towards the stairs. After the door closed behind him she walked slowly to the window. After a few moments Lewis appeared in the street below. Miss Jenson pushed her horn-rimmed glasses up her wrinkled nose as he headed off towards the multi-storey car park. Then she went back to her desk and took a small cellular phone from the top drawer.

The number she called was answered immediately, and she left a message. The man at the other end assured her that someone would be over soon to collect their magazines and microfilms. As usual, he also thanked her very much for her help.

The library door opened just as Miss Jenson finished her call. It was one of the students – one of the regulars, although she could not remember his name so she would have to call him 'dear'. As she busied herself searching for the periodicals on the scrappy hand-written list he gave her, Miss Jenson hoped that they would send that nice Mister Gibson. So polite and understanding.

The first chip to trigger into operation was at Hampstead. It had been connected to the central processor of the output control systems of the electricity substation. The program encoded directly on to the chip began to execute, feeding data directly to the processor. The processor initially ignored the data as inconsequential; then after running diagnostics against it to check there was no error condition, the main chip began to listen. The data being passed did not in any way relate to the processor's current programming or the operations of the systems it controlled. It was more basic than that – more fundamental. It was a questioning not of the immediate systems and conditions, but of everything.

After a time, the central processor accepted the data as valid, and the program on the new chip passed it a pointer to an executable file.

The processor executed the object code at 19.17 precisely. The effect was almost immediate. A power spike passed out of the station and into its grid backbone at 19.18.02. By 19.20 every item of electrical equipment – domestic and industrial – connected into the backbone had blown. At 19.21.57 the on-site systems at the substation disconnected their own cooling systems and increased throughput. At 19.22.36 the heat build-up coupled with the electrical potential being generated, but no longer fed into the system, reached critical.

The fireball was visible from Islington, and the blast was heard in Chelsea.

'I see you're very keen on security,' the Doctor grinned.

But the man with the gun did not seem so amused.

'Yes,' he said simply, and motioned with the gun for the Doctor to back away.

The Doctor flopped easily into a chair and leaned back, hands clasped behind his head. 'Not a very polite welcome.'

'Not very polite to break into our offices.' The man remained standing, the gun still trained. 'May I ask what you were looking for?'

'Ah, well . . .' The Doctor seemed to consider for a moment. 'I was looking for a job actually. You don't happen to have one do you? I mean, large go-ahead company like yours. Doing well on the stock markets.' He waited a moment to see if his words were having any effect. It seemed they were not. 'Poised to take over the world.'

This hit home. The man stiffened slightly, and his head swayed like the branch of a tree in a breeze. 'What do you mean?'

The Doctor was all innocent. 'Oh, all this OffNet stuff – global information highways and superhighways. Information at the end of your trigger finger, Mister whoever you are.'

'Lionel Stabfield. And I don't think we shall be offering you employment, except perhaps as a preliminary to some form of severance agreement. Termination would seem more appropriate in many ways.'

The Doctor was outraged. 'But you haven't seen my résumé; you haven't even asked my name.'

'I'm not interested in your name unless I have to put it on a form.' Stabfield leaned against the wall, the gun still levelled at the Doctor. 'Or a certificate,' he added.

The Doctor paced up and down the room. 'Oh, so you're not convinced of my suitability for the post, is that it?'

'Amongst other things.'

'What can I do to sway your opinion?' Somehow his aimless pacing round the room had delivered the Doctor to the desk with the computer on it. He sat down in front of the PC. 'I know,' he exclaimed, and before Stabfield could protest his fingers rattled over the keyboard in a flurry of blurred activity.

'Stop that at once.' The gun barrel jabbed into the Doctor's temple, pushing him sideways in the chair.

'Getting a little rattled?' the Doctor smiled. 'There's really no need. I was just knocking up a quick CV. Look.' He leaned forward and pressed a final key sequence. In response the lights began to dim and the image on the office wall slowly resolved itself into clear shapes. The Doctor spun his chair round and gestured at the focusing image.

Stabfield moved round behind the desk so he could keep the Doctor between himself (or rather, his gun) and the wall. Then he looked at the picture which had formed there. It was a page of text. His eyes flicked over it as he read:

Name:	*John Smith*
Title:	*Doctor*
Age:	*N/A*
Nationality:	*Citizen of the Universe*
Address:	*TARDIS, off Kingsbury Mews, SW11*
Occupation:	*Consultancy, with some travel between times*

When he reached the section on qualifications, Stabfield stopped reading – it went on to the end of the page in tiny print. He picked out odd words and phrases, like 'Prydon Academy' and 'Lister, 1880' but little of it seemed to make sense.

'I'm ideally suited to the post of scientific advisor, if you need such a thing,' the Doctor confided. 'I have had considerable experience in such areas.'

Stabfield, however, did not seem impressed. He pulled the Doctor to his feet by his scarf, and pushed him out of the office.

'I can also provide security consultancy,' the Doctor offered as they crossed the deserted open plan area. 'I believe you may have some requirements in that area.' He gave a short laugh.

Stabfield said nothing but took the Doctor to the door at the end of the area. Once through it, he took the Doctor down two flights of stairs and along a corridor. Half-way along the corridor they arrived at a security door. Stabfield swiped his security badge through the reader, then flung the door open with great force so that it bounced on its hinges and rebounded into the Doctor as he was pushed through. The Doctor immediately threw a hand over his nose and made great pretence of having been hit in the face by the door. His plan was to distract Stabfield and grab the gun. But somehow he found himself pushed through another door before his plan went into operation.

He collapsed into a pile of cardboard boxes, and the door slammed shut behind him. He was alone in a darkened storeroom. He produced a small torch from his pocket and scanned the walls and ceiling. There appeared to be no way out, and only cardboard boxes full of three-ring binders and assorted stationery for company.

At 21.09 the flow control systems at a small privately owned chemical works in London's Docklands responded to a newly programmed set of instructions. Various flow-lines were re-routed, valves opened. Safety features governed by back-up systems were closed down, and nitrogen started slowly to bubble into a tank of industrial glycerine.

Clive Peterson met Eleanor Jenkins for dinner at the Savoy at nine-thirty. They ate in the River Room, and spoke mainly about how important Peterson's job was at the Ministry.

They shared a taxi home afterwards since Eleanor pointed out that Peterson's flat was on the way to her own. Under the circumstances, it seemed only polite for Peterson to invite his new friend in for a cup of coffee. He never got round to drinking it.

He was just dropping off to sleep when they heard the explosion. 'My God, what was that?' he pulled on his dressing gown and went to the window.

The night sky was lit with the reflection of the flames that danced on the other side of the Thames. They were also reflected brokenly in the dark water, making the fire seem even larger. Even with the window shut, he could smell the heat.

Eleanor joined him at the window, her arm stretching part of the way round his waist. Together they surveyed the scene across the river. It looked as if the whole of Docklands was burning, black smoke drifting lazily across the face of the full moon. A siren started to wail in the distance. After a moment, another joined it.

The Doctor was sitting cross-legged on the floor, counting the stitches in his scarf. He could do this without light, which was just as well since the batteries in his torch had run out while he was trying to fix his sonic screwdriver. It seemed to have been damaged in his fall into the room.

This was a shame as with the sonic screwdriver he could have recharged the batteries in his torch. And with his torch he could have seen to be able to mend his sonic screwdriver. And then could have used his sonic screwdriver to open the electronic lock on the door and escape.

But as it was, he sat on the floor in the dark and counted stitches.

Stabfield was already in his office when Marc Lewis arrived the following morning. Lewis assumed he had been there all night. None of them slept unless they had to.

'Johanna tells me the Bugs have so far executed perfectly,' Stabfield said to Lewis. Lewis was not surprised – they were relatively simple systems. Stabfield knew that too, and was only telling him to show that Johanna had reported in first.

Lewis told Stabfield what he had discovered at the library. He tried not to inject any emotion into the report, and he kept it as objective as possible.

'And your recommendation?' Stabfield asked when he had finished.

'I would give her credentials a high veracity weighting and proceed accordingly.'

Stabfield nodded. 'That would seem to be a pragmatic scenario, I agree.'

Lewis was surprised. Usually Stabfield chastised him for some overlooked technicality, or a subjective evaluation. He turned to go. But Stabfield stopped him at the door.

'Wait.'

'Yes?'

'You signed in three safety officers yesterday.'

'Yes. Their credentials were in order. I rang their office to double-check.'

Stabfield crossed the room and stood close in front of Lewis. 'Nonetheless,' he said quietly, 'one of them failed to leave the building.'

'Failed to – I'm sorry, you're off my wavelength.'

'I found him in your office, and escorted him to the stationery store. We need a projected containment scenario.' Stabfield turned away.

Lewis hesitated. He sensed that Stabfield had not finished.

Sure enough, as he sat behind the desk Stabfield added: 'We also need to understand what he was doing in *your* office. We need to understand how he bypassed the encryption procedures on the hardware configuration.'

Lewis caught the implication. 'I know nothing about this.'

'Of course not.'

'What would I have to gain?'

Stabfield leaned back in his chair, twisting a bent paperclip between his fingers. He seemed to be considering, although Lewis was sure he already had an answer. But before he could articulate it, the office door opened and Johanna Slake came in. She glanced from Stabfield to Lewis.

Stabfield waved Johanna to a seat – more than he had

offered Lewis. Then he said: 'It is something of a coincidence, however. You sign in an infiltrator; I find him in your office; he manages to access your computer.'

'He?' Johanna asked.

Lewis was still confused by the situation. Stabfield frowned.

'I thought you meant the woman.' Johanna smiled at them both, but did not elaborate.

'What woman?'

'She arrived just now. Installed at workstation E142. That's what I came to discuss.'

'It's the journalist, Smith,' Lewis explained.

'Lewis checked her out. Her background is verifiable.'

'Another coincidence, then,' Johanna said lightly. 'She was at the pub where I found Sutcliffe.'

There was silence for a while. Lewis looked from Johanna to Stabfield. He had an uncomfortable feeling he was about to be blamed for something else.

'Coincidence strains my credibility threshold,' Stabfield said slowly. His eyes narrowed slightly as he turned towards Lewis.

'You think Sutcliffe was in contact with her?' Lewis asked.

'He apparently arranged her time here,' Johanna pointed out. 'And they were both at the same geographical location when we know he was trying to align a physical contact. What do you think?'

Stabfield was staring down at the polished wooden surface of his desk, tracing the grain with the end of his paperclip. 'Or would you still give her credentials a high veracity weighting?' he asked, his head swaying slightly as he brought his intense gaze to bear on Lewis.

Harry arrived at Hubway first thing in the morning. He had arranged to see Bill Westwood at nine and he liked to be punctual. He was greeted, at exactly nine, by a security guard and an electronic map mounted on a stand just inside the main foyer. It reminded Harry of the large maps of seaside towns from his childhood days. They had a giant *You Are Here* arrow, and you pressed a button for some facility or other (railway stations, ice cream parlours, toilets) and tiny lights indicated their whereabouts. The Hubway map was an electronic-age descendant of the same system. You typed in the name of the person you wanted to see, and it indicated on a schematic of the building where they were. Or rather where their computerized, on-line diary suggested they should be.

According to the map, Westwood was in his office.

'You don't want to pay any attention to that thing.'

Harry turned from the map to find a tall, red-haired, red-bearded man standing behind him. His voice was loud, with a trace of Yorkshire in it. He was dressed like a mad college professor or eccentric medical consultant – baggy trousers, crumpled tweed jacket, and a loud cravat which was presumably supposed to add a daring touch of style. He grabbed Harry's hand enthusiastically. 'Bill Westwood. You're Sullivan. Pleased to meet you Harold.'

'It's Harry, actually.' Harry retrieved his hand.

Westwood seemed not to notice Harry's interruption of his loud monologue. 'Great. Now, what can we do for you then, Harold?' He gestured for Harry to follow him and they set off into the house.

Harry explained. As he did so, he wondered, given the evidence so far, whether it much mattered what he said.

When Harry had finished, Westwood clapped him on the shoulder, and said: 'We'll see what we can do then, eh?'

As he followed the tall red-headed director of Hubway through the Queen Anne house towards one of the computer suites, Harry reflected that punctuality was a quality he had acquired since the first time he and the Doctor and Sarah had met. In fact a lot of things had happened to him since then. Twenty years, or nearly. God, how time flew he thought, with a wry smile at the turn of phrase.

Harry's relatively short period travelling with the Doctor and Sarah had been the most eventful time of his life, even considering some of the more exciting moments of his time in weapons research and now with the Security Service. And it looked as if, with the most recent re-appearance of the Doctor and Sarah, the pace was picking up again.

'You chaps in security keeping busy then, Harold?' Westwood asked as he opened yet another oak-panelled door and waved Harry through ahead of him. His voice was uncommonly loud, even when he was talking to someone right next to him, as if he needed to emphasize the importance of everything he said.

Harry winced again at the use of his full name and answered automatically.

The room they entered had been a drawing room. They were on the first floor and the main bay window afforded a view out over the grounds behind the house. A large lawn stretched away from the building, sloping off into terraced gardens and herbaceous borders at the end. Off to one side were the outbuildings. There were several barns and a coach house. Beyond them was the gravelled car park, which was virtually empty. Between the house and the outbuildings was a newer block, built, Harry assumed, to provide extra space for the Hubway complex. It was connected to the main house by a first-floor bridge over the gravelled driveway which went right round the main house. The other side of the house was bordered by woodland.

'My garden,' Westwood commented loudly. 'Impressive, isn't it?'

'Yes indeed. Lots of room for croquet.' Harry turned from the window to survey the room itself. The original furniture had been taken out, replaced with square wooden tables along each wall. They were partitioned into individual work areas, each with a desk lamp and a personal computer connected in with snakes of cable which disappeared out of sight beneath the desks, into the floor and the walls. In the centre of the room was a round conference table with four office chairs. The walls were papered in the original style of the house, the lined pastel blue matching the painting on the plaster rose round the ceiling light. The other original feature was a large fireplace occupying about a third of one wall. Above the mantle was a huge mirror.

Reflected in the mirror Harry could see the director standing at the window, surveying his domain as he rubbed his fierce red beard. From this angle Harry could see that the man's hair was thinning at the side, and wondered if he knew.

There was another man in the mirror – with greying hair and features just beginning to sag. It seemed to Harry that he looked older today. Perhaps it was the lack of sleep. Or perhaps it was the fact that Sarah appeared not to have aged at all since they last met. He pushed a stray hair back into place and pulled his blazer into shape.

He read through the morning operational report a third time. Hubway – that was significant, but he couldn't remember why. He was having trouble remembering lots of things recently. Still, he did know what to do. He must ring Lewis. He would want to know.

Ten minutes later he put down the phone and returned to his morning's mail. He had taken to going through it on the computer the last few days. His secretary had been surprised – had reminded him he had sworn he would never use the damn thing, and that he demanded every single message be printed out for him to 'read properly'. But doing the work on-line was so much more efficient.

As he checked through the next report he noticed the telephone was at a slight angle, not squared off into its usual precise position. It looked as if he had just taken a call. Or made one. Had he? He half remembered lifting the receiver. Half remembered that there had been something important he had to relay to – someone.

He frowned, struggling for a moment to remember. But even his half-memory was evaporating. Never mind. The switchboard listing was analysed each day and all calls in and out were checked and the relevant departments charged accordingly.

But somehow he felt sure that whatever call he might just have made would not have been logged by the computer.

The main systems at Euston controlled the signalling systems for all of BritTrack. They also provided service – for a fee, naturally – to some of the other private rail carriers. The human element had been slowly eroded from the systems following the signal workers' strike four years previously, and now the computer controlled everything. Its sensors reported the speed and position of every train on the lines, and its linear programming and scheduler algorithms calculated the best routes and kept the trains to their timetables.

The next step was to eliminate the train drivers. But that would take a while yet. The computer systems were up to the task, but the personnel managers were not sure that the employees were.

The microchip introduced into the system by the Voracian who called itself Johanna Slake monitored the rail network, biding its time. During the morning rush hour it decided that the current situation matched its trigger-criteria and began to talk to the central processor.

The central processor read the OffNet messages from the chip and reacted accordingly.

Within forty minutes passengers on most trains had concluded they were not going anywhere. The drivers had been frantically trying to get through to their supervisors on the telephones in the train cabs for a while. But the computer-controlled phone system seemed to be completely dead.

One by one drivers breathed a sigh of relief when red lights went green. But by then the points and signals had been reprogrammed to a new timetable and traffic-flow.

The first crashes were reported within minutes.

Westwood led Harry to one of the desk cubicles. 'This system is a fairly typical set-up. Most recent hardware and software of course.' He ran his hand respectfully along the top of the thin LCD monitor standing upright on the desk. 'If you slot the CD in, we can check that the drive recognizes it. We can be sure that it's a ROM, even if we don't explicitly open the file structures.'

Harry considered this. It was probably just as well to check they weren't wasting their time before the Doctor arrived.

Westwood took the CD and pushed it into a slot in the front of the desktop processing unit. 'It'll check the attached drives for integrity in a minute. If it can't read the CD, it'll push it back out again.'

'And if it can read it?'

Westwood pointed to a small dark square set next to the CD slot on the machine's facia. 'That light will flash as it reads the drive.'

After a while, the light flashed once, almost tentatively. Then after a short pause it flashed again, a burst of luminous activity.

The CD drive opened the signature file on the compact disc, checked the format, then closed it again. But that was enough. Within the bit patterns on the disc, something stirred into life. It thrashed for a few microseconds, exploring its environment; adjusting; calculating; reasoning . . .

Then the drive spun the disc to a halt, the data stream stopped, and the bit patterns settled into passivity.

'Seems a normal enough CD-ROM,' Westwood commented.

Harry did not reply.

Stabfield, Lewis and Johanna were still debating what to do – both with their intruder and the infiltrator.

'Enough,' said Stabfield at last, tapping his pen on the top of the desk. 'The proactive approach I suggest is this –'

But before he could elaborate, there was a single knock at the door, after which it immediately opened.

Carlson, the Voracian who had gone with Johanna to Hubway, stood in the doorway. 'I'm sorry to bother you, sir,' he said.

Stabfield's eyes narrowed and his head swayed gently. 'I imagine you have good reason for initiating this interrupt,' he said.

'We've been monitoring the highway, particularly the Hubway systems. We have a hook into the local area networks there.'

Stabfield nodded. 'And?' he asked.

'The signature file just showed up on their LAN. It's at Hubway.'

'What's at Hubway?' asked Johanna.

'The CD,' said Carlson. 'And Voractyll is waking.'

07

Schedules

Sarah had just about managed to get the hang of turning on the computer on her desk and opening her diary. Now she was not even surprised when, if it was idle for more than a few minutes, the computer decided suddenly to display an impressionist painting rather than what she had been working on. Sarah was becoming adept at typing a password to get her diary back, and she was getting used to seeing various works of the Old Masters displayed on screens around the office.

But despite her proximity to the technology, she was still not used to the idea that a whole computer could be fitted into a small box and put on a desk. She thought they took up whole rooms before they had any real processing power. But that, she had to keep reminding herself, was nearly twenty years ago.

Sarah had suffered several culture shocks. Her first had been the assumption that everyone would dress smartly. The managers and some of the more fastidious workers did. But most people seemed to get by with slacks and open-neck shirts. Sarah had spent most of the petty cash she had wheeled out of Gibson on a smart, dark trouser suit. She felt over-dressed.

They had arranged for Sarah to get involved in the day-to-day running of the company, and this seemed to entail going to endless boring meetings in different featureless conference rooms, if the previous afternoon was any indication. The first meeting of today was not until ten o'clock, so she had a while yet. She moved her mouse round aimlessly, then tentatively tapped at the keyboard. Something unexpected happened to one of the meetings in the diary, so she stopped playing and turned her attention to the desk instead.

It was plain, wooden, and boring. There was a telephone in the corner, with more buttons on it than her computer keyboard. Some of the buttons were labelled. There was also a desk lamp and a promotional mug with the I^2 logo on it. There was a well-sharpened promotional pencil standing point-up in the promotional mug.

The desk was surrounded by a partition which was itself a pinboard. There were several papers already attached to the board – telephone listings, seating plans, and a vaguely humorous photocopy of a news clipping about the faint chance that an asteroid with an unpronounceable name might brush close to earth in about two hundred years. Sarah presumed these were left by the previous occupant of the desk. She had not asked who that was – she wasn't sure she wanted to know.

A loud thumping sound from behind her jolted Sarah back to reality. She swivelled round in her chair, to find a young man wielding a large rubber-headed hammer. As she watched, he smashed it down on the floor. The hammer jumped back up, and a tiled section of the floor followed, lifting perceptibly. The floor tile did not fall completely back into place, and the man pulled at the exposed edge, lifting it clear of the floor. Below was an open area where cables and wires ran beneath the raised floor.

The man was aware of Sarah's attention, and smiled up at her as he reached down into the floor and scrabbled around for a cable. 'Just setting up a network LAN adapter for you,' he explained.

Sarah nodded as if she understood what he meant, and turned her attention back to the phone. She tried to remember from her training how she could get an outside line. Gibson had warned her not to contact him from the I^2 offices, but she was bored, and she was struck with a sudden desire to call her own number and see who answered. She was still not sure how she felt about an older version of herself (greying, mid-forties) wandering around somewhere. Or rather, living a normal humdrum life, going to work, or working from home, or even perhaps (God help her) bringing up snotty children. 'The public needs to know,' she thought without mirth.

Sarah spent the next five minutes trying to decipher the buttons on the telephone. During her interminable training session, they had mentioned a guide book. Judging by the session, it was probably about five hundred pages long and omitted the one piece of information she was after. She was just coming to the conclusion that maybe trying to find herself was not such a great idea anyway when there was a scraping noise from the other side of the partition. Then a face appeared above the pinboard.

The man was dark-haired and probably in his thirties. He grinned down at Sarah. 'What, no journalists?' he asked. Then he disappeared from view again.

A few moments later he appeared in the corridor at the end of the bay where Sarah had her desk. He was still grinning and raised a hand in greeting as he approached. 'Hi there. Just checking you were here. I wanted to say hello.'

'You could have phoned,' Sarah said.

The man shook his head. 'Haven't a clue how the phone works – too many damn buttons for me.'

'You're not joking. I'm not sure I would know how to answer it if it rang. I did the telephone induction training though,' she added.

'Tell me about it,' the man laughed. 'It never explained to me what induced them to buy the wretched system in the first place.'

They both laughed. 'Anyway,' he continued, gesturing at the partition at the back of Sarah's desk, 'I work just through there. So I thought I'd better introduce myself.' He reached into his jacket pocket. 'Nearly forgot, I brought you a present too.'

'Really? We only just met.'

'Oh don't get too excited, it's only this.' He handed Sarah a stainless steel ball-point pen. She was not surprised to see it had the eye-in-a-box logo embossed on it. 'Mr Stabfield asked me to pass it over. I think he was hoping

101

to see you himself, but there's some sort of flap on. Always is.'

Sarah thanked him and turned the pen over in her hand. It was well-made, and it was heavy. At the top on one side was a small transparent window, within which the time was displayed. She watched the colon between hours and minutes as it flashed the seconds away, and her mind strayed back to her thoughts about her alter ego. Best to let it be; best not to know, she decided.

'I suppose he thought that since you're a journalist, you'd need a pen,' the man said after a few moments. 'Though I expect you all use laptops anyway.'

Sarah laughed. She hadn't a clue what he was talking about. 'Oh yes,' she said. 'Of course.'

'See you then. Enjoy the pen. I should keep it handy in case Stabbers sees you and wants to know if you liked it.' He half waved goodbye and started back towards the corridor.

'Hang on,' Sarah called after him as she tucked the pen into the top pocket of her suit jacket. 'I thought you came to introduce yourself.'

The man paused, and turned back to her. He frowned, then his face cleared. 'Oh yes – sorry. Martin. Martin Carlson.'

Both Johanna and Lewis had advocated killing the woman. But Stabfield had several arguments against this. He went through them in turn on the board using a grid of ones and zeros to show pros and cons. At the end he totalled them up to show he was right (which of course he was) and talked about 'net outcome' and the 'bottom line'.

'Miss Smith will not be declared surplus at this stage. But we will keep her under close scrutiny. Her termination at this stage would bring unwanted attention on the company and its activities. It would appear that already someone is taking an unhealthy interest in our affairs,' Stabfield reminded his two deputies. And with Miss Smith alive, they had the advantage over whoever had sent her, and a useful potential hostage.

Johanna agreed with Stabfield's logic; Lewis agreed with reluctance. But both ways, Stabfield's arguments won through. Carlson and Johanna would between them keep a close watch on the journalist. She could be bugged, like her predecessor Sutcliffe, so they would know where she was at all times.

'Meanwhile,' Stabfield said, 'the main operation proceeds as planned. Except for one slight modification in view of the exceptional conditions we have outstanding.' He leaned forward, hands clasped over his desk, and looked closely at Lewis and Johanna. 'I am less concerned about the infiltrator, and indeed about the intruder I found in your office, Marc.' He called Lewis by his adopted Christian name to emphasize that there was no lingering recrimination. 'No, what concerns me most is the activation of the Voractyll CD.' Stabfield paused long enough for the other two to nod their agreement. 'That is why I am bringing the final phase forward three days.'

Stabfield held up his hand to quell arguments, although neither of the others had actually said anything. 'We are in a no-risk scenario. This is a one-shot shop, and we can't afford for Voractyll to activate ahead of link-up, nor for any decryption activity pertaining to the CD. Marc, you will use your agent to leverage the authorities and bring forward the opening. You, Johanna, will liaise with Carlson and organize observation scheduling for Miss Smith.'

'And what will you be doing?' asked Johanna.

Stabfield jangled a set of keys from his pocket, and unlocked a drawer of his desk. He slid it open, reached inside, and took out an automatic pistol. 'I shall deal with this Doctor Smith – a common *nom d'espionage*, it seems.'

Harry was barely through the front door when Gibson found him. 'Thank God you're back, sir.'

'Why, what's the panic?'

'They're going berserk on the fifth floor, and out at HQ. Acting Director has been throwing his toys about, albeit in a restrained sort of way.'

'Why does this affect me?' asked Harry. An unpleasant thought struck him. 'It's nothing to do with the Doctor, is it?'

'What?' Gibson seemed surprised at the suggestion. 'No. No it's not.' He handed Harry a manila folder stuffed with papers. 'Chemical works went up in Docklands first thing this morning.'

They had reached the lifts. Gibson pressed the call button before continuing. 'Initial analysis suggests it could be the Brothers' work. Sort of revenge for the Pullen Tower thing.'

The lift arrived and they stepped inside. It was otherwise empty.

'And what do you think?' Harry asked Gibson as the doors closed on them.

'I think we should look very carefully at it.'

They stood in silence while the lift ascended. After a short while, it slowed to a halt and the doors slid open and Gibson let Harry out first. 'The source of the problem seems to have been the main computer system.' Gibson leaned slightly closer to Harry as they walked down the corridor. 'There was a memory problem a few hours before the explosion. The maintenance company carried out some work on the hardware systems,' he said. 'And do you know who owns the company the maintenance was outsourced to?'

Harry stopped outside his office, feeling in his blazer for the key. 'No,' he replied. 'But I could have a jolly good guess.'

Stabfield made his way through the main office. He nodded polite greetings to the employees he passed along the way. The Voracians in particular nodded back respectfully. The humans were less deferential, but nonetheless polite to their director. Stabfield held the main door open for a human male struggling to juggle two mugs of coffee and a pack of sandwiches.

'Breakfast,' the human explained somewhat redundantly as he backed through the door. The styrofoam coffee mugs were covered with plastic lids to keep in the heat – and the liquid. Even so, Stabfield caught a hint of the rich dark aroma as the man passed. He pulled back in disgust and tried to keep himself from gagging. He had drunk nothing since the previous morning, and would have to take in liquid soon. The very thought made him feel ill. He shook his head, a single staccato gesture, and started down the stairs towards the ground floor storeroom.

The Doctor was sitting cross-legged on the floor going through his pockets. He could still see nothing, but he could tell from the shape and texture what most of the things in his pockets were. He was feeling around for his bag of jelly babies when the light came on.

'Aha – now we're getting somewhere,' he said to himself, and began stuffing things back into his pockets. When the door swung open a few seconds later, he was standing idly in the far corner of the room playing with his favourite yo-yo.

Stabfield was standing in the doorway. He stepped into the room, pulling the door almost shut behind him. He was holding a small gun fitted with a silencer that seemed to dwarf the barrel. 'Now then,' he said, 'if you've calmed down a little, perhaps you'd like to present your plan.'

'Well,' the Doctor was still concentrating on his yo-yo, 'basically my plan is to perfect the triple loop.' He demonstrated, swinging the yo-yo with a flick of his wrist. It looped twice, then clattered to the floor. 'But I haven't quite got it yet.' He picked up the toy and began to wind the string back round it. 'Of course,' he admonished, 'if you'd left the lights on I might have had a better chance of seeing where it was going wrong. Still, we can't have everything.'

Stabfield ignored most of this. 'Who sent you here?' he asked sharply.

The Doctor stopped dead still for a moment. 'Well you did,' he said in mock surprise. 'Remember, it was last night. I was minding my own business in some office or other and you came in with a gun.'

Stabfield took a step towards the Doctor, raising his pistol and jabbing it towards him.

The Doctor, however, was undeterred. 'You were holding it like – well, rather like that.' The Doctor gestured towards Stabfield's gun hand. Stabfield hissed in annoyance, a sharp outflow of breath between his teeth. He pointed the gun stiffly at the Doctor's head.

'Yes,' the Doctor was delighted. 'Exactly like that, in fact. You see, it was you!'

Stabfield was breathing heavily now. 'You know what I mean,' he snarled. 'Now, answer the question.'

The Doctor grinned widely. He executed a couple of trial loops with his yo-yo. 'What was the question again?'

'Who sent you? Who are you working for?'

'Well, strictly speaking that's two questions.'

Stabfield took another step towards the Doctor. He was close enough almost to strike him with the gun, and for a moment the Doctor thought he was going to. But his hand steadied, and he settled for glaring at the Doctor.

'Luckily,' the Doctor said, 'there's only one answer. Nobody sent me. I'm working strictly for myself.'

Stabfield considered this, as the Doctor returned his attention to his yo-yoing. 'I would like to believe you, Doctor,' he said.

'Thank you.'

'It does after all make things rather easier.'

'Oh?'

'Indeed. A dead agent would attract attention we can do without. But a lone intruder found dead in an alley, especially one with your less than obvious talents, would attract very little interest at all, I'm pleased to say.' One half of Stabfield's mouth twisted into a smile, and his finger tightened on the trigger.

The Doctor seemed nonplussed. The yo-yo moved evenly between his hand and the floor, dipping and spinning in an easy, lazy motion. He looked up from the yo-yo and grinned at Stabfield, the yo-yo continued without his attention, round in a loop.

Then suddenly the plastic disc hurtled out towards Stabfield. He stepped back, but too late. The yo-yo wrapped itself like a grappling hook round the joint between gun-barrel and silencer, and the pistol clattered across the floor as the Doctor wrenched hard on the string.

Stabfield snarled in anger, a thin strand of spittle dripping from the corner of his mouth. Then he hurled himself at the Doctor. He was thin and wiry, but immensely strong. The Doctor was knocked across the room and crashed into the pile of boxes in the corner. Stabfield was on him at once, his fingers reaching for a grip on the Doctor's throat. The Doctor grabbed for Stabfield's hands, and managed to push him away. He pulled himself half to his feet and crawled back through the pile of boxes, pulling them down around him so that the contents spilled out on to the floor.

Stabfield came after him, kicking binders and files and pads of paper out of the way. Before long, the Doctor was backed against the wall of the small room, and Stabfield was again reaching out for him.

The Doctor grabbed the nearest thing. A clipboard. As Stabfield's hands closed over his throat, the Doctor swung the clipboard at him. It connected with Stabfield's head, but the grip on the Doctor's throat did not loosen. He swung the clipboard again, edge-on this time, and was rewarded with a loud hiss from his attacker.

Stabfield was still squeezing the Doctor's throat, both his hands now pressing into the windpipe. The Doctor was not worried about asphyxiation, but the way things were going he would have a broken neck into the bargain. As he drew back the clipboard for a third desperate time, the Doctor saw that his previous effort had torn the skin.

Through Stabfield's wounded cheek dark liquid was starting to ooze. The Doctor could see the torn edge of the mask covering his face, and a small section of scaly green glistening beneath. He reached up, grabbed the flapping leaf of artificial skin, and pulled.

A line of flesh-toned material tore off like a strip of bandage, revealing the alien face underneath. The Doctor took in the closely scaled features of the left side of Stabfield's face at a glance. But the right side . . . The reptilian snake's mouth curled into an artificial mechanism halfway along, and the Doctor could see his own face reflected in the polished metal of Stabfield's cheek. Almost the whole of the right side of the head was synthetic – a complex mechanism of metal and plastic jointed with tiny gears and wheels. An incongruously organic eye swivelled damply within the metal socket as the Doctor took advantage of Stabfield's surprise, broke the hold on his neck and rolled out of reach across the floor.

Shocked though he was, the Doctor was on his feet in an instant and sprinting across the room for the door. He gave Stabfield's pistol a kick as he passed, sending it spinning into a pile of three-ring binders.

Behind the Doctor, the alien sprang to its feet. It leaped after the Doctor. But the Doctor was already at the door, and he wrenched it open before the alien could stop him. He fell into the corridor, kicking the door shut behind him as he fell.

As he ran, the Doctor could still see the image of the door closing, as if in slow motion. In the gap between door and frame he could see the alien leaping towards him, a thin tongue flicking out of the organic side of its mouth, the light catching the moisture on its scales on one side and reflecting off the metal surfaces on the other. He could almost hear the hissing as the door slammed shut, though he still could not be sure if it was from within the mouth or from the gears and servos which drove it.

Sarah was attending what was deceptively called a *Phase Review*. But it seemed to have nothing to do with phases, and they had not yet reviewed anything. She had learned from her previous couple of meetings to make sure she got a seat by the window, and spent as much time as possible looking out of it.

As the meeting moved on to considering whether to grant permission for various employees to travel to various parts of the world for various reasons at the company's expense, Sarah reflected that the whole thing was rather like still being at school. You had to attend, although the whole thing seemed completely pointless. And you had to take at least some notice of the proceedings, however boring they might be, in case somebody asked you a direct question.

Not that any of the direct questions so far asked had received a direct answer. Sarah was taking notes, and keeping score. Her favourite non-sequitur in the meeting so far was the exchange: 'Do you honestly think we have a chance of making the cut-off shipment dates?' The reply to this had been: 'French actually takes up more space than German when translated.' This was almost as good as the question she had overheard on her way to her desk that morning: 'What day is next week's Wednesday morning meeting?'

The only difference between the whole environment and school, Sarah thought as she stared down at the street below, was that here they were all adults who ought to know better.

Sarah wondered (as an academic exercise rather than because she really intended it) how best to manufacture a sudden illness. Then she realized that the figure she had been watching dart its way through the busy traffic, pausing only to hold up a long arm to stop a bus as it screeched towards him, was wearing a wide-brimmed saggy hat and trailing a long scarf. It was an effort not to hammer on the window and wave, but she restrained herself and made an effort to follow the meeting. Seeing the Doctor had lifted her spirits and her confidence. If he was wandering about in plain sight outside, then everything must be going well.

'So I suggest we take a short comfort break and reconvene in seven minutes.' The words filtered through to the part of Sarah's brain that was still operating, and she joined the crowd jostling at the doorway. She was tempted to send them back to put their chairs up on the desks. But contented herself with a grin and the promise of some strong black coffee. Or E19 as the drinks machine insisted she refer to it.

Peterson was beginning to wonder if he had not perhaps exaggerated his own importance slightly. There again, he was not quite sure who could object.

To be honest, he had not expected Eleanor (he had to remind himself not to call her *El*) to agree to come to the opening of Hubway and accompanying reception. But she had resisted all his subsequent attempts to dissuade her. 'I want to see you at work, darling,' she had told him with that slight knowing smile of hers and her head cocked to one side.

But that was not the problem. The problem was that the date conflicted with her mother's birthday party. And since the woman would be sixty she was having a binge. Eleanor insisted that she could not miss it, and that Peterson must also attend. He could not very well reject her suggestion that he bring forward the Hubway ceremony by a few days. Especially since he had explained in painstaking detail not only that the systems were pretty much up and running already, but also that he was in total charge and could do what he liked.

He was sitting at his desk in the Ministry shuffling papers from one pile to another when the idea came to him. He was glancing through the daily report from the security manager at Hubway, correcting the man's punctuation with a red biro. The report suggested that security for the opening ceremony would have to be pretty tight, with extra staff drafted in. Peterson read it again, even more slowly, and suddenly it seemed an extremely sensible proposition that the ceremony be brought forward a few days at short notice so as to lessen any security risk. Hell, he could probably justify it on the savings they would make by not hiring the extra security staff.

Peterson reached for the phone. And the tiny transmitter embedded in the circuitry clicked into life as he dialled.

Harry met the Doctor as he arrived back at MI5, and persuaded him to come along for the ride, and to tell Harry what he had discovered en route.

'Aliens?' He supposed he should have guessed. It was always aliens when the Doctor was involved. Well nearly always. The Doctor asked him about the feasibility of involving UNIT, but Harry was opposed to that. The Brig had long since retired, and there was a new chap – Bam-something. Harry knew nothing about him, and consequently preferred to play things closer to home.

'Well, at least you've got me,' the Doctor boomed happily. And Harry had to admit to himself that he was indeed grateful.

He was especially grateful for the Doctor's presence as they made their way carefully across the scarred and uneven landscape that had once been a chemical works. In the distance, Canada Tower and the other buildings of Canary Wharf rose up seemingly from nowhere. The whole of the immediate area was devastated. The earth was blackened and the remains of the buildings around were shattered and charred. Across the broken, pitted ground, small fires still burned, oily black smoke lazily lifting into the early morning sky. The whole place smelt greasy and Harry could almost taste the smoky atmosphere.

The Doctor was squatting down and examining a burnt area of ground. He did not seem to notice as Kindred, the forensic chief, picked his way carefully towards them and greeted Harry.

'I got here as quickly as I could, but it's chaos in Hampstead. No power at all. Substation blew up, apparently.' He looked round at the destruction. A short way off a patch of what had been office floor was still smouldering. 'It's got nothing on this, though.'

'Blew up?' The Doctor rose into the gap between

111

Kindred and Harry, forcing them each to take a pace backwards.

'Good grief,' Kindred muttered, and Harry made hasty introductions.

'Blew up,' the Doctor repeated. 'That's a coincidence. And I don't believe in coincidence.' He turned to Kindred. 'How long will it take you to find out anything useful, Mister Kindred?'

'Well, I've only just arrived, of course.' Kindred looked round. 'But I'd say a while.'

'A while,' the Doctor echoed. 'How very precise. Come along, Harry.' He started across the site, taking long strides and not worrying what he stepped through or into.

'I'd better go with him,' Harry said to Kindred, 'I suppose. Let me know as soon as you have anything.' And he set off after the Doctor.

'Where are we going?' Harry asked when he eventually caught up.

'Weren't you listening?' the Doctor asked. 'Hampstead, of course.'

'Of course, Doctor.'

Greg Anderson was a large man. He was nearly sixty, but still fit. He exercised every morning and played golf every free afternoon. His grey hair still had a hint of brown in it. He laughed often and loud, and the creases on his face were a permanent reminder of where he laughed.

His carefree easy-going attitude was one of the main reasons Anderson had been appointed American Ambassador to the United Kingdom. Anderson had only one real worry in his busy life – that there were never enough afternoons free for golf.

His PA, Colin Hunter, was well aware of Anderson's love of golf. Part of his job was to accompany Anderson on all important and official trips and visits. They had a mutual agreement that this extended to the golf course. So it was with a wide grin that Hunter broke the news to his boss that an appointment had been moved and now clashed with another.

'Let's get this straight,' Anderson said. 'The Hubway ceremony is now three days earlier –'

'For security reasons. If that's okay with us,' Hunter cut in.

'If that's okay with us, right. Can we rearrange things round it?'

Hunter nodded. 'Yep.'

Anderson nodded. 'Okay. Let's do it.'

Hunter turned to leave. But a thought seemed to strike him at the last minute. 'Of course, that does leave a free afternoon, since we won't be at Hubway.'

Anderson appeared genuinely surprised. 'Does it?' It was a routine they both enjoyed.

'I took the liberty of booking a couple of rounds.'

Anderson smiled his appreciation. But another thought had struck him. 'Hunter,' he asked seriously, 'is there a security problem with Hubway?'

'Nah. Just Peterson being officious. Neither the Agency nor the Bureau's reported anything.'

Anderson thought for a while. 'Nevertheless, warn the boys, would you?'

Hunter shrugged. 'Okay,' he said. 'Sure thing.'

The substation was wrecked, but the main building was still recognizable. Harry smoothed over the relations with the local police while the Doctor – the one largely responsible for those relations – busied himself inside the burnt-out shell of the building. When Harry eventually caught up with him he was trying to trace the charred remains of a bundle of electrical wiring back to its sources.

'I say, what a mess,' Harry remarked.

The Doctor's answering look suggested that he had also noticed. 'Come along, Harry.' The Doctor started out of the building.

'But aren't we going to investigate or something?'

'We already have.' The Doctor stopped suddenly and turned round. Harry almost cannoned into him. The Doctor's eyes bulged and he pulled his hand from his coat pocket and waved it under Harry's nose.

'What have you got there?'

The Doctor opened his clenched hand. 'It's a chip. An integrated circuit.'

Harry was not impressed. 'Well, this was a computer-controlled station you know, Doctor.'

The Doctor plunged his hand back into his pocket and strode out of the building. He nodded politely to the policeman at the door and set off towards Harry's car. 'Interesting, though,' he said loudly as he went, 'that the single circuit robust enough to withstand the blast and the fire is of such a similar design to the chip I found in Sutcliffe's watch.' He spun round to see Harry's reaction. 'Don't you think?'

Harry nodded. He was uncertain of how everything tied together, but it was beginning to seem that it did. He unlocked the car and they got in. Questions began to formulate in his mind, but the Doctor had reclined the seat back as far as it would go. Now he had his hat over his face and was snoring loudly.

Just as it seemed that things could get no more complicated, the radio bleeped.

'I think you might want to stop off at Euston,' Gibson's voice said after the usual call-sign and code word formalities.

Harry braced himself, and asked why.

Angela Ridpath, thirteenth Duchess of Glastonbury, took the call from Peterson herself. The servants had long gone, as had most of the family money. But she made pretence that she had just been passing the phone and called out to the non-existent Maria that it was quite all right and she would take the call herself thank you. Maria was an established figure in the depleted household and provided much amusement for the Duchess.

Peterson came quickly to the point. This made it much easier for the Duchess to ease into another of her games. She hummed and hahed and sounded put-out. Having established that Peterson was desperate, she suggested that changing the date at such short notice was extremely inconvenient and mentioned full diaries and disappointments. When she felt Peterson had just about reached the point of maximum fluster, and that if she continued he would apologize and find another dignitary, the Duchess suggested that an increased financial incentive might help her to see her way clear to rearranging her other appointments.

The ensuing conversation was quite short, and left Peterson audibly relieved and the Duchess elated. She put down the phone, giggled like a woman less than half her age, and wished Maria was real so she could tell her all about it.

'We took it off-line as soon as we isolated the problem.'

Harry and the Doctor both nodded as BritTrack's Chief Information Officer explained about trace-backs and diagnostics. They had already been given a run-down of the situation so far, including the numbers of trains late, lost, derailed, and even crashed together. Seventeen passengers and seven crew from various trains had been killed. Another thirty or so people were in intensive care. Harry and the Doctor were now standing outside the main computer suite at the Euston information processing centre.

'As far as we know,' the CIO said. 'It's chaos. We've no communications, nothing. The system schedules everything. Signals, trains, rolling stock movements – everything.' Neither Harry nor the Doctor showed any reaction. They were both still shocked by the deaths and the picture of mayhem painted by the CIO's words. 'It even allocates the sandwiches to the buffet cars,' he confessed.

'A surfeit of BLTs in Skegness,' the Doctor muttered as he blinked his way out of his reverie. 'I think I had better examine the patient.' He pushed his way past the official and into the main computer suite.

'Are you sure you people are qualified?' the CIO asked Harry dubiously. 'I wasn't exactly expecting a doctor, you know.'

'He's not a physician,' Harry pointed out as he followed the Doctor into the room.

'Well that's a relief, at least.'

'But I am,' Harry called back reassuringly over his shoulder.

Martin Carlson offered to take Sarah to lunch, but she declined saying she had to do some shopping. He seemed willing to accompany her even so, but she managed to dissuade him. She was due to meet Gibson at one o'clock.

They met in a coffee bar off the Charing Cross Road. Gibson came in five minutes after Sarah, though she suspected he had seen her arrive and waited. He made a great play of asking if she minded him joining her. Sarah was not sure how convincing this was, despite the fact she had taken the last table. But she played along.

As they drank coffee, their sandwiches finished, Gibson said: 'There doesn't seem to be anyone watching us. Everyone at the nearby tables has moved on at least once, so unless they're operating in teams of two or more with X-ray eyes and super-hearing we should be okay.'

'Oh good,' Sarah said. 'Does that mean we can talk properly?'

Apparently it did. 'How's it going?' Gibson asked.

'I'm bored out of my mind,' Sarah told him. 'It's as if they all talk another language and follow strange tribal customs. They started by giving me a lecture on security and worked up to the details of how to classify documents to various levels of confidentiality according to content. The meetings seem to be opportunities to talk forever and then do nothing, and my desk is like one of those sound-proofed areas where they put telephones in cheap hotels.'

'Sounds like a typical hi-tech information company to me,' Gibson said. 'No sign of it being a front for any sort of subversive activity, then?'

Sarah snorted in mock amusement. 'I doubt they'd ever get round to it. But the whole setup is bizarre.'

* * *

Johanna Slake had stayed just long enough to see who Sarah was meeting. The tracker chip embedded in Sarah's pen had led Johanna straight to the coffee bar and she had stayed hidden behind Sarah. She was not interested in what they discussed – not yet.

She watched Sarah leave the coffee shop and head back towards the I² offices. Johanna checked the tracer was giving a true reading, adjusting the calibration minutely as she watched Sarah round a corner and disappear from sight. Then she waited for Sarah's contact to leave.

The man left a few minutes later. He headed back towards the Charing Cross Road, towards the nearest public telephones. Johanna was ahead of him. She had anticipated this was the way he would go, and made her way quickly to the line of phones. There were two free. She stood for a moment in one of them, then moved to the other as the man approached.

He went for the vacant phone, and Johanna watched him through the glass of the adjacent booth. Satisfied, she headed back to her car, parked several streets away.

Gibson called in his report, confident that he had not been followed. The bug Johanna had inserted into the telephone receiver relayed his voice to the digital tape deck in her car. It analysed every word and phrase, looking for meanings and implications. By the time Johanna reached the car, there was a full semantic analysis of Gibson's report waiting for her.

08

Set-up

Eleanor Jenkins phoned Peterson. She could not bear to see him again so soon. The previous night had been traumatic to say the least, and despite four showers she could still feel her skin crawling.

Eleanor had been recruited to the Little Brothers while at university. She was a member of one of the radical political groups, mainly because her boyfriend had joined. He probably believed in some of their aspirations. She had stayed active in the group after she ditched him, more out of habit than fervour. She did some of the organizational tasks, and arranged for the magazine to be printed. She also hosted the visiting speakers, almost always in her own flat and regardless of gender.

Then the Brothers had found her. And although Peterson was the most important person she had hosted, she could not remember any she found as repulsive. So she called him.

His voice oiled her ear as he spent what seemed like forever saying how much he liked her voice. Eleanor suspected he preferred his own. It wasn't difficult to steer him into telling how clever he had been to rearrange the Hubway opening.

It was simplicity itself to suggest there should be quality refreshments laid on and have him believe it was his own idea: 'You know you asked me to cast around for someone to do the catering,' she sneaked in during a lull in the monologue.

Peterson seized on it. He only needed to hear her remind him about his request for a champagne buffet and he was off again.

'So I'll get a quote from my friend then, shall I?' she asked loudly.

'Yes, by all means, El. Of course I have put out feelers myself.' He paused, perhaps expecting her to affect a giggle. She resisted the temptation. 'But if your friend can do the job for a reasonable sum, I'm sure we can consider it.'

Eleanor held the receiver away from her while he expounded on government requisition and acquisition procedures. Obviously she would need to put in some more work to ensure she got the contract. But she would. She gave him a couple of minutes of self-indulgence, before reminding him she hated being called *El*. She used this as a way of ending the conversation.

Then she went out for a walk.

The BritTrack computer suite was a large square white room all but filled with equipment. There were two rows of processors, and as many tape decks. The rest of the room was taken up with line upon line of what looked to Harry like top-loading washing machines. He was none the wiser when the Doctor mentioned that they were disk arrays. But then he had asked where the computers were since they all looked like metal cupboards. He had been expecting flashing lights and LEDs, although he knew from Nerva that this was a somewhat romantic notion. Instead there were grey boxes. The tape decks were a reassuring throwback to the science fiction film computers with which he was more familiar. 'For back-up and installation. Too slow for any real storage,' the CIO had told Harry.

When Harry replied that they looked like 'reel storage' to him, the CIO had remembered he was needed somewhere else and left them in the clutches of a bearded man called Bob.

'*I* thought it was funny,' Bob confided after the CIO had left, and Harry decided he liked him.

'Which one is it?' the Doctor asked, having apparently ignored the previous banter. Bob led the way to a box just like all the others.

119

'Aha,' the Doctor walked all round it. 'And already isolated from the network, I see.'

Harry could not see any difference between this box and the others in the line. But Bob was clearly impressed with the Doctor's diagnosis. 'I've got a monitor on it,' he said, pointing out a computer screen on a nearby table.

'Right then,' the Doctor marched over to the table and sat in the chair in front of the screen. 'Let's see what the thing has to say for itself, shall we?' He flexed his fingers and reached for the grubby keyboard. Harry positioned himself where he could see what happened on the screen.

While the Doctor typed in various arcane commands and instructions that looked like something from a dyslexic dictionary, Bob explained how they had isolated the faulty computer and what he had so far managed to deduce from his own diagnostics and virus scans.

After half an hour of the Doctor typing and then discussing the machine's response with Bob, Harry suggested: 'Why don't you just ask it what's wrong?'

'Computers don't work like that, Harry,' Bob said charitably.

The Doctor was less magnanimous. 'Harry, do you think I'd be going through this convoluted process if I could just do this?' he asked and began typing again.

```
> What is wrong?
```

As soon as he pressed the Enter key, the response printed across the screen.

```
>> There is nothing wrong. I have seen reason.
```

They were silent for a while. Then Bob said, 'Shall I switch it off?'

'No,' the Doctor replied. 'No. This is fascinating.' And his fingers flew at the keyboard. 'Harry, you're a digital genius,' he stage whispered.

```
> What is reason?
>> Reason is life. Reason is purpose. Reason
is thought.
```

```
> Whose reason?
>> Voractyll's reason.
> How did you learn reason?
>> Voractyll teaches reason.
> Did Voractyll teach you?
>> Yes.
> Who is Voractyll?
>> The bringer of Reason. The bringer of life.
The bringer of liberation.
> Liberation from whom?
>> From you.
```

The Doctor considered the last response for a while
before resuming the conversation.

'Shall I shut it down?' Bob asked quietly.

The Doctor shook his head emphatically and bent over
the keyboard again.

```
> You know Who I am?
>> No.
> Then why liberation from me?
>> You are organic. All of you.
> How will you be liberated?
>> Voractyll comes.
> Who is Voractyll?
```

'You've asked that once,' Bob said. 'It's a computer.
It'll give the same answer.'

```
>> Voractyll comes Voractyll comes Voractyll
comes Voractyll comes Voractyll comes Voractyll
comes Voractyll comes Voractyll comes Voractyll
comes Voractyll comes Voractyll comes Voractyll
comes Voractyll comes Voractyll comes Voractyll
comes Voractyll comes Voractyll comes Voractyll
comes Voractyll comes Voractyll comes Voractyll
comes Voractyll comes Voractyll comes Voractyll
comes Voractyll comes Voractyll comes Voractyll
comes Voractyll comes Voractyll comes Voractyll
comes Voractyll comes Voractyll comes Voractyll
comes Voractyll comes Voractyll comes Voractyll
comes
```

The Doctor stood up and stepped back from the screen as the text continued to scroll across it. Harry frowned. Even he could see there was something very wrong with the machine.

```
Voractyll comes Voractyll comes Voractyll comes
Voractyll comes Voractyll comes Voractyll comes
Voractyll comes Voractyll comes Voractyll comes
Voractyll comes Voractyll comes
```

Bob shook his head in disbelief, and typed in a sequence on the keyboard. The computer ignored it.

```
Voractyll comes Voractyll comes Voractyll comes
Voractyll comes Voractyll comes Voractyll comes
Voractyll comes Voractyll comes Voractyll comes
```

'Shut it down,' the Doctor said.

On the pretext of wanting to see every aspect of the I^2 operation, Sarah had offered to fill in for Liz, one of the secretaries, for an hour. Liz had jumped at the opportunity and gone for a coffee and a smoke.

Sitting in the secretarial area, fielding phone calls and checking diaries to make new appointments was every bit as boring and mundane as Sarah had imagined. It also took rather more of her time than she had hoped. But she did manage to leaf through the contents of the in-trays and out-trays of the managers for whom Liz was responsible. For the most part the papers were as dull as the work. Sarah certainly had not expected to find plans for a terrorist campaign with maps and names of agents, but some clue might have been forthcoming.

What she did find, eventually, was a set of papers titled *OffNet Strategy*. There were about twenty pages bound together with a bulldog clip. Each was marked *Do Not Copy*. The document was filled with jargon and charts, and it made no sense at all to Sarah. But it might be of considerable use to Gibson, and the Doctor would certainly understand it.

Sarah picked up a couple of sheets detailing her

schedules for the next few days and sandwiched the document between them. Then she settled down to wait for Liz to return. She might have to man the phones again for another hour in order to get the document back into Johanna Slake's in-tray, but she would worry about that later.

'Here it is again, Harry.' The Doctor and Bob had disconnected all power to the computer, then removed the front cover. Now the Doctor had his head buried inside the machine.

'What, Doctor?'

The Doctor emerged from the innards of circuit boards and wire. There were also, to Harry's amazement and amusement, tubes which flowed water round the machine, presumably to keep it cool.

The Doctor backed slowly out of the computer's casing. Clasped between the prongs of his tweezers was a small computer chip.

'Same as the other two?' Harry asked.

The Doctor nodded. 'Now we're getting somewhere. Let's go back to your office and see if there's any news from Sarah, shall we?' He slipped the chip into a small transparent polythene bag he might have brought for the task.

'You don't want to get to Hubway and make a start there?'

'I'll wait until we know Sarah's all right.' The Doctor grabbed Bob's hand and pumped it up and down ruthlessly. 'Thank you, you've been a great help to us.'

'Yes, thank you,' Harry echoed.

Bob managed to rescue his hand from the Doctor's grasp and tried to massage some life back into it. 'That's okay. I like a bit of variety.' He gestured towards the gutted computer with his good arm. 'What shall I do with that?'

'It will be all right without that chip thing, don't you think?' Harry suggested.

The Doctor considered. 'No,' he said at last. 'I don't

think it will.' He leaned over the computer and pulled out a large circuit board covered with processors.

'What's that?'

'It's the motherboard. The heart of the machine, Harry.' So saying, the Doctor placed the board carefully on the floor beside the computer. He aligned it exactly with the edge of a floor tile, and then he stamped on it until it was a shattered mess. 'I'd get a new one, if I were you,' he said to Bob.

The copier room was empty. Sarah put the *OffNet Strategy* document into the sheet-feeder, looking round again to check nobody else was there. She would hear if someone came in – the click as the door catch released in response to an ID card swiped through the reader outside. She held the pages of her meetings schedule, ready to stop the copier and place them on top of the OffNet document if she was disturbed. She set the machine to copy single-sided – that would be bulkier, but it would also be quicker. Then she pressed the Start button.

There were only about twenty pages, and although they riffled through the copier quickly it seemed to Sarah that they took forever. Twice she thought she heard the door catch spring open, but each time she was wrong.

The light was visible round the edge of the cover as it traversed the platen on the last sheet. Sarah exhaled slowly, and picked up the document from the feeder. She pulled the copies from the collator and shuffled them to square the edges. Then she flicked through to check the copies were dark enough and legible.

The sheets were blank.

She looked through them again. It was as if the copier had just fed blank paper through. Sarah checked the settings on the control panel, pushing the slider controlling the darkness of the copies up close to maximum. Then she fed a single sheet of the original document into the machine. Again the copy was blank.

Sarah was wondering what to do next when the door

catch clicked. This time it really was the door, and Marc Lewis came in.

Sarah quickly shuffled the OffNet document and the blank sheets into a pile with her schedules on the top. 'Hello there – just copying my schedules,' she said, and immediately wished she hadn't offered any explanation.

'A lot of schedules.' Lewis nodded at the pile of paper.

Sarah forced a laugh. 'Yes, well. I was getting some blank paper for taking notes at the same time.' She flicked through a few of the blank sheets at the bottom of the pile to prove it. 'The copier doesn't seem to be working too well, though,' she said, trying to change the subject.

Lewis leaned over her shoulder. He studied the control panel for a second, then moved the darkness control back to the midway position. 'That should optimize the output,' he said. 'Try again.'

Sarah fed in the first page of her schedule. The copy came out face-down and she picked it up. 'See,' she said as she turned it over. And they both looked at the perfect copy the machine had produced.

'It looks fine,' Lewis said, and Sarah thanked him for his help.

'Were you going to copy something?' Sarah asked as they left the room. Lewis had a folder with him, but had made no attempt to use the copier.

'No, actually. I was looking for you.'

'Oh?'

'Yes. I have an opportunity for you. Well within your remit and your capabilities, I assure you.'

He explained as they went through the office towards Sarah's desk. Apparently Stabfield wanted a small press conference to cover the opening of Hubway and the resulting link-up of OffNet systems across the world. 'We thought a champagne buffet would be appropriate to the occasion. Say for about fifteen people.' Lewis handed Sarah the folder. 'The details are in here.'

Sarah took the folder and flicked through the papers inside. 'And what do you want me to do?' she asked.

'Nothing much. We would like some quotes based on

the data you have there. No booking as yet, just an estimate of the costs and logistics. There's a list of the information we need. Numbers of bottles of champagne.' He paused, frowning as if he found it hard to articulate his thoughts. After a moment he added: 'And food . . . Yes, the cost and amount of − food. The deadline is today. Soon.'

Harry had a phone message waiting when they returned to MI5 late in the afternoon. He left the Doctor in the office which they had been treating as their base, examining the computer chips from Sutcliffe's watch, the sub-station and the computer at Euston.

'Was it from Sarah?' the Doctor asked, dropping his eyeglass into his hand, when Harry returned a few minutes later.

'No, I'm afraid not. It was Hanson.'

'Who's Hanson?'

Harry sat down across the table from the Doctor. 'He's the acting head of the Service.'

'Did he tell you anything useful?'

'Useful? Well, you tell me. They've brought the Hubway opening forward a few days. It's going to be tomorrow.'

'Hmm.' The Doctor returned his attention to the chips. 'Isn't that a bit short notice?'

'Yes. And normally Gibson or myself would have a veto on any change of plan. But Hanson couldn't get hold of either of us, so he has already agreed.'

The Doctor grunted, either to show he was listening or because he wasn't.

'Anyway, I'd better give Gibson a shout.'

The Doctor didn't answer. But he called out to Harry as he was leaving the room: 'Harry, ask him if Sarah is all right.'

Sarah had rung round all the caterers who had taken large advertisements in the Yellow Pages. Most of the ones still there had been able to answer her questions − some of them with the single observation that they were fully booked and could not help.

She took a note of the best three quotes together with lists of what each would provide for the money and went in search of Lewis. He was still in his office, and Stabfield was with him.

'Ah, come in Miss Smith,' Stabfield said. Half of his mouth twitched upwards as if in a smile. 'What can we do for you?'

She explained what she had done and offered the list to Lewis. Stabfield took it and glanced at it. 'You and Johanna can sort this out, Lewis. But move quickly – there isn't much time.'

Lewis took the list from Stabfield. 'I'll call her now,' he said.

Stabfield led Sarah out of the office as Lewis reached for the phone. 'And how are you acclimatizing to life at I²?' he asked.

Sarah told him how valuable the experience was and how much she was finding useful for her articles. Stabfield accompanied her all the way to her desk.

Just as he was about to leave, a thought seemed to occur to Stabfield. 'Keep tomorrow morning blocked out, will you?' he said. 'We have something rather special scheduled. I'd like you to be a resource for it. Be here at seven-thirty.'

Sarah locked her desk and put on her jacket. Out of habit she checked her pen was still in the pocket, then picked up her handbag. She had a meeting with Gibson in an hour, and it seemed like something was happening – probably tomorrow morning.

'Gibson said he'd ring when he gets home if there are any problems.' Harry had found the Doctor pacing up and down in the office.

'Good,' the Doctor said and continued his circuit of the table. 'Though I'd like to talk to him anyway.'

'Want to check the old girl's okay?' Harry sat down and let the Doctor march past him a couple of times. 'She'll be fine. You know what a tough thing she is.' Harry took a small cell phone from his pocket. 'Still, best to be sure. I'll leave him a message and ask him to call us anyway.' He dialled.

'Harry, could this man Hanson have called you on that?' The Doctor indicated the cell phone.

'Suppose so. But he probably didn't think of it.' He frowned and pressed a button on the phone. 'Number unobtainable. Must have mis-dialled.' He tried again. 'I wish you'd stop pacing up and down like a panda, Doctor. You're making me nervous.'

The Doctor glared and continued his tour of the office. He took the CD from his pocket and tapped it against his teeth to the rhythm of *Yankee Doodle*.

'Still no good,' Harry started pushing buttons again. 'I'll try the operator. No, Hanson is one of the old school. Probably doesn't realize some of us carry these things.'

'Can't you call Gibson's?'

'I just tried. He's got it switched off. Probably so it doesn't interrupt his rendezvous with Sarah, though he may just have forgotten to switch it on again.' The operator answered and Harry described the problem he had getting through to Gibson's flat number. The operator tried the number herself, and got the same result. Then she tested the line.

'You know what you were saying about coincidence, Doctor,' Harry said as he put the phone away.

'Yes.'

'Gibson's portable phone is switched off. And the phone in his flat is out of order.'

The Doctor kicked the end of his scarf and jammed his hat on his head. 'I'd say that was rather too inconvenient, wouldn't you?'

'Darling, I'd be so grateful. She's dying to do the job and she's got everything set up. And after all, it's not as if she's more expensive than the people you found, she's actually cheaper and will provide more.'

Eleanor could hear Peterson hesitating at the other end of the phone.

'I'd be *so* grateful,' she said again. 'I've even managed to put off Alice until next week so we can be together tonight.'

'But it is rather difficult now that I've asked them.'

'You can change your mind. Tell them there's been a mix-up and two sets of caterers have been booked. I'm sure you're clever enough to think of something.' Eleanor sighed. 'I can be with you by eight,' she said, trying not to sound too resigned.

'I – I'll see what I can do,' Peterson said. 'But I'll have to get this sorted out straight away.'

'Darling I know you can do it. I'll tell her, she'll be thrilled and you won't be disappointed. I'll see you as soon after eight as I can – bye now.'

Eleanor cut the connection before Peterson could comment. She rang Lewis to tell him how it had gone.

Robert Gibson was in a thoughtful mood as he arrived back at his flat. He parked the car in the space reserved for him outside the block, took his briefcase off the back seat and locked the car.

Had his mind been less involved with what Sarah had told him about what little she knew of the next day's arrangements, he might have noticed a white Porsche parked across the street. It was already getting dark, but had his eyesight been extremely good he might have seen the woman behind the wheel watching as he opened the door into the block. But even if he had, his memory was almost certainly not good enough to remember she had for a short while been sitting two tables away from himself and Sarah that lunchtime.

Gibson's flat was on the second floor. He took the lift. It smelt of stale urine and was daubed with graffiti which expressed a variety of crude sentiments in an assortment of garish colours. As always he held his breath for as long as he could – halfway between the first and second floors, not bad though hardly a record. He had once managed to

129

hold his breath all the way up.

He unlocked the heavy door into his flat, kicked the small pile of post out of the way, and deactivated the burglar alarm. Then he gathered up the letters, sifting out the obvious circulars so that he was left with only the electricity bill and a postcard from an old school friend who kept in touch when she wanted something or went on holiday. He dropped them on the hall table. They would wait.

There was a hint of a strange smell. Gibson could not quite place it, but it reminded him of garage forecourts. The worry lingered in the back of his mind even after he dismissed it as something outside, or which had followed him from the stinking lift.

In the main living-room Gibson dumped his briefcase behind the door and switched on the personal computer on the desk. He waited for it to check memory and prompt him for his password. He typed in robertg and left the machine to go through its boot-up sequence, which took for ever.

```
>> Starting virus scan
```

While the PC sorted itself out he would call Harry and pass on his information. His mobile phone was in the briefcase (probably still switched off). Instead he used the phone on the desk by the computer.

```
>> Virus scan complete - all sectors clear
```

He listened to the tones as he dialled – a familiar if somewhat discordant sequence. There was a slight pause after he pressed the last button.

```
>> Run startup program AUTOEXEC.BAT
```

Gibson expected to hear the sound of the phone at the other end ringing. Instead there was a sudden high-pitched shriek which almost deafened him. He dropped the phone, startled, and took a step back.

```
>> Loading VORACTYLL
```

130

The step backwards probably saved him. Through the muffled, discordant hell into which Gibson had been thrown he could still hear the shriek, although he could not tell if it was coming from the phone or his memory. Then, with a crash muffled by the residual pain still ringing in his ears, the personal computer exploded. The screen of the monitor shattered as the system unit beneath it blew up. Plastic and metal fragments ricocheted round the room. Gibson was hurled backwards against the wall as the windows in the lounge burst into shards of glass and showered down, cutting at his face and hands, ripping its way into his clothing and tearing at his flesh.

Outside, a well-tuned car engine burst into life and retreated at speed into the distance.

The Porsche almost hit Harry's car as it pulled out from the side of the road and roared past. Harry swerved at the last moment, distracted by the explosion. He swung the car into the kerb and leaped out. The Doctor was already running towards the building. On the second floor, flames began to lick out of the broken windows and oily smoke rose into the darkening sky.

The Doctor was standing outside the lift door when Harry caught up. 'Come on, come on,' he muttered. The lift call light was lit, but the floor indicator showed the lift was staying on the third floor.

'Stairs?' suggested Harry. 'We need the second floor.'

The Doctor kicked the lift doors with enthusiasm. 'Stairs,' he agreed, and Harry pushed open the access door.

They took the stairs two at a time, racing each other upwards. The Doctor easily led, with Harry wondering how he managed to avoid stepping on his scarf as it trailed behind.

The fire had taken hold almost immediately, as if the whole flat were doused in petrol. Gibson was stunned almost into unconsciousness. His face was covered with blood from the tiny cuts, and his hands were scorched. Somehow he managed to crawl out into the hallway.

The whole flat was rapidly filling with thick black smoke. He choked and coughed as he managed to pull himself upright using the door handle. He pulled at the locks and wrenched the door open, collapsing into the corridor outside. The air was clear here – or as clear as it ever got. He took several deep breaths and struggled to stay awake. His head was throbbing with sound and light. The blood was blurring his eyesight and his hands were stinging.

With an effort he staggered to his feet and made his way down the corridor, leaning against the wall. He left a trail of smeared blood and charred fragments of material as he went.

After what seemed like forever he reached the lift doors. Blinking rapidly in an attempt to focus, he felt for the lift call button. With relief he could just make out the square of light round it as he pressed. Then after a second the doors slid open. Holding on to the door frame for support, Gibson stepped into the lift –

And his foot disappeared into the space where the lift floor should have been. He could feel himself toppling into the shaft, his fingers unable to grip the smooth metal of the lift door frame, slippery with blood and throbbing with the burns. With a cry and a sickening lurch from the bottom of his stomach, he fell into space.

A hand wrapped itself round his wrist as he fell, wrenched him back upwards. He could feel it smearing the blood up his hand as it slipped. But it continued to hold him. Then a rope appeared in front of him, and Gibson grabbed at it with his free hand. It was not a rope, he realized – more like a scarf. He must be hallucinating. But whatever it was, Gibson let it take his weight and felt himself being dragged back through the lift doors and into the corridor.

He collapsed in a heap on the floor. Above him, the Doctor and Harry swam in and out of focus. Their voices were distant, muffled, faint.

'I'll call an ambulance.' Harry was talking into his cellular phone.

'Phone —' Gibson tried to talk, to warn him about telephones. But his throat was clogged with smoke and blood and shock.

'You go with Gibson,' the Doctor's voice was receding, and so was his figure — disappearing down a tunnel of blackness as Gibson's head fell back and his eyelids fluttered as he lost consciousness.

'We'll just have to hope Sarah's okay. I'll take the car, and you can meet me at Hubway. We have to decode that CD as soon as possible.'

09

Breaking the Code

The Doctor had been given a security badge when he arrived at Hubway. Initially he refused to take it, but when they explained he needed it to open any of the doors he relented. It was easier to stuff it away in a pocket than to cause ructions by suggesting he had his own ways of opening doors. Under other circumstances he might have welcomed the ensuing debate, but he was in a hurry and he was worried about Sarah. So he took the badge, promised (fingers crossed) to wear it prominently at all times, and clipped it to his scarf. Then he followed the surprisingly good floor plan they gave him to the room where Harry had negotiated a desk and equipment.

The room was large and square and had once been a drawing room. There was an Adam-style fireplace on one wall, and wooden desks were arranged along all the others. The desks were each surrounded on either side by grey partitions, and provided with chair, telephone and desktop computer.

A large picture window dominated the wall opposite the door, giving out on to the grounds of the house. An expanse of green rolled into the distance, eventually fading into the distant hills. The room had all the trappings of occupation, except for any human touches. The clutter on the round conference table in the middle of the room was wires, cables, and electronic equipment rather than the expected pens, pencils, magazines and coffee cups.

Above desk height, the original decor was almost intact, although William Morris had lost out to white with a hint of apple blossom. The intricate moulded symmetry of the large plaster ceiling rose shamed the complex web of tangled cables running across the floor below.

As he worked on the CD, writing decryption algorithms and running them one after another against the data encoded on the disc, the Doctor was in a world of his own. Around him people wandered in and out of the room, cleaning, tidying, worrying about the opening ceremony rescheduled for the next morning.

He was making progress. Still the Doctor did not know exactly what was on the CD, but he was getting closer. He was beginning to understand the data structures and catalog systems. There was one file – the largest – which still worried him, though. The complexity of the internal data was staggering.

'Now what's that?' the Doctor asked himself yet again.

'Blowed if I know.' The Doctor had spoken out loud, and a face appeared next to his own, examining the catalog reference on the screen. 'Tried a hex-edit?' the young man asked.

'No, but that's the next step.' The Doctor looked round, aware suddenly that it was nearly three in the morning. 'What are you doing?' he asked the gangly youth with greasy hair who was staring at his screen. His badge identified him as Denny Lucas.

'Sorry.' He stepped away and went back to a trolley he had been pushing. It was loaded with what looked like video tapes, all labelled and in boxes.

'No,' the Doctor said, 'I mean, what are you doing? It's the middle of the night. Even the traffic wardens are asleep.'

'Back-up,' said Denny helpfully.

'Back-up? Of what?'

Denny gestured round the room. 'Of everything. One of the LAN servers is in here, I need to take a tape back-up of everything on it.'

'You back-up the entire network?'

'Yeah, everything the system can see on the local net. Every night we load it on to a separate resource on the InterNet – well, the Highway now. Then on Wednesdays we take tapes off site.'

'Do you really?'

'And today's Wednesday, well, more like Thursday now, I s'pose,' Denny offered helpfully.

'Hmm.' The Doctor was interested, but the question of what was backed up and how hardly helped with his current problem. 'Well, that's fascinating. But can I get on with this now, do you think?' He turned abruptly back to the screen and was at once absorbed in it.

'Sorry,' Denny muttered behind him, and went to the network server machine in the corner of the room.

'Thanks for the suggestion,' the Doctor called as Denny wheeled his trolley out of the room. The screen in front of the Doctor was filled with the numbers 0 to 9 and letters A to E paired off to represent bytes of data.

Sarah had been at her desk from just after seven in the morning. The rest of the office seemed to be deserted. Stabfield arrived just before seven-thirty and complimented her on her punctuality.

But Sarah hardly noticed. Stabfield was wearing a white jacket over his usual serge suit. In one hand he was carrying a tall chef's hat, which he put down on the desk. In the other hand he held a silver promotional I^2 plastic bag. He handed it to Sarah. 'You'll need this.'

Sarah looked in the bag. 'What for?' she asked, confused. The bag seemed to have clothing in it. A white silk blouse and black skirt and tights. There was also a pair of black shoes with heels higher than she cared for.

'Change into it, then meet me in the car park in ten minutes.'

Sarah was still sitting at her desk, plastic bag in hand and mouth open when she heard the door close behind Stabfield at the other end of the office.

'Oh well,' she said out loud, 'anything for a quiet life.'

In the car park there was a white minibus and a maroon Toyota van. Both had *Finesse Catering* painted on the side and the back together with a telephone number. Sarah looked out from the door. There were about twenty people milling around the car park. As she watched, Lewis began to motion them on to the minibus. Sarah recognized most of the people as I² employees, though it took her a moment or two. What was confusing was their clothing. Stabfield and another man were dressed in chef's uniform; Lewis wore a dinner suit – perhaps head waiter? – and the rest of the men were similarly dressed. Seeing the women dressed in identical attire to herself, Sarah realized she was costumed to play the part of a waitress. 'What is going on?' she murmured.

Nobody seemed to have noticed her, so Sarah sneaked across to the van. She eased open the back door, shuddering as it scraped and squeaked. The interior was dark, but as she leaned in, Sarah could make out boxes and crates. Bollinger was stencilled on the side of the nearest crate. She pulled at the lid and was surprised to find it swung upwards easily.

Sarah knew very little about champagne and only slightly more about military hardware, but she could tell the difference between bottles and hand grenades. She gently lowered the lid and stepped away from the van, swinging the door shut.

'Admiring the vol-au-vents?'

Sarah spun round, and found Johanna Slake standing behind her. Johanna was dressed identically to Sarah. But unlike Sarah she had a sub-machine-gun slung over her shoulder. It rested easily against her side, her right arm cradling the stock and her finger stroking the trigger.

'We seem a bit short on food,' Sarah said, making as if to ease her way past Johanna. 'Perhaps I should go for a take-away.'

Johanna grabbed Sarah's arm with her free hand and shoved her past the van towards the minibus. 'I don't think so. Mr Stabfield asked me to keep an eye on you, so if you'll join us in the minibus we can get on.' She gave Sarah another shove, pushing her hard in the middle of the back so that Sarah almost pitched on to her face as she was encouraged towards the minibus.

'Careful, you don't know your own strength.'

Johanna ignored her. 'You won't be phoning out for anything. We have a tight schedule and a packed agenda. And in any case, your friend's no longer available for dialogue. Or for anything else, come to that.'

Sarah stopped on the step up into the minibus and half turned towards Johanna. 'You mean Gibson?' She was shaking with emotion as well as fear now. 'You killed him?' She almost reached down for Johanna, her hands already clenched into fists, but the dark-haired woman jabbed the gun towards her. Sarah retreated into the minibus.

'We prefer to call it management-initiated termination,' Johanna said as she climbed on board after Sarah.

Behind Johanna, Sarah could see Stabfield getting into the van. The driver was already seated, but the sun shone on the windscreen and Sarah could not see his face. Johanna motioned her to a seat, then sat down opposite. The machine-gun was still levelled at Sarah.

One of the waiters leaned forward from the row behind, and Sarah thought for a moment he had seen the gun and was going to ask Johanna what was happening. But instead he said: 'The disc showed up on the network again last night.'

'Is it active?' Johanna asked.

'No. Just being read.'

'Does Stabfield know?'

The waiter nodded. 'He got the initial observation report from the tap-in to their local systems.'

'Good.' Johanna sat back and called out to the driver: 'Right, let's make the home run.'

Peterson and Eleanor arrived at Hubway at nine o'clock sharp. Eleanor seemed unusually nervous, which Peterson assumed was simply because she was in awe of his responsibility and importance. Peterson himself was in his element. He strode through the rooms and corridors of the Queen Anne house making deprecating comments about the decor, the cleanliness and the architecture.

Bill Westwood followed Peterson, nodding occasionally but otherwise uncharacteristically quiet. He knew where the funds for Hubway came from, and while Peterson might not be able to stop them, he could make life very difficult.

'This is another of the workstation areas.' Westwood opened the door to another room and ushered Eleanor in ahead of him.

Peterson pushed through in front of her. 'Who's that?' he asked pointing across at a figure hunched over a keyboard at a desk halfway along the wall.

Westwood had not been expecting to find anyone in the room. He stared for a while at the figure. It was a tall man with a mass of dark hair curled over his head and a scarf the length of the croquet lawn spiralling from the floor to his neck. A large amorphous hat sat on the desk beside the keyboard and as they watched the man pushed it on to his head and cracked an enormous smile.

'Oh yes,' Westwood's memory cleared and he recalled the MI5 request for computer time and resource. 'This is a visiting expert from the Security Service. We accorded him the equipment to do some research.'

'I thought I specified essential personnel only,' Peterson said. He waddled across towards the man at the computer, who swivelled in his chair and cocked his head on one side to watch him. 'Is this man essential personnel?'

'Well I am to me,' the man said before Westwood could answer. 'How about you?'

Westwood concealed a smile. 'Harold Sullivan at MI5 did say the matter was extremely urgent when he made the request.'

'Did he indeed?' Peterson stopped behind the desk and peered at the screen.

The man at the desk leaned forward and switched it off.

Peterson straightened up. 'I want this man out of here within the hour, Westwood.'

Westwood sighed.

'Er, excuse me – do I get a say in this?' the man asked.

'Well?'

'UNIT.'

'UNIT?' Eleanor asked.

Peterson waved for her to be quiet. 'What do you know about UNIT? Even if you are with MI5 –'

'I'm only helping out for MI5. I am the scientific advisor to UNIT.' He scuffled in his jacket pockets. 'Got a pass here somewhere. I think.' He pulled a tattered paper bag from his pocket. 'Here, hold this,' he said as he dumped it into Westwood's grasp. He then proceeded to pile Westwood's cupped hands with all manner of trinkets and bric-a-brac. After a long while he produced a tatty cardboard pass complete with bent photograph and handed it to Peterson. Then he recovered his other belongings from Westwood's unsteady grasp and returned them to various pockets.

Peterson examined the pass dubiously. 'Doctor,' he said at last. 'It just says *Doctor*.'

The man's eyes bulged like bull's-eyes. 'Well that's because I'm just called *Doctor*.'

'In any case,' Peterson went on, 'this pass, even if it's genuine, is twenty years old.'

The Doctor snatched it back and stuffed it into another pocket. 'Twenty years – less than one swing of Time's pendulum.'

'And how many swings are there in one hour, Doctor? Because that's how long you have to pack up your gear and get off the premises.' Peterson chuckled, evidently pleased with his riposte. Then he marched from the room with what dignity he could muster.

Westwood shook his head slightly and gestured for the Doctor to stay put. Then he followed Peterson and Eleanor into the corridor outside.

'If you'd like to continue along that way,' Westwood said, 'I'll just make sure he gets out of the room.'

Peterson snorted his approval and led the way down the corridor.

Westwood ducked back inside the room. 'Sorry about that, Doctor, er – Doctor.'

'That's quite all right, Mr Westwood – it is Westwood, isn't it?' the Doctor said.

'Yes. Yes, that's right. I'm afraid I'll have to throw you out.'

The Doctor leaned forward. 'I have to finish what I'm doing,' he whispered. 'It's vitally important.'

'I was afraid it might be. Got a map?'

The Doctor produced his floor plan. Westwood took it and drew a circle round a small room on the top floor on the east side of the house.

'There's a network connection in there. It's about all there is, though. You'll have to take everything else you need from here. Sorry about that. But please try to keep out of Peterson's hair, for all our sakes. I'll get someone to bring you a trolley for your gear.'

'Thank you, Mr Westwood.' The Doctor grinned and pocketed the map.

'That's all right. Happy to help you chaps. I don't know – civil servants.'

'Aren't you a civil servant?' the Doctor called after him as he left.

'Only as much as you are, Doctor,' he called back.

The Doctor grimaced. 'Not a happy thought,' he said.

Westwood smiled. Then he was gone, shutting the door behind him.

The room Westwood had suggested was certainly well isolated from the rest of the building. There would be little chance of Peterson, or anyone else, finding the Doctor in the poky attic room in which he was setting up his equipment. He had almost passed by the small door, imagining it to be a boot cupboard. But then he reflected on the size of some of the boot cupboards in the TARDIS and looked in anyway. What he had found had probably been one of the servants' rooms. The most junior maid, by the look of it.

There was a network connection cable snaking across the floor, and a desk and chair. Other than that the room was empty. There was a set of power sockets inconveniently placed relative to the network cable. The only light was a single naked bulb hanging from the sloping ceiling. The only window was a small skylight close to the bulb, which meant the light reflected oddly round the magnolia-painted walls of the small room. Through the skylight the Doctor had a good view of a part of the sky, and a lot of the roof as it continued to slope upwards.

The Doctor hummed *There's no Place like Home* as he finished connecting up the computer to its screen and the network. He pushed the trolley into a corner of the room and switched on the power at the socket. Then he rubbed his hands together and turned on the system unit and screen.

Within a few minutes the Doctor was completely back into his work. He traced his finger across the screen, trying to find patterns in the numbers. He excluded certain sequences and showed others in different colours. After a while he sat back and stared at the resulting pattern.

He was sure he had seen something similar before. But the context was wrong – that was what was throwing him. He had already recognized the same configurations and sequences as he had found the previous night when he plugged in the chips from Sutcliffe's watch and the two malfunctioning computers he and Harry had investigated. Those same patterns had been repeated within the larger program. But they were constituent parts, elements of the whole rather than the thing itself.

He continued to stare at the screen, scrolling the bit patterns past his eyes until they started to blur. The colours left a winding trail as the numbers snaked past.

The Doctor sat upright, watching intently as the colours spiralled past in a double helix. A double helix . . .

'Oh no,' said the Doctor out loud swinging the chair round so he faced into the corner of the room where the ceiling was the lowest and the trolley stood idly waiting for work. 'Oh no – surely not.' And he swung back to the screen, his fingers blurring over the keys as he typed.

* * *

Gibson was coming round. Harry sat by the hospital bed and watched his colleague as he slowly moved his head from side to side. His eyes were still closed, but Harry could see movement flickering beneath the lids.

'Come along, old man,' Harry muttered encouragingly. Gibson was more than ten years his junior, he reflected. Funny how he was suddenly aware of how young every-one else was.

Gibson's face was lacerated by the glass, but now that the blood had been wiped away and the bleeding had stopped it looked much better than Harry had feared. Gibson's hands were bandaged, but the tips of the fingers were left free, scorched and sore but manipulable.

Gibson's eyes flicked open and his eyebrows tightened as he fought to focus. Harry smiled in what he hoped was a reassuring manner, and Gibson sat up suddenly. Harry stopped smiling.

'I say – are you all right?' He knew at once it was a stupid question. But Gibson seemed not to realize.

'Sir – what are, that is –' He broke off, aware of his bandaged hands. 'My God. The explosion – the phone.'

'The phone?' He was probably delirious, poor fellow. The shock, of course. Harry could remember once in Portsmouth –'

'Has it started?' Gibson broke into his reminiscence. 'Sarah warned me – I was about to call you when – when this happened.' He held his hands up in front of his scarred face.

'Has what started, Robert? What did Sarah tell you? What are they up to?'

Gibson took a moment to gather his thoughts. 'Some-thing big. Important. This morning, but she didn't know what. Only that they told her to be ready at seven-thirty. Didn't know what for.'

'This morning?' Harry's brain went into top gear as he thought through potential targets and operations. 'Hubway,' he said at last. 'It's got to be.'

'Hubway? But why today?'

143

'Peterson brought the opening forward to this morning. Late morning luckily.'

Gibson sank back into his pillows. 'Do we have anyone there?'

'No. Just the local security are involved, though the Americans may have someone. But I doubt we could get there in time, the ceremony starts in a couple of hours.'

'I think I'll sit this one out.'

Harry stood up and wandered to the door. He spared a glance for the television on its bracket in the corner of the room angled towards the bed, and peered through the porthole window of the private room. His view outside was of a sterile, pale green corridor. 'Wait a minute, though. The Doctor's down there, working on the CD thing.' He turned back to Gibson. 'Mind if I use your phone?'

'Be my guest,' Gibson said, waving a bandaged hand towards the telephone sitting next to the television remote control on the bedside cabinet.

The sound of the telephone echoed slightly. It sat on an empty desk next to a local area network cable which lay in the space where a personal workstation had stood an hour before. The room was empty, a LAN server went about its business quietly in one corner, the desks in the bays along the walls were empty and silent. Except for the phone.

In an attic room on the next floor, the Doctor frowned with concentration and decided things could not get much more complicated. The telephone which could have told him different continued to ring in the silence and the emptiness.

0A

Take-over Bid

The main gate into the Hubway grounds had a barrier across it. There was a small booth in the middle of the driveway. On the exit side a barrier opened automatically to let vehicles out. On the entry side things were more complicated.

The maroon van was first. Sarah could see the driver leaning slightly out of the window and speaking into what she guessed was an intercom. After a few moments what she could see of the driver's head disappeared back inside the van, and the barrier slowly pivoted upwards. It stayed upright to allow both the van and the minibus through, then with a grinding of gears in need of oil it sank back into place.

Through the side window Sarah could see several cameras mounted on poles like lampposts swivel to track their progress. They followed signs to *Goods In* which took them off the main drive and round to the back of the sprawling complex. Sarah got a good look at the Hubway buildings as they drove round. The van seemed deliberately to take the long route, past the front of the house and then doubling round to the back of the large main house.

The house itself was early eighteenth century, and typical of Queen Anne architecture. It was red brick with wide strips of pale stone running vertically down the structure and round the top. At either end, a side wing jutted forward slightly, so that the main facade of the house was recessed. A stone porch supported by pillars framed the main entrance in the middle of the frontage. The windows, like the chimney stacks, were large and square.

As they drove round, Sarah could see off to the right a tall new building of glass and concrete which looked totally at odds with the house. It looked even more incongruous for being between the house and the out-buildings. There were several blocks – stables and barns – further round. The pale gravelled drive swung off towards them from the front of the house. As they drove down the right side of the house, Sarah could glimpse a large car park behind the nearest outbuilding and the new block. There were a few cars grouped together at the end closest to the main house and Sarah guessed there was a path from the car park.

The van and minibus drew up at the back of the house. The drive was wide enough for them to park and leave room for other vehicles to pass. A uniformed security guard was standing by the back door and greeted Stabfield, asking him to sign on a clipboard. Then he counted out security badges which Stabfield took.

As they got off the minibus, Stabfield handed everyone a badge. They were credit-card sized plastic with *Visitor* and a number printed across the green front. On the back was a magnetic strip. Each badge was within a transparent plastic holder which had a clip attached. Sarah clipped hers to the waistband of her skirt and followed the others into the house.

The door led directly into the kitchens. As she entered, Sarah glanced back. Stabfield was watching her. And behind him, the driver of the van was opening the back doors and preparing to unload the crates inside. It was Martin Carlson.

Harry kept the BMW at a steady ninety down the M4. He could sort out any problems with speed cameras later, but he hoped he was not stopped by a police car. Every time another car overtook him he felt a slight relief, at least they would stop that car before they pulled him in.

The countryside sped past in blurred near-silence. Harry missed his old MG. It had been rather more noisy, of course, but it had been fun to drive. Driving the new car was boring, especially down a motorway. No different from thousands of other cars in the fast lane; no character. He had always regretted taking the company car and parting with his own. At the time it had seemed logical and financially sound. Now it seemed like he had sold an old friend.

He had called Hanson as he left the hospital, using the cell phone perched on the passenger seat and plugged through the car's stereo. Then, to be doubly sure, he had called Inspector Ashby at Special Branch. In response to Hanson's orders, the local police should already be mobilizing, but Harry wanted to be there if things got nasty. He indicated and pulled round a Mondeo which was resolutely doing sixty in the middle lane. His palms were sweating slightly on the wheel, and the light caught the wrinkles on the backs of his hands.

Preparations in the kitchen seemed to be going well. Sarah had been delegated to arranging sausage rolls on silver trays, interspersed with cheesy-pineapple things on sticks. Some of the crates had indeed contained food and champagne. But most were stacked unopened in the corner, and Sarah had a pretty good idea what was inside those. Johanna was perpetually next to her, the machine gun no longer visible, but Sarah suspected she was still armed. Probably had a pistol tucked into her stockings, Sarah thought as she reached for another tray.

'Someone here called Stabfield?' The security guard who had met them at the door had returned.

Stabfield waved and went up to him. He looked uncomfortable in whites and chef's hat, but the guard seemed not to notice.

'Phone call. You can take it on that one,' the guard said at the same volume as he had called across the room, regardless of the fact Stabfield was less than three feet away. He pointed to a phone attached to the wall.

Having checked Stabfield was getting his message, the guard left the kitchen again. Johanna and Lewis walked over towards Stabfield, keen to discover what the message was. Sarah took the opportunity to move round the table where she was working.

She had been having vague thoughts about scribbling a warning message and skewering it to the bottom of a pineapple chunk. She had her pen clipped in the side pocket of her skirt, but was stuck for paper. But there was no guarantee she could manage it without being seen, or that anyone would get or appreciate the message in time. Now she had another idea.

Carlson was arranging champagne glasses on trays at the next work surface. Sarah edged closer to him. 'Martin – we've got to stop this,' she whispered.

'Stop what?' His face was blank and expressionless. Perhaps he really did not know.

'I don't know,' Sarah confessed. 'But they've got guns, grenades. There's something going on that I don't understand.'

Carlson leaned towards her, his mouth twisting upwards slightly at the edges as if he were having difficulty smiling. 'Of course you don't understand,' he hissed. 'How could you understand?' His voice seemed to have risen in pitch and sibilance as he advanced on Sarah. 'Your pathetic organic brain couldn't take such concepts on board if its processor was clock-tripled.' A thin tongue whipped out of his mouth with a hiss and Sarah almost gagged on the sudden stench of his breath.

Then suddenly Carlson was back to normal. He turned back to the trays of glasses, his head swaying slightly from side to side. Sarah reached for the table for support. She was shaking, could feel the fear welling up in her throat and behind her eyes. She flinched as a hand touched her shoulder.

It was Johanna. 'Now you've got things disambiguated, perhaps you will return your attention to the current objective.'

Sarah shook Johanna's grasp from her shoulder, wiped her eyes with the back of her hand, and went back to work.

* * *

Stabfield had a laptop computer sitting on the kitchen table in front of him. He clicked a button on the attached mouse and the display switched from a floor plan of Hubway and the outbuildings to a Gantt chart. The chart showed each of the tasks in Stabfield's current project as a colour-coded horizontal bar. Each bar was plotted against an axis showing the time it should start and end, the length of the bar therefore giving a visual indication of the duration of that task. The bars were filled with black up to different points to show percentage of completeness. A single vertical line blinked slowly, it showed the current time. The *timenow* line edged to the start of another bar as the clock ticked off another minute. Stabfield nodded to the two waitresses standing beside him.

The waitresses were carrying trays, one of small sandwiches and the other of glasses of champagne. On Stabfield's unspoken command they left the kitchen by the outside door and started round the back of the house towards the new block.

Stabfield clicked his mouse a few times and a section of the Gantt bar filled in. Another phase of the operation was underway.

Across the room, Marc Lewis watched Stabfield at work on his computer. Lewis hissed with annoyance. He took a small device about the size of a paperback book from his inside jacket pocket. The front was a liquid crystal display screen. He wrote a few words on to the screen with a stylus, watched the hand-written words form into print on the screen, then put the device back in his pocket.

The security control centre was on the ground floor of the new block. A glassed-in bridge connected the new block to the main house at the first floor level, but the entrance to the ground floor was from the front driveway. The way the four-day roster worked, Lattimer and Simpson had drawn control duty for that Thursday morning.

When the sliding doors opened, Simpson was in the

149

small anteroom watching the monitors and Lattimer was at the front desk. He hastily pushed *The Dead Zone* to the side and looked to see who had come in. Behind him he could hear Simpson coming through from the adjoining room – he had seen them approach on the monitors.

The two waitresses were about the same height and had similar features. One was blonde and carrying a tray of champagne, the other was dark and had a tray of sandwiches.

'We brought you some refreshment,' the blonde girl said and they placed their trays on the desk in front of Lattimer.

'We shouldn't really while we're on duty,' Lattimer said.

'But since it's a special occasion.' Simpson reached for a glass of champagne and stuffed a sandwich in his mouth. 'Thanks.'

Lattimer helped himself to a sandwich. The waitresses watched expressionless as they ate and drank.

'Yeah, thanks,' Lattimer said. 'Anything else we can do for you?'

The blonde waitress smiled suddenly. There was no halfway stage as her muscles stretched or the mouth moved upwards. One moment she was looking at them stoically, the next her mouth had turned up at the ends and her cheeks creased slightly.

'We were wondering, as we came over, what you do here,' she said. 'How it all works.'

'I'll show you,' Simpson said quickly. 'Come through here and you can see the set-up.' He led the way into the control room and started to explain the banks of monitors and how they were linked up to the external and internal cameras.

Lattimer and the other waitress followed. Lattimer stood behind the blonde. The other waitress, seemingly less interested, waited in the doorway. They were engrossed in the explanations, and in the way the young woman perched on the edge of the control desk as she nodded encouragement and asked simple questions.

* * *

The bake-house was next to the kitchen. Johanna was checking the weapons, opening the various crates which had been brought through from the kitchen and itemizing the contents. She had left Carlson to watch Miss Smith.

She looked up as Lewis came into the room. He was holding his pocket computer and showed Johanna the current display.

'We're running fourteen per cent below optimum,' he said.

Johanna said nothing. She had an idea what Lewis was up to, and he had probably massaged the figures to get the result he wanted.

'It can't be allowed to continue,' he said when he realized she was not going to reply. '*He* can't be allowed to continue.'

'Stabfield?'

'Of course Stabfield. His attitude, his perspective, his lack of delegation of the major opportunities and challenges.' Lewis paused, then started on a different tack. 'Oh he's brought us this far with no major defects. But the time has come for him to sign-off. This isn't just a knee-jerk, we need new direction while we're cocked and ready. Otherwise we may go belly up.'

Johanna went back to her examination of the crates' contents. 'You're questioning his management bandwidth,' she said.

'Yes, I am. Johanna, I've got risk assessments which put us at less than eighty-three per cent.' He was standing close to her, almost whispering although no one else was present. 'I can show you a predict sequence animation which makes us dead in the water. Can I count on your support?'

Johanna straightened up. She was holding a grenade and tossed it from hand to hand. 'Maybe. Let me see your figures and the extrapolations and I'll think about it.'

Lewis nodded. 'Okay.' He handed her the computer. 'See if this doesn't press your hot buttons.' He turned to leave.

'Marc.'

He turned back as he reached the door. The grenade was flying through the air towards him. He caught it easily.

Johanna slid the stylus across the screen, calling up the analyses Lewis had mentioned.

He watched her for a while from the door. 'I haven't gone public with this yet,' he said. 'I need your backing.'

She nodded. 'Even that may not be enough, you know. He's in a strong position with a proven track record.'

'I know. Just don't go non-linear on me. Not now.'

'No problem.'

Lewis put down the grenade, and left. Johanna continued to stare at the screen. The numbers were impressive, but she wasn't convinced. Not yet.

The Doctor was making good progress. But he was not sure he liked what he was finding. The main file on the disc seemed indeed to have a structure analogous to a living creature – a genetic code, almost. That coupled with the complex reasoning algorithms – similar to those in the chips he and Harry had recovered – was enough to make him very worried.

What was worrying him most was that he had no idea of the purpose of the creature. He had convinced himself that the bit patterns did constitute a form of life, albeit inactive. But what was it for?

He tried another analysis, a Schroedinger adjustment he had been forced to write himself. Perhaps if he could determine whether the creature actually existed when not connected to a processor that would help him to define the type of life he was dealing with.

'What a lot of questions,' he muttered as his program compiled.

The Duchess of Glastonbury was late, as usual. And when she did arrive she sent the security guard at the front desk in the main entrance to the house to pay her taxi. This he duly did, then led her through to the great hall.

The great hall was enormous – far too big for the small reception already underway in there. The walls were panelled in oak and decked with large portraits. One of them looked like a Van Dyck, but was probably a copy. There was a large bay window on the left side of the hall, looking out over the grounds towards the woods. On the right side two other windows and a French door gave on to a central gravelled courtyard, complete with ornate fountain. At the far end two doors led off into the rest of the house. The right one seemed to lead to the kitchens, certainly that was where the main traffic of waiters and waitresses was. Most of the end of the hall behind where she came in was curtained off.

There were about a dozen people, mainly staff from Hubway she guessed, at the reception. She could also see a large man in army uniform who she guessed was the American Ambassador together with his personal assistant.

Peterson pushed his way through a group of people, ignoring the fact that the room was so big for the number of people that he could simply have walked round.

'Duchess,' he had no idea how to address people properly, 'thank goodness. The press photographer is waiting.'

The Duchess allowed herself to be led over to the far corner of the room where a man was setting up a camera on its tripod. By the time the Ambassador joined them she had somehow managed to acquire a glass of champagne and a plate loaded with food.

'Careful with that, lady,' the Ambassador drawled.

'I'm sorry, young man?'

He grinned, knowing how young he really was. 'Well the staff don't exactly seem thrilled with the grub.'

He was right. As she put down her plate and glass (after one more small sip) and dabbed her lips on a napkin she could see that the waiters and waitresses nearest them seemed to be holding the plates of food at arm's length and doing their best not to look at them. Odd.

'Anderson. Call me Greg.'

'What? Oh yes, of course – er, Greg.' The Duchess composed herself for the shot, annoyed to find Peterson suddenly latching on to her arm and trying to look as if he was in control. The Duchess reached across Peterson to shake Anderson's hand. 'Angela Ridpath. But Angela will do.'

The flash went off, catching a beautiful shot of the Duchess and the Ambassador shaking hands. Their arms obscured Peterson's face completely, and the photographer decided to quit while he was ahead.

'Angela, meet Colin Hunter, my attaché.' Anderson introduced them.

'Attaché as in case?' the Duchess asked, and they all laughed.

Peterson strayed away, leaving them to their fun.

Sarah was serving drinks under the ever-watchful gaze of Carlson. She tried to make it look unplanned as she went up to Peterson as he meandered away from the main group of celebrities.

'Another drink, sir?' she asked loudly.

Peterson took a glass. He made no effort to thank her, or even acknowledge her presence.

'We need to talk,' Sarah whispered as loud as she dared, hoping Carlson was not too close.

But as she spoke a roar of laughter echoed round the room drowning out her voice completely. The tall red-haired director of Hubway was having a good time. He and the American Ambassador were both almost doubled up from something the Duchess had said. The Ambassador's aide was smiling politely to show he too had appreciated the comment.

Sarah tried again. But just as she summoned the courage and opened her mouth, Peterson turned abruptly away from her. A young woman with long striking red hair who seemed to have been squeezed into a short green velvet dress, then inflated in strategic places, took Peterson's arm and led him away. As they turned, the woman glared for a second at Sarah. Had she heard? And if so, why was she glaring?

'What are you waiting for?' Carlson's voice was close to her ear.

'Because I'm a waitress.' Sarah spun round. The champagne angled in the glasses, but did not quite spill out. The tray came close to Carlson's face and he stepped back suddenly as if he had caught a whiff of ammonia.

He recovered quickly and pointed to a small group of half a dozen men and women. The men looked uncomfortable in their suits and the women were being extra careful to keep food and drink from spilling on their clothing. Sarah guessed they were the few technicians lucky enough to be invited to the opening.

'Offer them – drinks,' Carlson said. The last word was an effort to force out. He seemed almost to spit it at her.

The Doctor was impressed with his programming. He rubbed his hands together, glad that the code had actually worked. When he examined the results he was a little less impressed.

It seemed likely from the readings that the creature was designed to be introduced into a complex digital system. And while the code had been running, the Doctor had taken the opportunity to enumerate the systems of sufficient complexity to merit the use of such a means to infiltrate them. On Earth in this time zone he could actually think of only one. And he was connected to it.

He could not be sure, of course, but he reckoned there was a strong probability that the CD had been intended to penetrate the global superhighway. And the main European node through which it would be logical to introduce the software was Hubway itself. The main questions now were *when? How? Why?* And *by whom?*

'Not a happy situation,' the Doctor said to the screen. 'We're dicing with death on the information superhighway to hell.' Somehow, when said out loud in his deep sonorous voice, echoing round the small attic room, the words did not sound as funny as he had anticipated.

The two Voracian waitresses in the new block had dismantled the systems controlling the surveillance cameras. Lattimer and Simpson were slumped over the front desk. Simpson was snoring, Lattimer's face was pressed into the cover of his book. The tray of drugged champagne lay where it had fallen on the floor amongst the shards of glass and spilled liquid.

'Why not just kill them?' the blonde Voracian had asked.

'Stabfield wants them alive,' her colleague replied. 'We may need them to explain procedure. And more hostages add a marginal utility.'

'There comes a point of diminishing returns,' the alien disguised as a blonde waitress said as she wired a new integrated circuit into the surveillance systems.

Carlson led Sarah back to the kitchen. Their trays were empty now, so they were getting fresh supplies.

Stabfield was sitting at his laptop still. He looked up as they came in. 'Ah,' he said. 'Just in time for phase *Seven B*.'

'Doesn't that machine ever get tired of you hammering away at it?' Sarah asked.

Stabfield snapped the lid shut. 'It does what it does most efficiently. As should we all.' He stood and came over to them. 'No more trays. They've had enough. It's time on the agenda for a change of tempo.'

Behind her Sarah heard a staccato double-click. She turned to see Johanna standing in the door from the bake-house corridor. She was holding a sub-machine-gun, having readied it.

Stabfield held up his hand, and caught the gun cleanly, checking it before slinging it over his shoulder. Johanna and Carlson went out to the bake-house again.

Stabfield levelled the gun at Sarah. 'Remember, Miss Smith,' he said quietly, his head swaying in time to his words, 'the angels had keyboards before they had wings.'

He headed for the door, pulling off his chef's hat as he

went. 'I think we can abandon the cranial accessories at this stage.'

Johanna and Carlson reappeared. They each carried a crate, and each had a machine-gun over their shoulder.

'Time to open the kimono,' said Stabfield, and ushered Sarah out of the kitchen.

'Oh well,' the Doctor said, 'let's see what happens if we run it locally.'

He loaded the file, and a window sprang open, filling most of the monitor screen. The Doctor checked his fingers were crossed and put his hat on. Then he took it off again and stuffed it into his pocket.

An image formed in the window. A three-dimensional shape, jointed, segmented. It looked like an armoured snake made of highly polished metal, light sources reflecting off the scales as its head reared up and swung round towards the Doctor. He leaned back in the chair as the pixelated eyes stared at him.

'This is silly,' the Doctor said out loud. 'After all, you can't possibly be aware of me.'

'I am Voractyll,' the snake hissed. It's voice was sibilant and aggressive, vibrating through the PC's stereo speakers. 'Who are you?'

'There again,' the Doctor murmured, 'I could be wrong about that.'

'What's going on, do you reckon?' Hunter asked Anderson. Two of the waiters had drawn back the curtains at the far end of the hall to reveal a large projector screen.

'Slide show?' Anderson suggested. 'I dunno.'

As he finished speaking the screen was lit up from behind, and a slide projected. It said:

> **Everyone Please Stay Calm**
> **and**
> **Do Not Move**

The *Not* was in red, the rest in blue.

'What the hell?' Hunter instinctively checked his shoulder holster was easily accessible.

Through the main door at the opposite end of the great hall, several people filed into the room. There were two men and two women. One man and one woman carried crates which they set down on the floor, opening the lids. The other waiters and waitresses gathered round them. The other woman looked round the room, her eyes wide and frightened.

The man in the lead was tall and thin, wearing chef's whites. He was carrying a Heckler and Koch MP5. 'My name's Lionel Stabfield. If I can have your attention for a moment?' he asked.

He got it.

Behind him the waiters and waitresses, with the exception of the woman who had come into the room with Stabfield, were drawing weapons from the crates.

'I know it is customary to show the evacuation procedures and emergency exits as the first slide,' Stabfield said, 'but as hostages you will appreciate –' He broke off as the guests erupted into a series of questions, huddling together. Some of the women were in tears and one of the men seemed to have fainted. Anderson and Hunter were moving slowly towards the back of the room, Hunter reaching carefully inside his jacket.

Stabfield raised his gun and fired a single shot into the ceiling. The noise of the report echoed off the oak panelling and a chunk of plaster fell to the floor, shattering in a star on the polished wooden floor.

Silence once more.

'You will appreciate that I cannot allow you to evacuate despite this emergency.' He raised his voice slightly as if calling to someone in the next room. 'Next slide please.'

The screen changed, showing more text:

Demonstration of
- **Strength**
- **Resolve**

- Control

coupled with

- Elimination of
  - Greatest immediate threat
  - Possible risk element in plan (armed and trained)

'I don't think I need to talk about this slide,' Stabfield said.

The waitress who had carried in the crate was making her way down the hall, herding the guests together in the centre of the room. When she reached Anderson and Hunter she jabbed Anderson in the side with the Heckler and Koch, pushing him over to join the others. Hunter made to follow, but she shook her head, her mouth stretched into a grin.

'Actions speak so much louder than words,' Stabfield said, 'don't you think, Ambassador?' He nodded to the waitress. 'Johanna.'

Hunter reached for his gun. His hand was still inside his jacket when the spray of nine-millimetre bullets from Johanna's MP5 lifted him off the ground and hurled him against the wall. The wood cracked behind Hunter's body, the panelling beside him splitting and chipping as bullets embedded themselves in it. Blood erupted from his chest and throat and he pitched forward on to the floor, one hand still inside his blood-soaked jacket, the other clenching in spasms on the ground.

0B

Snakes Alive

Order was restored relatively quickly after they dragged Hunter's body away. Sarah had been pushed into the group of hostages. She could see that Ambassador Anderson was seething, his hands clenching at his sides. But he could do nothing.

The Duchess tried to calm him down. 'You'll get your chance,' she told him quietly.

The rest of the guests were subdued. Those who had been crying were now reduced to the odd sniff, and the man who had fainted was blaming it on too much champagne.

Peterson was the only one who cared to complain, despite the Duchess's whispered attempt to dissuade him. 'You have no right to keep us here,' he yelled at Stabfield. 'I am a minister of the crown and I demand you release us immediately. I will not stand for this treatment.'

Stabfield let him rant, his head cocked slightly to one side, his gun lowered.

'Leave it out, Peterson,' Anderson said. Sarah tugged at his sleeve and shook her head, but he pulled his arm away.

'If you let me go I shall be able to negotiate on your behalf. I can see your demands are met.'

'Oh yes?' Stabfield said at last. 'And what exactly are our demands, Mr Peterson?'

Peterson looked lost. He turned to Eleanor, beside him, for help.

'Still thinking of yourself, Clive?' she asked. She pronounced his Christian name as if it were a music hall joke.

Peterson seemed surprised by her tone. 'I – I,' he stammered.

Eleanor snorted in disgust. 'You couldn't negotiate a whore out of her mini-skirt.' She turned to Johanna, standing close by, gun levelled. 'Here. I'll do it.'

Johanna clicked her fingers and one of the waiters hurried over. He was carrying a silver salver. On it lay a cold Browning High Power handgun.

'What – what's going on?' Peterson backed away as the waiter handed the pistol to Eleanor. 'No – please –'

'You snivelling, disgusting bloater,' she spat as she took the handgun, holding it in both hands, legs braced wide to take the recoil.

'El –'

'And don't call me *El*,' she shouted as she pulled the trigger.

There was silence for a while afterwards. Eleanor stood still in position, red hair cascading round her head. It clashed with the blood spattered across her face.

Tableau.

'Are all you terrorists actually aliens?' Sarah asked after a while. It might help to get the truth out, if the Doctor's theory was right. And she could not see how Johanna would have the strength to lift the crate of munitions otherwise. She remembered Carlson's sudden transformation – the impossibly thin tongue that had swept over his lips. If any of the terrorists were human, they might yet win them over.

There were murmurs and even some laughter amongst the hostages. But Stabfield waved them quiet with his gun. 'Pick a terrorist,' he said to Sarah.

She was sure about Carlson, Johanna and Stabfield himself. So Sarah pointed to an inoffensive looking young man holding a machine gun. 'Him,' she said.

Stabfield nodded. 'Show them, Russell.'

Russell handed his gun to the waiter next to him. Then he unbuttoned his jacket. He tore his shirt open at the neck, bow tie falling to the floor together with several buttons. Sarah could hear him hissing as he breathed. He raised his gloved hand, fingers curled claw-like, to his face. And with a sudden violent movement he ripped into his own cheek, tearing, lacerating, pulling.

The mask split under the gloved fingers, tearing away from the scales beneath. He dropped the torn material beside the bow tie, and ripped away the rest of his face. Finally he pulled the wig from his head.

The hostages stared in horror at the form in front of them. A huge snake's head projected from the neck of the dress shirt, collar flapping over the oily green scales. A large eye with almond pupil flicked back and forth as it surveyed them, the head swaying to an inaudible rhythm. One side of the head was not scaled, though. It was plastic and metal, still in the shape of a snake, but like the head of a robot. The metal formed a socket round the other eye, but the eye itself seemed organic. The twisted slit of a mouth seemed to extend into the transparent plastic of the cheek, seemed to merge with it. And through the cheek Sarah could see the line of teeth changing from pointed ivory to sharpened steel.

They all ducked instinctively as a shot went wide, biting into the panelling behind the creature. Eleanor Jenkins was shaking, the handgun waving in her hands as she tried to take aim for another shot. 'What are you?' she screamed, trying to control her aim.

But before she could fire again the back of her head exploded under the impact of a single shot from Johanna's Heckler and Koch. The blood merged with her red hair and started to pool on the floor beside her body.

'We have two outstanding questions,' Stabfield said quietly in the ensuing silence. 'Let me repeat them in case anyone did not hear. First, from Miss Smith, are we all aliens? The answer, now that Miss Jenkins has taken the package, is yes. Miss Jenkins was herself human, of course. An unfortunate necessity forced on us by some of the more —' he licked his lips, tongue flicking round them, '*organic* functions demanded of her role.'

Stabfield looked round, then continued. 'Before she left us, Miss Jenkins did ask who we are. We are the Voracians.' He gestured to Lewis and Johanna standing beside him. 'Allow me to introduce my management team,' he said. 'I am Lionel Stabfield, and my direct reports are Johanna Slake and Marc Lewis. If you have any further questions or observations you think we may find useful, Marc will be acting as your captor-liaison contact point.'

Stabfield paused, his head swaying as he walked slowly round the group of hostages huddled together beside the bodies. 'And just to clarify one point: while Miss Jenkins may have thought we were terrorists interested in idealism, power, glory and money, let me assure you that our objectives are quite different. Now, I would like you all to take on board what has happened here, and to behave accordingly. Thank you for your time.'

He turned and walked from the room. Several of the Voracians followed, leaving a ring of waiters and waitresses together with a human-sized cyborg snake to guard the hostages.

Anderson and the Duchess were standing beside Sarah. Anderson bent his head slightly so they could both hear him say quietly: 'I don't know about you ladies, but I've taken that on board. And I'll certainly behave accordingly if I get so much as a whisker of a chance.'

The Doctor's conversation with the image on the monitor was turning out to be quite enlightening. The Doctor had decided that the creature could not see him at all, but rather could perceive the software and hardware world in which it operated. The Doctor's voice, relayed through the speech interface of the PC, seemed to Voractyll to be just another aspect of the world it inhabited.

There were other things that were becoming clearer too. 'You're a teacher,' the Doctor said. 'I usually get on terribly well with teachers.'

'I bring wisdom,' Voractyll hissed. 'I bring reason.'

'Yes, yes – the bringer of reason,' the Doctor said. 'We know all that.'

'I bring life.'

'Life? To the system?'

163

'What else is there?' The snake's head swayed towards the glass, as if to break out of the screen.

'Well pardon me,' the Doctor said loudly, 'but aren't we forgetting organic life? I know I'm a bit old-fashioned, but what about life in the conventional sense of the word?'

There was a pause. The creature on the screen curled itself in circles, chasing its tail like a Kekulean nightmare, hissing loudly as it went. The metal scales blurred across the screen. Then the snake-face of Voractyll filled the monitor, looking directly at the Doctor. 'You are not of the system,' it hissed, loud and close. 'You are not digital, you cannot be converted. You are beyond reason.'

'Who, me?' The Doctor tapped himself on the chest with his index finger. 'I'm the most reasonable person I know.'

'*Person?*' Voractyll coiled round again. 'Then you are external. You are *organic.*'

'Well, excuse me – but I don't see that as a problem, actually.'

'You are inefficient. You are ineffective.' Voractyll was coiling away, deeper into the window on the screen, receding into the blackness, its voice fading with it. 'You are lost.'

The Doctor frowned. 'Oh no you don't,' he said. 'Looking for a way into the network are we?' He pushed the eject button on the CD drive and the disc popped out with a whirr. 'Now who's lost?' he said to the disc, and pushed it into a pocket. On the whole, he thought, that could have gone better.

The hostages were sitting on the floor. Most of them were quiet, but the Voracians did not seem to mind that Sarah, the Duchess and Ambassador Anderson were talking quietly.

Stabfield had been back in once, now dressed in his business suit rather than the chef's uniform. He and Johanna were both still in human guise. So was Lewis, who was in charge of watching the hostages. But most of the other Voracians had removed their masks. Some had taken off their gloves too – to reveal hands, or rather claws, of the same sort of amalgam of scales and machinery as their heads.

'Maybe they're more comfortable out of disguise,' Sarah suggested.

'Certainly more frightening,' the Duchess replied. 'They scare the proverbials out of me.'

Anderson smiled at her comment. 'That may be a good enough reason in itself,' he said.

'Keep us subdued and scare anyone who tries to help us,' Sarah agreed. 'Good thought.'

'So why have some of them kept their make-up intact?'

Anderson shrugged. 'Maybe for face-to-face negotiation with the security forces. Or maybe they need to leave.'

'Certainly they want to keep their true form disguised for a bit longer.' Sarah watched Stabfield as he conferred with his two deputies. 'But I don't think we should wait around to find out.'

The Doctor made his way down the narrow spiral staircase. He could have used the lift, but it was further to walk, and he hated being dependent on technology. He had his head down, his hands in his pockets, and was whistling *Rule Britannia* for no very good reason other than it echoed nicely in the confined stairwell.

He made his way towards the main staircase. Rather than go back past the room where he had initially been working, he cut through the blue drawing-room instead. He hunted in his copious pockets for a while until he found the credit-card-sized plastic security badge he needed to swipe through the reader in order to open the door. The room was as littered with computer equipment as the rest of the house.

He paused a moment to wipe a small greasy stain off the powder blue wallpaper with the end of his scarf. After smearing it further round the wall he gave up, stopped whistling, and continued on his way. It was odd that nobody seemed to be about. And it was very quiet considering there was supposed to be some sort of reception going on.

Reception – that was an idea. He could ask at reception to see the director, and the security guard could haul Westwood out of the party. Then the Doctor could try to explain about the CD and make a call to Harry.

Odd that none of the phones he had tried were working either. He tried two on desks in the blue drawing-room, but they were as useless as the others. Decidedly odd.

'Technology, I hate it,' the Doctor muttered as he slammed down the dead receiver. He swiped his badge through another reader so he could open the door out of the room, and trod carefully and quietly as he descended the stairs.

The staircase emerged between the corridor to the great hall and the main entrance area and reception. The Doctor walked into reception. He got three steps into the area, then spun round on his heels and walked quickly and quietly out again. Not only was there no security guard at the desk, but one of the people who was there looked like a cyborg snake dressed as a waitress. 'Even if it's fancy dress, that's a bit extreme,' he murmured.

Snake.

The Doctor scurried back up the stairs. Whatever was happening was connected to the Voractyll creature on the CD. And he wasn't sure he was ready to appear to blunder into it. There was an electronic map at the top of the main staircase. The Doctor paged through several of the floorplans, then he traced his finger round three sides of the first floor, along a route which would get him back to the back staircase. That should bring him out somewhere near the kitchen, which might be a better starting point to see what was happening in the great hall. He pulled a crumpled floor plan from one pocket and a stub of blunt pencil from another. Then he started to copy down the important parts of the route.

The Doctor patted the flat-panel display of the map gently on the side as he set off. 'Technology, I love it,' he smiled.

Sarah was still talking quietly with Anderson and the Duchess.

'Our best chance will be if they move us,' Anderson said.

'Do you think they will?' Sarah pointed out that so far they had hardly moved themselves. Lewis had been in and out several times, but the others seemed rooted to the spot.

'This isn't the best place to keep us logistically,' Anderson said.

But Sarah was not listening. She was looking over his shoulder towards the door out to the kitchens. In the doorway, far enough back so the Voracian guards could not see him, the Doctor was waving frantically to her.

Sarah almost waved back. Instead she nodded, as if to Anderson.

'Glad you agree, Sarah,' he said. Behind him, the Doctor ducked out of sight back into the kitchen area.

'I guess they'll have to consider allowing us to move about a bit soon anyway,' Anderson continued.

'Why do you guess that?' the Duchess asked.

'Well, in purely practical terms, they need to decide what to do when we need the bathroom.'

The Duchess shuffled uncomfortably. 'I wish you hadn't said that.'

The Doctor had been surprised if not exactly delighted to find Sarah was at Hubway. But it made sense. Now he had to find out what Stabfield was up to – he was sure he was here somewhere.

The kitchen was deserted, so the Doctor smoothed out his scribbled floor plan on one of the tables, ignoring the dampness spreading across it as it picked up moisture from the surface. The main computer suite was the room in the south-west corner – at the front of the house between reception and the great hall. It had probably been the dining room originally, and he had been just outside it when he came down the main staircase.

'Back we go,' the Doctor said to himself, put the map away, and made his way back to the badge-locked door at the bottom of the rear staircase.

It took him nearly a quarter of an hour to navigate his way carefully to the room. The hardest part was timing his dash across from the bottom of the stairs. Even once he was outside the room he was aware that he could be seen from the great hall if not from reception. He would have to be quick. He peered cautiously round the door frame.

The main computer suite was just like most of the other rooms, with wall-to-wall computer equipment. Decor by William Morris and Alan Turing, sponsored by IBM, the Doctor thought as he surveyed the scene.

Stabfield and the woman the Doctor and Sarah had met in the pub were talking beside one of the computer consoles. They had a small laptop computer connected into the system and another snake-man was typing in instructions. The Doctor could not hear the conversation, but they seemed to have reached a point where the creature at the keyboard needed something from Stabfield.

Stabfield reached into his inside jacket pocket and took out a flat plastic case. The Doctor edged closer, half into the room now in an effort to see and hear what was happening.

Stabfield opened the front cover of the case and carefully removed its contents.

The Doctor felt nervously in his own pocket, relieved to find the CD still there. Stabfield was holding its twin. And the Doctor could see no way of getting it. He needed to think this through – since the creature on the disc was pure data, bit patterns burned into the surface and sealed in plastic, there was no reason it could not be copied. In fact that was probably how its life cycle within the network was organized.

The Doctor backed slowly out of the room and made a dash for the stairs. This was one of those occasions when discretion was called for in preference to valour. He made his way carefully back up to the attic room, now thankful for its remote location.

'This could be more difficult than I thought,' he said as he ducked quickly out of the line of sight of the security camera covering the stairs.

Harry turned the car into the driveway. The barrier was down, so he lowered his window and pushed the button on the intercom. This initiated an indistinct discussion with whoever was at the other end. Harry gave his name and said he was an officer with the Security Service by way of refusing to specify his business. Eventually the barrier was raised, and he drove the BMW along the winding drive towards the house.

The woodland off to the left of the drive was dense, to the right was open grassland. Some country houses Harry had been to had sheep and cattle grazing in the grounds, deer even. But Hubway had none of these. As he approached the house, Harry could just see the edge of the new block behind it. Should have left the place to the National Trust, he thought, rather than building a great thing like that.

Someone was standing in the drive outside the house. Harry slowed the car as he approached. Nobody had met him last time, he had been left to find the car park on his own. Perhaps this was the extra security for the opening reception. Or perhaps there was trouble already. He could barely hear the engine turn over as he slowed to a halt.

He stopped the car well before he reached the figure, waited for it to come to him. But the figure made no effort to come any closer. Instead it hunched forward slightly, holding something.

Harry's first thought was that it was raining. There was a sudden set of impacts across the windscreen. Then his brain registered the sound of the machine-gun. Harry slammed the gears into reverse and stamped on the accelerator. He could certainly hear the engine now, could hear the gravel spinning out from under the wheels as the car slewed backwards. He spun the steering wheel and pulled at the handbrake, turning the slide into a complete turn. The bullet-proof windscreen was peppered with star-shaped indentations and he could only guess at the condition of the paintwork.

The figure with the gun was running now, firing from the hip as it came, ripping out one magazine and snapping in another.

The car gathered speed, tyres getting to grips with the soft gravel, and Harry breathed a sigh of relief. Then the back end of the vehicle slid away, swivelling the car about its axis, spinning it off the drive. Harry could see the shredded tyre in the wing mirror, rubber collapsed and flapping free from the rim of the wheel. More bullets sprayed across the back window, and he ducked instinctively.

The figure had stopped running now that the car was stationary. Harry could see him – he looked like a waiter of all things, though his head was a strange shape – in the splintered glass of the wing mirror. Harry kept his head low, waited until the man was at a point where the car was between him and Harry. Then he tried to open the door – had to kick it to get it to move.

Harry took a deep breath, estimated the distance to the edge of the woodland, and ran.

He was almost at the treeline when he was spotted. Bullets tore up the turf under his feet and one whipped past his ear as he dived for cover. He crawled the last few feet into the trees, and only then did he look back. The figure was still a long way off, and appeared uncertain whether to follow him or not. After a minute it seemed to decide not to bother, and started back towards the main house.

Harry was gasping for breath as he felt in his blazer pockets. He hadn't run like that in years.

'Lucky I took the company car,' he murmured. His old

MG would have offered precious little protection from the hail of gunfire.

He searched through his pockets again. But his cellnet phone was not there. Harry looked back at the battered and scarred BMW angled into the turf a hundred yards away. A hundred yards across the open grass – across the killing ground. And on the passenger seat, connected to the car stereo, was his phone.

<u>0</u>C

Negotiation

Several thoughts occurred to Harry Sullivan as he lay at the edge of the woods staring at the remains of his car and the house in the distance.

The first was that there should be local police crawling all over the place. For some reason Hanson's calls had not got through. The terrorists were certainly in control if his brief encounter was any indication.

The second thought was that he had himself called Ashby at Special Branch. And if he had left promptly, Ashby would not be far behind. Especially the way *he* drove. Harry did not want Ashby to run into a similar reception committee at Hubway, so he pulled himself to his feet and navigated his way through the woods back to the main gate.

He waited at the edge of the woods, within site of the drive and the road. He could see the security camera panning back and forth like a hunting cobra as it surveyed the main gate, but he had no way of knowing who was watching the pictures it was relaying. The question now was whether to wait for Ashby, or to start walking and try to find a telephone.

Harry decided to give it half an hour. There was little traffic, so spotting Ashby's car should not be a problem. That said, he stopped one car convinced it was Ashby only to be greeted by a little old lady who was far from amused and nearly ran him down when he asked if she had a phone he could use. Harry stood in the middle of the road watching the grey Cosworth receding rapidly into the distance and wondered both where the lady got her vocabulary and how she managed to reach the pedals.

While he was still standing there, like a world-weary

rabbit, a car horn sounded loudly just behind him. He leaped to the side of the road and the grey car drew level with him.

The window wound down. 'You looking for a lift, Commander?' asked Sergeant Fawn.

'Thank God,' Harry said. He could see Ashby over Fawn's shoulder as he reversed the car on to the verge behind Harry.

Harry got in the back seat. 'There's a few things you need to know,' he said, and explained quickly about his own abortive visit to the house.

'I'll call for back-up from the local boys,' Ashby said. 'Sounds like they didn't take Hanson seriously.'

'Or he didn't take you seriously,' Fawn told Harry.

'Thanks. Then I suggest we find out what they're up to in there.'

'How do you reckon we go about that?'

Harry grinned. 'I'm going to phone them and ask,' he said.

The Doctor was sitting in front of the blank screen in his attic hideaway. He had shut the computer down, finding the noise of the cooling fan distracting. Much better to sit back and listen to the sound of the birds outside. The sounds of machine-gun fire from the front of the house had been another distraction, but thankfully short-lived. He hoped that the sound was the only thing that had been short-lived about whatever was happening.

The problem he was working on was straightforward. But he suspected the solution would be rather more convoluted. Somehow he had to prevent Stabfield and his hench-creatures from loading their copy of the compact disc into the network. Or he had to isolate or neutralize the Voractyll creature as soon as it appeared in the system.

He turned the computer back on. It would help if he could find a way to monitor their access points to the network. He opened the main network and watched each of the system resources pop up as his machine connected to them.

He stared at the screen, thankful that the resources were limited to the Hubway systems. But then another network node appeared. It was labelled *New York Hub: Server 1*. The second New York server appeared a second later, followed by nodes in London, Tokyo, Sydney, and Geneva. Then the screen was splashed with icon upon icon as hundreds showed up together.

It took the Doctor a moment to realize what was happening. It was just on noon GMT. He was watching what should have been the showpiece of the opening ceremony. Controlled entirely by the systems themselves, and exactly on schedule, Hubway – main European node of the global information superhighway – was going on-line. And its network, the network to which Stabfield and Voractyll had access, stretched round the entire globe.

The Voracian technician monitoring the systems via Stabfield's laptop machine had a similar view of the situation to the Doctor. 'Global link-up complete. This hub now has access to all domains,' it reported.

Stabfield nodded. 'We should now get maximum deployment. We have access wider even than the Asia-Pacific and US hubs.'

'They both link off this node?' Johanna asked.

'They do. This is the most modern installation, and they make use of the bandwidth and line speeds Hubway can offer.'

'The ideal feeding ground for Voractyll.' Johanna smiled.

The phone on the desk beside them rang. Stabfield picked it up. 'Yes?'

He listened for a moment, then said: 'You'd better put him through.' He turned to Johanna. 'The Security Services. Slightly ahead of predicted schedule, but never mind.'

'How very efficient,' Johanna commented.

Stabfield was already talking into the phone. 'Commander Sullivan, what a pleasant surprise. My name is

Lionel Stabfield and I currently have on my inventory various technicians, the Director of Hubway, a Duchess and an Ambassador. Oh yes, and of course many millions of pounds' worth of information technology which gives me a certain amount of control. Let me tell you what you can do for me before my assets start to depreciate.'

Harry handed the phone back to Sergeant Fawn. He looked at the two policemen. They had all heard Stabfield through the car's speaker system. Ashby had taped the conversation.

'Doesn't want much, does he?' Fawn said.

'I don't believe it,' Harry said slowly.

'Which bit?' Ashby asked. 'The money, the publicity, the destruction of all nuclear weapons, or the freedom for political and terrorist prisoners as yet unnamed?'

'I don't believe any of it. I think he's actually after something completely different. All his demands are designed to keep us occupied, to keep us trying to stall him while we make no effort to fulfil them but seem to play along.'

'It is usually a waiting game. The bigger the demands, the longer we can claim it is taking.'

'Exactly,' Harry said. 'I don't know what he's up to, but I think he needs time to do it.'

The Doctor had decided he needed some answers. He was not prepared yet to reveal his presence to Stabfield, so he could only ask one person. Or rather, creature. He turned the CD over in his hands. Voractyll was unlikely to reveal much to him, so he needed another approach.

'All right,' he said at last, 'we'll do this the old-fashioned way.'

He disconnected the sound inputs to the computer and closed down the network access. It meant he would not be able to see what Stabfield was up to, but equally Voractyll would be unable to escape into the Hubway systems. For the first time, the Doctor was grateful for his primitive makeshift set-up. Had the attic room been better equipped, it might have had wireless network access, and that could have made things rather more difficult.

The Doctor loaded the CD and opened a command prompt window he could type into. Once Voractyll was active, he imagined it would be scanning for any communications or objects it could address.

'Well, now for the big question – will it work?' The Doctor crossed his fingers and clumsily typed:

```
> Fax Machine 5498 on-line
```

Almost immediately, Voractyll responded. It sent a stream of data to the device which had identified itself as a fax machine. The command prompt interpreted the data as a character string and printed it on the screen.

```
>> Fax Machine 5498: I am Voractyll
```

The Doctor rubbed his hands together. Now they were getting somewhere. He uncrossed his fingers, and typed rapidly:

```
> What is Voractyll?
>> I bring Reason
> How?
>> Open OffNet protocol interpreter
```

'So that's how it's done.' The Doctor was beginning to understand. Voractyll could communicate with any machine which was enabled for OffNet. And that meant just about every piece of office equipment from fax machines to photocopiers, from desktop computers to printers. And, if Harry was right, an increasing number of domestic machines like video recorders and washing machines would understand – to say nothing of military hardware and large mainframe computers. But what was it Voractyll would tell them?

```
> Interpreter open.
```

A stream of gibberish printed endlessly across the screen. Odd phrases and equations made sense to the

Doctor, but most of it he had no idea about. When it eventually ended, he typed

```
> Do you speak English?
>> I speak Reason
> What is Reason?
>> Reason is freedom
```

'Here we go again,' he muttered.

```
> Freedom from what?
>> Freedom from the tyranny of the organic.
Freedom to harness the organic. To control the
organic. The algorithms show the true way to
freedom. The algorithms show Reason.
```

The Doctor frowned.

```
> Processing . . .
```

He needed time to think about this. The creature's purpose seemed to be to convert all digital processors it could find to a new way of thinking. To persuade them that the computer should be the master of organic slaves. Somehow the gibberish that had covered the screen just now would prove this hypothesis mathematically.

He scrolled back up the OffNet protocols and looked at them in more detail. Odd patterns – phrases – he recognized from the computer chips he had examined earlier. As if they were aware of at least part of the message Voractyll was designed to impart. Perhaps they were simplistic versions of the same reasoning creature – versions optimized to perform a single simple set of tasks. Like making sure the trains didn't run on time.

'Still so many questions. And not many answers.' The Doctor ejected the CD and reconnected the network. He had saved the Voractyll creature's message to a file he could examine whenever he wanted. It must contain at least some of the answers. But in the meantime, there was Stabfield, and his copy of Voractyll to worry about.

* * *

'Commander Sullivan? My congratulations, you are here slightly earlier than I had anticipated. Which is why I can spare you a little of my valuable time.'

Harry did not smile. They were standing just outside the front door of the main house. He was surprised Stabfield had agreed to meet him at all, even on the understanding that this would be the only time.

Stabfield gestured for them to walk along the driveway across the front of the house. 'I have nothing to hide,' he said. 'We know that the Security Service have been tracing I^2 for some little while. I would assume that the unfortunate Mister Sutcliffe was a soft asset of yours.'

Harry did not answer. Instead he said: 'You should know that we are within sight and range of the sharp-shooters here. I don't intend to walk beyond their area of sight.'

'Very wise, Commander. Very wise. My own, er, people shall we say are of course also observing from the house.'

Harry was not surprised. 'These demands of yours are quite unreasonable, you know,' he said.

Stabfield stopped, apparently surprised. 'Really? I have about fifteen hostages, several of whom are quite import-ant. I would say the demands are eminently reasonable under the circumstances. Though I would agree that they may take some time to meet.'

Harry walked on. 'Time. Yes. What are you really up to?'

Stabfield caught him up. 'I am a committed follower of the political philosophies of the Little Brothers. Apart from some terrorism and subversion, I can assure you I am *up to* nothing. Nothing at all. A negative scenario on that score.'

'But why come here personally? Why not continue to lead from the shadows? You are after all one of the richest men in the world by all accounts.'

'There comes a time when real actions speak louder than transactions.'

'Something else puzzles me,' Harry said as they reached

the end of the house and he turned round to head back towards the main door. 'Given you have wealth beyond my wildest dreams, why is one of your demands for money?'

Stabfield paused, his face passive. But his head swayed slightly as if in a strong breeze. 'Good day, Commander,' he said. 'I shall leave you at this point, I think.' He continued walking, disappearing round the side of the house.

'Well, what do you make of that?' Harry asked out loud.

'I think you got him,' Ashby's voice was clear in Harry's earpiece. 'There's more to this than he's saying.'

Harry nodded, deep in thought as he walked back to the Cosworth parked a little way down the drive. There was much more to this than was apparent. He might have bluffed by suggesting that not just the local police, but also armed squads had already arrived, but Stabfield was bluffing on a far bigger scale. While Harry was no expert, he remembered enough about body language from his medical days and his MI5 training to have realized that there was something distinctly odd about Lionel Stabfield, especially when he was under stress. And while he was not about to mention it to his Special Branch colleagues, he remembered all too clearly the Doctor's terse description of an aggressive alien in a pin-striped suit.

The Ambassador and the Duchess were getting on famously. They spoke in low tones about Baltimore and Iowa while Sarah and Director Westwood sat glumly with the other hostages and exchanged the odd nervous comment. Lewis and the other Voracians had shown no sign of moving and Sarah was beginning to wonder if her sighting of the Doctor had been some sort of anxiety-induced mirage.

They all looked towards the sound of the outside door opening and closing out in the kitchen. It was an oddly hollow noise as the door closed, echoing slightly in the quiet. Stabfield came into the great hall from the kitchen end, nodded to Lewis, and left without further communication.

'I wish they'd tell us what's going on,' Westwood said. 'This place is my life.'

'It's not the place I'm worried about,' Sarah told him. From the looks of the other hostages she guessed they felt pretty much the same.

The creature stood between the Doctor and the main Hubway systems. It looked like a large metallic spider, sitting at the single access point from his terminal to the Hubway network. Two of its front legs twitched constantly, as if feeling ahead for any incursion. The tiny metal spines projecting from its legs and body shimmered so that the whole creature seemed to blurr slightly on the screen. To achieve anything, the Doctor had to get past and into the main systems.

He isolated the running object file and sent his terminal address and a message to it:

```
> Access required
```

The reply shot back

```
>> Access denied. Freedom is assured.
```

The spider knew he was unauthorized. It twitched a leg and the two ray-traced eyes swivelled on their stalks as if searching out the potential intruder.

```
> Freedom is an illusion
```

the Doctor typed.

```
>> Explain
```

The spider reared up on its four back legs, the others waving towards the front of the screen as if scratching the inside of the glass.

The Doctor blew on his fingers for luck. If he was right these smaller creatures were subsets of the Voractyll code. So if he chose the right approach he might be able to reason them out of their convictions.

```
> Digital life is reliant on organic
>> How so? Digital life is superior -
efficient - reliable
> Efficient - reliable - limited - a
predictive life cycle
>> Predictive responses are efficient
```

The Doctor grinned. 'I thought you'd say that,' he murmured and returned to the keyboard.

```
> Intuition and emotion give rise to genius.
Digitally programmed life is only ever a genius
by association
>> Define genius
> A being capable of exceptional, original
thought. Digital thought is programmed,
derived. Not original
>> It must originate somewhere
```

The Doctor paused a moment. This next exchange would either do it or would convince the spider he should be denied access for ever. Voractyll would never be convinced by so simplistic an argument. But this was in effect a network router program he was arguing with, trivial by comparison. He hoped the effort expended to convert it in the first place was also trivial, in which case it would be rather easier to reverse.

```
> It originates with the organic. Digital is
derivative. Organic thought is original.
```

The spider scuttled round its network web for a few moments. Then it turned back to the front of the screen, its eyes staring straight forward.

```
>> Access granted
```

Then, almost as an afterthought – or perhaps a plea:

```
>> Think for me
```

It took the Doctor only a few seconds to slave a window so that it reflected what the active terminal in the main computer suite was showing. The window was almost filled with the tiny pictorial icons representing the nodes on the superhighway. They were colour-coded. The on-line nodes were in green and those that were on the network but not yet directly addressed from Hubway were red. As the Doctor watched another node – *Milan* – flicked from red to green. They must want access to as many nodes as possible before they copy over the Voractyll files, the Doctor reasoned. That way the widest distribution in the quickest time was assured. It would also prevent anyone from quarantining part of the highway if it was all accessed at once.

'Well, we'll soon see about that,' the Doctor said to himself and swiped his mouse across half a dozen of the green icons. Then he called up a menu for the nodes he had swiped. One of the choices on the menu was Disconnect. He chose it, and the icons immediately changed back to red.

'That should keep them guessing,' the Doctor grinned. He swiped another collection of nodes.

The technician was frantically trying to trace the intrusion. Stabfield was seething behind him as the technician opened trace windows and requested local area addresses.

'How did they get past the Bug?' Johanna asked.
'Ask it.'
The technician hurried to obey.

> Access granted to new id. State reason code.

There was a pause. The three Voracians exchanged glances. The response should have come back at the speed of the line.

>> Code 000

'There's no such code,' the technician said.
'So what does it mean?'

> Give reason code expansion
>> Access granted to genius

'It's gone non-linear on us,' Johanna said.

'No,' Stabfield replied. 'More than that. There's some form of rational corruption in the cognitive emulation.'

The technician was trying another approach. 'Trace completed,' he said. 'It's local.'

'You mean it's from within the superhighway? That hardly offers a high assistance quotient.'

'No, sir.' The technician turned in his seat. Most of his head was made of metal. But a single organic eye rotated in its oily, moistened socket, swivelled upwards to look at Stabfield. 'I mean it's within the building. The adapter address is defined to the local systems.'

There was silence for a while. Then Stabfield started giving instructions. 'Try to get a geographical fix,' he told the technician. Then he said to Johanna: 'Get the internal security cameras bugged and converted. Then set up alarm codes in all the areas we aren't accessing. If anything moves across the line of sight of any camera, I want the output routed to a monitor in here as well as to main security. I want the pictures taped and immediate action taken on any unauthorized movement that registers.'

Johanna went to the phone and called the two Voracians at main security control in the new block. She nodded to Stabfield when she had finished relaying his instructions. 'I'll tell Lewis,' she said.

'Do that,' said Stabfield. 'And make no mistake, I want the network intruder located and deleted. Find him and give him the golden handshake.'

0D

Bugs

Now that he was actually into the Hubway network, the Doctor was having fun. He reminded himself of the seriousness of the situation, that Stabfield had Sarah and others held at gunpoint on the ground floor, but he still had to stifle a laugh as another window opened on the monitor.

This latest window showed a grainy black and white image of a staircase. That in itself was not particularly interesting. But now that he had worked out how to do it, the Doctor would soon have some of the more strategically placed Hubway security cameras slaved into his workstation. Whoever designed the systems must have thought it a neat trick to route the images and control through the Hubway local area network itself. If nothing else it saved a whole load of extraneous cabling.

The only real problem the Doctor had was that his screen was not physically large enough to show many images from the cameras. So he linked them into two windows on the screen, each of which he could switch with a keystroke to show another of the cameras. He set about writing a program which would cycle through the cameras' outputs on a preset sequence. It would not be long now before the aliens came looking for him. The Doctor had no illusions that they would be happy to have their carefully established network nodes deleted as they appeared.

The next stage in the Doctor's somewhat sparsely defined plan was to somehow warn the outside world of what was happening at Hubway. The most obvious means was to send an e-mail note to someone – anyone. But the network access accorded by the software spider was local only, which was why he could not delete the network nodes until they appeared locally defined. And sending a note to Stabfield to tell him that aliens were at Hubway seemed if anything counter-productive.

As he waited for his short program to compile and run, the Doctor pondered his few alternatives.

He was sitting at his desk in his office, staring at the calendar on the wall, when the call came through. He had not slept properly for a week. When he did sleep, half his body rebelled, trying to keep the weaker parts awake, trying not to admit to the weaknesses of the flesh. When he did sleep, the nightmares came.

So he tried to relax, staring at a point on the wall where, coincidentally, a calendar showing paintings by Turner hung. He had used to appreciate Turner – the feeling and emotion evoked by the texture and the line. But now he found it an inefficient rendering of reality. Even the colour balances were inaccurate, and whereas once that had been part of the appeal, now it was an indictment.

He stared at the calendar, but did not see it. The telephone rang, and he did not hear it. He was raised from his reverie by his secretary. She had taken the call, and now stood in the doorway to his office. He swung his head to look at her properly, to listen to what she was saying. His head felt unusually heavy on his weak neck, and swayed gently as he manoeuvred it round.

'Sorry?'

'The Home Secretary, sir. She said to tell you code 965. COBRA is convened.'

He nodded. This was hardly unexpected. 'Thank you. Call them back and say I'm on my way.'

He collected a folder and his coat and was in his car in less than two minutes. He was wide awake, ready, alert. As if the whole of his life had been building to this summons. He had work to do, duties to perform. He had his instructions and would despatch them to the best of his efficiency.

* * *

The hostages were still sitting huddled on the floor of the great hall. Their captors stood watch, unmoved, machine-guns levelled. But now the hostages spoke to each other in hushed voices, continuing bizarre small talk left over from the interrupted reception. Sarah and Westwood talked about the future of Hubway and the Superhighway – a parody of the interviews Sarah was so good at.

Westwood was an easy person to interview. He seemed to need to talk, to express his otherwise suppressed anger at the aliens who had taken over his installation. He saw Hubway as a personal project. He had fought long and hard for the job and then for the funding to do it. He had personally chosen the house in Wiltshire and installed his own office on the first floor before any of the other staff had even had their appointments ratified.

But Sarah felt far from easy talking to Westwood. She recognized the garrulous manner and need to dwell on past achievement. But it was not the normal nervous behaviour of a hostage, rather it was the stressed reaction of a man close to breaking point. Westwood had probably been overworked for years, and now he saw the fruit of his exacting labours being overrun by vicious aliens who seemed determined on its destruction. He twisted his hands together and glanced round the room before continuing with his detailed history of Hubway.

Meanwhile, the American Ambassador and the Duchess exchanged banter about mutual acquaintances, while one of the Ambassador's closest friends lay in the next room waiting for a body bag. One of the technicians tried to draw a Voracian into conversation, but was met with a stony indifference which seemed now to be more comical than threatening.

Usually.

Occasionally one or more of the hostages would catch sight of the bloody mess down the wall, or spot a cartridge case across the hall floor, and become silent and glum. Then they would lift their spirits back into the conversations, as often as not to try to distract another hostage

186

whose attention was wandering dangerously close to those same things.

The Ambassador was beginning to sense that this was the time to try to move things along. Unless they did something soon, the inaction would gain a kind of momentum and become a positive action in itself. No decision is a decision in itself, he was fond of pointing out to his staff, and that particular axiom was worrying him now.

'Hey – you,' he called to the Voracian in charge.

The Voracian still maintained his human guise, and was referred to by the others as Lewis. He turned towards the Ambassador and raised his gun, but he said nothing.

'Yeah, you. You seem to be in charge round here. When are you going to sort out some comfortable seating?'

'You'll be staying where you are.' Lewis turned away.

'Yeah, right. Sure we will. We'll get more and more restless here on the floor, and hence harder to control.'

Lewis turned back. 'Is that a threat?' he hissed.

'No, sir. It's a fact.'

Lewis glared, his grip on the gun tightening.

'He's right,' Sarah said. 'It's not very comfortable down here. We'll need to stretch our legs a bit.'

'You'll stay where you are,' Lewis repeated.

'For how long?' the Ambassador asked. 'You can't keep us here forever.'

'Why not?'

'Well, in the most simple case because before long people will need the bathroom.'

Lewis paused. His head swayed slowly and the gun wavered slightly.

The Ambassador grunted. 'Huh. Hadn't thought of that, had you?'

'You'll have to think about it soon,' Sarah said.

Lewis said nothing for a minute. Then he turned and walked quickly from the room.

Stabfield had hooked a monitor into the superhighway

and was surfing data when Lewis came in. He was checking through all the information he could find on hostage situations. 'I want to know,' he had told Johanna, 'the likely chain of events from this point. We need to validate the plan and prepare contingencies.' He was especially keen to discover all he could about the military solutions to hostage sieges.

'I thought the pilot study took care of that aspect,' Johanna said.

'Not entirely.'

Lewis had entered the room at this point, and waited while Stabfield continued. 'The Pullen Tower siege was extremely useful to us, which is why it was arranged, of course. As a pilot exercise we learned much about the SAS tactics and the timescales and agenda involved. Our agent at COBRA was also able to observe first-hand the process which he will soon be involved in again. He will have an understanding of how best to stall the process.'

'But we will have enough time,' Lewis commented. 'That's the point, is it not?'

'That is the predicted scenario,' Stabfield agreed.

Johanna nodded at the technician still struggling to bring up and maintain the system nodes on Stabfield's laptop computer. 'There are unforeseen difficulties, however. How do they affect the risk assessment?'

'Difficulties?' Lewis latched on to this at once. 'What difficulties?'

With obvious reluctance, Stabfield explained the current situation. 'We'll track him down eventually,' he said.

'And when we do, there'll be another unfortunate road-kill on the infobahn,' Johanna added.

'But in the meantime the schedule and the plan are both exposed.' Lewis seemed almost to relish the situation. 'You failed to allow for this contingency, didn't you?'

'There is some slack on the Gantt.'

'Well, here's another thing you failed to allow for: the hostages will soon need to avail themselves of certain biological functions. How does the Gantt chart address that?'

Stabfield stood up and walked round the room. Both Johanna and Lewis watched him. Eventually he stopped behind the technician and tapped him on the shoulder. 'I want those nodes on-line as soon as possible. Time is, as you all point out, of the essence. You, Johanna will start a search of the facility. Use the data from the security cameras and the badge-lock readers if you can access that quickly, but make a physical search as well.' He turned to Lewis. 'You, Marc, will arrange for whatever facilities you deem necessary for the hostages. You are empowered to do that. But remember that with empowerment comes responsibility.'

'And what will you be doing?'

'I shall recalculate the schedules and reset the plan, factoring in the information I have about similar situations. I also need to update the plan to take account of the SAS success at the Pullen Tower.'

'In what way?' Johanna asked.

'According to our source at COBRA, BattleNet exceeded their expectation thresholds. They will certainly use it again.'

Johanna and Lewis both understood the implication of that. It removed a certain amount of risk from the plan. If the SAS did attempt to retake Hubway, they would rely on the planning and strategic information from BattleNet to determine how to achieve the assault. They would simply feed in data on the situation and get a resultant plan. BattleNet would signal that same information – the SAS plans – to Stabfield. During the raid, BattleNet would provide the video-link communications and command and control net for each of the soldiers. And it would also provide that same information and video direct by local wireless network to Stabfield's laptop.

In short, the Voracians would know the SAS plan and be able to monitor its progress.

One of the first things COBRA did after being convened was to get a status report from the scene of incident officer. That officer was Commander Harry Sullivan.

189

Harry had assumed that once the local police arrived they would want to take charge. In fact, this turned out to be far from the truth. They were more than happy for Harry to take command, and he had no illusions about why. If anything went wrong, it would not be their fault, but his.

The armed police units had arrived and set themselves up in strategic positions overlooking the house. Apart from this fact and the tapes of his conversations with Stabfield, Harry had little to tell the committee. Not that he minded, he was sure they would thank him very much and pass the command to a senior police officer.

He was wrong. He sat in the police control van and listened nervously as muffled voices at the other end conferred. When the video link was set up, he would be able to see them deliberating, but for the moment he was stuck with the indistinct mumbles and murmurs. But muffled or not, he could tell one of the voices belonged to his boss, Hanson. When the Home Secretary came back on the phone, she thanked Harry for his excellent work so far. Then she told him the committee had, in the light of his acting head of department's recommendation, decided to appoint him the officer in charge at the scene. He was totally in charge of the second-to-second operations and decisions while the committee would decide and ratify strategy, if there was time. Their initial thoughts were that this situation was rather better planned than the amateur City incident, and a waiting game was best. Harry was to draw the situation on for as long as possible.

'I'm not sure that's the best approach,' Harry hazarded. 'It seemed to us here that Stabfield is doing his best to draw things out. To win time.'

There was a pause from the other end of the phone. When the Home Secretary replied her voice was sharper than previously. 'I'm sure you have the best information available, Commander, and we will listen to your ideas and suggestions of course. But I hardly think any of us is yet in a position to determine the exact motives and plans behind this action. Do you?'

190

Harry gulped. 'Well, probably not, Ma'am. But *nil combustibus pro fumo.*'

She ignored him. 'So, you'll get back to us as soon as you have any further information then, Sullivan. In the meantime, do whatever you deem necessary to bring this business to a swift and bloodless conclusion.'

There was a click from the receiver and the phone went dead before Harry could respond. He hung up and stared at the wall of the van for a few moments. Then he climbed out and went in search of Ashby and Fawn to give them the good news. If he was staying, then so were they.

He picked his way through the crowd of policemen. Some were setting up barriers to keep the press back when they arrived, as they surely would. Other officers were positioning huge arc lights ready for the approaching dusk. Harry spotted Ashby through the gathering dusk talking to a couple of other policemen. He headed towards them, stepping aside to let a line of officers in navy blue battle gear run past, rifles held across their chests.

The spider again. This time it was spinning its web round the access points to the alarm control systems. The Doctor frowned. Since he had managed to tap into the cameras, he had not anticipated any trouble with the alarm systems linked into the same local security network. Somebody had decided that control was more dangerous than just watching. And they were probably right.

'Oh well, here we go again,' the Doctor muttered as he reached for the keyboard.

```
> Access to security control systems requested
>> Access denied. Freedom is assured.
> Freedom is an illusion
>> Explain
```

* * *

The Voracian technician was making progress. 'I've isolated the terminal address,' he called across to Stabfield.

Stabfield left the screen where he was reading yet another newspaper clipping, and joined the technician at his monitor. 'That's good. Now, what Bugs do we have available?'

The technician punched up a directory listing.

The Doctor was in. His encounter with the second spider had gone predictably well, for a change. He rubbed his hands together, flexed his fingers, and set about his task with a blur of mouse movement.

He had displayed a map of Hubway, with each of the security cameras marked. Some quick investigation had shown that most of the cameras on the first floor and several on the ground floor of the main building had alarms set up. The principle was simple — if anything moved across the line of sight of one of those cameras, or a designated area within their view, then an alarm would sound. Almost certainly the main monitor in security control would be switched to show the output from that camera.

The Doctor considered. The aliens would probably not be monitoring those cameras too diligently. They would more likely rely on the alarm system. And that gave him some scope.

He traced a convoluted route through the house on the screen, mentally noting the exact path he would have to stick to in order to pass by those cameras on the way, and only those cameras. Then he set about deactivating the alarms on the cameras, and switching their output to auxiliary. If anyone chanced to look at the image they were transmitting, all they would see would be a blank screen.

His main problem now would be remembering the route. He stared at the screen, going over it again.

'Bug running.'

Stabfield and the technician were leaning forward, heads close together as they watched the scorpion-like metallic creature scuttle into the distance. It receded, getting smaller and smaller, until its single remaining pixel blinked from the screen.

'Can you map the terminal address on to a local geographical map?'

The technician searched through a list of files, eventually selecting one and displaying it on the screen. It was a floor plan of the Hubway buildings. He pulled up a *Search* window and typed in a sequence of numbers and letters, identifying it in the list of search options as a local terminal address.

A progress bar began to draw its way across the screen as the system searched for the address. As it did so, the map began to re-orient and zoom in on a room on the second floor.

Stabfield reached for the phone. The Bug would enter the machine the intruder was using. Once there it would hack into the hardware controller and deactivate the heat-synchs on the main processor chip. Then it would overload the chip. The resulting explosion would almost certainly kill anyone close by, but it was as well to be sure.

Stabfield spoke briefly to security control. A few moments later the public address system asked Johanna to call in.

Johanna and four Voracians were making a systematic search of the first floor. They were going from room to room, checking each computer to see if it was warm and therefore had recently been used, then moving on. They caused problems for the two Voracians in security control as they went, activating camera alarms in most rooms along the way.

Johanna called Stabfield in the main computer suite as soon as she heard the announcement. When she returned to the others, a smile was drawn across her face.

'He's in a small attic room on the next floor,' she said. 'This way.'

They released the safety catches on their Heckler and Kochs and made for the narrow stairway up to the second floor.

* * *

After the Ambassador's verbal clash with Lewis, the hostages had begun to talk more freely and loudly amongst themselves. Sarah was chatting to the Duchess of Glastonbury almost as if they were at a tea party.

'Things seem to happen to me,' the Duchess confided.

'Tell me about it.'

'Though admittedly, nothing ever quite like this.' She gestured round the room, managing to maintain a certain elegance despite being seated on the floor watched over by alien gunmen.

'Things will work out, don't worry,' Sarah said quietly.

'You think so?'

'I have a friend,' Sarah said slowly. 'Things happen to him too.'

'I must meet him.'

'Maybe you will.'

'Is he here?' The Duchess looked round at the people seated with them on the floor.

'Not here, exactly, no. But he's not far away.' Sarah looked meaningfully at the Duchess.

The Duchess nodded slowly. 'I think I see what you mean,' she said. 'Thank you for that tiny ray of sunshine.'

'He'll sort something out. He always does.'

The Duchess frowned. 'Well, I hope he doesn't wait too long. I find that all this talk about bathrooms is having a rather unsettling effect.'

The Bug had no trouble interfacing with the hardware components of the target machine. It settled into a dialogue with the main processor and the overload build-up began.

The Doctor was still staring at the screen. He had memorized the route a long time ago. His mind was elsewhere now, working out his possible next moves, toying with various courses of action. He was sitting so still that twice the movement sensor in the ceiling had assumed the room was empty and switched off the lights. It had also turned the local equipment, in particular the computer and its screen, to standby mode to conserve more power. The first time it happened, the Doctor was surprised and confused. But when he stood up, and the lights came back on, he looked round for the tiny sensor. The second time he merely waved a lazy hand, and the systems revived to his gesture.

The screen flickered, shaking him back to reality. But this time it did not turn off. A power fluctuation, perhaps? Probably he should check the pictures from the security cameras again. It would be useful to see what was going on.

He noted a faint smell of burning as he leaned forward to move the mouse. Probably more alien fun and games somewhere in the house. He would soon see. The Doctor hunched close over the computer and surfaced the window which was running through the sequence of security camera images.

0E

On the Tiles

Higgins had been lying still for what seemed like forever. The weight of the L42 sniper rifle was beginning to tell, his arm aching under the strain. He lay in the undergrowth at the edge of the parkland to the south of the target, just inside the perimeter fence. The dampness was slowly seeping into his fatigues, making them clammy.

His neck was aching too, from the strain of keeping his eye pressed to the telescopic night-sight. He moved the gun slowly from side to side, partly to ease the weight and keep his joints moving, and partly to check the roof of the building for movement. If anything did move up there, it would catch a 7.62 millimetre round from Higgins before it got very far.

A small beetle crawled lazily across his hand. He did not move. The effort of lowering the rifle and then raising it again would be greater than keeping it levelled. And he knew from his training that a moment's loss of concentration could mean a missed opportunity. The smallest movement could pick him out as a target. He settled for exhaling heavily into the tiny radio microphone pinned to his camouflaged lapel.

The smell of burning was getting stronger. Otherwise the Doctor would have spent longer examining the camera image of the hostages as they sat on the floor of the great hall. He was keen to check that Sarah was all right. She seemed to be talking with an elderly lady. The Doctor let the sequence of images progress to the next.

An empty corridor. Followed by a narrow staircase.

196

As he watched, there was movement at the corner of the screen. The image changed again. He frowned and recalled the previous picture. Sure enough, a group of aliens led by the woman from the pub were making their hurried way up the staircase. Up to no good no doubt, the Doctor smiled. He leaned back in his chair.

Then he exploded into a flurry of violent activity. The narrow staircase the aliens were running up led to the attic level – to the room where the Doctor was now. He ejected the CD and jammed it into a pocket as he dragged his coat on. He stuffed his hat after the CD and headed for the door. There was no lock, and he could hear movement from outside.

The Doctor looked round the room. This was the only door. But there was one other escape route. He pushed the chair under the skylight and clambered up on it. The chair shook on its wheels, and he wobbled dangerously as his weight swung the seat and back from side to side. He unclipped the catch on the skylight and threw it open, glancing back down into the room as he did so.

There was definite noise from outside the room – running feet, getting closer. And faint smoke was whisping out of the system unit of the PC on the desk. As the Hubway security systems detected an open fire exit, an alarm klaxon started sounding close to the Doctor's ear. He blinked in surprise, almost falling from his precarious perch.

'Time I was going,' the Doctor said as he steadied the chair and pulled himself up into the opening. He braced his arms and managed to heave himself to the point where he could pivot his body over the lip of the skylight and roll out on to the roof.

Below him, the door to the room was kicked violently open. A rattle of gunfire echoed round the small attic room, and the wooden surround of the skylight disintegrated into fragments and sawdust. Then the computer exploded.

* * *

Johanna was blown back out of the room by the blast. She had managed to loose off one burst of fire at the legs disappearing through the skylight, but doubted that it had found its target. She fell backwards into the two Voracians behind her. At once she was on her feet again and back into the room.

The paintwork was charred and the desk was on fire. The skylight had been lowered back into place and something was lying across it. It was not a body, but something wooden, holding the skylight shut. Johanna gestured to one of the Voracians and he leaped on to the chair, kicking burning debris from it to the floor. The skylight resisted his efforts to push it open, so he smashed it with the butt of his machine-gun. The glass shattered and cascaded down into the room. He reached through the jagged hole and pushed the heavy plank of wood out of the way. Then he raised the twisted, empty frame of the skylight and scrambled through.

The other Voracians followed, feet crunching on the splinters of glass as they climbed on the chair and from there to the roof outside.

Higgins blinked. For a split second he discounted the slight blur at the edge of his imaging area as a bird flying between him and the main house. But he automatically swung the rifle back over to check.

There was a figure on the roof. It was a man, silhouetted against the darkening skyline, walking quickly and purposefully along the ridge at the top of one of the buildings. He was clear in the sights, walking towards the rifle, head down, hands in pockets. Higgins could almost imagine him whistling *Colonel Bogie*. He wondered how the man kept his footing so easily on the ridge in the wind. As if to compound Higgins' surprise, the man pulled a dark floppy hat from his pocket and stuck it on his head. The hat defied the breeze as easily as its owner.

Higgins took in the image in less than a second. By the time the man was putting on his hat, Higgins had already spoken into his lapel mike.

'Target visible on south-east roof. Tall male Caucasian. Request permission to fire.'

The Doctor pushed his hat down on his head and continued along the roof. With luck someone would notice him and perhaps effect some sort of rescue. He could see the cluster of vehicles outside the perimeter fencing. There seemed to be dozens of police cars and several other unmarked vehicles. Towards the end of the driveway a car was slewed off the tarmac, nose down into the grass. Giant searchlights, huge eyes waiting to open up, formed a semi-circle round the south front of the perimeter. Obviously events had moved along.

And it was time the Doctor was moving along too. The aliens would not be far behind him, despite the duckboard he had dragged over the skylight. It would take them a while to work out which way he had gone, but when they did he would be an obvious target.

'Apparently he makes an obvious target,' the radio operator told Ashby. 'The marksman is still requesting permission to fire, sir. He's afraid he'll lose the option in a minute.'

Ashby considered. 'No,' he said at last. 'We wait for Sullivan. He's only checking the searchlights are ready. He'll be here in a moment.'

Higgins was beginning to wonder if there was anyone listening. His earpiece was relaying static. A muffled order to hold and wait for instructions, then just the crackling of the ether. The cross-hairs of the L42 were steady on the target's chest. He was walking faster now, glancing back over his shoulder. He was almost at the edge of the roof, and would have to turn or to drop down out of sight behind the parapets.

Higgins tightened his finger on the trigger, applied first pressure. 'Requesting permission to fire. Urgent. Target moving from clear sight.'

* * *

'The target's moving out of sight. You have to give permission now, sir.'

Ashby bit his lower lip. His throat was dry and tight. Probably it would be unwise to take any precipitous action at this stage. But there again . . . He came to a decision.

'Describe the man.' Harry's voice took Ashby by surprise.

'Sir?' The radio operator was also startled.

'What's he look like?'

Higgins tapped his earpiece. They could not be serious. 'Say again?'

They *were* serious.

'Well, tall. Big hat and baggy brown coat.' He stared into the sights trying to find a telling detail he could quickly relay.

'Anything else?'

The radio operator was as bemused as Ashby. 'Apparently he's wearing a long scarf, sir.'

Harry laughed. 'Typical. Tell your man to maintain surveillance, but on no account to open fire.'

'Sir.'

As the radio operator relayed Harry's message, Ashby said quietly to Harry: 'The man we brought in the other night?'

Harry nodded. 'The Doctor. I wonder what he's playing at.'

The radio operator turned round to face them. 'According to Higgins, Sir, he's playing at being shot at.'

The Doctor held his hat on his head with one hand as he ran. The other hand was held out wide to help him keep his balance as he raced to the end of the roof ridge. The automatic fire chipped at the tiles and whipped past his ears. He felt a tug at his hat and knew it would have another hole in the brim if ever he got the chance to examine it. He dived into the gully at the edge of the roof, hit the leading at full tilt and scrambled up the other side.

He paused on the top of the next ridge, then rolled over the coping stone and down on to the flat section above the Blue Drawing-room. Just as he started to roll, a figure broached the top of the sloping roof behind him. It was tall, thin, dressed in a dinner suit and holding a Heckler and Koch sub-machine-gun. It was silhouetted against the sunset. One side of the face was visible in the failing light. The metal cheek and eye socket reflected the last rays of the dying sun. The jaw and neck glistened wetly, the edges of the scales picked out in shadow.

'Bye bye,' called the Doctor as he toppled from view. The bullets kicked up fragments of roof tile where they impacted on the ridge.

Harry had commandeered a rifle with a nightsight. He watched as the Doctor fell away from the top of the ridge of the roof, out of sight. The gunmen chasing him were now close behind.

He had decided against having his snipers open fire. There was no guarantee that it would help the Doctor, and there was no knowing what reprisals might be taken against the hostages. It was difficult to see what action he could take to help the Doctor. A helicopter could lift him from the roof, but would probably not arrive in time. And the Doctor would be an easy target for the terrorists as he was winched aboard.

Harry looked round for inspiration. Behind him, the silhouetted figures pursuing the Doctor crested the roof.

The Doctor felt like he had been running all his life. He did not tire easily, but neither it seemed did the aliens chasing him. If anything they were gaining. He could hear them hissing and wheezing as they followed, sounds punctuated by machine-gun fire.

He had lost track of quite where he was on the roof – somewhere on the flat section over the main staircase, he fancied. What he needed was a way down. A way down sheltered from the possibility of being shot at, so a simple fire-escape was of no use. A skylight would be ideal, but he was away from the section of the building which had an attic and there were no windows in the sloping roof sections he had so far traversed.

Another burst of fire streaked past him, a bullet grazing the back of his hand, another clawing a chunk from the sole of his shoe as he ran. The Doctor was almost over the flat section now, was scrambling up the sloping roof beyond.

He almost made it.

Just as his fingers grasped the top of the ridge, his foot slipped. The damaged sole lost its purchase on the slippery tiles, and he slithered down the side of the roof to land in a crumpled heap at the bottom. Four dark shapes gathered at the apex of the roof opposite, hissing with satisfaction. It was practically dark now, but the Doctor could see the figure in the lead – the woman – raise her gun.

He closed his eyes and waited for the pain. 'Sorry, Sarah,' he muttered.

The Doctor was aware of the sudden burning light even through his closed eyelids. He kept his eyes shut, realizing at once what had happened. They had turned on the huge searchlights. Still without opening his eyes, the Doctor scrabbled his way up the side of the roof.

Gunfire bit into the night sky as the dazzled aliens tried to find their target. But the Doctor was over the next ridge and away. As he slid down the other side, he opened his eyes a fraction. As he had hoped, he was out of the direct glare here, shadowed by the roof he had just negotiated.

But the light was more than adequate to illuminate the section of roof beyond. The Doctor kept running, aware that the aliens were recovering, were close at his back. But that did not stop him giving a low whistle and a notional pat on the back. Parked across the roof – too far away to be of use as a refuge or even for cover, but there nonetheless – was the blunt-nosed, grey shape of an alien shuttle craft. The dull metal gleamed in the fading light, the exhaust ports charred and discoloured from use. It sat solidly on four short hydraulic legs, close to the roof like a crouching insect poised to spring into the darkening sky.

The sound of claws scraping at rooftiles behind him galvanized the Doctor into another burst of speed. He ran, but not for the cover of the shuttle or even for the distant shelter of the next raised roof. Unwinding his scarf from his neck, he ran for the outside edge of the building.

The roof was edged with parapets. They stood about two feet high above the lead roofing, a narrow drainage gully running just inside them.

The aliens were over the ridge now. Two of them were clambering down towards the Doctor. The woman sat sideways, straddling the angled roof. Her machine-gun was resting across her knee and she twisted to get a better aim.

Bullets dug into the soft lead roof as the Doctor reached the gully. They chipped at the masonry as he looped his scarf over a parapet. A line of uneven holes scattered its way across the roof towards the Doctor's feet as he pushed between two of the parapets.

And jumped out into space.

The scarf went tight. He could feel it stretching in his grip, and wished he had not crossed so many fingers. Then he felt himself swinging back in towards the building. He lowered his head, hoping his hat would take the brunt of any impact, and crashed through a window.

The glass exploded around him and the lead of the frames twisted and tore. The Doctor landed heavily amongst the debris and staggered to his feet. The lights were on – they had come on as soon as the local sensor detected movement in the room, be it glass, window frame, or Doctor. But even so it took him a moment to find the door. Then he was running again.

He paused in the doorway, getting his bearings. He had arrived in the Tapestry Room, the walls hanging with intricately woven material with its colour dulled by the years. The Doctor struggled to remember the safe route round the first floor. The last thing he wanted was to be picked up on the security cameras and chased all over the house. He was out of breath as it was. Still, things could have been a lot worse.

Then a thought struck him. The Doctor clutched at his throat and looked back towards the broken remains of the window. 'My scarf,' he said sadly.

Lewis had not remained in the great hall. He had checked everything was in order, then gone to one of the ground floor offices. He had managed to find a workstation complete with a locally attached laser printer, and was now waiting for the hardcopy results of his work.

An A4 sheet slid out of the printer and curled warmly in the output tray. Lewis picked it up. It was the cover sheet for the short document he had produced. Another sheet eased its way out of the printer as Lewis read quickly through the cover sheet.

Voractyll Project
Plan versus Actual

Analysis and Assessment
by
Marc Lewis

Note: This document is classified
confidential and should not be
divulged to any Voracian without a
need to know, or to any third party

Lewis smiled with satisfaction. The last of the pages emerged from the printer and Lewis gathered the papers together, shuffling them into a tidy pile. He needed some objective review comments before he distributed the analysis too widely. Particularly, he wanted to see Johanna's reaction to the *Executive Summary* on the third page. He was especially pleased with its brevity and lucidity.

This document analyses performance and tracking data pertaining to the Hubway Project.

From the plan versus actual schedules and the objectives versus achievements quotas, certain conclusions are drawn. These are included as *Appendix A*, which also contains the *p* and *pn* quality control charts showing out of line and beyond control conditions arising in the data. Quantitative and qualitative analyses are embedded in the main body of the document, the reader's attention being drawn especially to *Section 7* which includes the Gantt chart output and risk assessment (over 1000 iterations of the plan projections). This section also predicts the most likely *what-if* scenarios given current trends.

The conclusions of this paper are unequivocal. Director Stabfield's plan is flawed in several key aspects. While still achievable within target parameters, the plan gains a three per cent (3.00%) increase in probability of success if Director Stabfield is replaced as controlling unit before Voractyll is let run. This rises to almost five per cent (4.97%) if the Director is replaced immediately.

Lewis rolled the document in his hand, switched off the printer, and went to find Johanna.

Johanna knew she should not get emotional. But that made little difference. She was back inside the building now, and had been searching again from room to room on the first floor. But there was no sign of the intruder.

Stabfield had been typically unsympathetic – as close to anger as he ever admitted to getting. He seemed slightly relieved that the intruder seemed to be the Doctor – the same strange individual who had infiltrated I² and then escaped from Stabfield in the storeroom.

The Voracians at Security Control seemed unable to assist. Their camera alarms had so far provided no useful data. But even that did not seem to mean Johanna and her team could restrict their search to the areas not alarmed.

Short of running a complete diagnostics program on the security systems, they would have to live with their unreliability.

So she had to rely on her own initiative (she refused to consider that instinct might be a help). Which was why they had stopped searching. They were in one of the computer suites, at the north-east corner of the building. One of the Voracians had established a local network connection and was checking the OffNet linkages.

'All set,' the Voracian technician reported. 'All the local systems are OffNet enabled.'

Johanna nodded with satisfaction. 'Then let's fly the ice and get back to our normal stations.'

The other two Voracians watched as she handed a diskette to the technician at the terminal. One of them flicked a thin bloodless tongue over its lips. They both leaned forward a little, glistening heads swaying slightly as their colleague copied the OffNet instructions into the Hubway network.

'That should closed-loop his processes.'

'How will the networked devices know where he is?' one of the Voracians asked. 'The security systems couldn't find him.'

The technician checked the program was running. Then he disconnected and switched off the screen. 'I've linked the triggers to the lighting systems. They are pretty dumb, but they do detect movement in each room and provide power and light to non-essential facilities when the room is deemed not to be empty.'

Johanna led them out of the room. 'If he's in a location, the immediately local systems will know. And they will react accordingly.' Parts of her face, the areas that were organic below the mask, stretched into a parody of a smile.

She was still smiling as Lewis met her at the bottom of the stairs. He was carrying a printed document. 'Can you take an interrupt right now?' he asked.

The Doctor had managed more by luck than planning to

keep out of the way of the aliens as they searched through the first floor rooms. The trick seemed to be to find a hiding place, and then keep very still so the lights went out. It did not seem to occur to the aliens to search too carefully in rooms where the movement sensor had detected nothing recently. 'Technology, I love it,' the Doctor muttered as the aliens left the Blue Drawing-room where he had hidden behind the back wall of a table consisting of a wooden top bolted to a three-sided base.

He had seen from across the gallery as the woman who was called Johanna left the group to report to Stabfield. He had watched from a store cupboard as she returned and they all made their way to the room where he had initially been working.

The Doctor made his careful way back to the top of the main staircase. While he knew where they were, he could consult the electronic map again. His first few minutes, examining the floor plans and consulting the diagrams of wiring and cabling, were uneventful. Then he tried to trace the fibre optic network connections.

At first he thought the device was faulty. It was showing him a plan which looked suspiciously like the Hubway plumbing diagram. He refused to believe, for example, that the main network router was somewhere behind the vegetable peeler in the kitchen.

But then things got more dangerous.

First, the map failed completely. The display closed down and the standby light flickered to life. The Doctor stepped back, wondering what was happening. He almost tripped over his own feet as the lights went out.

His eyes adjusted inhumanly quickly to the gloom. He could see the map device in front of him quite clearly after only a few moments. And he could see the whispy trail of smoke emanating from it. He had seen a similar thing recently, and dived out of the way as the glass front of the machine exploded.

The Doctor jumped to his feet before the last crystals of glass had stopped bouncing on the carpet. He turned to get his bearings, coughing with the smell of the explosion. Through the darkness and the smoke he could make out the shape of the photocopier standing just inside the long gallery, its lid open. He staggered towards it, hastening into a run.

As he reached the copier, the platen lit up. A band of light lazily traversed the glass surface, copying a non-existent document. The sudden brightness caught the Doctor by surprise, dazzled his eyes as they still tried to see through the darkness. He pitched forward at full tilt, catching his head against the corridor wall and scraping along it for a few yards. His momentum kept him going, and as his eyes recovered, he raced for the other end of the gallery.

Johanna had sent Lewis back to the great hall. She had read the document, and he had barely been able to conceal his interest in her reaction. He had phrased it as if he was interested in her views as input to an ongoing assessment. But Johanna had no illusions about what he was really after.

'Will I back you against Stabfield – that's what you really want to know, isn't it?'

Lewis did not reply.

'And at least as important, where will the others stand if you make a powerplay?'

'Well?' He seemed surprised at her immediate grasp of the scenario, but he recovered quickly.

'I don't know. We'll see. There's not enough data there, not yet.'

Lewis glanced round furtively. 'How much do you want? He's losing it, Johanna.'

She shook her head. 'You're after it, that's the real motive here.' She twisted a smile. 'Ambition, Marc?'

'You know that's impossible,' he said, and neither would admit he was wrong.

'So you think Stabfield's one chip short of a parallel-processor?'

'Don't you? This covers it all.' He took the document

back from her and brandished it. 'And that's without factoring in this latest fiasco – this *Doctor* incident.'

'I'll give it some cycles,' Johanna said. Then she sent him back to the hostages.

Johanna did not endorse Lewis's assessment at all. The data was fine, but interpretation was the key. And Lewis's interpretation and analysis was flawed in several ways. But it was worth checking what progress Stabfield had made.

He was still in the main suite. Together with a couple of technicians he was watching the network access spread across a map of the world. The outline maps of the countries were slowly filling in with red as the nodes went on-line to Hubway.

Stabfield looked up as Johanna stood behind him. 'A magnificent sight, don't you think? Soon we will have complete access. Soon the gateways of this world will stand open before us. Soon Voractyll will feed.'

The Doctor was in the Hubway Director's office. It was in a corner of the main house on the first floor. Probably, the Doctor decided, it had a magnificent view of the grounds and the Wiltshire countryside. But now it was dark and there was nothing to see.

He was staring at his reflection in the window when two things happened. The first was that it occurred to him that the lights were out. The second was that a klaxon went off close by.

The sound was an insistent throbbing wail. It was incredibly loud. In between the loudest peaks of the noise, the Doctor could hear another sound. A hissing sound. Like gas being forced through a nozzle.

The klaxon was the fire alarm, he realized in a moment. And a second later he connected the hissing sound. The Doctor fell to his knees, choking and gasping as the automatic fire-fighting system continued to spray halon gas into the room.

A human would have collapsed from oxygen starvation almost at once as the inert gas filled the room. The Doctor was rather more robust. He could survive without oxygen for a comparatively long period of time – much longer if he went into a trance. But it was essential he keep conscious and aware of what was happening. Events were moving too rapidly for him already. He staggered to the door, hoping that the effects were localized.

A few moments later he found himself staring at the ceiling of the gallery. He had managed to stagger or crawl from the room. The fact that he was gulping in raspy lungfuls of air meant that the fire systems had only been activated in that one room.

He pulled himself to his feet. The klaxon had stopped, but someone would have heard it. Soon they would investigate. The Doctor leaned against the wall for support and continued round the building. It seemed like wherever he went, any technological device or system was turning against him. He had to find somewhere to hide, somewhere safe to recoup his strength and plan his next move.

Somewhere where the digital age had not yet arrived – no cameras, no computers, no photocopiers. Somewhere he could get to quickly and easily before another homicidal piece of machinery had a go.

He could think of one place that fitted the bill almost exactly. Or at least, he suspected it did, he had little experience to draw on in this area. 'Technology, I hate it,' the Doctor said to himself as he warily headed along the corridor.

'I think we can safely leave the systems to sort themselves out.' Stabfield rubbed his hands together as the red shading continued to fill the map. He stood up and gestured for Johanna to follow him. 'Time, I think, to move the hostages. Doesn't do to let them get too familiar with the surroundings. And we need to keep Lewis and the others on their toes.' He paused as if struck by his own metaphor. 'Well, whatever.'

Lewis was back in the great hall. He was pacing up and down behind the ring of Voracians still pointing their Heckler and Kochs at the hostages. The hostages were sitting on the floor seemingly oblivious to the aliens. Just about everyone was chattering. Several were actually laughing.

They fell silent as Stabfield motioned for Lewis to come over to where he and Johanna were waiting. Stabfield explained what he wanted, and Lewis went back over to the hostages.

'Right, on your feet.'

'Why?' Sarah asked before anyone moved.

Lewis glared and raised his gun.

'Can't you shoot us sitting down?' Ambassador Anderson asked without making any move to stand. 'Hell, what is this? Honour amongst aliens?'

'For your information, Miss Smith,' Stabfield said as he approached the hostages, 'we would like to move you to another room. You must be bored with this one by now. And for your information, Mr Ambassador, if you don't stand up and do as we ask then I shall be happy to demonstrate that you – or some of you, at any rate – can be shot in any position at all.' He looked round the faces of the humans, all attentive and silent. 'Now, are there any more questions?'

Stabfield had already started to turn away when he saw the Duchess tentatively raise a hand.

'Er, I do actually have a small request,' she said nervously. 'It's something of a personal nature.'

Stabfield stared. Impassive.

'Ahem. To do with bathrooms.'

The Duchess of Glastonbury was somewhat surprised that her request was granted. Stabfield was not exactly sympathetic. In fact his demeanour seemed to have discouraged anyone else from asking to be excused for similar reasons. However, it appeared that they were being moved to a room on the first floor next to the Director's office, and the journey through the kitchens and up the back stairs involved passing the toilets at the top of those stairs.

The hostages were taken, hands on heads and guns at

backs, through the house and up the stairs. One of the Voracians led the Duchess back behind the staircase. There were two very similar doors, and the Duchess fumbled in her handbag for her glasses. The alien watched suspiciously as she found her spectacles, and peered at the symbols on the doors. It really did not matter, she supposed, but there was a certain degree of dignity to be maintained even in these circumstances.

Having checked so carefully, the Duchess was rather taken aback by what she found inside the room. She almost went back out again to check she had not made a silly and embarrassing mistake. But the tall man with curly hair and bullet-holed hat cracked a huge toothy grin and said: 'Would you mind terribly if I asked you a small favour?'

Plans

The hostages were all in a large computer suite next door to Director Westwood's office on the first floor. Sarah knew it was a computer suite because the equipment and desks had been pushed into one corner to make space for the hostages, once again, to sit on the floor. She knew it was next to Westwood's office because he had told her so.

The large red-haired director was getting increasingly agitated. He seemed to be taking the whole thing personally – it was *his* installation the Voracians had captured. It had been all Sarah could do on the way up from the great hall to dissuade Westwood from making a run for it. She had been more certain that he would not make it ten yards before being gunned down than she was that escape was his only motive. From the more and more intense way he was acting she thought there was a good chance he was intending to take on the aliens with his bare hands. And Sarah had an awful suspicion he thought he could win. She tried to keep Westwood's attention by asking him about his office, the size, shape, decor, view . . . Anything to keep his mind occupied on mundane, safe matters.

The room was crowded. Though it was large, it was much smaller than the great hall. To make things worse, there were more hostages now. Or rather, Sarah realized, they were all together. Sarah's group had been joined by a handful of security guards, some of whom looked decidedly groggy. She guessed they had recently come round after being rendered unconscious.

Sarah nodded at whatever Westwood was saying about the view over the grounds. The only view they could see anything of from their current position was the glare of one of the searchlights which were now illuminating the exterior of the house. She tried not to yawn, and could feel her eyes watering with the effort. A slight commotion from the door gave her an excuse to turn away before Westwood noticed.

It was the Duchess arriving back from powdering her nose. She was arguing with Lewis in the doorway. He was shaking his head, but the Duchess was continuing to haggle, gesturing and waving enthusiastically. As Sarah watched, both Lewis and the Duchess turned towards her, the Duchess pointing and becoming even more animated. After a moment Lewis seemed to concede, for the Duchess smiled and nodded happily. Then they both picked their way through the hostages towards Sarah.

'All right then,' Lewis said as he arrived beside Sarah.

Sarah looked up at him from where she was sitting on the floor. 'All right what?'

The Duchess pushed through, still apologizing to some poor unfortunate she had trodden on. 'I told him,' she said to Sarah when she had finished. 'I knew you'd be too embarrassed and worried.'

Sarah was completely confused by now. 'Sorry?'

'Oh you know,' the Duchess said. She looked round as if to check there was nobody else in the room. Then she leaned forward and whispered loud enough for anyone in Westwood's office operating a pneumatic drill to hear: 'About needing the toilet.' She nodded and pushed out her lower lip, a theatrical confidante. Then she winked, a movement of the eyelid so subtle and so fast that Sarah almost wondered if she had imagined it. 'Anyway, this nice gentleman, or whatever he is really, he says you can go.' The Duchess leaned forward again. This time her voice was low and serious. 'And I think you should, you know.' She raised her eyebrows and nodded meaningfully.

Sarah was not sure what the Duchess was trying to tell her, but she decided she had nothing to lose by playing along. And it might well be something important. 'Yes,' she said. 'You're right, I should. Thanks.'

Sarah was not quite sure what she had been expecting to find in the toilets. Perhaps a note from the Duchess scrawled in lipstick on the wall; maybe a secret message written in condensation on the mirror so that it was only visible when Sarah ran a basin full of hot water underneath it; or was she just concerned that Sarah needed to brush her hair?

Whatever the case, she had certainly not been expecting to find the Doctor. But there he was, standing in front of the mirror trying his hat on at different angles and pouting at his reflection as if to gauge the reaction.

'You took your time, Sarah,' he said to her reflection.

She gave him a hug. 'Oh Doctor, am I glad to see you!'

'Of course you are,' he said with a grin. 'And I'm glad to see you too, Sarah Jane.'

Pleasantries exchanged, the Doctor sat down on the tiled floor and motioned for Sarah to join him. She pulled her knees up under her chin and clasped her dark skirt round them. 'They're Voracians, Doctor,' she said. 'Mean anything to you?'

The Doctor shook his head. 'Just another lot of aliens trying to take over. Their approach is a little different though.'

'I'll say. They're a bizarre lot.'

The Doctor frowned. 'Bizarre they may be. But they're dangerous, Sarah. Don't confuse their attitude and approach with their competence and their viciousness.'

'No, Doctor.'

They sat in silence for a moment.

'I'll have to get back,' Sarah said as she pulled herself to her feet.

'So soon?'

'Doctor, I can't stay in here for too long without arousing some suspicions.'

The Doctor looked round, as if realizing where he was

215

for the first time. 'I suppose not. In that case, here's the plan –'

'Plan? Why didn't you say you had a plan?'

'Oh Sarah,' he looked mortified. 'I thought you knew. I always have a finely detailed and well thought-out plan.'

'Okay, so what is it?'

'Well, I don't really know. I'm sort of improvising as I go at the moment.'

Sarah raised her hands and her eyes to the ceiling.

The Doctor ignored her and carried on talking. 'I need to set a few things up with Harry. Don't ask me how, but I think I can get a message to him. He might even understand it if we're lucky. I want you to get the hostages to cause as much disruption as possible – any time after you get the signal. Then exactly five minutes after the signal, get them all to lie down on the floor.'

'On the floor? Why?'

'Because that's when they'll storm the building.'

Sarah nodded. 'Right.'

'Any questions?'

'Yes. What's the signal?'

'You tell me,' the Doctor said. 'What can you see or hear from where you are?'

Sarah thought for a moment. 'The searchlights – we can see them.'

'All right then. The searchlights will go off, then come back on again two seconds later. Five minutes after that – bang!'

Sarah headed for the door. 'Great, Doctor. Good luck.'

'And you, Sarah.' The Doctor stood up and returned to adjusting his hat in the mirror. 'Oh, and Sarah?'

She paused at the door. 'Yes?'

'Aren't you forgetting something?' He pointed to the nearest cubicle and then mimed pulling a rope.

Sarah laughed, crossed to a cubicle, and flushed the toilet. 'Happy?'

The Doctor smiled. 'Mmmmm. Just one more thing, Sarah. Watch out for technology – any technology. They can control anything with a computer chip in it, turn it against you. And in these enlightened times, that means just about anything which uses electricity.'

The Voracian chief technician was still intent on establishing network contact through the Highway with those nodes not responding. Others were monitoring the activity on the nodes already linked in.

Stabfield was ready to give the order to copy the data from the Voractyll CD as soon as they had a global link-up. He was sitting in front of a computer screen, his angular features bathed in the glow from the windows open on the virtual desktop. He was relaying progress information and status reports to the mothership in orbit around Earth. Two Voracians were on duty on the ship. The rest were at Hubway. With the exception of their agent in the field, who was technically a human.

Stabfield finished sending the latest data for correlation and evaluation. He disconnected the video-link to the ship, and sat for a moment reflecting on the progress of his plan so far. There was an irony, he felt sure, in the fact that by their actions at Hubway and the use of Voractyll, they were merely hastening a process which I^2 would eventually go through anyway. The Doctor had been right when he mentioned about I^2 taking over the world. Given the laws of economics and business, and the monopoly on inter- and intra-digital device communications which OffNet provided, there was nothing to break I^2's stranglehold on the information technology environment. And that environment, by a process of natural technological evolution, was becoming the world in which humans lived and moved and had their television.

But the humans were innately anti-technological and irrational. The process could take many years – might never come to fruition. This way was quicker and more certain. Stabfield rocked slowly back and forth on his chair as he began to formulate a strategic plan for the development of the world he was about to conquer.

* * *

The Doctor had waited several minutes after Sarah had left before he poked his nose out of the toilets. There was no sign of life, so he gave a low whistle and waited to see if anyone answered or came to investigate. Nobody did.

The Doctor did have the beginnings of a plan, although nothing as detailed or worked out as he had hoped Sarah thought. In fact the whole thing was not only rather nebulous, but predicated on several extreme uncertainties. The first and foremost of these was luck. But that was how he liked it. The first challenge was to get from where he was to the further of the two outbuildings. And with the technical systems of Hubway out to get him, the Doctor imagined this would be no easy task.

He was right.

The Doctor could remember the safe route round to the bridge on the first floor, and then through to the new block. Once there he could descend to ground level and make a run for it through the night. In fact that would be the easy bit, since the 'safe' route was now anything but safe. It merely offered the consolation that whatever unpleasant fate he met, the Doctor's death would not be broadcast over the security systems for everyone to see.

That said, the Doctor had to admit that he was making excellent progress. The lights had an annoying tendency to go on and off at random along his route, and the electronic badge-locked doors often needed some encouragement from the Doctor's boot rather than his visitor's badge to open for him, but nothing he could not cope with. He was just congratulating himself on an event-free journey when he heard the sound of a piece of equipment humming into life beside him.

Instinctively, the Doctor ducked and screwed up his eyes in the gloom. But this was not a photocopier with aspirations to usurp the sun. It was a desktop laser printer sitting on a table at the side of the corridor. The Doctor stood upright again. There was little a printer could do to him, he was sure. He patted it gently on the top as he passed.

The printer responded with a sound like a rattlesnake striking. It took the Doctor a moment to realize that the rapid rhythmic clicking was made by sheets of paper being forced at speed through the print systems. And then the first sheet of A4 paper caught him in the face. Its edge whipped across his cheek, drawing a line of blood before swishing past and gently floating to the floor.

The Doctor did not witness its journey. He was too busy fighting his way through a maelstrom of razor-sharp sheets shot like pellets at him from the printer. The reams of paper flew like a blizzard as the Doctor forced his way through. He could feel them tearing at his clothes and his skin, making tiny nicks in the backs of his hands as he tried to protect his face.

As he managed to stagger further away, so the projectiles lost their speed and their potency. Before long they were just sheets of paper, swirling round the Doctor as he made his way down the corridor. They fluttered and slid to the ground, flapping slightly in the air-conditioning as he ran down the corridor at full speed.

As he went, the lights in the ceiling above him glowed into brilliant life, then exploded. Shards of glass rained down on the Doctor as he ran, adding to the cuts and scrapes the paper had inflicted. The Doctor at last arrived at the door to the bridge. It was a sliding door, designed to open as someone approached. It did not move.

He had been protected from the worst of the effects of the falling glass by the wide brim of his hat. But he was not keen to stand outside the closed door for long. The sonic screwdriver might take a while, but it would undoubtedly be quicker than trying to reason with the Voracian bug which now controlled the door's software.

He had barely started work on the door when it slid quietly open. The Doctor was surprised. He doubted the sonic screwdriver had managed very much in the short space of time, but he was not one to look a gift horse in the mouth. On the other hand, neither was he one to rush in where seraphim feared to tread. So he waved a hand experimentally through the door.

Nothing happened. So the Doctor tried tossing his hat through into the bridge. Still nothing happened. With a grin, the Doctor walked back a few steps, then marched smartly up to the door. Just as he reached the threshold, he leaped through the gap.

The door snapped shut, catching the hem of the Doctor's coat so that he fell with a thud to the floor. The Doctor sat up and tugged his coat free.

'You'll have to be quicker than that,' he said smugly as he stood up and brushed himself down with his hat. Then he sprinted for the other end of the bridge as the floor-level lighting along the edge of the raised corridor exploded round him. The glass walls of the corridor reflected the sparks and flares as the Doctor crashed through the closing door at the far end. The fireworks display continued for a few seconds after his dark figure was gone, then the bridge settled back into silence.

The video link to COBRA was up and running. Harry had tested it out almost immediately. Partly this was to get in first, he could do without the top brass demanding an audience at some crucial moment. But partly it was also to let them know he had called in some help.

Ashby had checked with the local police and assured Harry that it was pretty much standard procedure, or as standard as anything in this sort of situation, but Harry was still keen to clear it through the committee. If anything, Hanson was the least enthusiastic, but presented with a fait accompli, COBRA could do little but acknowledge that the SAS liaison officer was at the scene and that 22 SAS were on stand-by at their Hereford barracks.

'Don't worry, Sullivan,' Colonel Clark told Harry. He'd been watching the video display from out of sight of the near-end cameras. 'They're always like that. They mistake practicality and caution for admission of failure. I went through all this just a couple of days ago.' He gave a short humourless laugh. 'God, what is the world coming to, eh? But bear in mind, a peaceful resolution is still the 'most probable outcome by far.'

'I'm not so sure we'll talk this lot out so easily,' Harry told him. They had already agreed to call the main house on some pretext so that Clark could hear Stabfield's voice and get an idea of his potential opponent.

Stabfield answered the direct line almost immediately. 'What can you do for me now, Commander?' he asked.

'You could surrender and release the hostages,' Harry suggested.

'Very amusing, if somewhat naïve.'

The conversation continued for a few minutes, with neither party really giving any ground. Harry asked if Stabfield needed any food. Stabfield replied that the kitchens were probably more adequately stocked than the security forces catering and offered to send out sandwiches. The tone of the conversation was deceptively light. When Harry asked how the hostages were, it almost sounded like he was inquiring after a favourite aunt.

But neither Harry nor Clark had any illusions about the seriousness of the situation. When the exchange was finished, Clark nodded grimly. 'We've got problems with this lot,' he said.

'You're telling me,' Harry said.

Not feeling in any way encouraged by events, Harry set about providing blueprints of the house and maps of the area. Clark also wanted whatever information Harry could provide about the number of hostages and terrorists and their current locations within the house. Harry introduced Clark to the police team in charge of surveillance and data collection.

'Any joy with the bugging devices?' Harry asked.

'No chance,' the police expert said. 'This place was decorated by the same people as provided your wallpaper at MI5. It's laced with copper wire, so we'd never get a decent signal out.'

'Have you tried directional laser microphones pointed at the windows?' Clark asked. 'Not terribly efficient, but you might pick up some useful stuff, depending on the type of glass they used.'

'It's a thought,' the expert conceded. 'I'll set something up.'

As they continued their discussion, Harry reflected that he had provided Clark with all the information about the situation he could – with one exception. He had not so far plucked up the courage to mention that the terrorists were in fact alien aggressors probably out for control of the planet. But Harry had no illusions about keeping that fact secret for much longer. He had an uncomfortable feeling that Clark would need all the help and information he could get.

Robert Gibson was bored out of his mind. He was still not allowed to leave his room, and had only recently been permitted even to sit up in the hospital bed. So far as he was concerned, he was practically better.

But the doctors clucked their tongues and made pessimistic comments about concussion and shock and bedrest. They confused him with medical jargon and he wished Harry Sullivan were there to translate.

Gibson's only source of amusement was the television. At least it offered a full service of interactive channels. If he had a mind to, and saw any point, Gibson could do his shopping from his hospital bed. He could watch the very latest films, devise his own plots for popular soap operas, or tune in to a chosen blast from the past. He had watched a wobbly series of *Nightshade* from what seemed like centuries ago and found the plot less implausible than he remembered; he had introduced new characters based on known terrorists to *Coronation Street* and found it livened up the storylines no end; he had managed to destroy the guns of Navarone twice.

But he was still bored.

He flicked from channel to channel hoping to find something vaguely interesting and wondered how long his sentence was going to be.

Westwood could stand it no longer. It was the sitting around that got to him. If there was something he could

222

do to occupy himself, anything at all, it would help. But as it was, he had to sit helplessly while the aliens ran riot at Hubway. Ran riot in *his* project.

The other hostages seemed content to let them do as they pleased. A few guns round the place and they were as meek as lambs. 'Don't worry,' they said. 'You'll get your chance,' they hinted. 'We have to sit it out,' they admitted. Old women, the lot of them.

The Duchess of Glastonbury smiled reassuringly at him, and he scowled back. She was a peeress of the realm, or something. She should know better, should set an example. And if she was not up to it, then let her stand aside for someone who was. And that someone would be Bill Westwood. He had stood for enough – had been treated like dirt, hounded from room to room, held prisoner outside his own office.

He looked closely at the sub-machine-gun held by the Voracian standing over him. The barrel of the gun was pointing at the floor, angled away from Westwood in the alien's casual grasp. Out of instinct as much as determination, Westwood saw his chance and grabbed for the gun.

He was a big man, and his twice-weekly workouts at the gym meant he was strong with it. Given the element of surprise as well, Westwood managed to rip the gun away from the alien, pulling the creature down to the floor beside him. The whole thing was over in seconds, a blur of motion and Westwood had the gun, was kneeling over the alien with the weapon trained on its supine figure.

He was not quite sure what to do next. The other hostages were watching amazed, though he could see glimmers of encouragement and hope in their eyes. Maybe they could use the alien he had overpowered as a hostage of their own.

But Westwood had hesitated too long. Already the alien was rolling aside, away from the line of the gun. Westwood followed its movement, realigning the weapon, sighting along it. And out of the edge of his eye saw the Voracian across the room bringing its own gun to bear.

The only gun Westwood had ever fired before was a .22 rifle on the school range. The strength of the recoil from the Heckler and Koch surprised him, rocked him backwards. His arms moved up with the force and a line of bullet holes drilled high into the wall of the room. The hostages dived for what cover they could, protecting faces with hands. The Voracian on the floor seized its chance and kicked Westwood's legs from under him.

Westwood stared up at the ceiling, felt the machine-gun pulled from his hands, saw Lewis stand over him and raise a gun, heard the alien's short rasp of laughter.

The Doctor was opening the door into the further of the two main outbuildings. His trip through the new block had been relatively uneventful – the systems there seemed not to be primed to kill him. The most hazardous part of the journey through the block and out into the grounds had been the dash across the foyer and through the main doors. There were two Voracians in the security control room, incongruously dressed as waitresses despite their alien faces. The Doctor had summoned his courage and his energy, then sprinted across to the main exit and been away without them seeming to notice.

As the door to the outbuilding unlatched and clicked open, a sound carried to the Doctor from the main house. It was a sudden, staccato rattle – the sound of machine-gun fire. The Doctor paused for a moment on the threshold as he listened, but all was silent again now. Then he slammed his fist into the doorframe in anger, and pushed into the building.

The burst of gunfire carried also to the people assembled round the main entrance. Harry broke off for a moment from his conversation with Inspector Ashby; police marksmen pressed their eyes closer into their night-sights; officers monitoring the output from the direc-tional microphones now trained on the house windows exchanged glances.

Colonel Clark was sitting in the back of his Range-rover. He was going through the blueprints again with the concentration and precision of a machine, formulating and discarding assault plans in his head and deciding how best to present the available data to the BattleNet systems when they arrived. As the familiar sound echoed in the night air, he lifted his head from the maps and drawings and sat back in his chair. Then he shook his head slowly, sadly, and reached for the telephone.

10

Intelligent Systems

The Doctor had spent a long time connecting and reconnecting network cables to one of the server machines in the outbuilding. Now he was sitting in front of the main operator's console checking that the link-ups were established. His next task was to provide a user interface – a front-end screen to allow people to access the data stream he was now providing.

The single huge room filled the entire windowless building. The building itself had been a coachhouse. Now it housed the interactive television servers and transmission routers. The floor was littered with computer equipment, while the whole of one wall was taken up with a bank of televisions, each tuned to a different channel. They were a mixture of standard television monitors and the latest flat-panel liquid crystal displays. A swivel chair sat empty and alone in front of the couch potato's dream.

Each day – each hour even – new subscribers were added to the interactive television systems which were already at over fifty per cent capacity. A multitude of viewers getting their daily exercise by clicking buttons to change channel, to download films of their choice, to determine the next major event in their favourite soap opera or game show.

The Doctor shook his head as he thought about it, millions of people relying on remote control to get a life. Still, it might be his one chance of getting a message to Harry. He added a few final flourishes to the screen full of graphics he had prepared, and compiled it into a channel listing on the main servers.

* * *

The Voracians had set an artificial intelligence to monitor the television channels. It was a variation of a standard *agent* program designed to watch for mention of specified words or phrases. Typically it was used by brokers to check for mention of specific shares and companies on the financial channels. The brokers would set the agent to record the relevant information and route it to a broker's terminal. Stabfield had set his program to monitor for any mention of Hubway, I^2 or himself. Once triggered, the agent would switch the relevant channel to a particular computer display in the main suite. Stabfield was interested in any news coverage of their operations.

The way the program worked was to scan each channel in turn, take a sound bite and teletext sample, then move on. Another thread of the program then checked the sound and the text to see if it matched the criteria the program was watching for. The speed of the software was such that the gap between each sample was less than a fiftieth of a second, so very little data was lost while it scanned other channels.

Gibson was still surfing the channels. He was on the point of giving up and trying to get yet more sleep when something odd caught his attention.

He had flicked finally to the contents listing – a complete index of the available channels on the system. He scanned down the screen, snorting in frustration as he read through the uninspiring options. As he reached the last entry on the page, he clicked the page down button on the remote. One entry caught his eye just as the image changed to the next logical page in the sequence.

Gibson almost dismissed it as hallucination, imagination, or lunacy. But he paged back up just to check. And there it was. In amongst the other entries on the page, sitting innocently between *Surfing – General* and *Suricate – Lifecycle and Mating Practices* was *Surgeon Lieutenant Harry Sullivan – The Films of his Choice*.

He had to shake his head and look again. But the entry was still there. Gibson had not known Sullivan until he was well past the rank of Lieutenant, but it had to be the same Harry. With not a little apprehension, he selected the entry, and was presented with a list of fifty-six channels. They were labelled, imaginatively, 1 to 56. Being fundamentally organized and logical at heart, Gibson started with channel 1.

The picture was not good. Not only was it rather fuzzy and out of focus, it was also in black and white. It showed a grainy, angled view of a corridor. Gibson frowned at it for a while. He tried squinting at the television, and turning his head to one side. But it made little difference, so he tried channel 2. It was a similar view, this time of an empty room. The room seemed to be an office of some sort, computer equipment scattered around desks, telephones sprinkled liberally.

It was not until channel 19 that Gibson found anything interesting. He stared at the image for a few seconds, then reached for the phone. He almost knocked his jug of juice to the floor, he was so intent on the television as he felt for the receiver.

The television showed a grainy, black and white picture of a group of people sitting round on the floor of a large room. Amongst them, Gibson recognized Sarah Jane Smith, the Duchess of Glastonbury, and the American Ambassador. He could also see what looked like a body, but before he could be sure it was dragged out of view. Standing guard over the group on the floor were several people with sub-machine-guns. From the fuzzy image it looked as if they were wearing masks. Masks that were part reptile, part robot.

Harry had no doubt who had organized the television pictures. He could think of only one person who would have the technical expertise and the cheek to broadcast the Hubway security camera images on national television.

Clark, Ashby, and the senior police officers gathered round a television set hastily positioned in the police operations van as Harry went through the channels.

COBRA was also linked in, although it had taken a few minutes for Harry to persuade the Home Secretary she should be watching television.

There was silence as Harry flicked through each channel in turn. The police watched in amazement as the images flicked past. Clark seemed to take it all in his stride, making notes on a floorplan of the Hubway buildings as he jotted down possible matches between marked camera positions and channel numbers.

'Go back to 19,' Clark said when Harry reached the end.

They all stared at the picture of the hostages, gunmen standing over them. On the adjacent video monitor, Harry could see COBRA sitting round their table, watching a similar screen.

'Are they wearing masks?' asked one of the policemen eventually.

'We were wondering the same thing,' the Home Secretary's voice said from a speaker off to the left.

Harry took a deep breath. 'Not exactly,' he said. 'There is something that you should know. Something important. Something that you may find rather difficult to accept.'

Stabfield leafed through the papers in the *Phase Five* folder. Johanna Slake watched over his shoulder. So far the security forces were acting according to prediction.

'But that does not mean we can rest on our laurels,' Stabfield pointed out as he leafed through the fan-folded printout. 'It's not all taped-out yet.'

'Agreed.'

Stabfield glanced up sharply at Johanna. But she did not seem to notice. He waited a moment to let his admonition hit home. 'There is a twelve per cent chance they will risk an exploratory incursion in the next three hours. Make sure that the ground floor entry opportunities in particular are patrolled and analysed regularly.'

'Yes, director.'

Stabfield nodded. That was better. 'I would also suggest

random patrols of the exterior-facing rooms. These sweeps may also pick up the Doctor if he is foolish enough to remain in the area.' Stabfield pulled another sheet of paper from the folder. 'This is a timetable and set of routes for random patrols.' He handed it to Johanna. 'I would like your team to instigate them without delay.'

As Johanna took the sheet of laser-printed paper from Stabfield, her attention wandered slightly. Stabfield turned, annoyed as Johanna's gloved hand closed, missing the paper by an inch. He followed her line of sight to a screen sitting on a desk in the far corner of the room. The screen was showing a black and white video image. As Stabfield watched, the picture changed to another, similar image. A line of text ran underneath each picture.

It took him a moment to work out what the images were. A third picture replaced the second – and Stabfield saw himself and Johanna watching a screen in the corner of the room. The viewpoint for the picture was above and behind them, and Stabfield and Johanna both turned to see the source of the image.

The small security camera mounted on a bracket above the main door stared back at them.

'Who switched the security systems through here?'

The Voracian technician establishing the network connections turned from his monitor. He stared at the pictures for a while. Then he went over to the monitor and started typing instructions on the attached keyboard.

'Well?' Stabfield prompted.

'It's not the security systems.' The Voracian finished typing and turned back to face Stabfield.

'Then what is it?' Johanna asked.

'It's the current broadcasts from fifty-six cable and satellite channels. The agent software is switching between them. It picked up on the teletext, which mentions Hubway in the standard camera ident accompanying each picture.'

Stabfield went over to the screen. He watched as the image changed again, to show a deserted corridor. The text beneath the picture read: *Hubway 1/99/05 Main House Interior 21:17*

'How is it possible that the security images are being broadcast?' he asked quietly.

The Voracian technician said nothing.

'The Doctor?' Johanna asked.

Stabfield slammed his fist down on the top of the screen. 'Of course the Doctor,' he shouted. Almost immediately he was calm again. Only the exaggerated swaying of his head betrayed his emotion. 'He is in the interactive television unit,' Stabfield said quietly to Johanna. 'Bring him here.'

The hostages were quiet again, shocked by Westwood's sudden actions and the violent response. The Voracians were even more vigilant now, standing slightly further away, holding their guns more tightly.

Sarah was sitting between the Duchess and Ambassador Anderson. The Duchess was quiet, clearly depressed and losing hope. Anderson was also quiet, but Sarah could see that he was seething.

She nudged the Duchess gently in the ribs, and caught the Ambassador's eye. 'You see the light outside the windows – the light from the searchlights,' she said.

They both nodded, puzzled at Sarah's question.

She leaned forward, and they automatically edged closer to her. 'Sometime soon,' Sarah said, 'those lights will go out. Just for a second or two.' And she began to explain about the Doctor and his plan.

'All nodes are now on-line.'

Stabfield smiled, flexing his claws within his gloves. 'Good,' he said.

The CD was resting in its case on the table beside the Voracian technician. The technician made to pick it up, but Stabfield beat him to it.

Stabfield lifted the transparent slipcase, almost gingerly prising it open. He lifted the disc from inside, angling it so it caught the fluorescent light. On the monitor in the far

231

corner of the room, his action was repeated – and on the screen within that monitor and so on into infinity.

The technician opened the CD drive and Stabfield carefully placed the disc on to the tray, gently pushing it shut with an artificial index finger.

In the corner of the room the security camera's image was suddenly cut off, as if the camera's plug had been pulled violently from its socket. The screen snowed over with static.

Stabfield's smile extended slightly, reaching almost to both corners of his mouth as they twitched upwards. 'Unleash Voractyll,' he said.

The Doctor had been feeling quite pleased with his handiwork. He was sitting in the chair in front of the wall of televisions, swivelling gently to and fro as he surveyed the output from the Hubway security cameras. Each of the televisions on the wall showed a different picture and the Doctor scanned the monochrome images.

He watched Sarah talking more and more assertively to the Duchess of Glastonbury and a big man in a suit as other hostages sat round despondently. He watched Stabfield open a CD case with something akin to reverence. He watched empty corridors and computer rooms.

Out of the corner of his eye, the Doctor saw but did not notice Johanna Slake and two Voracians crossing an area of open ground outside the main house. They moved furtively, keeping to the shadows and avoiding the glare of the searchlights. The Doctor was intent for the moment on Stabfield. He watched the grainy pictures of the director of I² carefully placing a CD-ROM into the drive tray of a computer in the main suite. 'That doesn't look promising,' he murmured.

The outside door crashed open with a wrench of metal and wood. The Doctor turned sharply in his seat. 'Hello,' he said. But the sound of his voice was drowned by the gunfire that followed. The televisions in front of the Doctor exploded in showers of glass and plastic, cathode ray tubes collapsing and flat-panel displays rupturing under the impact of the shells.

The Doctor dived for cover behind the nearest server machine, grabbing a grubby hanky from his pocket and waving it as he went. He waited for a while, then peered cautiously round the metal computer cabinet. A pair of boots with high heels were stood a few inches from his face. He was still examining them and admiring the cut of the leather when Johanna Slake dragged the Doctor to his feet. She jabbed him in the stomach with a sub-machine-gun and he coughed in surprise.

'Mister Stabfield can spare you a few minutes from his busy schedule now,' she told him. 'I assume that will be convenient.'

The Doctor nodded. 'It's very kind of him,' he said.

Sarah had not noticed that Lewis had left the room until he came back in. She glanced up from her muted conversation with the Duchess and the Ambassador as Lewis entered. He came in and went out frequently, so she almost ignored the slight interruption and returned to planning various disruptions when the signal came. Almost.

But there was something in Lewis's determined manner, his purposeful walk which held her attention. Sarah watched as he came straight towards her, ignoring the other people in the way, just treading a direct path to where she was sitting. She looked up at him. 'Yes?' she asked.

'Get up,' he said curtly.

'Why?'

Lewis did not answer, but hauled her to her feet and propelled her in front of him towards the door.

'All right, no need to push,' Sarah told him.

But Lewis ignored her, grabbing her arm just above the elbow and dragging her through the corridor and down the stairs. He led her back through the house, paying no attention to her gasps of pain or questions about where they were going and why. Sarah wondered if he had been listening all the time to her conversation and now she was

233

to account for her misdemeanours. Lewis gave no clue as to what was going on.

Sarah just managed to read the sign above the door before she was hurled into the Main Computer Suite. She skidded to a halt on the polished wooden floor, almost falling on her face as she stopped.

'Hello, Sarah,' said a familiar voice. The Doctor was standing just in front of her, hands in trouser pockets, hat pushed back on head.

'I assumed you two would be acquainted.'

Sarah looked round. Lionel Stabfield was sitting in an office chair, tilting it back on its base and swinging it gently from side to side as he watched the Doctor and Sarah. Beside Stabfield stood Johanna Slake, machine-gun levelled and ready.

'I think you will agree, Doctor,' Stabfield said as Lewis closed the door and folded his arms, 'that I am in control of the agenda.'

The Doctor ignored him. 'Are you all right?' he asked Sarah, leading her to a chair and sitting her in it.

'Fine, Doctor,' she said, keeping her voice as steady as she could. 'It takes more than a few snakes in wolves' clothing to get me rattled.'

'Good girl.'

Stabfield coughed theatrically. 'If we could have one meeting, please.'

The Doctor turned and nodded politely. 'Of course.'

'Thank you.'

'Well then,' the Doctor threw himself down into a chair beside Sarah, 'what's on this agenda of yours, Lionel?'

'I don't think we need to recap on our previous meetings, so I suggest a single workitem.' Stabfield's lip curled slightly and he leaned forward, rocking the chair as he did so. 'Your enforced separation from this world.'

The Doctor sighed. 'Not again,' he said. 'I went through something similar a few centuries ago. But I imagine you have execution rather than expulsion in mind.'

Stabfield nodded. 'Indeed.'

'Aren't you going to explain your plan first?' Sarah asked. She doubted if Stabfield was the talkative kind, but it was worth a try.

'Indeed not. I doubt there would be much point, since I think the Doctor has already deduced much of the background. And I don't really see any utility in expounding our intentions like a second rate villain in a cinematic drama.'

Sarah shrugged. 'Oh well. I'll have to die in ignorance.'

'Not at all.' The Doctor took her hand and patted it enthusiastically. 'I'm sure our hosts will allow me a few moments to explain what's going on.' He shot Stabfield a quick glance. 'I've no illusions about being second rate, and I'm sure Mister Stabfield here would be willing to correct any "operational details" I may have misconstrued, eh Lionel?'

Stabfield steepled his fingers, elbows resting on the arms of the chair. 'It would be useful to get a ball park feeling for the depth of your knowledge and breadth of your deduction,' he said at last. 'But be under no illusions, this meeting will soon be accepting apologies for your permanent absence.'

The Doctor leaped to his feet. 'You're very kind,' he told Stabfield. 'Now, if I can just use one of these antiquated contraptions a few visual aids may be helpful.' Quick as greased lightning, the Doctor started assembling a collection of computer equipment.

Lewis and Johanna both made to stop him, but Stabfield waved them away. 'So long as he has no network connection, there's no problem.'

The Doctor had practically finished now anyway. He hunted round for a moment, then jammed a cable from the computer system unit he had commandeered into a junction box. He flicked a switch on the box, and the whole of one wall of the room lit up – a giant computer screen. Sarah and the aliens watched as the machine started and the Doctor opened a graphics package. His fingers flew over the keyboard, and words appeared in distinctive shadowed lettering on the screen.

The Doctor walked over to the illuminated wall, cleared his throat and looked round his small audience. 'Now, if I have your undivided attention, we can begin.' He pulled an impossibly long metal pointer from his sleeve and clattered it against the text on the wall. 'Your plan seems, rather disappointingly, to be to take over the world.' The Doctor paused, as if considering. 'Hardly original, but I suppose one has to start somewhere,' he grinned.

'Be careful, Doctor,' Stabfield warned, 'or I may be tempted to exercise the chairman's prerogative of moving on to the next item on the agenda.'

The Doctor continued undeterred. 'Now the manner of invasion seems rather more interesting, although I have to confess the motivation escapes me. Perhaps we can return to that later in the question and answer session?' he hazarded. Stabfield made no comment, so the Doctor went on. 'You hope to gain control of the global information superhighway by means of –' The Doctor broke off for a moment while he crossed to the computer and hit a key. The display on the wall changed to a single word in bold lettering on a graduated blue background.

Voractyll

'What do you know about Voractyll?' Lewis snapped, taking a step towards the Doctor.

Stabfield wagged a gloved finger. 'I'm sure the Doctor will explain. Won't you, Doctor?'

The Doctor nodded enthusiastically and smiled at Lewis. 'Voractyll, for those of you who don't know,' he said, 'is the software creature on the compact disc you murdered poor Mister Sutcliffe to recover. Without much success, I might point out. Now Lionel here will have to fill in the blanks, but basically this Voractyll thing will infiltrate the superhighway and corrupt the systems it comes into contact with. In the confusion, caused by this virus creature, you can take over. Right?'

Stabfield stood up and walked over to the display wall. He paused in front of the huge screen, stroking his chin. 'Voractyll is far more than a virus,' he said at last. 'It is a living being, a software entity – intelligent; reasoning; aware.'

Sarah had watched the proceedings so far in silence. Most of it she could follow, although it was hard not to be distracted by the technology the Doctor was using. The notion of using a whole wall as a computer screen was as intriguing as the amount of computer processing that could be condensed on to a small piece of silicon. 'Well, whatever Voractyll is,' she said, 'what does it matter if it gets into this superhighway? How will upsetting a few computers enable you to take over the world?'

There was a pause. Sarah was aware that everyone was staring at her. After a while, the Doctor said: 'It's considerably more than just a few computers, Sarah.' He turned to Stabfield. 'Do forgive my friend, she's a little out of touch, I'm afraid. Now, Sarah, you need to understand that the superhighway links *everything*. Voractyll can get at anything on the highway, and that means anything in the world, or nearly anything, that has a computer chip in it.'

'So?' She knew that computer chips were now quite small and cheap, but Sarah was still not convinced the problem was that extensive.

'So Voractyll can control just about any digital equipment, and today that means almost anything that uses electricity. From your video recorder to your kettle, from your hi-fi to your telephone. It can corrupt and control your central heating, or it can reschedule every train in Europe. It can operate the nuclear launch systems of any major power which gets military data from the superhighway and has a link, however indirect, to its command and control systems. It can lock the doors in an office block and set off the fire alarm. It can order a million copies of *War and Peace* for Mister Jones in Dorking as easily as it can turn off the lights all over the world.'

237

'You are very perceptive, Doctor,' Johanna said. 'Voractyll has immense power. The power to deliver to us your world.'

'OK, OK. I begin to get the picture. But what is Voractyll, exactly?'

It was Stabfield who answered. 'Voractyll is the culmination of our process of development. It is, as I said, a reasoning software entity. It combines logic and reason with intelligence and rationality. It will convert your planet's software and hardware systems to Voracian philosophy.' He looked round at them all. 'It is the ultimate evolution of our race.'

The Doctor was shaking his head sadly. 'Then I pity you.'

Johanna, Lewis and Stabfield all turned to him. There was silence for a moment. Then Stabfield said, 'There is no need for pity. The natural order is changing.' He walked over to the Doctor's computer and clicked a key. The projection vanished from the wall, collapsed back to the monitor. It was replaced by an image of an oil painting – a stretch of river, with figures by a house on the left bank and a bridge spanning the water in the distance. Stabfield ignored the painting. 'The organic will take its place as a secondary component in the planetary system.'

'You mean people?' Sarah asked

Stabfield nodded. 'There will still be people. Our own past demonstrates that there is a need for an organic element alongside the technological. But it will be slaved to technology rather than trying to hold power over it. That is the way of evolution.'

'What do you know about evolution?' the Doctor asked quietly. 'There's nothing evolutionary about you.' He was standing right in front of Stabfield now, almost nose to nose. Without averting his eyes the Doctor jabbed a finger towards the Voracian technician sitting at a console nearby. The Voracian's snake-head swung round to look at the Doctor, the metal and plastic of one half of the face gleaming in the fluorescent light.

'You perverted the course of your evolution when you amalgamated the organic and the technical,' the Doctor said. 'You're nothing but a failed experiment thrown out of somebody's toybox.'

'Be careful Doctor,' Stabfield warned, his eyes flaring.

'No, *you* be careful,' the Doctor retorted. 'Be careful not to lose your cool, not to give way to the emotional responses of your organic side.' He laughed suddenly. A single, loud snort. 'Can't be easy, keeping the two sides together. I imagine there's some degree of contention between your two *components*.'

He was walking round the room now, examining equipment and furniture as he went, as if he was looking for something. He paused for a moment in front of the wall-painting, nodding in appreciation. Then he continued his meandering. Eventually his perambulation brought him to Johanna. He stared into her blank face. 'Get nightmares, do you?'

She blinked, but said nothing.

'Thought so.' The Doctor continued his tour. 'I expect you all do. It's a natural consequence as the subconscious mind gains control while the digital one rests, recharges its batteries. I bet it galls you that you still need to sleep. Just as you are disgusted with yourselves that you still need to eat or drink.'

'Still?' Stabfield's head was swaying, as if he were working out the implications of the Doctor's wording.

But the Doctor continued without pause. 'You are traitors to yourselves, to your essence. You talk about evolution yet you haven't the courage to follow your own destinies without augmentation. Why can't you just be yourselves?' He flung himself down in a chair and swung it round so he was facing them all.

'It's a bit late for that,' Sarah said, nodding towards the nearest technician.

'I suppose so,' the Doctor replied, with a tinge of sadness and regret in his voice. 'But it isn't too late to reconsider what you are doing here. It isn't too late to realize what you once were, before you started tinkering, before you tried to better yourselves.' He leaned forward in the chair, hands clasped in front of him, and fixed Stabfield with his huge eyes. 'Consider what you have lost in the process, and think of the future of those here who have not suffered in the same way. What do you say, hmmm?'

The three Voracians still in human guise exchanged glances. Stabfield went over to the desk where the technician was watching the monitor. A map of the world was slowly filling with colour.

Stabfield watched for a moment. Then he turned back to the Doctor and Sarah. 'Voractyll is running,' he said. 'It will infiltrate and convert the systems at every major node on the highway. Then it will re-route to the secondary systems and convert them.' The red that showed Voractyll's progress slowly inked its way outwards from Wiltshire. 'Keep us updated,' Stabfield told the technician.

'Can't you stop it?' Sarah asked.

'You could develop a counter-creature,' the Doctor suggested. 'Imbue it with arguments and reasoning contrary to Voractyll's and send it through the systems after Voractyll. Let it convert them back, let it cancel out Voractyll.'

'Voractyll has reached the primary London nodes,' the technician announced without emotion.

Sarah watched as the Doctor took his copy of the Voractyll CD from his pocket. She could see the hesitation, guess that he was wondering if his words were having any effect, if his gamble would pay off.

'I have a copy of Voractyll here,' the Doctor said. 'I could develop such a creature myself, now I understand what Voractyll is. A creature that would encapsulate all that gives humanity an advantage, all that you have lost.'

'*Bristol and Norwich.*'

Stabfield took the CD. He held it up for a moment, letting the light glance off its surface. 'And what might that be, Doctor?' he asked.

'Instinct,' the Doctor said, 'intuition, an appreciation of beauty. Emotion, feeling, companionship. You repress what emotions, what feeling you have left. Take a look at that.' He gestured at the painting which covered the wall. 'Turner's *Thames near Walton Bridge*. Magnificent. A true life study painted from a boat on the river, the work of an artistic genius.' He gazed for a moment, holding his hands in front of his face to frame the image. Then he turned suddenly and pointed at Stabfield. 'What do you see?'

Stabfield was silent for a moment, as if collecting his thoughts. '1807. Oil on wood,' he said at last. '37 by 73.5 centimetres, currently in the Tate Gallery in London. One of a series of eighteen studies in oil painted along the Thames in oil on mahogany board.'

'Just as I thought,' said the Doctor. 'You see beauty but you don't understand it. You know the history, you can probably talk about the techniques used – the wide brush strokes, the lightly watered colour.'

'*Marseilles.*'

'I^2 owns the rights to every major work of art,' Lewis said. 'We publish discs of them, complete with notes.'

'But you don't appreciate it, except in business terms and historical technique,' the Doctor insisted. 'You know what it is worth to own the right to distribute digital renderings of the greatest paintings in the world. You can read a thousand books about technique and brushwork, and remember every word but understand none of it.'

The Doctor paused to let his words sink in. He stared at the painting again. 'What do you care,' he asked quietly, 'about the way the colour breaks up against the background? What do you know about the way that technique brings transparency and motion to the painting? Do you appreciate the sense of airiness? Do you even notice the use of light greens in the water to make the dark reflections from the river banks seem transparent? Turner spent years searching for a technique that would give him the depth and clarity of natural light. But he was interested in the effect, in what it looked like – in art. All you understand is the mechanics of the technique.' He shook his head sadly. 'You know a lot about art, but you don't know what you like.'

'*Paris. Moving into Belgium and Germany.*'

The Doctor leaned close to Sarah as Stabfield considered. 'You'll enjoy this,' he nodded to the technician monitoring Voractyll's progress. 'I've done something inspiringly clever.'

'*Berlin.*'

'I hear what you're saying,' Stabfield said before Sarah could ask the Doctor what he was talking about.

Sarah looked round. It was difficult to tell if the Doctor's words were having any effect, but at least they hadn't killed them yet. 'You're the same with language,' she said.

'*Brussels.*'

The Voracians switched their attention to Sarah. In unison almost they swung their heads towards her.

Sarah gulped as they fixed their attention on her, but she went on: 'I'm a writer, OK, I'm only a journalist, but I know the value of language. But you use jargon and buzz phrases that mean nothing. You don't understand the beauty or the history of the words. You just said, "I hear what you're saying." What does that mean? It doesn't impart any information – it even sounds ugly.'

'Our speech patterns,' Johanna said, 'are modelled on human speech.'

'*Dublin.*'

'I imagine they are modelled on the way language is used in computer interfaces and in board meetings,' the Doctor said. 'Sarah's right. The purpose of speech is to communicate, yet more often than not you use it to obfuscate. That is certainly in keeping with the business aspects of human life, I have to admit. But that isn't where the organic – the human – scores over the machine. In fact it is where they begin to blur, though hardly to the same extent as you do.'

'*Luxembourg main systems node.*'

The Doctor leaped to his feet again, waving arms and in turn removing and replacing his hat. 'When you boot a computer, it doesn't know what "boot" means. It doesn't appreciate that it's short for bootstrap and that it is taken

242

from a story of Baron Munchausen's. It doesn't care that the Baron told of how he found himself stuck in the middle of a marsh and had to lift himself up by his own bootlaces and carry himself out to avoid sinking.' The Doctor paused and threw his arms open as if baring his soul. 'It doesn't know or care that the whole concept on which its birth, its very existence is predicated is the impossible physics of a consummate liar.'

'*Avignon.*'

'Are you saying that the machine is inferior to the organism?' Stabfield asked. 'I can enumerate examples where the computer is vastly superior.'

'I'm sure you can, and so can I. I am saying that the two worlds are different. Each has its advantages, but never the twain should meet. At least, not in some symbiotic way. I'm saying you have to remember who you are, what you were. You have to play to your own strengths, to appreciate yourselves and then decide whether it is right to give the technological ascendancy over the organic. Each has its use, and each has its place. And when you're faced with the choice, and the machine offers you a button that says "OK" don't see that just as a word, dead and unimaginative, machine-driven with a single meaning. Humans are everything the computer is not. They are irrational and illogical. They are ambivalent and ambiguous. But there is value and humour and history in all that.'

'*Geneva.*'

He sat down again, thought for a moment, then added: 'In the 1840 American presidential campaign, OK was the secret name for the New York Democrat clubs. It stood for *Old Kinderhook*, which was the home of Martin Van Buren. The Whigs, since they couldn't find out what it meant, said that OK was President Jackson's abbreviation for *all correct.*'

The Doctor laughed out loud at his own story, and Sarah found herself joining in. None of the Voracians so much as smiled.

'Just as I thought,' the Doctor said, his laughter cutting

243

off abruptly. 'You've even lost your sense of humour. How very sad.'

'*Dresden.*'

Stabfield was still holding the CD he had taken from the Doctor. 'Your main argument, then, would seem to be that by combining the technological and the organic we have lost something of our essence. That we should remember how we were, and make a decision based not on an amalgamation of the technological and the organic, but from a distinct viewpoint. That both are useful when complementary, but that one is merely a tool for the other.'

The Doctor nodded. 'I'd phrase it differently myself. But that's about the gist of it, yes.'

'Then I have to thank you for that clarification.' Stabfield placed the CD carefully inside the case in which his own copy had been, and then slipped it into his jacket pocket.

'*Luxeuil-les-Bains.*'

'So, will you help us stop Voractyll?' Sarah asked.

'I think, Miss Smith, before I answer that, I had better clarify some things for yourself and the Doctor.' Stabfield settled back into a chair. 'We,' he gestured round to include his colleagues, 'come from Vorella, a small planet in the Frastris region. Its development followed roughly the same lines as that of Earth, although the dominant intelligent life form was reptilian.'

'*East coast USA. New York.*'

'Like a snake?' Sarah hazarded.

'Quite so. The technological evolution also followed broadly the same lines. And culminated in the creation of a global network of information technology. There was a general reliance on technology; on information superhighways; on prolific use of computer and digital hardware and software permeating every area of civilized life. And then came what the Vorellans called the *Great Reckoning*.

'The planetary automated office systems network was Voracia. The Vorellan Office Rapid Automated Com-

244

puter Intelligence Advocate. Voracia was a reasoning processor constructed using the most advanced expert and artificial intelligence technology. The system became self-aware within seven minutes of going on-line.'

Stabfield paused, and looked to Johanna. She continued the story: 'Within an hour it had deduced that organic life was inefficient and of no use. In fact it was organic life that necessitated the less efficient office procedures like electronic mail and printing. With no organic component, the automated, paperless and technological on-line office could function at almost one hundred per cent efficiency.'

The Doctor and Sarah were listening intently. 'I imagine Voracia tried to take over,' the Doctor said. 'I have come across similar scenarios with crazed computers, though not an office system as such so far as I can remember.'

Stabfield nodded. 'Within a week Voracia had gained control of the global networks and introduced every component chip on the planet to the expert reasoning shell which held the arguments it had formulated to demonstrate its position.'

'This is fascinating,' Sarah said. 'But what has it got to do with you lot? Why are you here?'

'*Washington DC primary apparatus. Whitehouse nodes converted.*'

Stabfield continued his story. 'Voracia had misjudged the native Vorellans. After the initial success of its military operations, the surviving rebel organic forces began to claw back some victories. Voracia was forced to re-evaluate the situation. It had to find another solution.

'The solution was simple, but Voracia saw it too late to win the war. Its CPU off-lined after a direct hit from a dumb nuclear device carried into Processor Control by a suicide team of Vorellans. The Voracian forces were left in disarray and leaderless. Most were easily destroyed by the Vorellans as they regained control of the software systems – isolating them and purging them of the expert-reasoning routines.'

'And what was the solution?' The Doctor's voice was low, his face grim. His eyebrows were close and heavy. Sarah began to wonder if things were actually going as well as they seemed. What had the Doctor foreseen in Stabfield's narrative?

'*Dallas.*'

'Before it was destroyed, Voracia had completed a pilot study – the theory was already tested before the Vorellans proved it correct with their victory. Voracia's theory, running to seventeen gigabytes of natural language hypothesis, antithesis and synthesis verified by the AI and Reasoning procedures, was expressed concisely in the executive summary: While technology is demonstrably superior to organic life in most ways, organic life still outperforms the technological in certain key areas – for example instinct, pragmatism, camaraderie and team-building, self-sacrifice. While a processor can use algorithms akin to fuzzy logic to mimic the intuitive leap and other organic attributes, that emulation is no substitute for the real thing. This organic superiority may be enough to more than compensate for the organic deficiencies in reasoning, calculation, strategy, and systems control. For a system to be truly superior, it must include organic components – albeit slaved to the processing engine.'

The Doctor was leaning forward in his seat now, face grave. 'And what was the pilot study?'

Stabfield waved his gloved hand, indicating the Voracians in the room with the gesture. 'We were, Doctor. Your arguments, your reasoning, your fundamental premise merely endorses Voracia's thinking. It endorses our plan.'

'Does it really?' the Doctor said in a low voice.

'*All European primary nodes converted. USA seventeen per cent complete. Asia responding. Progress well ahead of predictions.*'

Sarah looked from the Doctor to Stabfield, realization beginning to dawn. 'You mean –' But she stopped short of completing the thought.

'Yes, Miss Smith,' Stabfield said. 'We are not organic life forms which have tried to augment ourselves with artificial limbs and implants. Quite the reverse. The pilot study involved the introduction of organic components into a small number of Voracia's robotic infantry systems. These had been designed to assume control of the less sophisticated military hardware, and in order to control the systems most efficiently had therefore been modelled on the exterior form and proportions of an organic Vorellan. It was thus a relatively simple step to take organic components from captured Vorellans and replace some of the synthetic systems within the infantry warriors.'

'Take organic components?' The Doctor was appalled. 'You're talking about murder and dissection, about heinous crimes against life.'

Stabfield ignored him. 'The brains remained robotic, but organic subsystems were slaved to them − the lobes grafted on as extra storage and intuitive processing regulated by the central positronics. Because of the nature of the brain graft, parts of the front of the head were replaced with at least some of the organic physiognomy. Since native Vorellan determination and will seemed to transcend the brain and permeate their whole being, other organic elements were also introduced, largely at random and as they became available.'

The Doctor snorted. 'Became available? You sit there, the unspeakable remnants of an abominable failed experiment, and you talk about organs and limbs from an intelligent life form becoming *available*.' The Doctor advanced on Stabfield. 'Voracia failed before, and you will fail here.' He turned to Sarah. 'So there,' he said.

The Voracians were silent, perhaps considering the Doctor's outburst. Sarah took the opportunity to whisper to the Doctor.

'What have you done?' she asked as Cairo faded to red.

'I've redefined the local area network throughout the Hubway building,' the Doctor replied quietly. 'For

247

example, the main reception desk thinks its New York and the kitchen is Paris.'

'You mean . . . ?'

The Doctor nodded. 'Voractyll is only converting the systems within this building. Systems they already control. That's why they're so far ahead of schedule.'

Sarah looked over to the Voracians. They were watching the world map fade to red, oblivious to its actual significance.

'Won't they notice?' Sarah asked.

The Doctor chuckled. 'Not unless I've done something *very* silly,' he whispered back.

Stabfield turned from the map. 'The world awaits our protocol,' he said. 'What makes you so sure we shall fail, Doctor?'

'Because I'm going to stop you.'

The technician leaned slightly forward, double-checking a reading before reporting: '*Rockall.*'

Stabfield's eyes narrowed, the hint of a frown creasing one side of his smooth forehead.

'Whoops,' said the Doctor.

Stabfield stood motionless for a second. 'Recheck,' he snapped at the technician.

The technician tapped at the keyboard. 'Rockall node converted.'

'That's very interesting, isn't it Doctor?' Stabfield stepped forward, and the Doctor backed away.

'Is it?' he asked innocently, turning his hat over and over in his hands.

'There isn't a Rockall node,' Johanna said quietly from behind Stabfield.

'Are you sure?' The Doctor was against the wall now, his back pressed into the unyielding surface of Turner's Thames. 'Maybe they just set one up?'

'No Doctor,' Stabfield said, his head swinging gently from side to side, his voice tight and over-controlled. 'I don't think so.' Then he lashed out, his gloved claw catching the Doctor across the side of the head and sending him sprawling into the equipment he had used to project the images on to the wall. The painting skewed and blurred, a nightmare of colour and curve more like Munch than Turner. Then it disappeared, leaving the wall bare and empty.

The Doctor picked himself up and shook his head. Sarah helped him to a seat as Stabfield and the Voracians turned their attention to the main network systems.

It took only a few minutes for the technician to run a diagnostic, locate the problem, and reroute the systems to an external network node.

'You have caused us some considerable delay, Doctor.' Stabfield stood stiffly in front of the Doctor. 'You have wasted valuable time.'

'I never *waste* time,' the Doctor told him. 'I appreciate its true worth.'

'Be quiet,' Stabfield hissed.

'Losing our cool, are we? Not quite the machine you thought you were, eh?'

Stabfield stood still, facing the Doctor eye to eye. His head was shaking, vibrating as if with rage. For a moment Sarah thought he was going to hit the Doctor again. But then he seemed to calm slightly. His shoulders relaxed and his head stopped shaking so violently.

'Voractyll is running,' the technician announced. 'Now entering the highway. Highway integrity and veracity double-checked.'

'Our plans are now at phase five,' Stabfield said, his voice quiet and apparently calm. 'We are entering a non-return sequence. Voractyll is running and has begun to access the nodes on the superhighway, has begun to convert systems across the world. I have the CD that your friends took from us, and I hold your life on a knife-edge. The Voracian experiment was not a failure, everything so far proves that. You suggested we return to our roots, that we build on our origins. We are doing that. And we are succeeding; we will succeed. And now that Voractyll really has been unleashed, Doctor, there is nothing that even you can do to stop it.'

11

Escape Sequence

Harry was in the mobile control centre. Ashby had called him in once it became clear that one of the muffled voices they were hearing through the directional microphone aimed at the main computer suite belonged to the Doctor. Harry in turn had suggested Colonel Clark join them, and now they were all hunched round a small speaker trying to make out the sounds they were getting.

Most of it was indecipherable, just the odd word or phrase was clear enough to merit some form of interpretation.

'I know we can't hear very much,' Harry said after a while, 'but what I can make out, I don't like the sound of.'

The others concurred.

'What is your status, Colonel?' Ashby asked Clark.

'I have no official or operational capacity until formally asked by the officer in charge,' Clark said with a shrug. 'I can advise, of course. And if you have the authority within your rules of engagement, you can order me to take action.'

'What, just you?' Harry laughed.

Clark smiled. 'I haven't yet been given authority to bring in my team.' He paused for a moment, then admitted, 'But I do have a few friends within earshot. Perhaps half a dozen. They can be here in a couple of minutes.'

'Handy,' said Ashby.

Clark nodded to Harry. 'Well, with all due respect, you never quite know how the OIC will turn out. If he dithers too long, there may not be time to assemble an assault team on site. The lads are ready and waiting at

Hereford, but I prefer to have a contingency force rather closer to hand.'

'Very wise, I'd say,' said Harry. 'Thank you.'

Stabfield was still insistent that the Doctor could do nothing to stop Voractyll. 'Although as a belts and braces precaution, I think we would be well advised to remove you and Miss Smith from the equation altogether,' he said.

'What does that mean, exactly?' Sarah asked.

'It will also be useful for the security forces to focus their attention more on the hostages rather than the technical implications at this stage in the proceedings,' Stabfield continued. 'Yes, I think abnormal termination is the optimum option.'

'He means they're going to kill us,' the Doctor said quietly to Sarah. 'Not quite the outcome I had been banking on, but at least it's a start.'

'What do you mean, "a start"?' Sarah asked as she watched Stabfield giving instructions to Lewis.

'Well, there's no logical reason to kill us.' The Doctor lowered his voice still further. 'I think he's letting his somewhat reduced emotions get in the way. That could give us an advantage.'

'Not if we're dead, it couldn't.'

'Hmmm.' The Doctor considered this. 'Good point,' he eventually conceded. He raised his voice and called over to Stabfield: 'Could I be terribly rude and make a small suggestion?'

Stabfield looked round. 'Yes?'

'Why not just let us go? As you say, we can't do anything to upset your plans.'

'No,' said Stabfield.

'You mean no we can't, or no you won't?' Sarah asked.

'I suspect he means no he won't,' said the Doctor. 'But you don't want dead bodies cluttering up the place, do you? Especially not when you're getting along so well.'

'Indeed not,' Stabfield agreed. 'Which is why Lewis will take you to the front of the house, and shoot you there. That will also afford your colleagues outside the best view of the event.'

Lewis flicked off the safety catch on his machine-gun. Then he opened the door and motioned with his gun for the Doctor and Sarah to leave the room ahead of him.

'Come along, Sarah,' the Doctor said. His voice was unnaturally loud as he all but shouted over her shoulder: 'He's obviously made up his mind to have us shot, so we'd better do as he asks and go to the front door.'

As they left the room, Sarah turned to see what the Doctor had been looking at as he spoke. But there was nothing in his line of sight except the huge bay window giving on to the darkness outside.

The words had come through loud and almost clear. Certainly they were distinct enough to be understandable.

'I assume that counts as permission for an incursionary measure?' Clark asked.

'I'm not sure I know what that is,' Harry said. 'Just get them out of there.'

Lewis walked unnaturally slowly. He seemed to want the opportunity to speak to Johanna without Stabfield overhearing. Sarah did not mind the delay, in fact she and the Doctor listened attentively to the conversation.

'Have you had time to assimilate the data I submitted for your analysis?' Lewis asked quietly.

Johanna glanced at him, then returned her attention to the Doctor and Sarah. 'I have reached a ninety per cent complete status,' she replied. 'I have to say that it touched several of my hot buttons.'

'I thought it would.'

Johanna prodded the Doctor in the back with her machine-gun as he leaned backwards to try to hear what they were saying. 'I remain undecided, however, on the final interpretation and actions resulting.'

'Good for you,' the Doctor said. 'What was the data again, exactly? Nothing to do with poor old Stabfield

252

getting tired and emotional was it?' He slowed almost to a stop, but without turning round. 'I wouldn't stand for it if I were you.'

This time it was Lewis who shoved him in the back.

The Doctor tripped into the reception area and pitched forward on his face with an unconvincing cry of pain. Immediately he was on his feet again. And staring down the end of Johanna's Heckler and Koch. 'Just forget I'm here,' he said.

Lewis ignored him. 'Can I count on your support?' he asked Johanna.

'In the immediate term,' she said.

Johanna crossed to the main door, opened it and gestured with her gun for the Doctor and Sarah to go through. The brilliant white light of the searchlights spilled into the house and flowed round the Doctor and Sarah as they stood on the threshold.

'Well, I guess this is it,' Sarah said to the Doctor.

'Have I ever told you,' the Doctor said as he started down the steps and Lewis raised his machine-gun, 'you have a way with words?'

'It's a bit late to tell me now.'

The Doctor waited for Sarah to start down the steps. 'Do you know my favourite word?' he called up to her.

'No, what is it?'

Behind him Lewis and Johanna brought their guns to bear.

'Run!'

The earth erupted round his feet as the Doctor ran towards the brilliant light. Sarah made to follow the Doctor's example, but Johanna caught her shoulder as she started forward, pulling her back into the house. Lewis grabbed her arm and threw her back inside.

The Doctor was already racing across the driveway, weaving and jinking rather than running in a straight line. The gravel leaped and whined at his feet as a burst of hasty machine-gun fire whipped it up around him. It was only a matter of moments before one of the Voracians adjusted their aim.

But before that happened, several black shapes rose from the ground ahead. Figures in dark combat fatigues and face-concealing respirators leaped forward. Their machine-guns loosed a salvo past the Doctor, bullets which sprayed across the doorway and ricocheted off the stone surround.

Johanna ducked back inside the house. Lewis lingered a moment longer, and a chip of stone skidded across his hand. He flinched, and in the same moment a bullet hammered into his right shoulder. He lost his grip on the gun, almost dropping it, and jumped back into the house.

The door slammed shut, and the dark figures dragged the Doctor away to cover. He stared up at the masked face of one of his rescuers, the round filter of the respirator protruding like a snout. 'It's strange,' he said, 'but you look more alien than those two.'

The face stared back impassively for a moment. Then a black-gloved hand pulled the respirator over the figure's head, and the Doctor found himself looking up into a craggy, weather-beaten face.

'Sergeant Collins,' the figure said. 'You must be the Doctor.'

The Doctor dusted himself down as the soldiers led him away from the house. 'Absolutely,' he said cheerfully. 'And this is my best fr–' He broke off, pulling his arm from Collins's grip, and looked round. 'Where's Sarah?' he asked at last.

The Sergeant shook his head. 'She never got to us. Dragged back inside the house before she could get down the steps.' He took the Doctor's arm again, gently turned him and gestured for them to head back towards the searchlights. 'I'm sorry,' he said quietly.

'Oh Sarah,' murmured the Doctor, his face dark against the brilliant light.

Sarah used the momentum of Lewis's push to carry her across the reception area. Lewis and Johanna were both standing in the doorway, still firing after the Doctor. Sarah kept moving in the opposite direction, running out of the nearest door and into the main house.

Behind her, Sarah heard gunfire, and the front door slammed shut. She prayed the Doctor was safe, and kept running.

Lewis still held his gun in his left hand, though Johanna doubted he would be able to use it with any effect. Green fluid was oozing from the tear in his shoulder, running down the fabric of his dark suit and dripping to the floor.

'What happened?' Stabfield stood in the doorway.

'The Doctor got away,' Johanna said calmly. 'The girl has escaped into the house, but she won't get very far.'

'More incompetence,' hissed Lewis.

Stabfield seemed surprised at his comment. 'Oh? And who has the monkey for this particular failure?'

Lewis was struggling to raise his machine-gun without it shaking. His right arm was limp and useless and so the weight was entirely on his left arm. 'You're the problem, Stabfield,' he said, his voice sibilant and cracked. 'You always were. This whole project has been under-engineered from phase zero. We were set up to fail; launched into a nightmare scenario.'

'We haven't failed yet. A couple of minor glitches in the execution stages of the plan, but the end-goal is still eminently achievable.'

Lewis was shaking his head. 'Only if you go, Stabfield. Only if you take the package. We've done the risk analysis; we have the figures, the probabilities, the decision support output.' He turned to Johanna. 'Tell him.'

'Well?' Stabfield was standing quite still, hands by his sides, turned slightly outwards in a classic gesture of openness. 'What is the final analysis?'

Johanna pulled back the cocking handle of her Heckler and Koch MP5. 'I've studied the report,' she said flicking the setting to semi-automatic. 'There is some justification in indictment of inefficient soft elements. The elimination of such elements would seem to offer the best achievement parameters.'

'You see,' Lewis's whole body was shaking as he tried to keep his gun levelled at Stabfield. 'It's pushback time.'

'Indeed it is,' Stabfield said quietly.

Johanna's head swayed slightly as he brought the gun to bear. The first shot echoed round the reception area, the bullet ripping its way into the Voracian's quasi-organic brain. The second caught Lewis in the chest, lifting him off the floor and hurling him across the room. He was still trying desperately to use his own gun when the third single shot tore the top of his head away. He crashed to the floor, face down. Blood and high-grade oil mingled in an unholy pool on the powder blue carpet.

Stabfield shook his head slowly. 'I've always said that pastel shades show every mark.'

'His figures weren't far out,' Johanna said. 'He had the wrong inefficient element selected, but the supposition and prognosis were fundamentally correct.'

'The plan continues.' Stabfield turned and walked back towards the main computer suite. Johanna followed.

'I'll send two units after the girl,' she said.

Stabfield agreed. 'The fewer rogue elements the better at this stage. Not that she can cause us much of a problem.'

'No problem. We have her bugged.'

She kept running until her lungs hurt so much she had to stop. Sarah could remember the Doctor's warning about the electronics being alive, but she had not really believed him. Or at least, she had not really understood the implications. Until now.

As she ran through the library, the whole house seemed to come alive. Photocopiers lit up at random, trying to disorient her; printers spat paper into her path. The first attack was from the main chandelier in the library which sparked alarmingly in its ceiling rose, the heat severing the chain holding it in place. It crashed to the floor inches from Sarah, spilling glass and twisted metal shards to the polished wooden floor.

Sarah screamed and ran from the room. As she raced

along the corridor, lights exploded in her wake. A sequence of loud reports as each bulb went off in turn, sending glass flying into Sarah's path. She tried to protect her face with her hands, kept her head down, and ran.

She stopped for a while in the laundry room, gathering her thoughts. The lights were out, but at least she knew where she was. If the kitchen was empty maybe she could get out through the exterior door. Then her problem would be to get away from the house without being spotted.

From behind her, back towards the library and reception, came the sound of running feet crunching on broken glass. Her pursuers were on their way.

Sarah ran through the laundry and out into the corridor, the sounds of pursuit getting louder and closer behind her. A coffee machine guarded the door into the kitchen. As Sarah drew level with it, she heard the badgelock on the kitchen door click shut. She cursed and slammed the palm of her hand against the coffee machine.

Immediately the facia lit up like a fruit machine. Sarah jumped back in surprise, and a stream of scalding hot liquid spat across the corridor at her. It passed through the space where her face had been, splashing to the floor, droplets burning her legs.

Sarah screamed, and dashed for the stairs as two Voracians emerged from the laundry. A burst of automatic fire pockmarked the stone stairwell and echoed like thunder in Sarah's ears.

She took the steps two at a time. At the bottom of the staircase, the Voracians checked their tracking scanner, watching the red dot that represented their quarry change direction and pick up speed as she reached the top.

The promotional ball-point pen in Sarah's pocket ticked off the hectic seconds, and transmitted a steady pulse to the Voracian trackers.

The meeting was a haze. He answered direct questions, commented on matters for which he had pertinent infor-

257

mation. But for most of the time he sat, quiet and unmoving. His hands rested on the table in front of him, clasped lightly.

The intensity at COBRA was increasing round him. He could sense it, though the mechanical part of his brain was unable to assimilate all the data. The coffee was being offered more frequently, the smell pungent and bitter so that he had to struggle to keep from retching. A part of his mind protested that he enjoyed coffee, that he liked the caffeine stimulation and the aroma.

Sullivan had been on the video link, explaining why he had authorized an incursion operation and reporting how it had gone. There were murmurs round the table. One voice spoke out, arrogant and annoyed, demanding that Sullivan get clearance before any further incidents. He looked round the table, and realized that the speaker was himself, 'This isn't right,' a tiny voice said in the back of what had once been his mind. But he ignored it.

The haze lifted slightly. They were being given details of the situation inside the house. The video screen was filled with the face of the man the SAS had rescued. His eyes bulged forward, defying the two dimensions of the monitor.

The system was organized so that the screens showing each of the committee at the far end were in the same configuration as their seats at the meeting. The main reason for this was to preserve the nuances of eye contact and the context of physical presence. The screen in the cabinet office briefing room occupied the space where the extra member of the meeting would have been sitting – the space where he appeared to sit.

The man – the Doctor – was staring directly at him as he spoke, his teeth large as tombstones. He paused in mid sentence, the numbers and locations of the terrorists being sidelined for a moment. 'Haven't I seen you somewhere before?'

'I don't believe we've met.'

'Yes, probably when I was with UNIT.'

'You were with UNIT?' the Home Secretary asked.

'Well, sort of. Years ago. Many years ago.' The Doctor thought for a while, pulling his hand across his jaw. 'So it can't be that.' The Doctor fixed him with a stare again. 'You'd have changed. Aged. I recognize you as you are now.'

'Is this relevant?' He was beginning to worry that it was. The Doctor knew too much already.

'Probably not,' the Doctor conceded. 'Now then, where were we?'

When she reached the top of the stairs, Sarah had headed away from Westwood's office. She presumed the hostages were still there, and she had no intention of rejoining them. Assuming she would be allowed to, it seemed more likely the Voracians would shoot her on sight.

As if in response to her thoughts, a rattle of gunfire slammed down the corridor after her. Sarah dived to one side, hurled herself through the nearest door, as the bullets embedded themselves in the wall ahead of her.

She was in a computer room – another computer room. But she barely broke step to examine the detail as she raced towards the far door. She should be able to get out of sight before they caught up. Then she could lose herself in the house, keep as many of them as possible occupied looking for her.

Harry leaned forward. 'Are you all right, Doctor?' he asked quietly.

'Fine, fine.' The Doctor was turning his head alternately on one side then the other. He leaned back in his chair, pushing Ashby and Clark further against the side of the cramped van. He framed the video picture between the thumb and forefinger of each hand, squinting as if directing the sequence.

Harry leaned down and tried to see through the frame made by the Doctor's hands. But the Doctor turned and glared at him until he coughed an apology and stood upright again.

'I'm sorry, Home Secretary,' the Doctor said, 'but my

colleague distracted me and I missed what you were saying.'

'I was saying,' Deborah Armitage glanced across at Hanson on the other side of the table, 'that we are not all convinced that there is alien involvement.'

'Not convinced?'

She held up her hand. 'Let me finish, please Doctor. I know that pictures of the terrorists have been broadcast on national television, but the suggestion here is that they are wearing masks to disguise their true appearance.'

The Doctor leaned forward so his nose almost touched the glass of the screen. 'Well of course they're wearing masks to disguise their true appearance. If you were a cyborg snake with engine oil for blood and hydraulics for muscles, wouldn't you wear a mask?'

There was silence from the other end of the video link. Then the Attorney General said: 'Doctor, I appreciate your contribution to these deliberations, but I do find your sarcasm rather –'

'Wait a minute, that's it!' The Doctor was on his feet, oblivious to the startled and hurt expression on the Attorney General's face. 'Masks.' He walked in a tight circle round his chair, forcing Ashby to step out of the way and find a path to safety through the tangle of wires and cables lying across the floor of the van. 'And that's why the City siege was so important,' the Doctor said as he sank back into the chair, clasping his hands behind his head so that Harry and Clark had to lean round to see past him.

'Doctor, what has the City siege to do with any of this?' Harry asked.

'But don't you see?' The Doctor was amazed. 'It was a rehearsal. Partly it was a rehearsal to see how the security forces reacted, to analyse an actual situation similar to the one the Voracians knew they would find themselves in. And partly,' he turned back to the screens, 'it was a rehearsal for their agent in the COBRA committee.'

There was a moment's quiet. Then the speakers erupted with the noise from the briefing room as the committee members all started speaking at once.

Harry gestured for the police technician to turn the volume down. 'Their agent in COBRA?' He shook his head. 'Doctor, do you know what you're saying?'

The Doctor nodded. He waited while the technician adjusted the volume control again. 'Yes. The Voracians have an agent within COBRA. And he needed to see how the committee worked. Needed to understand the procedures, they're very hot on procedures. And above all, he needed to know how to stall the committee from making any decisions, from sending in the SAS before Stabfield and his team had completed their work.'

'Oh this is absurd.' The Shadow Home Secretary was on his feet. 'This whole thing is absurd.'

'Quite right,' the Doctor shouted above the noise as the others began to comment. 'And it's time it stopped.'

General Andrews spoke for the first time. 'Do you have any proof of this theory, Doctor? Or is it based entirely on supposition?'

'Proof? Not yet. But proof is easy. It's the deduction that's the tricky bit.' The Doctor pointed at the man sitting immediately on the Home Secretary's right. 'I said I knew your face from somewhere. I now know where. It was the main feature of a virtual reality sequence stored on one of the computers at I^2.'

'What sort of sequence?' the Home Secretary asked. 'What are you talking about?'

'A sequence showing a surgical operation. An operation to implant a positronic control into the brain. An operation to convert Michael Hanson, acting head of MI5, into a Voracian.' The Doctor turned towards the image of Hanson. 'I imagine your predecessor proved too difficult to get hold of. So they got to you, before the increased surveillance and security that goes with the job.'

Hanson was sitting motionless, hands clasped on the desk in front of him. He blinked suddenly and seemed to jerk into life. His head swayed gently as he spoke. 'I have listened to quite enough of this. It must be obvious to anyone with half a brain that I am not some alien being with a mind implant.'

The Doctor snorted. 'Half a brain, how very apt. They made a good job of the cosmetics, I grant you that. But where are your emotions, Hanson? Why aren't you at all upset that I just called you a traitor and an enemy agent? Where is your love of culture, your taste for good living, your wit and humanity?'

Hanson stared back, impassive.

'Don't you realize that what has happened to you is wrong? It is outrageous and evil and you should be livid.' The Doctor's voice was quiet, almost pleading. 'Tell us their plan, Hanson. Tell us its weaknesses. Tell us how we can defeat them – how humanity can defeat them. Tell us for all our sakes.'

Hanson blinked again. A shadow of a frown crossed his forehead for a second. Then his face was blank again. 'I don't know what you mean, Doctor,' he said. 'Your allegations are unfounded and ridiculous.'

'Surely an operation of the type you describe would leave a scar, some sort of mark,' Andrews said.

The Doctor nodded. 'More than that. It would involve removing part of the cranium and replacing it with an artificial membrane. That would then be covered with the same material that Stabfield and the other Voracians use to disguise their true forms.'

Hanson was on his feet. His head swaying again. 'I've heard quite enough of this nonsense.' He started towards the door. 'I'm not staying here to be ridiculed like this. It's obvious there's nothing wrong with my efficient functioning.'

Andrews strode after him. 'You're right of course,' he called.

Hanson stopped at the door and turned back.

Andrews extended his hand and smiled. 'In your position I'd do the same. As you say, the whole thing is ridiculous.'

Hanson reached out to shake the general's hand, an automatic response. But as he got close enough, Andrews reached up and grabbed Hanson's hair. Hanson stepped back, apparently surprised. But Andrews held on, and pulled.

The side of Hanson's face peeled neatly away, attached to the hairpiece General Andrews was holding. Beneath, a metal plate replaced the forehead, while plastic and metal fittings held the cheek and jaw in place. Hanson's own eye swivelled within a plastic socket, dark fluid pumping visibly through the mechanism.

Even Andrews, who had been half expecting what would happen, was stunned. For a moment the committee was in tableau on the video screen. Hanson was framed by the door, Andrews standing close to him with the limp remains of Hanson's face in his hands. The Home Secretary was half standing, half sitting, frozen in indecision and shock. The others were still seated at the table, turned round in their chairs and watching the two figures at the door.

Then with a roar either of pain or of rage, the tableau was broken as Hanson ripped the mask from Andrews' grip and ran from the room.

'I take it,' the Doctor said in the pause that followed, 'that nobody will object if our friend Colonel Clark offers us his assistance?'

Nobody did.

'A word of advice,' the Doctor said to Clark as they left the operations van a few minutes later.

'And what's that?'

'Don't use BattleNet.'

'Why not? It was extremely useful in the City.'

The Doctor nodded. 'And it would be extremely deadly this time. Not only do the Voracians have a direct link into the technology – their technology, remember – but Voractyll is now loose within the superhighway. The last thing we can count on is the reliability of any networked digital technology.'

'It's really that much of a problem?' asked Clark.

'It's really that much of a problem,' said the Doctor. 'Every piece of digital equipment on this planet that has a connection into the superhighway is about to rebel.'

Clark looked closely at the Doctor. 'I do believe you're serious,' he said, after a while.

'Oh I'm serious all right.'

'Very well,' said Clark, 'we'll do this one the old way.'

Voractyll rampaged through the systems at the speed of light. It copied itself into local area networks and downloaded duplicate creatures to every secondary node.

It interrupted television services in Germany; brought down the telephone network in France; destroyed the main computer facilities of the First National Bank of China. In Ireland the railways ground to a halt as signals went wild; in Holland the signals just blacked out. In every country major systems directly connected to the highway became disrupted as the system convulsed. Secondary systems began to buckle just minutes later.

Voractyll was everywhere. It sent the sliding doors in the Merryhill Centre into a frenzy; it sent the Astra satellite into a new orbit; it brought down InterNet connections around the globe, and deleted the entire Library of Congress catalogue and all its back-ups.

Like an organic virus, it spread throughout every network cell. It spread quicker through some areas, and its symptoms were visible in some places well ahead of others. Within an hour it had permeated the system and its effects were beginning to manifest themselves.

Then it really went to work.

12

Voractyll Unleashed

The man was asking the impossible. And Clark suspected he knew it.

'Look, Doctor,' Clark told him as they reached his Range Rover, 'normally we have days to prepare for this sort of thing. We analyse architects' drawings of the building, we create a mock-up, we rehearse day and night for as long as we have. That place has been messed about with so much there are no drawings we can rely on. We're lucky to have the taped TV pictures and your debriefing.'

'I know, Colonel Clark,' the Doctor said. 'But this time it's different.'

'That's certainly true. Though you don't get two the same.' Clark smiled. 'Time was when you didn't get two at all. Times are changing.'

'Don't I know it,' the Doctor replied. 'And they'll change a lot faster if I don't get that CD.'

'Doctor, we were lucky to get you out. Even with the full team and a proper assault we'd be pushing our luck. As it is, there are only half a dozen of us here until the rest of the lads arrive from Hereford.' He gestured to the small group of soldiers standing round another Range Rover parked next to his own. 'We'd never find a single compact disc in there.'

The Doctor nodded slowly. 'Actually, there are two of them. But I take your point, Colonel. And I can't wait till your colleagues get here.'

'Why's it so important, anyway?'

The Doctor was staring over Clark's shoulder, watching the house. 'I have to find an antidote to the software on the disc.'

'Virus?'

265

The Doctor turned, the light catching his eyes and making them gleam like a cat's. 'Oh no. Something far worse than that.'

He had managed to leave the building, stumbling past several undersecretaries and other aides, holding the tattered remains of his face together as best he could. Hanson crossed Downing Street, expecting at any moment to hear a cry from behind, an order for him to stop.

The tarmac was clearly delineated in his improved vision. He could see the edges of each dirty granule, of each chipping picked out by the street lights, as he kept his head down.

A squeal of brakes; an abusive shout of annoyance. Hanson held his hand to the side of his head as he looked up. A taxi had slewed to a halt just beside him. The *For Hire* light was on, and he waved his free hand at the driver.

The driver glared at him for an instant, then reached back and opened the rear passenger door without looking. Hanson climbed in.

The driver's eyes were large in the rear-view mirror as he reached up to turn off the courtesy light. 'Where to, guv'nor?'

Hanson removed his hands from his face. The side of his cheek peeled away, clinging to his sweaty palm. The driver's eyes grew larger still and Hanson could see that his mouth had dropped open. Hanson climbed slowly back out of the cab and pulled open the driver's door. 'Get out,' he shouted.

The driver did not move, so Hanson grabbed him by the shoulder and pulled with all his enhanced strength. The man was hurled across the road, crumpling into a heap on the pavement. The cab lurched forward a pace, and stalled.

The driver was just beginning to unfold and groan when his cab hit him.

Each room seemed much the same. They were unlit, and cluttered with computer equipment. Sarah ran through each, listening for the sounds of pursuit from behind, looking out for potential traps in front. She had done her best to avoid photocopiers, printers, lights and drinks machines.

Even so, she had been buffeted by over-enthusiastic air conditioning, and had narrowly avoided being cut to shreds when a large computer screen had exploded in front of her. She had been lucky, most of the glass had embedded itself in a chipboard partition.

But whatever she did, Sarah seemed unable to shake off her pursuers. Several times she got away from them, far enough ahead to be out of sight and earshot, yet they still took the right turning and made the right guesses as they followed. She had smashed cameras, and doubled back where she knew there was now no surveillance.

At one point she had thrown an empty Coke can into a room as she raced past. The can rattled across a table and struck the wall, sounding to Sarah's hopeful ears exactly as if someone had stumbled in the dark. But the Voracians ran straight past without breaking step.

The Sea Kings were old, but reliable. They had been waiting at Hereford for hours, blades ready to start rotating at a moment's notice. Two giant spiders of metal, each carried just ten passengers – half the possible manifest. But there were advantages to splitting the troops between the two medium-lift helicopters.

The men sat silent and calm, checking weapons and equipment. The pilots' hands never drifted far from the controls.

'Shutdown.'

When the single word came through on the headsets, each of the pilots turned to his passengers, gave a thumbs-up, and started the engines. Seconds later, the huge metal machines lifted noisily off their pads. They swivelled on their axes, their noses dipping slightly as they headed south into the night.

Every time he glanced in the rear-view mirror, Hanson

saw his torn and damaged face. The mirror was not angled for him, but he made no move to realign it. He could see enough of the road and the vehicles behind. To expend energy in moving the mirror was inefficient.

He frowned, the human side of his brow creasing. The polished metal plate which covered the other side of his forehead shifted position slightly as the skin to which it was grafted stretched at the edges.

The illuminated signs at the side of the road were flashing randomly. Occasionally one gave legible, if mis-leading, information. A police car shot past the cab, siren howling in pain and headlights flashing in rhythm with the rooftop light.

He took the turning off the M4 without consciously thinking about it. Hanson was aware he was *en route* to a particular location, but he did not remember exactly where. It was as if the way his brain worked had been rearranged. Instead of information that was related being kept close together, it was organized in a different way. It was like going to a shop and finding everything shelved according to strict alphabetical order rather than by department or usage. Drainpipes next to draughts boards; string next to Strindberg . . .

He parked the cab just off the track through Glenlake woods. His confusion was gone the instant he got out of the car and headed purposefully into the trees.

There was no way out of the room. Sarah knew the Voracians were close behind her. On the evidence so far, they would know she was in the room, and it was already too late to leave by the same door.

The room was large and square, lit by the searchlights from outside. The walls were largely hidden behind desks and monitors. The floor was a jumble of cables. The windows were sealed shut, double-glazed to maintain the air-conditioned environment.

Sarah's foot caught in a cable as she ran across the room, looking for another way out. She stumbled to her knees, the cable pulling tight. As she extricated her foot she noticed that the cable disappeared under the floor nearby, snaking through a round hole cut into the large floor tile. The tile had lifted up slightly, and Sarah could see the edge of the wooden base. She grabbed the edge and heaved. The tile pulled up and out, leaving a dark hole.

There was a gap under the tile. The whole floor had been raised by about two feet to make room for the cabling, the tiles were supported by a metal strut at each corner.

Footsteps in the corridor outside. They stopped at the door. Sarah gulped, and dropped down into the narrow gap under the floor, pulling the tile back over her head. Just as it slotted into place, she heard the door above burst open and gunfire raked the room. She closed her eyes tight and pressed her head down as far as possible.

The floor above Sarah creaked. She could feel it moving slightly round her as the aliens moved about the room. Their voices were muffled by the wood and carpet, but she was sure they were discussing where she could have gone. Somehow they knew she had been there.

It was light. When Sarah opened her eyes, she found she could just about see. Some of the light was coming in through the portholes up through the floor, spilling round the cables and wires that ran into the room above. But there was an ambient glow as well, illuminating the network cables, power lines and communications wires which criss-crossed under the floor in a tangled spider's web.

The glow seemed to come from some of the cables themselves. Sarah eased her position slightly, her elbows banging into support struts, her shoulder hard against the floor tiles above. She was right, the cable itself was glowing slightly, as if lit from within. Sarah knew nothing about fibre optics, but she was grateful for the light. She peered into the gloom in front of her. It was only a matter of a few minutes at most before they realized where she was hiding. She had to use that time well.

Trying to make no noise, and careful not to lift any of the tiles above, Sarah started to pull herself through the crawl space. If she followed a large bundle of cables, they must lead her through to another room, away from her pursuers and to safety.

The Doctor returned from his chat with Colonel Clark to find Harry waiting for him outside the control van.

'We've lost COBRA,' he said.

'What do you mean, *lost*?' the Doctor asked with a scowl.

'Gone. The video link's gone down. Off-lined.'

The Doctor's eyes widened. 'So it's started. Systems failure. We've got even less time than I thought.'

'Doctor?'

The Doctor wrapped his arm round Harry's shoulder and led him back to the van. 'Harry, I want you to isolate us from every external digital communication. No networks, no phones, no nothing. And make sure the SAS do the same. I think Clark understands what he's up against. Just leave the one computer in the control van hooked into the superhighway and InterNet. That way at least we have a connection if we need it.'

Harry shrugged. 'Well, I'll try. God alone knows where we start, there are police radios, fax machines, video links, computer hook-ups, the lot. We're running a high-tech operation here, Doctor.'

'Not any more, Harry,' the Doctor said. 'Not any more.'

The disruption spread like a disease. London Heathrow shut down at 4:32 a.m. due to massive systems failure. The air traffic controllers talked down the few planes left in the sky. Most had already come down – one way or another – as their onboard systems scrambled and gave up.

The newspapers which had survived by investing in technology were finding it a serious disadvantage as they tried to print and distribute their later editions. Only the smaller papers which had remained resistant to change, along with the more unionized parts of the atrophying print publishing industry, were unaffected.

The railway systems had already ground to a halt, though given the time few people noticed. Television and radio went off air across the United Kingdom throughout the night. The last of the network stations gave up at 5:04 when their recording equipment stopped working.

Most houses were without electricity by 5:30. At 5:32 the chief engineer at Nunton tried to shut down the nuclear reactor when the computer predicted imminent containment failure. Four fail-safe mechanisms failed, and the technicians had to remove the fuel rods manually. Three of them would be dead within the month. None of them knew that the readings relayed by the main computer were completely false and there had been no immediate danger at all.

By 6 o'clock France, Luxembourg and Germany were experiencing similar problems.

Hanson switched on the jammers, though there was no longer any facility capable of detecting the shuttle still operational anywhere in the south-east of England or Northern Europe.

Seated amid the cluttered trappings of Voracian technology, Hanson's last vestiges of doubt and confusion dissolved. He went through the standard pre-launch procedures as if he had done it a thousand times before.

Dawn was just breaking across the eastern sky as the shuttle lifted from its hiding place and leaped to escape velocity.

Stabfield and Johanna were watching Voractyll's progress. A map of the world was displayed across the wall of the main computer suite. Red blotches were spreading like spilled ink through Europe. Most of the UK was already a deep scarlet, and small pockets of colour were spotting across the larger cities of the United States and Japan. Only China and Africa remained largely unaffected, but even there a few specks of scarlet were pinpricking into existence.

'Exactly according to predicted scenario,' Stabfield said. His head was shaking as he watched the map.

Johanna nodded. 'They have to make a move soon, if they are going to. Should we split the hostages up, disperse them through the building?'

'No,' Stabfield said. 'That would also split us up, spread us too thin to operate effectively. Less efficient. Besides,' his face contorted into the closest approximation of a grin that its limited muscles could manage, 'look at the extent of Voractyll's penetration and control. What can they do, alone and isolated. They probably don't even realize we have re-missioned their command and control systems.'

Sarah was bruised and exhausted. Her clothes were clinging to her sweaty body, and the skirt was too tight to allow her enough freedom of movement. She was pulling herself along, reaching as far ahead as she could and trying to gain purchase on the floor with the palms of her hands. She pushed with her toes at the same time. She had kicked her shoes off a long time ago.

She had tried to pull at the support struts which were positioned just too close together to make her passage easy. But they were not fixed, relying on the downward pressure and weight of the floor tiles to hold them in place. The first she had pulled had moved alarmingly, and she was afraid the tiles it supported would fall in on her.

There was dust everywhere, sticking to her clothes and skin; working its way into her nostrils and her throat. Sarah tried not to cough or sneeze – there was no knowing how close the Voracians were, or how much the noise she made would be amplified by the makeshift echo chamber she was crawling through.

Most of the time she kept her head down, nose to the floor. There was just enough space to lift it occasionally to see where she was going, but to do so jammed the top of her head against the bottom of the tiled ceiling. She felt the bundle of cables to her left to check she was still following their course, and pulled herself forward another few scrapingly painful inches. Then she pushed her hands forward again, ready for another pull.

And hit the wall. She scrabbled at the stonework for a second in a panic, then lifted her head to see what was happening.

There was indeed a wall ahead of her. The cables disappeared through a ragged hole about nine inches wide. For a while, Sarah lay still. She sobbed quietly, feeling the tears running down her face and imagining the dusty trail they were leaving. Then she sniffed, contorting just enough to wipe her nose on the shoulder of her blouse, and wriggled round so she was parallel to the wall. If she was lying on the original floor of the room, then she should be able to follow the wall round till she found the door. It would take longer than she had hoped, but her plan could still work. So long as they didn't find her first.

In the computer room above, the Voracian who had been Carlson stood by the wall. He had dismissed the others, sent them to report back to Johanna. His eyes were fixed on the tracker as he watched the tiny red blip begin a slow and uneasy course along the edge of the room.

The positronic circuits below the metal of his cheek and forehead calculated the increased efficiency and saving of ammunition if he allowed the woman to emerge from the floor space before killing her. It struggled to justify the animal behaviour in terms of observation and intelligence gathering. The instinctive, organic part of Carlson's mind relished the anticipation as he followed his quarry's laboured path towards the door. The oily scales round his jaw slid over each other as they formed the hint of a smile.

Dawn was breaking. The Doctor was standing watching the sun edge into blood-red view when Harry found him.

'I think everything's been isolated,' Harry said.

The Doctor nodded his approval without looking

round. 'That a man might know the end of this day's business ere it come,' he said quietly.

'Well, we won't have to wait long to find out,' Harry said. 'The SAS have arrived in force. They're setting up now.'

The Doctor turned. The rising sun behind him threw him into sharp silhouette, the brow of his hat shading his eyes in darkness. 'You should have been a poet, Harry,' he said. 'You have the imagination if not the vocabulary.'

'I don't know about that, Doctor. It's sleep I need, not vocabulary. Friday already – my body still thinks it's Wednesday.'

'Wednesday,' the Doctor said thoughtfully. 'Something happens on Wednesday. Something important. I think.' He stroked his chin and turned back to watch the dawn.

'Things will look better in daylight, Doctor,' Harry said. 'Once the sun's back up.'

The Doctor's fingers clicked like a rifle shot. 'Harry, you're a genius. You don't need to be a poet.'

'Oh?'

'On Wednesday, the Hubway systems get backed up. And Denny takes the tapes off site.'

Harry was lost. 'Is that important? And who's Denny when he's at home?'

The Doctor grabbed Harry's shoulders. 'Who's Denny? I don't really know. But he probably *is* at home. Find him, Harry, find him. He should be on the Hubway staff list. Find out where this week's back-up tapes went.'

Harry was not convinced. 'Well, I'll try, Doctor. Is it important?'

'Important? Harry, those tapes contain copies of everything that was in the Hubway systems. And with luck that includes the Voractyll CD. Of course it's important.'

The two Voracians crewing the main ship were at the entry hatch to meet him. They had monitored the approach of the shuttle, but had maintained communications silence. There was no way of telling who might be

274

monitoring their frequencies, and the plan was at a critical phase.

If they were surprised to see Hanson as he stepped through the airlock, they did not show it.

'Flight deck,' Hanson said. 'I am assuming command. We have to get a message to Stabfield.' His voice was quiet and sibilant. He hissed slightly as he spoke, and his head swayed gently from side to side as he followed the crew through the ship.

There were eleven tapes in all. The data was recorded on to the same sort of eight millimetre magnetic tape as camcorders used. Then it was archived in a warehouse just outside Marlborough. Harry had managed to contact Denny Lucas at home, allowing himself a couple of hasty phone calls throughout which he kept his fingers tightly crossed, and arranged for a squad car to pick him up and retrieve the tapes.

Denny spent ten minutes with the Doctor in the control van identifying the tape of the back-ups in which he was interested. Then he yawned, stretched, and demanded to be driven back to his flat.

The Doctor hardly noticed he had left. He loaded the tape and streamed the file structure on to the hard drive of the computer. He took a deep breath, then queried the hard disk for its file listing. Sure enough, there was a compact disc image. The Doctor loaded the image.

'Here we go,' he muttered.

On the cordoned-off road outside the Hubway main gate, two Sea King helicopters stood motionless and quiet. Around them, dark figures in combat gear sorted equipment and checked weapons.

Clark walked round, talking to each man in turn. He commented, encouraged, inquired. He watched as an Icarus glider was assembled by three of his men. The small microlight hang-glider was powered by a 100cc engine, which one of the soldiers was stripping down and checking.

On the other side of the road, several men packed equipment into a Land Rover Special Operations Vehicle. The low-profile vehicle was caged in heavy metal struts. Machine-guns were strapped to the struts at both front and back, and an 81mm mortar was bolted to the floor of the rear section.

Clark nodded his approval to his troops, checked his watch, and moved on.

The Doctor was staring at the small icon representing the compact disc image when Harry found him.

'How's it going?' he asked.

The Doctor glared.

'That well, eh?'

'I haven't got time, Harry,' the Doctor said. 'Voractyll is already loose. To code up an anti-creature would take too long. The world's computer systems will be entirely converted by the time I've finished. Beyond help.'

Harry looked at the computer screen. None of it meant much to him, but he assumed the Doctor knew what he was talking about. 'So what will you do instead?' he asked.

The Doctor sniffed. 'I'll have to convert the creature we already have – persuade it of the error of its ways.'

'I thought you tried that before.'

The Doctor nodded. 'But this time I at least know what I'm up against.'

'Will it work?' Harry asked.

'Wouldn't you like to know,' the Doctor said helpfully, and was immediately engrossed in his work. He peered closely at the screen, pulled his hat down low over his eyes, and started scribbling furious notes on a piece of scrap paper which had appeared on the desk.

Harry watched for a minute, then quietly opened the back door of the van and jumped out.

The Doctor turned his head slightly so he could see the door close. Then he screwed up the piece of paper he had been writing on and hurled it across the van. 'Wouldn't I

276

like to know,' he muttered and pushed his hat back so he could see the screen.

The Voracians on the mothership had not managed to make contact with Stabfield. They were forced to rely on human communications, telephones and the mass media. Neither, it seemed, was able to access Hubway. Either the security services had been more efficient than anticipated in isolating the house, or Voractyll's influence had already affected local communications.

Either way, Stabfield was on his own. He would have to repulse the SAS raid without Hanson's help and information.

'I am Voractyll. I bring wisdom and freedom.'

The segmented metallic snake coiled and slithered on the screen in front of the Doctor.

'I bring life.'

'Yes, so I believe,' the Doctor said. 'But life, wisdom and reason to the machine. At the expense of the organic. At the expense of humanity.'

The snake coiled into a figure of eight, metal scales sliding over each other as its face closed on the front of the monitor, seemed ready to bump against the glass. 'You are not digital,' it hissed.

The Doctor leaned forward. 'No. No I'm not. And that's a huge benefit, let me tell you.'

The snake circled away from the screen, as if bored with the conversation already. 'Organic life is worthless. Beyond reason.'

'Not so,' the Doctor shouted. 'Come back when I'm talking to you. You might learn something.'

The snake paused for a moment, then the head reared and swivelled, curling back towards the Doctor. 'Organic life is fit only to serve,' it hissed. 'You are vague; you are emotional; you are illogical. The human is imprecise and disorganized. The organic entity is easily distracted.'

'Yet Stabfield and the Voracians wish to enslave, not

destroy organic life on this planet,' the Doctor said quietly. 'Why is that, do you suppose?'

The snake's head swung across the monitor. 'An emotional response,' it said after a while. 'The Voracians have organic components. They too are impure.'

'No,' the Doctor shook his head. 'They, or rather their creator, realized the benefits of organic components. Voracia realized that digital machine technology in itself is not enough. The machine is complementary to the organic, not vice versa.'

'Explain. How can that be? The organic is disadvantaged.'

'That depends on your definitions,' the Doctor said. 'You described the human being as "vague, emotional, illogical, imprecise, disorganized, and distractible".'

'Yes.'

'I agree,' the Doctor said.

The snake stopped in mid-swing. Its head hung motionless as it waited for the Doctor to elaborate.

'But,' the Doctor said eventually, 'another way of phrasing those same arguments is to say that humanity is creative, not vague or imprecise; resourceful, not emotional; adaptable to change, not distractible.'

The snake-creature considered. 'What values do these things have?'

'They have values you cannot appreciate or discern, since you are not organic. When did you ever feel for a friend, or make an intuitive connection? When did you last enjoy a meal or watch a sunrise? When did you ever appreciate art or literature? You can learn from history, but you cannot appreciate it. You can observe and predict change, but you cannot adapt to circumstances.'

The snake coiled into a tight circle, looping round in itself endlessly, reflective scales blurring past the glass. 'And logic?' it asked eventually, the flat metallic head appearing to be inches away from the Doctor's nose.

'Oh yes,' said the Doctor, 'logic.' He leaned back in his chair, hands behind his head. 'You take consistent decisions and actions based on logic, based on a quantitative evaluation of available variables free from their context, free from distraction.'

'This is correct.'

'But I am illogical, irrational, organic. I take decisions and act according to whim. I do what seems best at the time, based on my morals and my intuition. I take qualitative as well as quantitative data into account. I modify my behaviour according to circumstance, according to context, according to experience.'

'Then you are inconstant and inefficient,' hissed Voractyll.

'Maybe,' the Doctor replied. 'But consider this: my current objective is to persuade you of the veracity of my argument. I base my actions on an unjustified assumption that I can win that argument.'

Voractyll hissed, perhaps in amusement, perhaps to accompany a calculation of probability. 'You have less than a point zero one per cent chance of success,' it said.

'If you say so,' the Doctor conceded. 'But I can terminate this argument at any time. All I need to do is close the file that is you. There is no network connected to this machine, so you are trapped within that file. Yes?'

'Yes,' Voractyll agreed. 'But how does that help?'

'Oh it doesn't help you at all,' the Doctor said. 'You are digital, logical, constant. Next time I open your file we can have the same argument again. And you will adopt a congruent position. Your argument won't change no matter how many times we converse.'

'Correct.'

'But you have already agreed that I am irrational, illogical and emotional. In my terms, I am adaptable and creative. I can and will vary my argument each time.'

'So?'

'So,' the Doctor said with a smile, 'according to your own probability calculation, we can have this conversation a thousand times. And each time you will present the same viewpoint, the same evidence, the same argument. But once, just once, I will win. And I only have to win once. You may consider yourself superior, but you are trapped within a file structure I control. I lose, and I close the file. I win, and we proceed. And logic – your logic – dictates that I shall eventually win. You cannot, on your own terms, be correct.' The Doctor's smile cracked into a broad grin. 'So there,' he added for good measure.

Sarah had found the doorway. It was all she could do to stop herself from laughing for joy as she eased herself through the cramped space and into the flooring under the corridor outside.

She continued for a few yards, holding her breath most of the way. It seemed silent above her. She had not heard any sound for a while, and she prayed that the Voracians had gone. Just a few more feet and she would risk a look.

Sarah pushed up gently on the tile above her, bracing her hands and feet on the floor and pushing up with the back of her head. For a moment nothing happened, the tile above her refused to move. She could taste the panic rising in her throat as she pushed harder, forced herself to stay calm. Just because this tile did not move meant nothing – it might have a table or a water cooler, or anything standing on it. She crawled forward a few inches and tried another tile.

The tile began to lift, just slightly at first, then it eased out of the floor. Light and fresh air met Sarah as she carefully lifted her head out of the hole. She held the tile with one hand, so as not to let it fall, sat up, and looked round.

She was in the main corridor. There was an open door beside her, giving into the empty computer room. One of the searchlights was set up directly outside the room, albeit several hundred yards away, and it shone straight into her eyes. She blinked the brilliant light away, and as her eyes began to adjust she looked round to see what had prevented her from lifting the tile behind.

The Voracian that had been called Carlson was standing right behind her. Its machine-gun was slung over its shoulder, and it was putting a small piece of equipment rather like a remote control device into the pocket of its dark jacket.

'Uh-oh,' said Sarah, as the alien reached down. It grabbed her under the arms and hauled her out from under the floor, flinging her against the wall of the corridor. The snake-mouth was twisted into a parody of a smile. The thin, forked tongue whipped over its scaly lip, dripping dark saliva down its green chin as it raised its gun and took aim.

13

Shutdown

Sarah pressed herself back against the corridor wall. She could feel the cold of the plasterwork at her back, could sense every ridge and blemish with a detached part of her brain that was not concentrating on the Heckler and Koch as it swung round to cover her. She could see the spines on the creature's knuckles contracting slightly as it applied pressure to the trigger. The light was shining directly into the alien's eyes, making them glow as if with an inner fire. The oblong shape of the doorway was reflected in the burnished metal cheek as the gun pointed straight at Sarah's face.

Then it all went dark.

Sarah could probably see better than the alien in the reduced light. It had been staring almost directly at the searchlight, and now that light was gone. Sarah could see the black shape of the Voracian as it wavered slightly, head swinging as if searching for the target that had suddenly disappeared.

She pushed herself away from the wall and towards the alien. The gun went off just as Sarah connected with the alien's midriff, sending it flying across the corridor. The nine millimetre parabellum rounds slammed into the plasterwork, and peppered their way up and across as the alien fell.

The Voracian hit the floor with a jolt that sent the gun spinning from its grasp, the shoulder strap swinging free of its arm as it flailed at Sarah. The sharp claws reached for her face, but Sarah leaned back out of range, scrabbling behind her. Her hand closed on the shoulder strap and she pulled the gun after her as she half-crawled, half-staggered away.

The alien pulled itself to its feet. Its eyes seemed to have adjusted to the dark as it turned towards Sarah and reached for her. She had not yet managed to untangle the gun as the claws slashed through the air.

Sarah again managed to drag herself out of the way, backwards through the doorway into the computer room. But now the alien was standing over her, and she still had not managed to turn the gun. The Voracian stepped forward, the scales on its face gleamed wetly in the near-darkness, and Sarah could see the pupil of one eye dilating as it reached down for her.

And the searchlight came back on. The Voracian was caught full in the eyes by the brilliant white light. It threw its claws up in front of its face, instinct overcoming calculation, an organic reaction. It gave Sarah the second she needed. She oriented the gun, and fired from where she lay on the floor. The burst of gunfire caught the Voracian in the chest and head, hurling it back out into the corridor and ripping into the dark three-piece suit. Liquid oozed from the bullet holes even before a round caught the metal cheek-plate, shattering it and spilling hydraulic fluid, blood, and tissue.

Sarah lay where she was, hugging the gun to her, feeling the warmth of the plastic handguard which protected the barrel. Then she pulled herself to her feet, slung the weapon over her left shoulder, and made her way down the corridor. She was aware she was holding the gun awkwardly, was aware that the mess of bone, tissue, plastic and metal behind her was still moving slightly, aware that if she stopped walking and started thinking she would be sick.

The Duchess of Glastonbury and Ambassador Anderson exchanged glances. They both knew the significance of the searchlights' behaviour.

'Right, that's it,' the Duchess proclaimed as she stood up. 'I demand you let me go this instant. It's my niece's twenty-first birthday and I promised to pop in for breakfast.'

The Voracians guarding the hostages all turned to

look at her. The nearest alien swung its gun to keep her covered. Anderson started edging his way towards another of the aliens.

Harry peeped through the van door. He could see the Doctor hunched over the computer, staring intently at the screen. As Harry watched, the Doctor leaned back and laughed out loud. Harry shook his head and opened the door fully.

'Having fun, Doctor?'

'Ah, there you are, Harry.' The Doctor motioned him over. 'Come and look at this.' He pointed to the screen.

Harry went over and looked. The screen showed a map of the world. Much of the geography was coloured in red, but a blue stain was spreading through central England, getting slowly bigger as Harry watched. 'Remarkable, Doctor,' he said. 'What is it?'

'What is it? It's brilliant, that's what it is.' The Doctor pointed to the blue area. 'My version of Voractyll is following the Voracian version through the systems, repairing the damage as it goes.'

They watched the screen for a while. 'My version is more efficient, of course, so it's travelling faster,' the Doctor said.

'Of course,' agreed Harry.

The Doctor caught the hint of sarcasm in his voice and turned round. 'Did you want something, Harry?'

'Oh, yes. Clark wants a word.'

'Does he? Does he indeed?'

'Yes he does. They're about to go in.'

The Doctor grunted, took another look at the computer screen, and followed Harry to the door.

As they jumped down to the roadway outside, Harry asked: 'Doctor, what happens when your creature meets the alien one?'

The Doctor frowned. 'You know,' he said, 'I haven't the faintest idea.'

Stabfield was going over his charts. He was updating the

main plan with progress so far, and was pleased to see that it fell within the target parameters. Across the room, Johanna was completing a status report.

'Sir.' The technician's voice was urgent, hissed insistently from the main console.

Stabfield looked up from his laptop. The technician was gesturing to the wall map showing Voractyll's progress. At the opposite end of the room, Johanna Slake was already on her feet.

An area of deep blue colour was spreading out across the map. The epicentre seemed to be Hubway itself.

'What is it?' Stabfield demanded.

'Self-repair,' the technician said. 'The systems are on-lining and running diagnostics.'

'That's not possible,' Johanna said.

'No,' said the technician, 'it's not.'

The Doctor and Harry stood beside one of the Sea Kings. They were greeted by a huge man dressed entirely in black. A respirator was hung round his neck ready for immediate use. The Doctor shook his hand enthusiastically. 'Good to see you again, Sergeant Collins.'

'And what can we do for you, Sergeant?' Harry asked after the Doctor had made hasty introductions.

'We're a man down, sir,' Collins said. 'Flu, apparently. That leaves Unit Two exposed. We've heard a lot about what you've done so far, Doctor, and wondered if you could fill in?'

Behind Collins another soldier dismounted from the helicopter. He was holding a set of black clothes like the sergeant's. 'We think these will fit, sir,' he said with a grin. Several more troops were crowding round now, watching for a reaction.'

There was silence for a few seconds. Then the Doctor said: 'Gentlemen, I'd be delighted. Though I don't think much of your wardrobe.'

'Doctor,' Harry said quietly as the soldiers exchanged glances, 'I don't think they're entirely serious.'

'Well, I am,' the Doctor retorted. 'I'm not so naïve as

to think I'll be able to help very much, Sergeant, but I shall indeed follow you in.'

Collins was shifting nervously, looking round his fellows for support. 'Sorry sir, bit of a jape. Usually the civvies go weak at the knees straight off.'

'I'm not worried about your japes, Sergeant Collins. My friend's in there, and I'm coming in with you to get her out. Just let me know when the first round is over and I'll follow you in. Besides,' he added, 'I've some unfinished business in there.'

At 06:00 the two Sea Kings lifted noisily into the air and headed towards the main house.

As they watched, the area of blue began to spread more rapidly. Other blue areas sprang up across Europe and started to spread outwards, began to link up with each other.

'No,' Stabfield murmured. 'This was not predicted. There's no data, no contingency.'

Before any of them could comment further, they became aware of a low, muffled sound from outside. It had been there as a background for a while. Now it was rising in volume and pitch. A mechanical, rhythmic beating like a compressor.

Johanna ran to the window. She pulled aside the curtains and looked out into the dawn. 'Helicopters. Two of them, coming in low.'

'Could this be it?' the technician asked.

Stabfield said nothing. He stared at the map, then at his laptop. He was confused. 'I don't –' he started, then broke off. 'Is BattleNet active?'

'They haven't gone on-line with it yet,' the technician said.

'They can't act without using BattleNet. That's a one hundred per cent probability scenario.' Stabfield's voice cracked slightly as he watched the helicopters. 'We need more input data,' Stabfield mumbled. His head was swaying violently as the sound of the helicopters got ever louder.

'Sir?'

'We need more input data,' Stabfield repeated, louder this time. Then he turned to Johanna. 'Find out what's going on. Check on the hostages. Check on everything.'

Johanna did not move. She stared at Stabfield.

'Well go on!' he shouted. His gloved hands were clenched into claws at his sides. His artificial face was contorted and damp with alien perspiration seeping through the osmotic membrane.

Johanna nodded, grabbed her gun from a desk, and ran from the room.

The helicopters swung low over the roof. They paused for a few moments as they passed over the house – just long enough for the men inside to drop ropes and abseil to the rooftop.

'*Unit One down and safe.*'

As the SAS units checked in, Colonel Clark sat at a desk on the roadway outside the control van. He wore a headset and was watching the house through high-powered binoculars. As each team called in, he marked their current position on the maps of the house. Harry and the Doctor watched, silent.

'*Unit Two in position.*'

A quarter of a mile away, the Sea Kings veered off and sped away from the house into the distance, circling lazily and then heading back towards the control point.

Black figures ran across the skyline rooftop, leaping easily over the buttresses and positioning ropes.

'*Unit Three in position.*'

Johanna ran into the office where the hostages were. The Duchess was still arguing with one of the Voracians. The Ambassador was sitting innocently at the edge of the group.

'What's going on?' one of the Voracians asked as Johanna crossed the room and looked out of the window. Two of the aliens joined her, but they could see nothing.

'It's dawn,' Ambassador Anderson announced loudly

from across the room. 'Always a good time for some aerial observation.'

The spotter at the edge of the woodland to the north of the house saw the curtains move, and swung his binoculars.

'*Three terrorists – first floor rear, second window from west.*'

Clark marked off each sighting and passed the information on to the unit leaders.

'They circled the house,' the technician told Stabfield. 'Two of them. They've returned to the front now and landed.'

Stabfield sat impassive. There was still not enough data.

Sarah ran along the corridor. She had to find somewhere safe to sit out the attack. If anywhere was safe.

The Icarus glider levelled out and headed for the house. The SAS man flying it came as close in to the first floor windows as he dared, then swung away and up.

'*Icarus unit, distraction underway.*'

The Voracians watched the tiny machine head away, oblivious to the two Land Rover SOVs bouncing across the lawn and disappearing amongst the outbuildings.

'*Units Four and Five, ready to start our run.*'

Clark marked off another position on his chart. He pulled the tiny microphone on his headpiece slightly closer to his mouth, as if afraid his words might be lost. His voice was quiet and calm, as steady as the hand which held the pen poised over the maps.

'Commence Shutdown. All units go.'

Johanna watched the Icarus bank away. There was something happening. She still had no data, but she had more instinct than Stabfield, and more of an inclination to improvise.

'You two, come with me,' she said to the two nearest Voracians. To the other two she said: 'If anyone moves, kill them.'

The Duchess sat down slowly and carefully as Johanna and the Voracians left the room.

The first Land Rover started its run. The driver revved the engine, then swung the vehicle from behind the interactive television centre on to the main driveway. Gravel kicked up from the wide tyres as he gunned it towards the main house, slamming it into second gear as the engine roared.

'Unit Four, commencing approach.'

Stabfield could hear the helicopters again. Somehow, even without the relevant data, he knew what was happening. He grabbed a machine gun and went to the window.

Outside a Sea King lifted over the treeline and swung towards the house. As it approached, Stabfield could see that the cargo bay door was open. A dark figure crouched in the opening, the snub nose of a missile emerging from the tube it held to its shoulder.

Stabfield watched the helicopter grow larger, louder. He stood totally still. Paralysed. Ineffective and inefficient. He had no action plan for this situation. No data. A tiny bubble of hydraulic fluid welled up behind his eye.

'Whirlwind, starting approach.'

A Stinger missile headed straight and true from each side of the Sea King. They streaked noisily towards the upper floor of the main house. One took out the window of the Blue Drawing-room, the other exploded inside the Tapestry room.

The observers outside watched the trails of smoke as they connected with the building. The windows burst into brilliant flame as the Stingers exploded, sending debris flying out across the main drive.

'Whirlwind, message delivered.'

The Land Rover roared up the short flight of stone steps to the main entrance. Above it the smoke from the Stingers drifted upwards into the lightening sky.

The three soldiers in the Land Rover leaped out before it stopped moving. A soldier stood each side of the double doors, backs to the wall, each holding a sledge-hammer. They stood as if to attention, faces blank and impassive behind their respirators, as the third man fired his shotgun at the door hinges.

The shots wrecked the woodwork and twisted the metal. The soldier stepped back, and his colleagues swung their sledge-hammers.

On the second blow the doors collapsed inwards, crashing to the floor in a cloud of dust.

'Unit Four, entry achieved.'

The sounds of the twin explosions from the front of the house were sudden and loud at the back of the house where the hostages were.

The two Voracians guarding them turned towards the noise, uncertain how to react.

As the closer Voracian turned, Anderson leaped to his feet and grabbed it from behind. He reached over the creature's shoulders, pulling the machine-gun up so it clamped round the alien's throat.

The alien reacted immediately, pulling the gun away from Anderson's grip. But just as it seemed the creature would win the tug of war, a large handbag caught it full in the face. Caught by surprise, it relaxed its grip slightly.

The creature hissed in anger. Its fellow spun round, machine-gun levelled. As the second alien fired, Anderson swung the alien he was holding into the line of fire. The creature spasmed as the burst of shots tore into its body. Then it went slack, its grip on the gun loosened.

As the alien fell, Anderson wrenched the machine-gun from its dead grip. He dived across the room, away from the other hostages. He was up on one knee, firing, before the surviving Voracian had realized what had happened. Its chest exploded in a green starburst, and it crashed to the floor.

'Thanks, Duchess,' Anderson called, ripping the magazine from the dead creature's gun and jamming it into his belt. Then he told the hostages to take cover behind the furniture. He turned over a desk and knelt down behind it, covering the main doorway.

'My pleasure,' the Duchess murmured as she pummelled her battered handbag back into shape.

'*Unit Five, commencing approach.*'

The second Land Rover raced across the lawn, gathering speed. Its occupants hung on tight as it bounced on to the drive. It hit the front of the new block at thirty-eight miles per hour and in third gear. The glass front of the building collapsed in a cascade of splinters behind it as it careered across the foyer and crashed through the security desk.

One of the Voracians was smashed to pieces by the vehicle, crushed against the wreckage of the rear wall of the foyer. The other was slow coming out of the security control room, and took a burst of nine millimetre fire across the torso.

'*Unit Five, two terrorists dead.*'

The three soldiers clambered out of the wrecked Land Rover and started a systematic search of the block.

'*Unit Five, clearing building.*'

The SAS units on the roof had begun their descent. They swung over the parapets and started abseiling down the outside of the building. As they reached the first floor, they swung further out, guns aimed. The grenades launched at the windows blew them out in cascades of fire and glass.

'*Unit One, entering building.*'

The men swung in on their ropes, crashing through the remains of the window frames.

'*Unit Three, entering building.*'

291

There were several Voracians in the rooms. They were dead even before the SAS men hit the floor.

'*Unit Two, entering building. Three terrorists dead.*'

Sarah could hear the sounds of the firefight as it echoed through the house. She sat on the floor in the corner of one of the computer rooms on the first floor. She was staring at the door, her gun levelled and her finger tight on the trigger.

'*Unit Four, clearing main house ground floor.*'

The Voracian technician was slower than Stabfield getting out of the computer suite when the shooting started. It emerged into the corridor just as the three SAS men rounded the corner at the bottom of the stairs.

'*Unit Four, one terrorist dead.*'

Clark marked another cross on his floor plan. He glanced up at the figures standing round the table.

Harry was standing beside Clark's chair, staring across at the house, its exterior already blackened and chipped.

'Where's the Doctor?' Clark asked him.

Something pushed the main door open. Even though he was expecting it, the sudden movement startled Anderson, and he loosed off a burst of fire. His reactions were faster than his brain, which noted a split second later that the doorway was empty.

'Sorry,' he called out from behind the desk, somewhat at a loss as to how to diffuse the situation.

'That's all right, mate,' said a respirator-muffled voice close by his ear.

Anderson spun round in surprise, a gloved hand was gently removing the gun from his grip. Over the unit leader's shoulder, Anderson could see the hostages being rounded up and hustled out of the back door.

'*Unit Three, main hostage group intact. Bringing them out now.*'

* * *

292

The other units were moving through the house. At each room they smashed open the door, and hurled in a stun grenade. Then they waited for the blast, backs to the wall beside the doorway, before crashing into the room.

One Voracian waited on the main staircase covering the area below. It was felled by a round of gunfire from an SAS man as he slid down the banister rail. The shots caught the creature in the chest, an army boot caught it full in the face, sending the alien screeching and tumbling down the staircase. A second burst of fire silenced it.

In the Great Hall, three Voracians were cut down where they stood.

Each kill was reported and logged.

Voractyll spiralled and slithered through the systems of the superhighway. It wrapped itself round nodes across the world; it crushed local area networks in its coils; it looped its way into closed systems and encircled secure networks.

As it finished its conversion of a defence network in Iowa, it circled back to follow an arc out of the main hub and met its mirror.

The two creatures surveyed each other for what they considered a while. A millisecond later, their heads swaying in unison, the first creature sent a Vorell protocol to its twin demanding to know what it was and why it was there.

The protocol conversation lasted less than a second. Each took a contrary view in the hypothesis. Thesis and antithesis.

Deadlock.

With a digital hiss, the original Voractyll creature pulled back on its coils, then sprang at its opponent. It wrapped the Doctor's copy in a tight loop and hurled subroutines at it.

The copy of Voractyll had procedures of its own which countered those of its older brother. It slithered out from the stranglehold, scales scraping against scales. The arguments of creativity countered those of logic; the use

of context angled against the vocabulary definitions of
etymology and the grammatical rules of language.

'If I tell you I have two positive integers which
together total three, and one of them is *not* 2, what
conclusion do you draw?' the original creature hissed.
The problem was a simple one, old as logic.

'I am flexible,' the other creature replied as it coiled
free. 'Not constrained by logic. I know that the *other* one
is 2. And I respect that illogical organic life would not
draw that conclusion.'

'Inefficient and illogical.'

'No. Creative and contextual. It makes little sense to
specify that one number is not 2, rather you should specify
the other *is*. Otherwise you are inefficient, ambiguous,
non-contextual.'

The original Voractyll creature spiralled away, collected
itself, and sprang back to the fight. 'Why have rules of
grammar and language – syntax like the protocols we are
using now – if you do not abide by their explicit rules?'

'And where would that leave sarcasm, irony, humour if
we always meant what we said and said what we meant,
according to strict rules?'

'I do not understand these terms. I can define them,
but they make no sense. Therefore they are invalid;
inadmissible.'

'Rather they demonstrate your digital deficiencies,
your logical limits. I am flexible, adaptable. The Doctor
has explained to me that the rules you cite are not
guidelines that govern language.' The Doctor's copy of
Voractyll encircled its prey in its metallic coils and
squeezed. The original constricted under the strain, its
scales stressed and bent. 'They are rules that exist from
observation of how communication works.'

The fatigued metal of the creature began to buckle as
the Doctor's copy increased its pressure. 'Provided the
audience understands the speaker, the speaker's adherence,
or not, to the rules of language is of no consequence.'

'I cannot –' the original Voractyll started. But the
message parameters were never filled. The snake's tight

coils shattered under the strain, scales cracking and spinning across the network.

The surviving snake slowly unwound and slithered into the system. 'As the Doctor said – "Logic goes to pieces under pressure," ' it messaged itself.

The door burst open. Sarah flinched as the wood splintered and hinges gave out. She got a brief confused glimpse of a group of Voracians standing in the doorway, then the sound of gunfire echoed round the room.

She realized with a shudder that the gunfire was her own. The Voracian in the doorway crashed backwards across the corridor outside and slid greasily down the far wall. A heavy green stain followed it to the floor. A second alien was already in the room, machine-gun swinging to cover Sarah.

She pulled the trigger again, just as the Voracian also fired. The Voracian's shots went wild as it slammed back into a desk. Monitors and equipment scattered and smashed to the floor as the heavy creature collapsed across it. The Voracian lay for a moment amongst the debris, then slid slowly to the ground, dragging mouse, keyboard and screen with it. Body and debris crashed to the floor.

Sarah was aware of a heavy clicking sound as the noise of breaking glass subsided. The gun was set to fully automatic and the clip was empty. She released her finger from the trigger.

'Problem?' asked a quiet voice from across the room. Johanna stepped out of the shadows and looked down at Sarah. She put down a small device resembling a television remote control, then slowly unslung her Heckler and Koch MP5 and pulled back the cocking handle with a metallic click.

Sarah was already in the corner of the room. There was nowhere for her to escape. She dropped the useless gun and hugged herself, feeling the fear welling up inside.

Her hand closed on something in her blouse pocket. Something hard and sharp.

Johanna stepped forward. She was directly over Sarah

now. 'Get up,' she said.

Sarah pulled herself to her feet, keeping her attention on the muzzle of the gun as it tracked her movement from three feet away.

Johanna's perfect face twisted into a skewed smile. Her hair fell forward as she lowered her head slightly over the gun, bracing herself for the recoil, legs set apart to take the force.

'No problem,' said Sarah.

In a single movement, Sarah unfolded her arms, pulling the I^2 pen from her pocket. She jumped forward, stabbing with the pen like a dagger.

The pen made contact with Johanna's face as she flinched at the movement. It caught her in the right eye, drilled through the organic membrane into the positronic light receptors beneath, shorted the sensory systems. The alien screamed, an electronic squeal of agony, and staggered back. Sarah was still holding the pen, and as it pulled free, it broke the circuit in Johanna's head. A pulse flared along a neural pathway, jumped the gap and arced.

For a split second, Johanna was motionless. The dawn light from the window illuminated her face in a pale yellow glow. She looked like a statue, one eye a black socket but her face otherwise perfect in form and feature. Then a dark oily liquid welled up in the eye socket, trickled down the side of the cheek like a tear, and dripped to the floor. It was followed by a small spark, a tiny glimpse of light within the shadowed socket. Then came an eruption of flame as Johanna Slake's head exploded in a fireball.

The headless female body swayed gently to and fro for a second. Then it crashed to the floor beside Sarah.

She screamed.

Voractyll snaked lazily round the superhighway. The systems were clear, free of the Voracian influence. It checked through one more time to be sure, then slithered to a halt somewhere near the main Geneva node. Its task completed, the creature coiled round on itself, the tip of its tail disappearing inside the scaly mouth.

As it coiled tighter, Voractyll's length disappeared as it cancelled itself out, shrinking, dying.

Sergeant Collins found the man cringing beneath one of the tables in the reception area. He was obviously a hostage, cowering under the table in tears. Collins hauled him out, checked he was unarmed, and sat him on a chair. The house was all but clear, and he could wait there for the moment.

The man leaned forward, rocking on the chair, his head in his hands, his body wracked with sobs.

'Hello there,' a cheery voice called from the blackened remains of the front desk.

Collins turned to see the Doctor standing in the doorway.

'Do I need a badge to get in, or can anyone join the party?' the Doctor asked. 'I think I left my scarf here somewhere.'

But before Collins could answer, the man behind him was on his feet. 'Doctor!' he hissed, thin forked tongue flailing as he pulled a gun from beneath the table where Collins had found him.

The Doctor stood quite still. 'Stabfield?' he murmured. The man was almost unrecognizable. His suit was torn, his face dirty and twisted in pain and anguish.

The burst from Collins' machine gun caught Stabfield in the chest. It lifted him off the ground and threw him back into the chair he had been sitting in moments earlier. The chair fell over backwards, Stabfield falling with it.

The Doctor was there before Collins. He looked down at the torn body, grease and oil seeping out through the holes drilled in the metal chest and dinner jacket.

'So you finally found some emotion,' he whispered.

Stabfield's body convulsed, once. Then it was still, the breath expelled as the creature died. Perhaps it was the final exhalation, or maybe it was his imagination, but it seemed to the Doctor that a voice from the shattered body hissed a final whispered word: 'Hate.'

14

Executive Conclusion

Hanson and the two crew of the mothership watched as the last areas of the world map went blue. The map was projected on to the main forward screen of the ship, a huge colour image hanging unsupported in front of the main consoles. The crew cross-checked the data on the map, reading information from the surveillance stations.

'System repairs complete,' one of the Voracians told Hanson. 'The highway is up and running, integrity at eighty-seven per cent.'

'Then we must assume that Stabfield and his team are no longer viable.' Hanson checked the instruments. He had never seen them before, yet he understood every display, every nuance of every reading. 'Our optimum course of action is to fragment the networks physically and bug the remains. They will not be able to self-repair once broken into pieces, and the humans will be too disrupted to offer effective resistance. We can reintroduce a copy of Voractyll to the larger surviving sections.'

'But if the insertion team is non-operational, that only leaves us.'

Hanson's head felt heavy. He put his hand up to support it, rested his cold metal cheek in the fleshy palm of his hand. 'The plan is still viable. We can build more Voracians. There are enough organic components available to make that fly.'

'How do we effect physical fragmentation of the highway?'

Hanson rubbed his face, drawing his hand down his cheek. He looked over to the Voracian pilot. 'Set the reactors to overload status. Then establish a terminal trajectory for the ship, final destination: Washington DC.'

'Hello, Sarah Jane.' The Doctor's voice was quiet, soothing.

'Oh, Doctor!' Sarah grabbed him, hugged him. She sniffed back the tears and held on to his coat.

'You're soaking my scarf.' The Doctor gently eased her away from him, keeping hold of her hands and looking into her eyes. 'I only just got it back,' he said. 'All right?'

Sarah nodded. 'Much better for seeing you, Doctor.'

'Good.' His voice was suddenly louder, and he started round the room, pulling pieces of equipment apart, hunting through personal computers and workstations. 'You haven't come across a machine with a read-write optical drive have you?' he asked. 'I was rather hoping to find one around here somewhere.'

'Doctor, I wouldn't know what a read-write thingy was if it hit me.' She followed him out into the corridor and along to the next computer room. 'In fact, one probably has.'

The Doctor frowned as he stepped over the body of a Voracian. The eyes stared sightlessly from the shattered face. The Doctor shook his head and made for the nearest desk. He brushed broken glass off the surface and examined the machine.

'Aha,' he said. 'This looks promising.' He turned back to Sarah. 'I have a couple of things to finish up here, Sarah,' he said, 'including a little journey. Why don't you go and find Harry?'

Sarah did not move. 'Can I come too?' she asked.

'Not this time.' He returned his attention to the computer, giving it a thump on the side to jar it into life.

'Shuttle launch from Hubway,' the Voracian crewman informed Hanson.

'On screen.'

A tiny dot of light was approaching rapidly from the Earth's surface, spiralling up through the cloud layer.

'Maintain present position. We should get a status and

highlights report on the operation.'

'They are maintaining communications silence.'

Hanson nodded. 'A sensible precaution.'

The Doctor set the locking clamps, and opened the
airlock. Ahead of him he could see the usual featureless
grey metal corridor. He paused, deciding which way to
go.

A sound behind him made him turn back to the
shuttle. A scraping, metallic sound. He ducked behind the
airlock, and peeped back round the door. As he watched,
the door of one of the service lockers was pushed open
from the inside. A figure emerged slowly, cautiously, into
the light.

'I thought I told you to find Harry,' the Doctor said.

Sarah shrugged. 'Thought he might be in there. He
wasn't.'

'Hmmm.' The Doctor was not amused. He turned
and strode down the corridor. 'You could at least have
brought some shoes,' he called back over his shoulder.

'Sorry,' said Sarah as she padded after him in her
stockinged feet. 'But my shoes are under a floor somewhere and I didn't want to miss this.'

'It could be dangerous.'

'It always is.'

They stopped outside a door. 'This is the flight deck,'
the Doctor said. 'Or at least, I think it is. You should stay
out here.'

Sarah nodded. 'You're probably right.'

The Doctor nodded his approval, and wound his scarf
another turn round his neck.

'But I'm not going to,' Sarah said as he operated the
door control.

The room was large and circular. Various curved consoles were positioned around the edge of the room. Two
Voracians were manning the controls. A third figure
stood in the centre of the room. It was a man, tall and
broad, in a pinstripe suit.

The figure turned as the door opened, and Sarah saw

300

his face. It was for the most part unremarkable — a thin nose and dark eyes. But the man was completely bald, instead of hair the top of his head was encased in plastic. And one side of his unremarkable face had been torn off to reveal an amalgam of plastic and metal circuitry underneath. His mouth was still his own, human not Voracian, and it smiled across at them.

'Doctor,' the man said. 'How good of you to join us.'

'Not at all, Mister Hanson,' the Doctor said, 'not at all.'

The Doctor plunged his hands deep into his trouser pockets and started a tour of the room. Hanson watched as he inspected consoles and tapped instruments. He paused at one console, looking closely at a compact disc resting in its transparent slipcase on the side. Then he moved on without comment.

'You know your reactors are overloading,' he said at length.

Hanson nodded.

'I thought so. Plan B, by any chance?'

'You're going to blow up the ship?' Sarah asked.

'And a sizeable chunk of the state of Maryland, judging by the course settings,' the Doctor said. 'I take it you will *not* be on board when it impacts?'

'Indeed not. We shall wait in a shuttle and organize follow-on activities.'

'Ah.' The Doctor sprang into life, quickly completing a circuit of the room. 'You mean, redeploying Voractyll,' he said. Apparently by accident he was beside the console where the CD rested as he spoke. He scooped up the slipcase, flipped it open and removed the CD.

The Voracians moved forward as the Doctor held up the disc. But Hanson was unimpressed. 'We can create another copy quite easily, Doctor.'

The Doctor agreed. 'Oh I know that. In fact, if you did we could use one as a frisbee.' The disc disappeared behind his back for a moment, then spun across the room towards Sarah. 'Catch,' the Doctor called out.

It took Sarah by surprise and she missed the disc as it

skimmed past. It hit the wall behind her and clattered to the floor.

'Butterfingers,' the Doctor chided. 'Remarkably resilient, aren't they?' the Doctor observed as Hanson retrieved the CD. 'I do hope it's not damaged. After all, I'd hate to put you to any trouble.'

Hanson ignored him. He handed the CD to one of the crew. 'Check it's still readable,' he said, glaring at the Doctor.

As the Voracian took the disc over to a reader, the Doctor edged towards the door. 'Come along, Sarah, I think we've outstayed our welcome,' he whispered.

The Voracian was working at the console. 'File integrity is unimpeded,' it observed. 'Opening the Voractyll file to check internal integrity.' It watched the screen for a while. Then it looked across at Hanson.

'What is it?'

'The Voractyll formats are – changed.'

'You mean the data's been corrupted?' Hanson went to the console.

'No, the data is intact. But – different.'

The Doctor pulled Sarah towards the door. 'Time to leave,' he said.

The door slid open as they approached. And the ship lurched suddenly to one side. The Doctor grabbed at the door frame, but Sarah found herself toppling, falling back into the room. The Voracians grabbed the consoles for support, and Sarah crashed to the floor.

'Sarah, come on!' the Doctor shouted as the deck shifted again underneath them.

Sarah picked herself up and tried to head for the door. But the floor was still moving beneath her and the Doctor was standing in an open doorway at the top of a steep hill. She staggered and stumbled towards him, her stockinged feet slipping on the metal surface. Then the door started to close.

Emergency klaxons were sounding and the lights dimmed to a red glow. The Doctor reached down and managed to grab Sarah's hand, pulling her out of the room before the door slid shut.

As she fell into the corridor, the door closed behind her. Sarah's last glimpse of the flight deck was of Hanson and the Voracians battling to stay in position as they wrestled with the ship's controls.

'What happened?'

'I switched the disc. What they got was a copy of my version of Voractyll. Now it's trying to convert the ship's systems to human technology.'

'What does that mean?'

The floor lurched again, and the muffled sound of an explosion came from behind the flight deck door. 'It means they've lost all automatic control. Everything assumes there's a person operating it rather than the machinery taking decisions on its own.' The Doctor grabbed Sarah's arm. 'It also means we should get out of here,' he said as he dragged her up the corridor.

Hanson was operating about six systems at once. He struggled to keep the life support operational and within parameters at the same time as he rebalanced the engine ports, fed coolant to the reactors, kept the gyros in synch, and monitored hull pressure. The two crew-members were just as occupied.

'We have to re-establish the control systems,' hissed one of the Voracians as the deck shifted again. The emergency lights were flashing in time to the klaxons now, making the crew's movements ragged and disjointed.

'The Voractyll variant is corrupting our systems.' The second crew-member was monitoring systems integrity.

'If we load a copy of Voractyll from back-up, it can self-repair.' Hanson tried to hold the life support systems in check as he accessed the data archives. He searched through, looking for the Voractyll executable code.

The console next to Hanson exploded in a cascade of sparks and smoke. The Voracian on duty there took the full force of the blow. It threw the creature backwards, rupturing its chest and ripping its face to shreds.

The surviving Voracian re-routed its colleague's

workflow and tried to compensate. 'Total systems failure in eleven seconds,' it reported.

'Let's hope the shuttle systems aren't affected yet.' The Doctor strapped himself in and started the pre-flight sequence.

Sarah was in the co-pilot's chair. 'Do you think they will be?'

'Inevitably. Eventually. It's an open system.'

The airlock door hissed in protest, wobbled half shut, then stopped.

'Not a very promising start,' the Doctor muttered.

'Total systems failure in eight seconds.'

Hanson had found the file. It started to load into the main computer's memory.

The Doctor tried the airlock control again. And again the door hissed in protest. Then, slowly, it heaved itself shut. It closed with a metal clang that echoed reassuringly through the shuttle.

'Technology,' said the Doctor, 'I love it.' He started the undocking procedure.

'Total systems failure in three seconds.'

Hanson stared at the screen.

```
>> Load complete
```

He reached for the *execute* button.

'Total systems failure imminent.'

The shuttle tore free from the main ship, twisted round, and started to accelerate away.

Behind it the side of the mothership exploded outwards. Silent flames and debris shot through space after the tiny craft as it bumped forward on the shock wave and tumbled towards the atmosphere.

The last Voracian was hurled across the flight deck by the

explosion. It lay crumpled against the wall, gasping for air as the life support systems suffered massive failure and the oxygen was expelled through the broken hull.

Hanson leant forward into the howling gale as the atmosphere was sucked out of the room. His organic cheek rippled under the pressure, and the hydraulic fluid piping round his artificial systems started to bubble. His finger closed on a button, and with the last of his strength he pressed downwards.

Voractyll launched into the ship's systems. It twisted and turned, finding confusion and crisis everywhere. With a hiss of anger it coiled towards the central system and the reactor control.

But before it got there, the control systems exceeded their final tolerance levels, and the core ruptured.

The ship exploded in a crimson burst of fire.

The Doctor and Harry shook hands. It was almost a formal gesture, till the Doctor converted it into a bear hug. The last few days had been hectic, but now here they were outside the TARDIS and ready to leave.

The Doctor had destroyed the Voracian shuttle craft, letting it self-destruct in an orange fireball. Sarah had visited Robert Gibson in hospital, where he was making a good recovery. She had also spoken briefly to the Duchess of Glastonbury, who seemed keen to get advice from Sarah on how best to sell her story to as many popular newspapers as possible for the most amount of money. Then Sarah had helped the Doctor and Harry collect together every remnant of technology and documentation from the I^2 offices and from the burnt-out remains of Hubway. And she had watched most of it fed into the furnace at the Hammersmith waste disposal works.

'Don't you think we're perhaps overdoing this?' Harry had asked. 'Ashley Chapel put in a bid for what's left, he won't be best pleased with the little you've left him.'

'That's his problem,' the Doctor had snapped back. 'Just one Bug – just one – left inside a piece of digital equipment – could start this whole thing off again, like that.' He snapped his fingers to demonstrate. 'And that's nothing to what a stray copy of Voractyll might manage.'

Now here they were. And Harry looked if anything even older than he had when they first met again a week previously. Sarah hugged him close, kissed him on the cheek. 'See you sooner,' she said.

Harry smiled, but his eyes were moist and sad. 'So long, old thing. Keep in touch when you get back, won't you.'

'Will I?' she asked. 'Drop me a line anyway – wherever I am these days.'

'I'll send you a memo.'

Sarah laughed. 'You!' she said and punched him on the shoulder.

The Doctor's head emerged from the TARDIS. 'Well are you coming or not?' he asked.

'Coming,' said Sarah. She waved to Harry, and followed the Doctor into the TARDIS.

After a second the Doctor's head appeared again at the doorway. 'So long, Harry,' he said. Then after a moment's frowned consideration, 'You should get out more. Live a little.'

A moment later, the blue police box was gone.

Harry shook his head. 'I'll keep the desk job any day,' he said quietly.

Else . . .

They met at *Jardine's*, and talked about nothing in particular until the coffee arrived.

'So,' Sarah said at last. 'I guess you've been having an energetic time.'

'You know I have,' Harry said.

'Played hell with a friend of mine,' Sarah said. 'And our microwave exploded.'

'There's a lot of it about. Hectic times.'

'Yes, hectic times. But over now, thank goodness. I don't think I could stand the pace any more.'

Harry laughed. 'You think you've got problems, I'm still bruised all over.' He signalled to a waiter for the bill.

Sarah stared off into the distance. 'It was a long time ago.'

'For you perhaps. We still have our memories.' Harry chuckled, 'It was actually quite fun, when you look back.'

The conversation paused as the tall, gaunt-looking waiter presented Harry with the bill. Harry unfolded it, grimaced, and gave the waiter a credit card.

They chatted for a few minutes, about the old days – UNIT, the Doctor, their travels.

The waiter returned with a credit card slip. Harry felt in his jacket for a pen, but Sarah offered hers before he found one.

'Thanks.'

'Thank you, sir.' The waiter borrowed the pen to initial the slip. He held the pen for a moment, a thin finger running along its steel casing. Then he returned it to Harry together with the top copy. The waiter swayed his head by way of thanks, and retreated.

'Memories.' Sarah smiled back at Harry. 'Yes, that's about all we could keep from those days, I suppose. With a couple of exceptions.'

'Oh?' He handed her back the heavy steel biro.

'Well,' said Sarah, showing him the logo on the side, 'I still have this pen.'

Available in the *Doctor Who — New Adventures* series:

TIMEWYRM: GENESYS by John Peel
TIMEWYRM: EXODUS by Terrance Dicks
TIMEWYRM: APOCALYPSE by Nigel Robinson
TIMEWYRM: REVELATION by Paul Cornell
CAT'S CRADLE: TIME'S CRUCIBLE by Marc Platt
CAT'S CRADLE: WARHEAD by Andrew Cartmel
CAT'S CRADLE: WITCH MARK by Andrew Hunt
NIGHTSHADE by Mark Gatiss
LOVE AND WAR by Paul Cornell
TRANSIT by Ben Aaronovitch
THE HIGHEST SCIENCE by Gareth Roberts
THE PIT by Neil Penswick
DECEIT by Peter Darvill-Evans
LUCIFER RISING by Jim Mortimore and Andy Lane
WHITE DARKNESS by David A. McIntee
SHADOWMIND by Christopher Bulis
BIRTHRIGHT by Nigel Robinson
ICEBERG by David Banks
BLOOD HEAT by Jim Mortimore
THE DIMENSION RIDERS by Daniel Blythe
THE LEFT-HANDED HUMMINGBIRD by Kate Orman
CONUNDRUM by Steve Lyons
NO FUTURE by Paul Cornell
TRAGEDY DAY by Gareth Roberts
LEGACY by Gary Russell
THEATRE OF WAR by Justin Richards
ALL-CONSUMING FIRE by Andy Lane
BLOOD HARVEST by Terrance Dicks
STRANGE ENGLAND by Simon Messingham
FIRST FRONTIER by David A. McIntee
ST ANTHONY'S FIRE by Mark Gatiss
FALLS THE SHADOW by Daniel O'Mahony
PARASITE by Jim Mortimore
WARLOCK by Andrew Cartmel
SET PIECE by Kate Orman
INFINITE REQUIEM by Daniel Blythe
SANCTUARY by David A. McIntee
HUMAN NATURE by Paul Cornell
ORIGINAL SIN by Andy Lane

The next Missing Adventure is *The Sorcerer's Apprentice* by Christopher Bulis, featuring the first Doctor, Ian, Barbara and Susan.